TRAIL
through
TIME

LIBERTY VALLEY LOVE: BOOK 5

JOSIE MALONE

ISBN: 978-1-955784-53-5

Published by Satin Romance
An Imprint of Melange Books, LLC
White Bear Lake, MN 55110
www.satinromance.com

Published in the United States of America.

Cover Design by Lynsee Lauritsen

PART I

"This too shall pass."

— NINA ARMSTRONG, HORSE-RESCUER AND
PHOTOGRAPHER

PROLOGUE

Peoria, Illinois – Summer 1871

THE TRAIN RUMBLING THROUGH THE DARK, HEADED WEST.
Fourteen-year-old, Kyle Morgan sat near the open doors and stared
out into the night, watching the miles click by. His right cheek still
burned under the bandage. He suspected the deep cut slicing his
face would infect unless he kept it clean, but that would have been
impossible at the farmhouse. His so-called mother tried to come up
with a story for him to tell the neighbors and the inspector from
the Orphan Aid Society that sent him west on the train two years
ago and her husband threatened him with a whipping if he told the
truth about their son striking him with a hay hook during chores.

Would the injury have meant a new home if he'd stayed and
talked with the old man from New York? Kyle doubted it. This
was his third placement and each was worse than the one before.
He'd heard that some of the orphans on the train from his original
trip had decent homes with real good folks. They even went to
school, but not him. He'd worked from dawn to dusk on three

3

different farms, wearing ragged clothes, surviving whippings, and eating food scraps he wouldn't have given a dog.

None of those homes matched that of the middle-aged couple who originally adopted him when he was barely three, taking him from the orphanage and leaving his older brother behind. After they died in a fever outbreak, their property went to their grown children who returned nine-year-old Kyle to the orphan's home in New York City. Five years later and not much had changed. Still unwanted, still unloved, still unnecessary anywhere except for the back-breaking labor he performed as not much more than a slave, but nobody fought a war to free him, Kyle thought bitterly.

By the time he was back in the New York home for abandoned and orphaned children, Rad had been long gone to fight in the war for the Union, and once again, Kyle wondered if his brother survived. No way of knowing, but there was a distant memory of Rad talking about going West so that was where Kyle headed now. Somehow, some way he'd find his brother and they'd be a family again. A real family with people who loved and cared for them.

Liberty Valley, Friday, July 13th, 1888

The ridge rose before them. Huge granite boulders lined the path while smaller fragments covered the trail. A light sprinkling of dirt covered the slick gray stone, and a tiny evergreen clung precariously to the side of the hill. Fog shrouded the top of the ridge, hiding the steepest part of the ascent and the gateway to the future.

Daylight had faded and the moon would soon rise. Bethany Chambers-Morgan sat on her gray Arabian stallion, Tigger, studying the steep hill, and the hoofprints left in the mud by Gary Smith's stolen horse. She'd hunted the suspected killer for so long. Her German shepherd, Luke, a retired K-9 service dog, sniffed at the trail then trotted back to stand next to her horse, whining softly. Tigger backed up, and she felt the tension in his body. Neither animal wanted to go forward, and she didn't blame them, not since all three of them died on the trail on the other side of the ridge in 2018.

Goddess chosen, she'd crossed through *Time* to come here from the future. She hadn't expected to find her destiny, much less the man of her dreams and she didn't intend to leave Marshal Rad Morgan and the life they had together. She glanced at his younger brother sitting on a strawberry roan gelding next to her. "I followed my heart when I married Rad. You don't have to go after Smith, Kyle. I trust the cops from my precinct to capture him."

"I want to see your world and know for myself that killer is under lock and key." A frown creased Kyle's forehead and he rubbed the jagged scar on his right cheek. "If it doesn't work, I'll come home the next time the door is open."

"I don't know that I can open the portal for you next time," Beth said. "It may take both me and the *Guardian* in 2018. And I don't know who she is. All I can do is tell you again to see my father, Will Dawson. Tell him that I'm all right and ask him for help. Maybe, he will be able to help find the *Guardian*. He knows more than he acts like he does."

Kyle nodded. "I'll find him as soon as I arrive."

"Fair enough." Beth leaned over to hug him. "I promise I'll try to bring you home in September of 2019. That will give you a little more than a year. You can see to it that Smith gets arrested and stands trial for his crimes, at least the ones in the twenty-first century. Don't tell anyone other than Will where you come from."

"I know. You've told me that three times already. They'll think I'm crazier than a bedbug if I say I rode in from 1888. Anything else?"

Beth hesitated for a moment remembering the night she'd shown him a photo of a petite brunette in jeans and a bright red western blouse standing next to the light-yellow Appaloosa horse. "Do you remember my friend, Nina? The one Smith attacked? The reason I came looking for him?"

"Yes. He left her for dead and took the horse she'd nursed back to health, the one belonging to Trace Burdette."

"That's right." Beth lifted her chin. "See if you can find a way to let her know Wonder is back home and I'm happy too."

"I'll do my best," Kyle said.

"Okay then." Beth reined Tigger to the left and concentrated on the hill. In a few moments, silver moonlight shone on the trail, lighting the way up the hill. "The way is open. Go carefully if you wish."

"It's what I want," Kyle repeated. "Take care of Rad and name the first baby after your pa and me." Obviously eager for a new adventure, he urged his horse forward.

———

Kyle Morgan turned in the saddle to check his back trail. He hadn't heard anyone or anything since he rode over that strange hill at dusk, but the winding trail didn't take him anywhere near what he expected to find in Beth's world, after reading the books his older brother gave him. Yet, Kyle couldn't shake the feeling that someone or something lurked behind him, pursued him. Why? Gary Smith should be hours and miles ahead of him.

He reined S.O.B. back onto the moonlit path between the evergreens. The strawberry roan Appaloosa pinned his ears, crow-hopped twice, and then stomped down the track. The horse seemed angrier about traveling into the dimming light than fearful. A breeze rustled through the pine boughs. Off to Kyle's right, a creek chuckled over rocks. A squirrel chattered.

And the fog rolled past the giant cedars. Vapor cloaked the trees in foggy shrouds. The gray cloud thickened, and Kyle made his decision. He'd stop for the night. He swung out of the saddle and led the gelding forward. Eventually, the trees parted on a clearing. Knee-high grass would provide a meal for the horse. And there was water from the creek.

Well, since he wasn't getting anywhere, he might as well set up camp. Maybe, he'd catch a fish for supper. Perhaps, he was stuck in this place for a reason. It could be like the elevator he'd ridden in New York City. The door to Beth's world might take a while longer to open. So, he'd read the books that Rad gave him again, the ones Beth's adopted cousin wrote. Maybe, there would be time to work on his own story of a gunfighter who had a secret.

He'd settle for a cold camp tonight. Smoke from a fire would draw Smith to him and Kyle wanted to be ready for the killer, not end up one of his victims. Being left as a carcass for the coyotes to eat didn't figure in his plans. He had places to go and a new adventure to pursue. Hunting his older brother for nearly sixteen years hadn't ended the way Kyle believed it would back when he was a boy. Neither had living with Rad on the Morgan ranch for the last year.

He'd ride careful, Kyle thought, just as he promised his new sister by marriage, Bethany. He was almost thirty-one years old and somehow, someday he'd find a home, a life he was meant to have, even if he didn't know the details yet.

1

CIVILIAN AND POLICE CARS FILLED THE PARKING LOT AROUND THE funeral home, although the memorial service wouldn't start for almost two hours. Nina Armstrong parked her twenty-year-old Ford Ranger in the space reserved for her and switched off the engine. She dreaded facing everyone, but what choice did she have?

My best friend died trying to bring the man who raped and battered me to justice. Quit whining and whinging and go for it. She would do the same for me.

Taking a moment, Nina reassured Pooka, her half-grown, tri-color collie mix who sat in the passenger seat that she would be back as soon as she could manage it. She knew she was adhering to an old-fashioned code of conduct that most service dog trainers would say was unnecessary, but somehow, she couldn't take a puppy into a memorial service. There would be other times and places to socialize Pooka.

Nina clambered out of the truck and lingered for a moment,

locking the driver's door. At least, she was off the crutches. She hadn't been able to make herself wear anything but black jeans, a subdued top under her black western-style jacket. Regardless of the occasion, she doubted she'd ever wear a dress again.

Last month, she'd had hysterics when her brother-in-law tugged gently on her braid at a horse show, causing onlookers to stare at her. Her mother and stepfather suggested she continue to avoid crowds if she couldn't control her emotional meltdowns. The following afternoon, she'd visited Ginger Taylor and demanded the former hairdresser shave her head. Ginger refused, saying a cap-style cut was enough, and promised to deliver the chocolate brown, waist-length braid to the local *Locks of Love* wig-making drive.

It was time to quit stalling, Nina told herself sternly. Sooner or later, someone would see her standing by the truck in the parking lot and try to escort her inside. Taking a deep breath, she headed into the lobby and looked around. A photograph of Beth Chambers in her formal cop blues stood on an easel near a door. Nina winced, remembering the day she'd taken the picture. Afterward, the two of them had gone to lunch at Beth's favorite restaurant, Billy-Bob's where they enjoyed giant slabs of cheesecake with their coffee, not bothering to feel guilty because they'd split one of the huge, specialty burgers and a mountain of hand-cut, crispy French fries first.

In the room, several other easels held large pictures of Beth. Many showed her in different Army uniforms. In one corner was a candid shot of her in jeans and a Western shirt, holding her horse's reins while Luke, her retired K-9 partner stood by the pair. The light gray Arabian nuzzled her arm and Nina recalled her friend always had horse cookies in a coat pocket reserved especially for Tigger.

Blinking back the tears, Nina went past the cluster of police officers to the front of the room. Beth's foster father, Will Dawson, stood there with one of his many relatives, a petite brunette that Nina recognized as Audra Dawson, Beth's favorite cousin.

Despite wearing a formal black suit, he looked like a silver-haired, singing cowboy with one of his favorite Stetsons. Will smiled and reached out to hug Nina when she joined him. "Thanks for coming. I'm glad you made it."

Nina slipped out of the sideways embrace, hoping she didn't offend the older man, but she couldn't bear to be touched, even five months after the attack. "Beth would hate all this fuss."

"Yup, she sure would. She always threw a fit about the 'falderal' when we got together every time before she deployed." Will smiled, all the way up to warm brown eyes. "But, this way her friends can say goodbye and wish her well."

"And the family can, too," Audra said, turning with a friendly nod. "I'm Audra Dawson-Watkins now. Don't worry about missing my wedding. Joe and I eloped and the relatives don't know what to make of that."

Nina nodded, glancing around and seeing several more members of the Dawson clan. "I saw Joe at the vet clinic when I took in my puppy for his shots last time. He was nice. He even gave Pooka the teddy bear that he'd chewed up."

"That's my husband," Audra agreed happily. "Animals first and people barely second. He'll be back as soon as he straightens out the chaplain. Joe will find a tactful way to explain that nobody will be happy if he opts for one of those surface speeches that are so popular and make it obvious that he really didn't know Beth even if she was sent to him for counseling for her P.T.S.D."

The conversation eased some of Nina's nervousness, but she still had to ask, "Have you heard anything more from the District Attorney? Does he have anything new to say about Gary Smith?"

"Oh, the fellow still claims Beth is alive and well in 1888," Will said. "Detective Watkins assures us that Smith's trying for an insanity plea, but he won't get it. He had her coat and everything she kept in the pockets for trophies, plus there was more evidence when they found his saddlebags and that dead horse in the National Forest."

"There's no way Beth would give up her things," Nina said.

"She got her man. Smith will spend the rest of his life behind bars once he goes to trial."

Will drew an antique gold watch out of his pocket, rubbing the case with a calloused thumb. "You're right. She did get her man. And all of the Dawsons can live with that. Time to stop blaming yourself for what she did, sweetness."

"But, it's my fault she tracked him into the National Forest and got herself killed," Nina said. "I'd never want her hurt."

"Same goes for you," Audra said. "She'd hate it if she thought you blamed yourself. She always took care of everyone even before she became a cop. It was her job and she stepped up. Again, no blame attaches to you."

Not for the first time, Nina wished she believed that. The topic changed to her horse rescue operation and she repeated the party line she'd come up with last spring. "It's fine. Donations are up and horse abuse is down so everything works. I've been adopting out some of my rescues, but that takes work too."

Audra nodded. "You bet it does. Trying to sell luxury items in a down economy is never easy and it may not be politically correct, but horses are tough to support even when people aren't worrying about mortgages and taxes. And looking for homes when the animals are psychologically damaged can't be easy at the best of times."

Nina felt some of her tension ease. She'd prepared to be criticized and judged, not hear this much understanding on so many levels. She glanced across the room and saw Joe Watkins coming toward them. He never had been a big guy, barely six foot. He was still lean and wiry, accompanied by a younger man in a dark suit, carrying a black cowboy hat. Was that the minister? It couldn't be, not with that hat.

Audra turned her smile on them. "Nina, you remember my husband, don't you? And this is a friend of ours and Beth's, Kyle Morgan."

Nina tensed for a moment, concerned he might try to shake her hand. Instead, he stood still, and then slowly smiled until it touched his dark brown eyes. While she didn't smile back at him, she relaxed again. He wasn't a giant of a man, shorter than both Joe and Will, but three inches taller than she was at five-feet-four. Faint amusement trickled through her. No wonder he needed the hat to make himself bigger. Sun-streaked blond hair reached his broad shoulders and she realized it was longer than hers. She noticed the faded line of a jagged scar that sliced his right cheek and wondered what happened. Was it some kind of a war injury? Had he and Beth served together in Afghanistan?

"Where did you meet Beth?" Nina asked. "I don't remember her mentioning you."

"In the woods on one of her hunting trips."

Nina met his gaze, wary now. "Beth didn't hunt."

"He means a camping trip," Audra said. "You're her best friend. You know she used to head for the hills around the holidays. She hated fireworks after all those Army tours in the Middle East. They triggered her PTSD."

"Then, why didn't he say that?"

Kyle shrugged. "Wasn't sure what you folks called it. And she was downright unsociable when I stumbled into her camp looking for my brother. Her dog attacked me. Knocked me down and held me in the dirt."

"Not really?" A burst of rare laughter bubbled up inside Nina. "What did your brother do?"

"Laughed. He never was the sensitive sort. Probably why he and Bethany get along so well."

"You mean got along." Tears stung and she blinked hard. Now, she had another reason to hate herself. She'd deprived her best friend of a man who undoubtedly would have been her soulmate and given her the 'happy ever after' she dreamed of and rarely mentioned. Nina glanced around the room. "Is he here?"

"No. Rad isn't much for ceremony."

Another thing he and Beth had in common, Nina thought, glancing at the others in their small group. She saw a faint smile crease Will's face and realized he enjoyed hearing the reminiscences. It still came as a surprise that he wasn't blaming her. She knew she ought to move around the room and talk to the other guests, including the police officers who continued to arrive, but she couldn't make herself do it. The same went for the rest of the Dawsons. Sooner or later, someone would point out that if Beth hadn't gone after the man who attacked Nina, there wouldn't be a need for this memorial.

As if her thought conjured him up, a big blond man in a dress police uniform came toward them. Nina shuddered, recognizing Detective John Watkins. He'd investigated her case immediately after the attack and while he never said anything offensive, she'd always been grateful the nurses in the hospital didn't leave her alone with him. Nina hated his censorious looks as if it was her fault that she discovered an intruder on the Armstrong property and tried to stop him from stealing one of her rescue horses.

"I wanted to express my condolences again," John Watkins said. "Detective Chambers was a good person. She'll be missed."

"Thank you," Audra said, in a polite tone, too polite. "That means a lot."

Will nodded agreement and Joe stepped forward. "Let me show you where we'd like the officers to sit, John. Perhaps, you could arrange that for the Dawsons."

"Sure. I'd be happy to do that. I just wanted to say—"

"Now isn't the time for anything else." Joe escorted his cousin away.

Audra glared after the detective as the pair headed into the chapel. "If he'd stepped up when she was alive instead of throwing up hurdles during the initial investigation and sabotaging every-thing Beth did, you wouldn't have been hurt, Nina. When he acts like he was her best friend, instead of her 'bête noire,' it just pisses me off. I'm so glad that Joe and Art don't do holidays with his family because I'd be majorly tempted to let Brigid put ipecac in his gravy."

"Want me to take him outside and kick his tail, Mrs. Audra?"

"No, Kyle. But, thank you for offering. Instead, would you

please keep him from harassing Nina? He's one of those men who thinks when a woman is attacked that she asked for it and I don't want to embarrass everyone by screaming at him for being such a backward ape."

"I suppose I should opt for being P.C. and say I don't need a protector," Nina said, her tone even, "but I appreciate the support."

"It's what Beth would want and that's why we're all here," Audra said. "Besides, I'll just write him into one of my books and let a renegade werewolf kill him gruesomely. That will make me feel much better since we can't poison him."

Kyle chuckled. "Do you do that a lot, ma'am? Kill off folks in your books?"

"All the time, but I always change the names and the morons usually don't recognize themselves, much less try to sue me." Audra glanced toward the door, frowning at the newcomers, a young woman followed by a man with a TV camera. "I don't believe this. We told the funeral home, no reporters. Come on, Uncle Will. Let's go kick them out of here. This is a memorial, not a circus. Kyle, take Nina into the chapel. I don't want them seeing either of you."

"Yes, ma'am." Kyle inclined his head toward the elaborately carved wooden doors. "After you, Miss Nina."

She started toward the inner chamber, glancing at him, grateful he was close to her height and didn't tower over her. "I think I know why she wants me out of sight, but why is she sending you?"

"Because Smith tried attacking me and stealing my horse up in the hills when the one that he'd taken broke a leg and he had to shoot it. If nobody else told you about it, that's because it wasn't the one that he absconded with from your barn. Emancipation is safe and sound with Trace Burdette. Don't reckon she'll ever let him out of her sight again."

"Emancipation? Do you mean, Wonder? That's what I called him since it was a wonder he was alive when he came to my place."

"Well, since my brother gave him to Trace after his ma died

and she raised him from the time he was three months old, guess we should use the name she gave him. She was real perturbed when Smith stole him and brought him here. Like I said, now she has him back and he's safe and sound in her barn. Granted, she'd like Smith hung for horse stealing, but that's not likely to happen."

"Not when they're building a case against him for murdering Beth," Nina said. "I still can't believe he got bail."

"He hasn't been convicted yet," Kyle said. "Have you seen him anywhere?"

"No. My uncle's lawyer got a restraining order so he can't come near me." Nina shuddered. "What about you? Has he approached you? Threatened or attacked you again?"

"Not yet. Some folks saw us fighting up on the mountain back in July and called the police. If it hadn't been for that, they never would have arrested him. Those reporters are interested in sensation, not real stories. They don't understand he'll watch their stories too."

"I've been avoiding them as much as I can and blocking their calls on my cell phone." Nina drew a deep breath, hoping a change of subject would keep thoughts of her attacker out of her mind as they walked into the chapel. They headed up the main aisle between the wooden pews, footsteps muted on the dark gray carpet. A soft melody filled the air, and she knew Beth would have called it 'elevator music' preferring her favorite classic country or old-time rock and roll, especially Helen Reddy's songs. Bouquets of flowers surrounded the altar, including some of the long-stemmed roses her best friend loved.

Blinking hard to hold back the tears, Nina flicked a quick glance at Kyle. "What kind of horse do you have?"

"S.O.B. is a strawberry roan, Appy gelding."

"Does his name stand for son-of—?"

"Yes, ma'am. My brother named him because he's nasty and has a bad attitude. Sooner kick you than eat. Spends most his time with his ears flat back, threatening to bite folks. Rad says he was a stinker when he was a colt even before he had a run-in with a porcupine and lost."

"How did you end up with him?"

"He threw and stomped one too many of Rad's hands and my brother was going to shoot him. Didn't seem fair to me since the fellow still had blood on his spurs and S.O.B. was a mess. Blood all over him and cracked ribs. Told Rad I'd take the horse and he could fire the man when he healed up or I would."

Nina slid into one of the seats closest to the side door. "What did the vet say about your horse? Did Joe or his dad look after him?"

"Didn't need them." Kyle sat down next to her. "No, I doctored him. Got kicked a couple of times, but once Señora Ortiz started giving me old biscuits for him, we made friends. He likes those better than anything."

"Who is Señora Ortiz?"

"She runs Rad's house for him. She and her husband are good folks."

"And she makes biscuits for your horse." Nina smiled. "Where's their place?"

"Oh, it's a fair distance up in the hills. I've been working for the Jamisons at the Rocking J, but their place is getting revved up. Pretty soon, S.O.B. and I will have worked ourselves out of a job and have to move on."

"What kind of work are you doing?" Nina eased back in the chair and listened while he talked about building fences, repairing barns, and looking after all sorts of livestock. His deep voice rumbled softly and reminded her of an old-time cowboy in a classic movie. For the first time in a long time, she felt safe.

She didn't say that. She usually didn't say much anymore. Then, whatever she did say couldn't be held against her. She let his low conversation provide a barrier between her and the other guests as the room slowly filled during the next hour. She recognized Sean Killian, the local horse-shoer with his new wife. That was another wedding she hadn't attended, but he'd understood when she gave him a gift basket the next time he came to trim the horses. He'd brought her Pooka last spring, promising a puppy could make almost anyone feel better, especially a rough-coated collie mix who loved to snuggle and who protected her from the monster in her nightmares.

More of the Dawsons filtered into the chapel including Clancy and Kate escorted by their former fiancés, Sean's older brothers. It looked like the broken engagements weren't working either, but Nina didn't share that. The Jamison family slipped into the row beside them, seventeen-year-old, sandy-haired, Orion taking the seat next to Kyle, nodding at Nina, but not speaking.

She heaved another breath, then glanced over her shoulder when she heard footsteps. Behind her, Marlene Dawson, the leader of one of the largest horse 4-H clubs in the county for almost forty years, took a seat. Her sister, Darlene who didn't look old enough to have six adult daughters sat next to her along with Joe's father, Dr. Art Watkins.

Slowly, Nina realized they had her surrounded and protected. Tears burned, but she managed to nod at them. "Thank you."

"Beth would want us to look after you," Marlene said, "and this is the first chance we've had in a while."

"What she said." Darlene leaned forward. "I haven't seen your family yet. Where are they?"

"They're not coming. They said that Beth was my customer, not theirs."

"No point in being stupid if you don't display it." Marlene heaved a sigh and shook her head. "I'll try to run interference for them so they don't piss off the entire Dawson bunch and all their kith and kin."

"Why bother?" Darlene demanded, narrowing her blue eyes. "You and Earlene never cut me slack when I screw up."

"You're a Dawson like me since we married into the clan. We hold you to a higher standard and you know Earlene changed her name to Estelle when she left home. Stop being such a turd."

"I'm not and I don't see why you always take her side."

Nina felt a smile edge her lips as the two older women squabbled like teenagers. She flicked a sideways glance at Kyle and saw amusement filter into his face, making lines crinkle around his eyes. She wanted to thank him for providing a distraction but wasn't sure how. Telling a stranger how frightened she was by the people who had known her for years made her sound like the nutcase her family claimed she'd become, not a thirty-two-year-old woman who'd successfully operated a horse rescue for almost a third of her life.

She glanced toward the dais where the choir lined up and a young man began to play the small grand piano. She choked back a nervous giggle when she recognized the tune as Helen Reddy's signature song, *I Am Woman*, the anthem of women's liberation, one of Beth's favorites.

Following the song, the chaplain greeted the crowd and thanked them for coming to celebrate a life taken too soon. He spoke about the woman he'd known, the one who served her country as a medic in the U.S. Army, and then came home to continue her service as a law enforcement officer. Afterward, it was the turn of Beth's police captain and several detectives.

Kyle stirred beside Nina and leaned over to whisper, "They're making her sound like a saint. She'd be telling them to spit in the wind and call it a shower."

"Hush." Nina bumped him with her elbow. "They're creating their own reality. If they admit how much they hated her or the fact that the captain didn't stop the guys from harassing her or they never backed her up, they'll look like even bigger jerks than they are. Nobody believes their crap anyway."

"Want me to take them out and slap them around, Miss Nina?"

"No, that's overkill." She nudged him again. "Watch this. I think Clancy Dawson is about to kick tails and take names."

Without waiting for the last officer to finish speaking, Beth's cousin strolled up to the dais, a red-headed Amazon in a dark blue, western-style dress and fancy cowgirl boots. She took the microphone from an unwilling John Watkins, although she didn't need it. As a horse show judge during the spring and summer seasons, she was accustomed to commanding an audience in a much larger arena. "Wow, I never knew our Beth walked on water when everyone around her made it rain. Comes as news to me and I'll bet it does to you too."

That brought a round of laughter and Clancy favored the crowd with her sunshine smile. "I'm not going to give you a bunch of hogwash about the Bethany Rose Chambers these cops knew that always protected the weak regardless of the cost. I'm going to tell you about the little girl my uncle adopted and the first time he brought her to a family picnic and the way she loaded up her pockets with food because she never knew if or when she'd have another meal which was why my mother and sister always sent her home with leftovers. And when I get done, I want the rest of you to get up here and share your stories about our Beth too. The real person, not the one who had to be perfect at the Eagleville precinct because all of us know a woman has to be twice as good at everything she does to earn half as much recognition."

Nina glanced over her shoulder at Darlene. "I didn't know she went hungry as a kid. She never told me."

Darlene shrugged, blinking dark blue eyes to hold back tears. "I hope someone shares the way Beth kicked butt and threw coffee cups when she lost her temper. Otherwise, she'll sound like even more of a saint when my daughters get done."

2

COFFEE CUP IN HAND, POOKA ROMPING AROUND HER, NINA headed for the barn to feed the eight horses that still depended on her. She couldn't say she'd enjoyed the memorial the day before but was glad she'd attended. She hadn't been able to go to Billy-Bob's, the restaurant where the Dawson family and all their relatives intended to have food and continue the celebration of Beth's life. She'd told Audra that she needed to get home to look after the rescued animals, but the other woman's look was understanding, too understanding, although there hadn't been any pity.

For that, Nina felt gratitude. She took a deep breath, forcing away fear as she opened the door and stepped inside, immediately heading for the light switch. Nickers and whinnies greeted her and she paused for a moment to look down the row of stalls. No humans, just four-legged critters wanting breakfast. Pooka whined softly, brushed by her to charge ahead to inspect the old barn.

Nina sighed. Her stepfather and stepsisters said she always overreacted to everything, calling her a drama diva even before the assault, so they didn't care for the changes she'd made in her daily life. One of them complained constantly about her taking over a downstairs bedroom because she was on crutches and couldn't make it to her old room upstairs when she returned home from the hospital. A second griped about the way she looked between surgeries when her face was still healing. The third and her husband had frequent discussions about what a 'bitch' Nina was and how she played the 'victim' card when they knew she'd overhear. The youngest said she'd overstayed her welcome in 'their' house.

As usual, her mother opted for another glass of wine and silence, choosing the 'go along to get along' routine that made Nina crazy for more than twenty-five years ever since the marriage to Deke Zacallah that brought him and his four disgusting, spoiled daughters to the Armstrong ranch. Nina knew the bottom line was that she was expected to leave her home to them so they could sell the three hundred acres to the developers. Somehow, she couldn't make herself do it, not when it was her family's place passed down from the first Armstrongs who arrived in the late 1880s.

Nina settled the latest war by moving out of the large, three-story house to the original, homesteader's one-room, log cabin adjacent to the old barn her great-grandfather built. It didn't matter that she heated her new place with an antique wood cookstove, kept her food in an ice chest, and used kerosene lamps for light. Because the house hadn't been lived in for so long, it didn't have electricity or running water. Luckily, there was a bathroom in this barn with a toilet and shower. She used the washing machine in the barn to do her laundry and hung her clothes to dry on the closest fence.

More complaints when she moved the horses to this building near the cabin, but it wasn't what they said. She wasn't on the 'pity pot' and trying to make all the clientele feel they had to choose up sides between her and the Zacallah clan. She simply couldn't bear being in the indoor arena where she was attacked and moving the horses meant she could sometimes go for hours without a flashback.

I didn't ask for Smith to assault me. No woman would. She shuddered, remembering the mantra Estelle Jamison, the new age therapist taught her. *Cancel, cancel. Bad thoughts away. Good memories only today.* Focus on breakfast for the eight horses looking, waiting, stomping and bashing their doors. Water first, then hay and grain.

She flipped the shut-off valve at the end of the expensive hose, the one she'd bought because it was 'drinking water safe' and wouldn't cause cancer in her rescue horses. They'd suffered enough already in their short lives. She lifted the handle on the standpipe and headed for the first stall where Georgia pinned her ears and snorted.

"Get over yourself," Nina told the small bay mare, who was officially measured as a pony even though she was half Arabian and half Morgan. "I've never sprayed you with cold water. I only use warm when you need a bath and if you hadn't fought with that skunk two months ago, we'd have gone with grooming just like we have for the last year."

She continued talking to what remained of her menagerie as she filled their tubs. Minnesota had crapped in hers and that delayed Nina since she had to drag out the gray Arabian's tub to do a dump and scrub. "Honestly, I keep your water spiffy clean so why you do this at least once a week and sometimes once or twice a day is just annoying."

The mare tossed her head, stamping impatiently before nosing Nina's jacket pockets in an obvious search for a carrot. "Like you deserve a treat, Miss Potty in the Wrong Place."

She always chopped up two or three carrots in rounds like her grandmother had done for stews and brought them with her to the barn on every visit, morning, noon, evening, and even on late nights. It was a training technique to teach the abused animals that all people weren't evil. Nina gave Minnesota two pieces and moved onto Alabama's stall. He and his brother, Alaska were old and arthritic palominos in their late twenties who could be trusted to teach any young riders, but they weren't fast enough to remain popular with their high school riders who'd passed them around a gaming club and finally abandoned them when they couldn't barrel race or do games at a dead run anymore regardless of how much they were whipped and spurred.

Nina had taken them in last January and didn't expect to find them homes. They'd just live out their days with her. They didn't bite or kick or do anything wrong, adoring whatever attention she managed to give them, especially grooming. Alaska sometimes had trouble picking up his legs to have his hooves picked, but it was an old age issue, not a behavioral one.

Onto the ponies, Arkansas, California, and Colorado that Nina privately called, 'the three musketeers.' They had adjacent stalls because they were so bonded. Marlene Dawson brought them up in February when she found them starving in a pasture after their owners sold their property and moved out of state. Some of Nina's visitors called them, 'black beauties,' but only California was truly black. Colorado was a dark brown, such a rich color that she looked like her buddy instead of the liver chestnut that she truly was and Arkansas was a blue roan, black with white hairs mixed into his coat. Arkansas and California were typical Shetlands, but her sturdy build, height, and bill of sale showed Colorado was a Welsh Mountain pony.

Missouri, the last horse was one of her all-time favorites. A former show horse, he'd come with a stall mate that she'd managed to adopt out just before the assault. A tall, nearly pure-bred, flashy chestnut with white markings, the registered Arabian had serious issues whenever he had to leave the barns or arenas. However, he was amazing in the ring. Over the past year, Nina managed to teach him to go to the paddock outside his stall, but he still rolled his eyes and spooked when she tried to ride him outdoors.

Nina finished filling his water tub and fed him the last six carrot pieces. "Someday, we'll be able to ride with the big boys and I won't give you to anyone who thinks you're a robot pony who should just go, stop, turn, have perfect gaits, and not have a personality."

Missouri crunched the last carrot, flicking his ears at her. He never nuzzled her or demanded attention, but he liked it when she stroked his white blaze and talked to him. Unlike many of her rescues, he didn't have any physical scars. All of his were psychological.

Pooka woofed a low warning and streaked down the aisle to stand guard against her leg, a tri-colored, collie protector. Nina glanced toward the far barn door in time to see Gretchen Zacallah, her youngest stepsister stalk inside. The petite blonde in breeches and a sweater stormed toward her, slapping a crop against her knee-high English boots. "What did you do yesterday? All three of my morning students cancelled today and your mother is still fielding phone calls."

Nina stepped warily around the woman, keeping an eye on the whip. "I reminded your entire family about Beth Chamber's memorial service more than once. I went to it along with most of the county. Even the police and firemen showed up since she was a detective, a medic, and an emergency first responder as well as an Army veteran."

"So, what? She was one of your students, not mine."

"She was a Dawson, adopted but still one of their clan. I told your family that again when all of you were at breakfast yesterday." Nina dragged the hose back down the barn and began to coil it, the dog beside her. "As Estelle Jamison says, 'what goes around, comes around' and of course, you should expect consequences for any choices you make."

Gretchen raised the whip and Nina lifted the end of the hose. "Don't go there. I don't start battles but the cops yesterday told me I had a right to defend myself and I will call them if I'm attacked again."

Pooka growled in agreement, showing white teeth. One more glare and Gretchen turned, stomping from the building, muttering curses. Nina dropped the hose and grabbed the half-grown puppy in a tight hug, shaking. Granted the police had been talking about what to do if Smith came through the restraining order, not the Zacallah bunch, but they wouldn't know it was a bluff.

Black plumed tail wagging, Pooka wiggled and tried to lick her cheek. He had the traditional black and white coat with golden brown eyespots, tan cheek spots, and tan markings on the legs, but his heeler blood meant he also had mottling or speckles on his white ruff and paws. Nina accepted one more doggie kiss and hugged him again. "Come on, we have horses to feed, and then we'll go make bacon and eggs for us. The stove should be warm enough by the time we get back inside."

She picked up her insulated travel mug, took one last swallow of coffee, and continued with the chores. On the way to the two-story hay-room, Pooka brought her his ball and she tossed it down the hallway. He raced after it, earning a snort from Georgia but the rest of the horses ignored the game in favor of whinnying for alfalfa and grain.

Nina knew traditional horsy people would have issues with playing 'doggie fetch' in her barn, but she figured anything that desensitized the abused horses was a plus. She'd loaded a bale of hay the night before so it didn't take long to push the wheelbarrow down the aisle and pass out flakes of alfalfa grass to the hungry mares and geldings. She followed that with their grain and then she strolled toward the cabin. She'd let the horses eat while she and Pooka did. After that, she'd groom them before Sean Killian arrived to trim their hooves.

She stopped on the back porch and collected an armload of firewood on her way inside, grimacing. The memorial stressed her so much she'd forgotten to buy a bundle of wood on the way home from the grocery in Eagleville. It meant she could fix breakfast, but she'd have to run out today for more wood if she wanted heat and meals later. Oh well, if it wasn't one thing, it was another.

Pooka headed for the daybed in the living room. He jumped up and snuggled with his teddy bear while she built up the fire in the wood cookstove. Enough light streamed through the windows that she only needed to light the kerosene lamp on the kitchen table.

Using warm water from the teakettle, she washed her hands. She took the lid off her travel mug, dumped the remains of the coffee into a regular cup, and added hot, replacing the blue enamel pot on the stove. "Okay, our food's next."

She found classic country music on her cell phone, put it on the counter so she could sing along while she fried bacon and scrambled eggs in a cast-iron skillet. In the three months, she'd lived here she'd learned a lot and now she placed two pieces of sourdough bread directly on the clean cooktop behind her pan. Granted, she had to watch the toast closely so it didn't burn, but she was good with that.

"Pioneer folks, that's us." She dished up her food and dribbled the remaining grease on Pooka's kibble. She had to wait for it to cool before she fed him so he didn't burn his mouth, but meantime he got the piece of toast she used to wipe out the skillet. He took it under the table and she sat down to eat her own meal.

After she ate, she added her leftovers to Pooka's dish and fed him in what he considered his den. Then, she cleaned up using hot water from the reservoir on the stove to wash her few dishes from yesterday and today. She'd have to bring over a bucket of water from the barn to refill the small tank and wondered again how her great-grandparents managed to have water inside before digging the well or installing a pump. Her father was the one who updated the barn but hadn't seen any sense in installing pipes in the cabin when they'd freeze in winter. She put a batch of sourdough bread to rise, started a pot of potato soup, and ran the carpet sweeper over the rug in the living area.

She glanced at her watch. Ten o'clock and all was well. She had approximately an hour to groom the horses. She checked the fire in the stove and added another two pieces of wood. Now, her soup could simmer all day. She glanced over her shoulder as she slid into her down vest. "Let's go, buddy."

Pooka eased out from under the table and they headed for the door. She stopped on the porch long enough to lock it since she didn't want to return and discover any intruders inside and that included members of the Zacallah clan. She collected a bucket of brushes and a halter from the hay room, then went into Georgia's stall. Pooka flopped outside the door, chewing on a stick.

Not even a year ago, Nina would have turned on her favorite country music station while she groomed the horses, but not anymore. She needed to be able to hear if anyone approached. She talked softly while she cleaned the bay mare's hooves, oozing compliments about how pretty the horse was and Georgia flicked her ears in apparent agreement.

Pooka dropped the stick, rose, and stood outside the stall, growling. Nina nodded and glanced toward the door to see Yekandra, Gretchen's older sister approach. In her mid-thirties, small with waist-length brown hair neatly braided and pinned in a coronet, the woman always had an edge. Being in the second trimester of a first pregnancy didn't help. Nina wondered if her stepsister would have been happier if she'd chosen a kinder husband, but Roland was just as nasty. Did the two of them make each other worse or did their marriage stop them from harming two decent partners?

"Good morning, Kandra." Nina paused, body brush in hand and petted Georgia's neck, glancing at the woman in the barn aisle. As usual, she wore a calf-length, loose-fitting flowered dress because her father didn't approve of women in pants and her husband backed up his archaic, patriarchal views. "How are you feeling today?"

"I'd be better if I didn't have to come to hunt you down and you showed up on time for meals."

"I don't eat at my mother's house. I eat at mine." Keeping a wary eye on the older woman, Nina ran the brush over Georgia's shoulder. "Is there some reason you want me to visit?"

"Sean Killian called looking for you." Yekandra narrowed brown eyes, fury spreading across her face, causing her cheeks to turn red. "He said he wanted to give you a heads up that he's bringing an apprentice today and he told Roland that he won't have time to shoe for us anymore. When Roland suggested the apprentice take over, Sean said, 'no' and he hung up."

"I wonder why he didn't call me on my cell," Nina said. "I charged it up yesterday when I cleaned the barn." She put the brush on the wall, dug out the phone, and checked messages. Surprisingly, she didn't have any from the shoer so she texted him. He'd respond when he wasn't under a horse. "That's different. I don't recall Sean having an apprentice in years, not since Laredo Hawke and he's working up in Baker City now. Sean didn't say anything about it yesterday."

"Why did you see him then?"

"At the memorial." Nina put away the phone and picked up the brush again. Often, she felt like she spoke a foreign language that none of the Zacallahs understood. "His family has always been connected to the Dawsons even before his brothers got engaged so of course, the Killians showed up en-masse. Their father, Senator Killian couldn't make it back from the other Washington, but he sent an immense floral arrangement on its own easel, all-white mums, roses, and tulips with greenery and two of his high-ranking aides came with Mrs. Killian."

"I don't believe this. Why are we being targeted because you didn't tell us how important some stupid detective was?"

"Beth was my friend, not just a customer." Nina struggled to keep her tone even. "And I did tell you that it was low-class not to come with me to the memorial since she'd boarded her horse here ever since she bought Tigger four years ago. Besides, you've treated Sean rudely for years and Roland told him that he over-charged. What's the big deal about Sean firing you as clients now?"

"He's the best farrier in the county, if not the entire state. How's it going to look to our customers when he won't shoe for us, but still does your pity ponies?"

"Like he needs a tax write-off." Nina knew it wasn't true, but it worked. It provided Yekandra with the excuse she needed and she flounced out of the barn.

Nina heaved a sigh. "Why do I think the peace and quiet is over? I hadn't seen them in nearly two weeks except for yesterday morning when I went to their house. Now, two of them in only a few hours?" She shook her head, brushing Georgia's back. "I'll bet the rest of them show up to bitch and moan before the end of the day."

3

BACK IN THE DAY, HIS BROTHER ARRANGED FOR HIM TO LEARN horseshoeing from Lars Swensen, the blacksmith at the Lazy B, but Kyle Morgan didn't say that to Sean Killian. He hadn't been thrilled with the idea of taking Kyle to the Armstrong place. Sean told Audra Dawson-Watkins that he didn't see the point when he planned to drop them as clients. He was downsizing since he intended to pursue his veterinary career at long last and would be taking more college classes after Christmas.

Sean shot a sideways glare at Kyle before focusing on the highway once more. "I'll say again this makes no sense, Nina's suffered enough."

"I'm only aiming to help her like I promised." Kyle leaned back in the passenger seat of the pickup, pulling his hat to shade his eyes. He didn't say the promise was to his sister by marriage. Few folks in these parts knew his story and he wasn't sharing it with a near stranger.

"Keep in mind that if it comes to you or her, I made my choice long ago." Sean signaled for a right turn off the highway. He drove through wooden gates, down a long, paved driveway toward a large, gray, and white house complete with a porch that wrapped around two sides, covered by a huge balcony supported by giant white pillars. It looked like it belonged to a southern plantation, not a property nestled in the Cascade foothills.

Kyle whistled softly. "Some folks have more money than sense."

"It's always the way." Sean drove past the house toward an enormous barn. "Of course, the Zacallah's don't waste it by paying their bills on time. They always want me to submit an invoice. When I get their checks, I still have to call their bank to see if the funds are available."

"That's why you told them I wouldn't shoe for them, isn't it?"

"Even if I think Joe and Audra have a stupid idea, I wouldn't put my worst enemy in a 'can't win' situation." Sean parked the truck in front of the building. He climbed out and walked toward the back of the rig.

Kyle followed. He waited while Sean put on a pair of leather chaps, caught the worn pair the other man threw at him, and did the same. Gloves came next. Kyle stepped up, took two buckets of tools.

They started toward the arena. Sean stopped when a tall, lanky man in a tweed jacket, high-necked sweater, and pants tucked in fancy knee-high boots sauntered toward them. Sean nodded. "Morning, Roland."

"Thought you weren't coming today, Killian." Roland's smile didn't touch brown eyes. "You said we needed to find another farrier."

"You do, but I'll still handle Nina's rescues. They need special treatment."

"Well, they're not here and neither is she." He turned his head, spat. "About time too."

A tense silence mounted between the men. Sean reached in his denim jacket, pulled out a cell phone, and pressed buttons. "Nina, it's Sean. I'm here. Roland says you've moved out. Where are you?"

Kyle watched as a faint tinge of red crept into the other man's face. Had he thought they'd leave on his say-so?

Roland scowled at Kyle. "What are you looking at?"

"Nothing much," Kyle drawled, narrowing his own gaze. He didn't bother to put down the buckets of shoeing tools. Roland didn't seem the type to start a ruckus with another fellow and most folks around here talked rather than resorting to fisticuffs. "Figure a *real* man don't declare war on women, or children, or critters."

That earned him a scathing glance before Roland turned and headed back to the barn. Kyle hoped there wasn't a horse who'd suffer the consequences of the man's temper, but standing silent wasn't a Morgan trait. Kyle eyed Sean. "So, where is she?"

"At the other side of the ranch. She didn't say as much, but they kicked her out of the house a couple of months ago." Sean took one of the buckets. "Let's load up and drive over. Roland hires his beat-downs done."

"Hope he pays them better than he does his shoer." Kyle followed the older man back toward his pickup. "Else, they'll come after him."

"Anything scare you, Morgan?"

"Yup. My brother and his wife. They'll tear out my innards and serve 'em for supper if I don't step up and look after Miss Nina."

"Sound like my kind of people." Sean chuckled. "Give their phone number to Elinor so she can invite them to our next barbeque."

Kyle nodded and put the tools in the rear of the truck, then strolled to the cab, opening the passenger door. He wasn't going to do it, but he couldn't tell Sean that Rad and Bethany were alive and well in 1888 Liberty Valley without sounding loco. As they drove past the house, Kyle spotted an older, gray-haired man in a dark suit standing on the porch. "Who's that?"

"Deke Zacallah. He came to run the ranch twenty-five years ago, married Nina's mother, Rhonda, and moved his family in here. Could have been a good match, but if Nina's relatives hadn't raised hell when he sent her off to boarding school and involved a bunch of lawyers, the Armstrong ranch would be one more housing development."

"Wouldn't the spread belong to Nina's ma?"

"So most would think, but it was homesteaded by the Armstrongs before the turn of the century, the 20th century and those folks were pretty darn smart. They set it up so the ranch goes through the Armstrong line and it has to be blood relations, not those who married into the family. When Nina's father died, the land went to her. If something happens to her, it goes to her cousins, not the Zacallah's."

Sean turned right, down a narrow dirt track barely visible through tall evergreens. The truck bounced from one rut to the next. He came to a stop in front of a tiny log cabin with a corral off to the right, adjacent to a small barn.

"Looks cozy." Kyle spotted Nina in the corral with a bay horse. "Like home."

"How can you say that after seeing where she should be? She's the one entitled to the big house and fanciest show barn around."

Kyle pointed to the smoke rising from the chimney of the cabin, the young dog romping toward them, the woman waving. "Seems happier here. I bet that driveway keeps most city slickers from visiting. From what I've seen since I arrived in July, folks here tend to think more of their cars than they do their kin or kinder."

Without waiting, Kyle opened his door and strode to the corral. It wouldn't be proper for him to mention how pretty she looked in work pants that outlined round hips and long legs before being tucked into laced-up riding boots or the green plaid shirt that clung to her bosom making her hazel eyes appear more green, than brown. "Mornin', ma'am. You sure have a fine-looking horse there. Got a name for her?"

Nina smiled, then laughed. "Of course, Georgia has a name. Why wouldn't she? Your horse does, even if some people wouldn't call it politically correct."

"Reckon so, but S.O.B. will take me where I want to go all day long. Don't matter how rocky or muddy the trail gets, or what comes at us, he doesn't have a speck of 'give up' in him. We mosey through, so his name fits."

"That makes sense." Nina glanced past him to Sean. "Sorry about the confusion. I thought you knew I moved back to the old place. Marlene came with her sister for coffee last week."

"No worries." Sean shrugged and took the toy cloth disc from the collie and gave it a toss. Tail wagging, the pup raced after it. "Guess if I'd asked, she'd have told me. Like Kyle says, you look happy and it's all that's important. Shall we get these trims done?"

"Happy?" Nina blinked, then gave Kyle a long, steady look. "I hadn't considered it. How did you know?"

"Anybody but a fool would be happier here than living some-where with that greenhorn and you don't appear to be lacking in sense."

"Greenhorn?" Nina tilted her head, eyeing Kyle, then Sean. "Who is one?"

"Roland." Sean climbed through the corral fence. "Well, come on, Morgan. Let's see what you know and if you can trim this girl or if she kicks your head in before you finish with the first hoof."

"And here I figured Miss Nina liked me a little. Thanks for the warning."

Nina giggled. "He's talking about Georgia. She hates men and barely tolerates Sean."

"Too bad I don't have any of Señora Ortiz's biscuits. We could make friends." Kyle buckled the belt on the leather chaps, then fastened the snaps that held the leather in place over his legs. "Reckon, I'm ready if she is."

———

She didn't remember the last time she'd laughed but admitted silently that Kyle Morgan had his own brand of charm. Nina tight-ened her grip on the lead line as he approached the mare so the horse couldn't bite him. Georgia flicked her ears, then pinned them flat against her head, giving the man her ugliest, menacing look.

She clicked her teeth when he stopped and stood nearby. He didn't reach for her hoof or leg. He simply stood stock still for a moment, then began to scratch the filly's neck. Eventually, she heaved a sigh and rotated her ears to a sideways position. He kept rubbing and petting, before glancing at Nina.

"What's her story? Bound to have a reason to be riled up."

"I'm not sure. She came with her dam who was the sweetest mare I'd ever seen despite being starved until she was the proverbial rack of bones. Florida passed on last winter. Dr. Art Watkins said old age combined with prior neglect caused her to have heart trouble and she went in her sleep. A lot of my rescues are abused by men, so they have serious issues with your gender. I've only had one gelding in the last fifteen years that arrived with a serious hate for women and he just attacked blondes."

"I remember him." Broad-shouldered in his flannel western shirt, Sean leaned against the corral rail. "Died out in the pasture for no apparent reason. You had Art take him into the Snohomish clinic. We did a necropsy on him and discovered he had advanced liver disease, brought on by ingesting buttercups."

"Any of your horses not have misery in their pasts?"

"Afraid not, Kyle," Nina said. "When I inherited the Armstrong trust at eighteen, I started rescuing abused, starved horses. There are plenty of people that go to the kill pens to stop animals from going to Canada for slaughter. I stick around the western part of the state and take the unwanted ones, horses left behind by those who claim to *love* them."

"One of your cousins does the same for dogs and another does it for cats," Sean said, warmth filling his gray eyes.

"Yes, and my aunts and uncles do a lot for foster kids, troubled teens, and the homeless too." Nina stroked Georgia's face. "The Armstrong family philosophy runs along with what President Kennedy said, 'For of those to whom much is given, much is required.'"

"Comes from the Bible too." Kyle ran a hand down the horse's brown leg. "Jesus said in Luke, 'For unto whomsoever much is given, of him shall be much required; and to whom men have committed much, of him they will ask the more.'"

The quote surprised Nina. She waited while he picked up the hoof and cleaned it. "Sounds like you know the Bible really well."

"Not much choice where I was raised." He didn't look over his shoulder at her. Instead, he dug out the dirt, studying the inside of the hoof. "Families always had the *Good Book* even when they didn't have anything else to read and I could listen to their preachifying before supper or take a whipping and go to bed hungry. After a day working in the fields, I'd have my ears wide open even when it was hard to keep my eyes that-a-way."

"Your parents did that?"

"No, ma'am. My ma passed on when I was little bitty. Don't know who my pa was, but he wasn't around. My brother and I ended up in an orphanage and I was adopted early, 'cuz I was a cute bugger. When my new folks died, their kin returned me to the orphan's home. Lived a half-dozen different places until I lit out when I was fourteen. Figured I could take better care of myself than anyone else did."

Nina nodded. "That's pretty much what my aunt hears from the homeless teens on the streets. Unfortunately, it's a common story nowadays."

"Reckon so." Kyle switched to the hoof knife and scraped away a thin layer of the sole. "Killian, want to take a look afore I nip off anything?"

"Yes." Sean stepped up, all professional horseshoer. "Show me what you have in mind."

It took a little more than two hours for Kyle to complete the trims on all eight horses while Sean supervised. Afterward, Nina led the way to the cabin so they could have coffee. She carried in the last of the wood and added it to the fire in the stove before filling three cups with coffee from the blue enamel pot and putting out the plate of chocolate chip cookies Brigid Dawson gave her the day before. "I'll follow you out when you go. I forgot to pick up a bundle of firewood on the way home yesterday."

"You have trees all around, Miss Nina. I'll stock up for you."

"Thanks, but it's easier to go to the store than deal with the family drama if I have the loggers cut wood for me."

"Oh, you don't want green standing timber, ma'am. It'll creosote up the inside of the chimney and cause a fire. No, you want me to fetch dead branches and there's bound to be some under those fir trees." Kyle drank some of his coffee. "Señora Ortiz collects corncobs and saves them for when she wants a hot fire to bake biscuits."

"I'll go to the Lazy B, take care of their horses, and come back for you later, Kyle," Sean said. "It'd give you time to fill the woodshed, not just the box on the back porch."

"If you call Orion Jameson, he can come with his saw to help me," Kyle said. "We could fill Miss Nina's whole woodshed and keep those downed logs from rotting away."

"How do you know there's downed trees?" Picking up a spoon, Nina headed for the stove to stir the pot of soup simmering on the stove. "You didn't walk through the woods to get here."

"If nobody's cleaned up in there for a year or so, there's bound to be a load of 'widow wood', suitable for heating and cooking."

"'Widow wood'?" Sean chuckled. "Haven't heard that phrase since my great-grandma's day."

"I never have." Nina checked the bread dough on the warming oven. Since it was ready to be punched down, then shaped into loaves, she carried the bowl over to the counter. "What does it mean, Sean?"

"My grandma said it was small pieces of wood she could gather herself because it didn't need sawing or chopping. She used to bring the little branches up to the porch and burn them in her tiny airtight stove. It saved on the electric bill. Made my dad crazy because he was always afraid people would see her and say if he didn't take care of his own grandmother, he couldn't be trusted to look after other seniors."

Kyle drank the last of his coffee and set the cup by the sink, picking up his hat. "Which wheelbarrow do you want me to use for wood, Miss Nina? If you're like Mrs. Audra, I reckon you have one for horse feed and one for their droppings."

Nina finished putting the second loaf of bread into the greased pan. "You're right. I use the green one for mucking. Are you sure about this? I don't want to impose."

"No need to fret about that, Miss Nina. I owe you for letting me practice my hoof-trimmin' on your stock since I hadn't done it in a coon's age. Good to know I ain't lost my touch and still have the eye for it." He put on the hat, tipped it courteously, and started for the door. "Sean, reckon now would be a good time for you to speechify with Miss Nina about those horses that your wife wants her to find."

"I reckon so." Sean grinned appreciatively. "Nina, do you have any more of that coffee?"

4

SEAN WAITED UNTIL THE DOOR CLOSED BEHIND KYLE. "I THINK HE watches too many classic cowboy movies, but he seems to be a nicer guy than I figured earlier today. He's not afraid of Roland Wrinn."

"Why would he be?" Nina topped their cups and replaced the coffee pot on the woodstove. "Roland's got a nasty mouth, but he's never struck a woman."

"Only because your step-daddy would kick his butt out of here and Roland knows that better than anyone. He'd have to get an honest job instead of sponging off your mother and the Armstrongs."

"Fair enough." Nina sat down at the kitchen table, across from Sean. "Now, what kind of horses does Elinor want? And why? Doesn't she have enough stock for Silver Lake Pony Ranch?"

"She did, but she's opening a smaller version over at my place in Snohomish. She brought her horse, the kids' ponies, and Blaze who is still recuperating after being shot a couple of months ago, but she needs about six more."

"What's she going to do with them?"

"Lessons, leasing to beginning students so they can practice what they learn, and pony rides. She'll keep doing camp and trail rides over at Silver Lake."

Nina pulled out her notepad and a pen, taking notes. Definitely old school, but she didn't want to waste the battery on her cell phone, for this task. "Skill set for the livestock? I'm assuming they need to put on their *happy faces* and never bite or kick regardless of stupid human mistakes."

Sean chuckled. "You got it. Elinor's students spend more time walking than galloping and more time grooming than riding, but the majority are children."

Pooka lifted his head from where he napped under the table and woofed softly, a low warning bark. The back door opened and Kyle carried in an armload of small branches. He stacked them neatly in the metal holder near the stove. Lingering in the room, he adjusted the dampers on the chimney, added fuel to the fire, closed up the stove, and readjusted the dampers again so heat would circulate through the cabin.

After he left, Nina eyed Sean. "It took me a couple of days to learn how to do that so the place didn't fill with smoke. He was really nice yesterday at the service, but this guy is way different than other men I've met."

"Well, maybe he learned it living on the streets," Sean said. "He shared more with you than he did with me when we trimmed your stock. If you keep asking questions, he'll keep talking. Now, about those horses—"

Nina nodded. "Does Elinor have specific colors she wants? Some people are really prejudiced against black horses, the same way they don't want black cats or black dogs."

"Elinor's not that way. She prefers good personalities to colors or markings, but no spooky ones so we may want to avoid flighty Arabians or smart-alecky Morgans who have no patience for silly riders or young Quarterhorses who still buck."

"Sounds fair." Nina wrote down that information. She wouldn't tell him she appreciated the equine assignment and the money it'd bring. She hated seeing her Uncle Omar once a quarter and running the budget for her rescue by him, although he never quibbled on costs and always offered more money than she said she needed.

She felt like a real charity case since she'd stopped teaching lessons and working as a consultant for potential horsebuyers. Sean was the first client she'd had in months. Granted, Uncle Omar never said that and of course, she didn't either. She glanced at the wall calendar and spotted the note. The next foundation meeting was a week away. Crap! That meant she'd have to spend tonight updating her financial records by hand.

Tomorrow, she'd take her laptop and go into town where there was Wi-Fi. Then, she could enter the figures in the spreadsheets and email the attachments to Omar. He'd pass them onto the rest of the board of directors. It wouldn't take that long, but she still hated the trips to Portage or Eagleville. Of course, if she combined it with buying groceries and grain, she'd only waste a day. The difficulty was dealing with the constant stares. Worse was the sympathy.

She took a deep breath, focused on Sean again. "What sizes does Elinor want?"

————

Kyle whistled softly as he broke up a dead fir branch, then loaded the pieces into the full wheelbarrow. He'd almost filled the wood box on the porch. He wouldn't finish filling the woodshed next to the cabin today unless Orion came with his chainsaw, but she'd have enough firewood to last a few days and keep her warm. He pushed the wheelbarrow out to the driveway.

"Who are you and what are you doing?" A female voice demanded.

Kyle turned, saw a woman with short, dark hair standing in the road. He still wasn't quite accustomed to gals in the work pants

Mrs. Audra called 'jeans' or tight-fitting, low-cut shirts. He nodded a greeting. "Afternoon, ma'am. I'm fetching wood for Miss Nina."

"I didn't know she'd hired help."

"I'm not hired yet. Just helping out after the coffee and *with-it* she provided." Kyle pushed the wheelbarrow up the rutted drive toward the cabin. "Reckon, a lady alone can use all the help she can get."

"She's not alone. Who the hell are you?"

"Kyle Morgan and I didn't see anyone else living with her, 'cept her critters. And your name, ma'am? I'll tell her that she has a caller."

"Leah Zacallah and what do you mean by a caller?"

"Maybe, I oughta say a visitor." Kyle kept walking, kept pushing the wheelbarrow across the yard to the porch. "I'm still learning how you folks talk here. You did come to visit, didn't you?"

Another long look and then she nodded. "Did you arrive with Sean Killian? Are you his new apprentice?"

"I came with him." Kyle parked the wheelbarrow, climbed the steps, and walked across the porch to tap on the door, before opening it. "Miss Nina, you have a visitor. A Miss Zacallah is here to see you."

"Thanks, Kyle." Nina stood and came across the room to the doorway, the dog at her heel. She glanced at the woman in the yard. "We're having coffee, Leah. Would you like to join us?"

"I wanted to talk to Sean about trimming and shoeing the rest of the stock," Leah said. "Is he with you?"

"Yes." Nina stepped back and waited, taking a moment to eye the firewood neatly sorted in the large wood box on the porch. "I can't believe you found all this, Kyle. Where was it?"

"In the grove under those evergreens. When I come back, I'll bring an ax and split kindling for you. It will make it easier for you to start your cookfire, Miss Nina."

"Why don't you just get an ax out of the toolroom, Nina?" Leah climbed the steps, heading for the open door. "We have several, don't we?"

"I don't like drama," Nina said, keeping her tone even, "and I don't want to be accused of stealing or anything else if I go in the buildings over by the big house."

"Don't see how it's stealing, Miss Nina," Kyle stacked wood neatly. "It's your place and your tools and your buildings. It's even your fancy house although lots of folks would like this cozy one better. Reckon, you tell me to fetch one of your axes for you and I will. I'll bring one of your hatchets too."

Leah froze on the porch, glancing between Kyle, Nina, and Sean. "What are you saying?"

"He's not from around here so he doesn't know to keep his mouth shut about your family taking her inheritance when she was little more than a baby," Sean drawled. "And the talk around Liberty Valley is bound to get worse since everyone knows your family blames her for that crazy man assaulting her."

"Smith is evil, not loco," Kyle said. "If Miss Nina hadn't been home, he'd have killed Mrs. Audra. Bottom line was finding one of Bethany's best friends and butchering her to break Bethany's heart and spirit."

Nina ignored Leah's gasp of shock and outrage. "Why are you really here, Kyle Morgan?"

"To watch over you, Miss Nina. That devil is outta jail now and no piece of paper will stop him. But, I will."

"You mean you'll protect her until the police get here?" Leah asked.

"Reckon, that's another option," Kyle agreed. "Not my first choice or Rad's, but it'll do."

Nina rested her hand on Pooka's head in an obvious attempt to calm the growling pup who stood between her and the other woman before stepping closer to Kyle. "He told you to kill Smith, didn't he?"

"Yes, ma'am." Kyle removed his hat, ran a hand through his hair, and replaced the Stetson. "Don't aim to scare you though. Rad wouldn't want me doing that, doesn't cotton to men who disrespect women."

"It doesn't frighten me." Nina smiled up at Kyle. "I wish he was here so I could thank him for sending you."

"Once Smith is out of the picture, I'll take you to Rad's place and you can thank him yourself."

"I'll look forward to that." Another smile, one that touched her eyes this time. With Pooka at her heel, she turned to take her guest into the house.

Kyle returned to stacking wood. He flicked a quick glance at Sean who stepped up to help unload the wheelbarrow. "Reckon, you didn't want me telling her that I'm here to kill Smith, not coddle him."

"I don't have a problem with it after what he did to her. You need help disposing of the body, let me know."

———

While she filled another coffee cup, Nina remembered all the buzzwords about another person not being able to make her feel anything, but oddly enough Kyle Morgan's matter-of-fact attitude made her feel safe for the first time in ages.

"I'll tell the family you need to be in the house with the rest of us." Leah took the cup, frowning at the strong, dark brew. "Do you have any cream or sugar?"

"Yes, but don't do me any favors." Nina crossed to the camping cooler, opened the lid and took out the carton of flavored creamer, then pointed to the sugar bowl on the table. "I don't want to be in that house any more than the rest of you want me there. Instead of fighting with the Killians, you'd do better to use your energy to find a different shoer."

Leah doctored her coffee, then took a cautious sip. "You don't understand anything about people, do you? If they see you as a victim, then we're cast as the villains. I'm sure when Sean goes home and tells his wife that you're living in a backwoods cabin, she'll decide that's our fault too, not your choice."

Continuing to stand near the stove, Nina counted silently to ten so she wouldn't show the older woman to the door. "My choice? Was I supposed to throw a fit and say it was *my* house? Did all of you want to hear I'd sleep in whichever room I wanted? Arreana freaked when I didn't climb the stairs to the guestroom and borrowed her bedroom on the first floor while she was away."

"Don't be silly. Uncle Omar offered to install an elevator in the house and you wouldn't let him. Of course, that upset your entire family."

"You're not my family." Nina took a deep breath, keeping her tone even. "I don't see the point in the Armstrong foundation paying for regular updates on the big house when the money would be better spent on our causes."

"You and your causes." Leah sniffed in blatant disgust. "What about your mother? She deserves a decent life, not constant scrubbing and cooking because we can't pay a housekeeper or maids."

"Not my circus, not my monkeys," Nina said with utter calm. "I told Uncle Omar the foundation doesn't pay for the upkeep while she lives there with your family. She made her bed. She can lie in it with your father, but I'm not the Zacallah cash cow anymore."

Leah gasped. "You bitch."

Nina nodded, folding her arms. "Yes. Your family should have sucked up to me when I was seven instead of sending me off to boarding school. I could have been taught to love you, but instead, you screwed up. After the way you treated me when I was hurt by what Kyle calls that nutcase, I made sure to tell the board of directors not to spend one red cent on the Armstrong house while any of the Zacallahs are in residence. And I really don't care if Sean continues to spread the word that I'm here in the cabin."

"We may not understand you, but we do love you, Nina."

She didn't even take time to consider that nonsense. She had at least a hundred memories that proved the falseness of such a notion including skipped birthdays, no presents for Christmas, not even a letter when she was at boarding school making her an object of scorn by some of the other students. "Show me. Bring over those tools for Kyle."

"Like what?"

"Oh, let's start with the ax and hatchet he wants. Then, a hammer, an assortment of nails, rolls of wire, and lumber to repair the barn paddocks and the pasture fences."

Leah sipped her coffee. "I'll talk to Dad about it and you'll arrange for Sean to shoe the horses in the big barn."

"Like I said, that's his choice, not mine. You'll have to talk to him. He may be tired of waiting for the Zacallahs to pay him, especially since he has a new family to support."

"What are you talking about?"

"Come on. Didn't you think Uncle Omar would ask me about the shoeing bills when he went through my accounts last quarter? I told him I only have eight horses and Sean tends to write those off as a charitable donation. You're running a boarding and training barn. Pay for what those horses need out of what you charge their owners. The Armstrong foundation isn't your cash cow either."

That earned another scathing look before Leah put the cup on the wooden counter by the sink and stalked out the door, slamming it behind her.

Nina took a deep breath. Standing up wasn't her favorite thing to do, but she couldn't keep being a doormat for the entire family. Once Leah spread the word that sponging off the foundation was over, she could expect more drama from the Zacallah bunch. She'd bet it wouldn't end with their family. Sooner or later, they'd send her mother over with a fresh batch of guilt, but this time Nina wasn't buying.

Someone tapped on the back door and Pooka gave a yip of greeting, moving out from under the table. Kyle petted the dog. "If you make us a list, Miss Nina, then Sean will go with me to fetch those tools for you and we can lock them in your woodshed for now."

"What if Roland pitches a fit?"

"Ain't like he packs a gun, Miss Nina and it's your things. We'll just fetch them for you."

5

THE NEXT AFTERNOON, NINA TURNED INTO HER DRIVE. POOKA lifted his head but didn't shift from where he lay on the passenger seat of the pickup, an unconcerned co-pilot. She slowed as she saw another truck and two men shoveling gravel into the ruts closest to the cabin. As she neared, she recognized Kyle Morgan and Orion Jamison. She pulled closer and slowed to a halt, but didn't turn off the engine.

Kyle rested his shovel against the other truck, then strode toward her. Removing his hat, he waited until she unrolled the window. "Afternoon, Miss Nina."

"What are you doing?"

"Fixing your road a mite to make it easier for you to get in and out."

"If you fix the road, it also makes it easier for company and I don't want any."

"Yes, ma'am. I reckoned on that so we're only putting rock in the deepest chuckholes. Then when the rain comes, you won't get stuck in the mud. Figured if it was all right with you, Orion and I would build a gate for the far end and fence off the drive so nobody could come to call without your say-so. He brought his chain saw and we'll drop a tree for posts, plus clear out a couple of those dead ones for firewood and finish filling your shed."

Nina eyed him warily. All of his ideas were good ones. She didn't see anything beyond reasonable concern on his rugged features. He didn't shift from his stance, all broad-shouldered patience in low-heeled cowboy boots. She nodded. "All right. Thank you, Mr. Morgan."

He smiled, his dark brown eyes warming. "Yes, ma'am. Your ma's waiting on the porch to see you. She brought your sister."

"Which one?"

"I don't know, Miss Nina. It wasn't Miss Leah, the one who came to call yesterday when I was here."

"Okay. I appreciate the warning."

He nodded, replaced his hat, and then turned to rejoin the young sandy-haired man who'd continued to work. Orion offered a friendly wave as Nina drove past him to the house. She took a deep breath, rolled up the window most of the way so Pooka could breathe, but wouldn't be able to jump out to join her.

She switched off the engine when she parked behind the side-by-side ATV in front of the cabin. She left the groceries in the back of the truck, grateful for the first time that she didn't have a refrigerator so she hadn't bought her favorite ice cream. She'd unload everything once she'd dealt with her so-called company. Gawd, she hated visitors, especially those with their own agendas.

She pushed Pooka back when he tried to climb out with her. He'd be safer in the rig. She locked the driver's door, then headed up to the porch where her mother waited with Arreana Zacallah, as blonde as her youngest sister. For a moment, Nina wanted to return to her pickup, race down the driveway and hit the highway until she found somewhere safe from the entire bunch. She couldn't, not when she had horses depending on her.

Instead, she continued putting one foot in front of the other until she stood on the stairs, eyeing the two women in the plastic chairs on the porch. Both wore jeans and sweatshirts. Still slender in her late fifties, Rhonda Zacallah didn't look her age, but that was undoubtedly due to her last facelift. She'd been a proponent of cosmetic surgery forever and Nina wouldn't have cared except that her mother always wanted the foundation to pay the cost.

Nina inclined her head. "Well, I wish I could say this is a surprise. It's not. What do you need?"

"I wanted to talk to you about the new man you hired," Rhonda said. "Your father is upset because the toolroom is empty."

"That's a shock." Nina folded her arms, keeping her gaze on the tall dark-haired woman who'd given birth to her, but preferred her stepdaughters to her own flesh and blood. "My father died twenty-seven years ago, when I was five. He hasn't complained about anything since then and I'm sure he wouldn't have cared about a few old hand tools when he was alive. Besides, his grave looked just fine when I put flowers on it an hour ago."

"You know she means my dad." Impatience filled Arreana's tone and her green eyes. "He runs the place. It's ours, not yours."

"Then, take the Armstrong name off it and see what happens," Nina said, struggling to keep her tone even. "Uncle Omar will have his lawyers on your doorstep before dinner."

"There's no need to involve your uncle." Rhonda shot a worried look at Arreana. "If you have the tools taken back, everything will be fine."

"No. Everything here is mine. I can do whatever I want. Right now, I want you to leave. I have work to do."

Utter silence while the two women gaped at her. Nina shifted slightly and pointed to the expensive ATV, one more toy bought with Armstrong money. "Stay and I'll call Uncle Omar on my cell phone and ask him to have the entire Zacallah bunch evicted. I'm tired of your hijinks and since you're in my face when I've done nothing that affects you, then it's time for you to go."

Arreana rose angrily to her feet. "We're leaving, but this isn't the end. I don't know who you think you are—"

"You've been sponging off me for too many years and I'm done being your cash cow. You should have listened to Leah when she told you that yesterday. Coming here and bitching about two shovels, two hammers, three handsaws, one bucket of bent, rusty nails, a five-pound carton of fence staples, a double-bitted ax, a hatchet, an antique post-hole digger, an old fence-stretcher and two spools of recycled hog wire is totally inappropriate even for you people."

Rhonda cast an annoyed glance toward her stepdaughter. "I thought—"

"What? That I wouldn't run an inventory when Sean Killian and Kyle Morgan came back from their scavenging trip? I learned to do that when you gave my clothing and toys to Arreana and Gretchen before shipping me off to boarding school without my teddy bear. If I didn't keep track of what I owned, I lost it."

A tear streaked down Rhonda's perfectly made-up cheek. "I can't believe you're still blaming me for that so many years later."

"What goes around, comes around and you should have expected consequences when you sold my pony and dumped my dog at the pound after Daddy died."

Arreana stalked past Nina toward the ATV. "You're such a drama diva. Of course, Dad got rid of that stupid dog when it bit him. It was vicious."

"He shouldn't have kicked it or cracked its ribs." Nina flicked a glance past her stepsister to her mother still standing on the porch. "What? Do you think I don't remember that? I was seven when you moved your lover in here. I never was stupid. It's why I called and ratted you and Deke out to Uncle Omar and why I got him to take my cat and her kittens. I didn't want them killed too."

Another long look before her mother started toward Arreana. "Will you please come for dinner tomorrow? We need to bridge this gap before everything escalates. Half the county is up in arms because you're living in this shack. The rest will be after the meeting with Omar and the Armstrong board of trustees hits the news media."

"Sorry, I already have plans." Learning to lie well was one more lesson taught in the boarding school world. Taking another breath, Nina shrugged. Most people expected a liar to stand perfectly still and maintain an unblinking pose so she strove to appear calm and perfectly normal, not jerking her head or shuffling her feet, but still rocking on her heels.

"Well, please don't tell them all our business. I didn't evict you from the house."

"No, you didn't have the guts for that," Nina agreed, folding her arms while she gazed at her mother. "You just allowed your husband, his children and their hangers-on to treat me like dirt until I left."

Nothing more was said and she waited until they stomped past her to the ATV, till it roared to life and Arreana drove across country before heaving a huge sigh. Grateful for the respite, Nina strode to the truck where Pooka waited, standing on the bench seat. She unlocked the passenger door and allowed the puppy to jump down.

He pushed against her affectionately, tail wagging and she leaned down to pet his white ruff. "I know, buddy. You wanted to protect me, but I couldn't bear to see another animal hurt by those people."

Tears burned and she blinked hard to keep them from falling. Crying meant spiteful remarks by the other girls at boarding school as well as some of the teachers. She didn't do that either, not anymore. One more heavy sigh and she reached in the back of the truck to lift out two cloth bags filled with groceries. She really did have work to do, but once she finished, she'd groom Missouri out in the corral. If he remained calm, perhaps she could longe him. And if she succeeded with that, he might let her ride him in the small corral.

———

Orion kept shoveling rock. "You planning to move in here, Kyle?"

"I haven't decided if it's needful yet." Kyle frowned, gazing toward the cabin. He didn't hear raised voices, but that didn't mean everything was peaceful. He'd seen wariness creep into

Nina's face and it wasn't because of him or Orion. "She said we could put up a fence and a gate at the end of the drive."

"That won't stop the Zacallahs from visiting." Orion paused, leaning on the shovel handle. "You should ask if we can fence off the back trail from the rest of the ranch. We know full well those women didn't come by us to get to the house. If I hadn't sensed the change in the energy flows and you hadn't heard the ATV, we never would have known they were here and you couldn't have told Nina when she came home. My sister, the lawyer, always says to 'follow the money' and since the Armstrong board of directors meets next week, the Zacallahs are going to be in Nina's face until the next budget is released."

"She doesn't want them around, but they keep visiting."

"Which means there's something they want." Orion wiped his forehead on his t-shirt sleeve, then returned to work. "Meteor sees the two youngest Zacallahs when she caters local parties so I'll ask her to do some spying. I'll pass on what she hears and get my mom over to renew the 'warding' on the cabin."

"Won't your sister lose customers?"

"Nope. She doesn't like Arreana because she always goes after the waiters figuring they can't turn her down. So far Meteor and her friends have been lucky, but they don't want to be sued for having a hostile work environment when their employees are sexually harassed."

"You folks certainly have lots of laws. Wouldn't it be easier if people just learned the difference between right and wrong?"

"First, you have to define what's right and what's wrong, Kyle, and that's been argued for eons."

———

Gary Smith had been watching the house, but he never saw her. One witness, a yapping, little witch who'd spilled her guts to the police and accused him of the attack when he hadn't managed to kill her. Well, it was a mess he intended to clean up before leaving the area for good. Eliminating this last witness in Liberty Valley was in his best interest even if he intended to travel to new killing places. California was nice this time of year and so was Alaska.

It wasn't like the cops in different towns and states talked to each other. They hadn't back in the day and they didn't here either. She couldn't keep hiding in that big house forever. Sooner or later, she'd have to come outside and when she did, he'd grab her. Once he had her, he'd take her to his place near Corbettstown where nobody would intervene. He'd leave the body in the woods for the scavengers.

Since that irritating detective who'd pursued him non-stop remained behind in 1888 with her new lawman husband, it wasn't like anyone would find the remains of her do-gooder friend who thought she was so wonderful for treating horses as if they were people. He missed his club, a black nightstick. He'd had it since his first cop kill years ago when he took it as a souvenir, but it'd been seized by the detectives who arrested him in July. Well, the new cedar club he'd carved would just have to do.

If they'd had results from the lab, he knew he'd be back in jail facing multiple murder charges, although he personally didn't see anything wrong with silencing women who yapped worse than coyotes, constantly bitching about their rights. He'd make every moment of his freedom count before that stupid idiot, John Watkins learned that Chambers bitch was right. Gary Smith lowered the binoculars, stretched, and leaned against the tree again. Where was Nina Armstrong hiding?

6

MORNING CAME EARLY AND SHE MISSED THE CONVENIENCE OF electricity. Some days, it seemed to take forever for coffee to brew in the enamel pot on the woodstove. Nina sighed and reminded herself that the stress and annoyance of living with the Zacallahs made everyday life impossible. At least she didn't start her day by being constantly harassed. Since she had kindling and firewood, courtesy of one Kyle Morgan, it didn't take as long to have fresh coffee in the morning as it had when she moved into the cabin.

Carrying her travel mug, she headed for the door with Pooka an eager escort. Eight horses waited for breakfast and she needed to take care of them before she fixed her own meal. She unsnapped the chain on the barn door and walked inside, freezing in place when she saw the overhead bulbs already lighting the hallway. She didn't see anyone, but she knew she hadn't left on the lights last night after her shower. Someone was here, lurking in the building.

Who was it? Gary Smith?

Pooka tilted his head, curious. Then tail wagging, he emitted a cheerful bark and dashed down the aisle toward the far end of the barn. Apprehensive, ready to turn and run, Nina forced herself to take one more step so she could see what her dog did. Garden hose in hand, someone stood outside Missouri's stall.

Nina slowly approached. As she neared, she recognized the wiry dark-haired man in jeans and a dark blue Armstrong Horse Rescue t-shirt.

Hector Ortiz, a part-time catch rider in his twenties usually worked in the main barn. He glanced at her and smiled. "Morning, Nina. Your brother-in-law sent me over to help you today."

"Why?"

"Don't know." Hector shrugged, still smiling as he reached down to pet Pooka. "There's a lot less drama here so I followed directions. I've filled all the water tubs, dumped, and scrubbed Minnesota's. She's still a super poop diva, isn't she?"

"Always!" Nina sighed, before taking a sip of her coffee. "Don't expect this to be a permanent assignment, Hector. The foundation board meets this week so everyone is trying to get on my good side." Another sip of coffee and she added, "I can talk to Uncle Omar about having you work here if you want although it doesn't have the *cachet* of the big barn."

"I'd prefer being here so please do that. I get enough fame riding the Xanadu Arabians on the circuit during the season. Do you want me to feed the hay while you do the grain?"

"Sounds great." Nina headed for the feed-room. After one last pet from Hector, Pooka raced to join her.

With Hector's help, feeding took a lot less time. She left him to scoop the manure out of the small corral while she went to breakfast. When she returned, he was in Georgia's stall grooming the bay filly. While Nina saddled up, he moved on to prepping Minnesota.

She walked Georgia in both directions around the corral a few times so the skittish mare could see they were safe. An older pickup pulled up in front of the cabin. This time Kyle drove. Orion Jamison was in the passenger seat. Georgia snorted and tossed her brown head, black mane flying for an instant.

"Morning, Miss Nina." Kyle strode across the lawn, pausing to pet Pooka, but not throwing the ball the pup offered. "Want me to hold her while you mount up?"

"She's not quite ready yet." Nina nodded to Orion. "Why are you guys here?"

"We want to work on the gates for your driveway," Orion said. "Be prepared for a major fit from Deke when he hears about it. We checked in with Omar and he told us to get what we needed. We picked up new lumber, nails, and hinges at the hardware store in town, put it on the bill for Armstrong Horse Ranch."

Nina winced, then stroked the mare's neck. "I didn't mention moving to the cabin when I emailed in my reports."

"Reckon he'd do the same thing if it came to choosing between your family and peace and quiet," Kyle said. "I told him we wanted to fix the pasture fence for the horses so they could graze when you weren't training them. It'd save on hay."

"And the individual paddocks off the stalls too," Orion added. "My mother asked me to tell you that she'd be by later today so the two of you can chat. She said there wasn't any need for you to drive over to our place when she'd enjoy a peaceful visit."

"I'll look forward to it." The horse heaved a dramatic sigh, then relaxed and Nina shared an amused look with Kyle. "I think she's ready to work now. Hector Ortiz is in the barn if you need an extra pair of hands. He's helping me out today."

"Ortiz? I wonder if he's related to Gabe. I'll have to ask." Kyle eased through the rails on the fence, straightened, and strode to the right side of the horse, snagging the rein and off stirrup. "She's ready when you are, Miss Nina."

"I don't know all of his relatives, just that his older brothers run the family lumber business, but Hector prefers horses." Nina checked her stirrups. Although nobody else used her saddle, it was still a good safety precaution. Then, she swung up onto Georgia's back. The mare stomped a front foot, pinned her ears, and kicked out with her right hind leg, then with her left before stretching out in what was almost a bow. With the version of horsy yoga complete, she listened to Nina's cues and began to walk around the corral, ears flipped downward in airplane mode, still sulking.

Nina relaxed in the saddle and allowed the mare to sort through her angst as they circled the small ring. Georgia liked grooming, hand-grazing, treats, and lots of attention, but hated riding for some reason known only to her. If she could talk, she'd undoubtedly be on Estelle Jamison's couch for hours, doing emotional laundry while the therapist provided silly little rhymes to keep away tormenting bug-bears. As it was, Nina just made sure all of the equipment fit and didn't hurt the horse before she rode. It wouldn't be possible to find her a forever home until the bay stopped the temper tantrums.

"You ever think about just taking her on the trails?" After he climbed back through the fence, Kyle leaned on the top rail. "She looks bored to me. Can't blame her. Who wants to walk in circles all day?"

"We jog and lope some too." Nina bent to pet the brown neck when the mare settled to a walk, rather than stomping her hooves. "I don't like heading off into the woods by myself. Accidents happen even to the best riders."

"That's fair." Orion stopped petting Pooka and strolled up to the corral. "If you have another stall, we could haul over Kyle's horse or he could ride one of yours."

"Missouri is the only one that could carry him for any length of time, but he's super spooky outside. Alaska and Alabama have arthritis and wouldn't last more than an hour or so and climbing the hills is too difficult for them."

"Let me make friends with Missouri first," Kyle said. "Meantime, we'll go hit a lick on the gates. We dropped the trees yesterday. Will the sound of the saw cutting posts upset Georgia?"

"Nothing annoys her, not cars or trucks or motorcycles, so small engine sounds won't." Nina petted the mare again, considering the question. "You're probably right about letting her get out and go across country for a bit."

"All right. We'll figure out how to make it work, Miss Nina."

———

Liberty Valley was less than two hours away from the F.B.I. branch office in Seattle, but Tasha Endicott thought it was like entering the remote regions of a backwoods enclave when they reached the Cascade foothills. She didn't say that to her partner, Special Agent Brad Newsome. She'd heard the talk that years ago, he'd been excellent on the job. Now, he was good at bellying up to the bar at the end of the day. When they arrived, she'd let him lead the conversation at the Eagleville cop shop. He and Detective John Watkins did the 'good old boy' routine until she was ready to gag, but she kept her nausea and disgust to herself.

"There it is, up ahead on the right." Tasha pointed to the large black and white carved sign, reading 'Armstrong Horse Ranch'. In smaller letters at the bottom, it said, 'Home of Armstrong Horse Rescue.'

"I see it. Couldn't miss it." Brad slowed for the turn, drove through wooden gates, down a long, paved driveway toward a large, gray, and white house complete with a porch that wrapped around two sides, covered by a huge balcony supported by giant white pillars. "Let me do the talking."

"Of course," Tasha said. She didn't have his seniority, but after seven years with the agency, she wasn't new to the job. She took a deep breath and nearly told him that a woman who'd survived a vicious assault would undoubtedly be more comfortable with a female investigator, but they weren't here to reopen that can of worms. They'd leave it to the detectives in Eagleville.

"Our case is Beth Chambers." Brad parked the black SUV in front of the house. "We want to know who killed her, where and when. Nothing else."

Tasha nodded and opened her door. They walked together to the steps where a tall, dark-haired woman in her mid-fifties waited.

———

Astra Jamison grimaced as she turned off the wide paved driveway to a rutted, narrow gravel one. She didn't want to think about what this would do to the shocks of her new Lexus and flicked a side-ways glance at her mother in the passenger seat. "Why am I driving you to see Nina Armstrong on my one day off this month? You could have come by yourself."

"I could, but you know the rules. The *Lady* told me you were needed here and no, I don't know why yet."

A few minutes later, Astra parked in front of the old log cabin. She reached in the back seat for her black jacket. She shrugged into it, feeling the comfort of its power as she fastened the buttons. She wasn't a judge yet, but somehow her dark lawyer suit of black pants, sleeveless navy shell, and a fitted black coat made her feel as if she'd donned the robes of justice. Her sisters had their defenses. The law was hers.

Leaving her mother behind, Astra sauntered across the yard toward the corral where Nina Armstrong rode a small bay. Ears pricked forward, the mare nickered a welcome and Astra inclined her head at the respectful greeting. "It's good to see you too. You're looking well."

———

Nina reined the horse to a stop, eying the slender redhead in the dark suit on the other side of the corral fence, recognizing her as Astra Jamison, one of the triplets she'd seen at the memorial. "Did I ever arrive at your family's ranch looking as frazzled as I feel sometimes? If so, I'm sorry."

"I am too. Please forgive my rudeness. I was talking to your horse since she greeted me first."

"I'd forgotten we both showed up to rescue Florida and Geor-gia. Why did you let me take them if they wanted to go with you?"

"Because you'd brought your trailer and a bag of carrots and all I could provide was a promise to come back after I investigat-ed." Astra stroked the horse's brown face, straightened the black forelock. "She smelled grain on you even though you hadn't offered any. There was alfalfa-grass hay waiting for her in the trailer and she hadn't eaten in three days because she and her mother finished off the last of the manure in the paddock then and licked up the last mud puddle that morning. Her dam opted for 'food now rather than a possible meal later,' and Georgia went along with what her mom wanted. Good choice."

Nina winced at the memory of the scrawny, skeletal mares she'd found a year and a half ago. "I hate people who mistreat animals, especially the ones who refuse to take responsibility. They didn't have a bale of hay in the barn or a sack of grain and claimed the horses were too 'stuck up' to eat what they provided."

"What goes around, comes around." Astra narrowed sunset-dark blue eyes. "They got their comeuppance when I dropped an email with pictures of the two mares to Beth Chambers. She had different deputies checking on them for months, along with social workers."

"Why social workers?"

"People who abuse animals often abuse their children. Their kids didn't appear starved or mistreated, but I knew the people Beth sent wouldn't back off until they discovered what they perceived as the 'truth' and a couple of them would manufacture dirt." Astra stroked the horse's face again. "She likes it here and loves you, but she wants to do some real riding across country. She says if you'll go with her, she'll quit the tantrums in the ring."

Nina blinked, more than slightly bewildered. "That was the same advice Kyle had, but he didn't claim to be talking to her."

"He probably read her body language. She isn't exactly subtle and you don't have to be a witch to understand animals."

Nina laughed. "Are you really a witch?"

"Yes, but most people spell it with a capital 'b' when they talk to or about me." Astra shrugged a thin shoulder. "It's better than the lawyer jokes, many of which aren't funny."

Nina leaned forward to pet Georgia's neck. "Well, I appreciate the advice. I know I should get out and ride the trails, but after last spring I'm scared."

"Trust Georgia's instincts. Watch her ears. She'll signal you if there's anyone or anything dangerous around." Astra glanced toward the puppy chewing on a stick in the middle of the yard. "Take the dog and he'll guard both of you."

Nina nodded. "I can do that, but I don't want Pooka hurt."

"He won't be. I see a long life for him and outcomes are my business."

The way she treated Georgia as if the horse was another person was weird, but oddly enough it made Nina trust the other woman more than anyone in her family. Still, visitors meant staying home for now. This afternoon would be soon enough to ride out of the corral and travel on the well-manicured paths that her stepfather maintained for the boarders. She didn't like the guy, but it didn't mean he totally failed at taking care of the Armstrong property.

"I've got coffee on the stove in the cabin." Nina swung out of the saddle. "Let me put Georgia in her stall and we'll go have some."

"That works for me, but my mother prefers tea."

"No worries. I have hot water and teabags too."

Astra smiled. "Sounds good although she prefers her tea prepared English-style."

A short time later the three of them settled on the porch with their chosen beverages and store-bought molasses cookies, since her previous visitors had finished off the ones Brigid Dawson sent.

Finishing a cookie, Estelle sipped her tea, then heaved a dramatic sigh as she gazed across the yard. "Time to do some work, I suppose. Nina, tell me about living here. Is it what you expected?"

Nina nodded. "It may not have all the conveniences, but the lack of daily drama makes up for it. I've seen my mother and step-sisters a lot this past week, but that's their choice because I haven't sought them out and I haven't cut them any slack."

"Telling them to respect your boundaries is appropriate as long as you're consistent."

"In other words, don't back down or they'll totally trample

you," Astra said. "You'll also want to avoid the temptation to show them how they make you feel. Emotions are tricky."

"I'm confused." Nina eyed the pair. "So, do I tell them to leave or not?"

"You tell them whatever you want to tell them." Astra's attention appeared to be on the strong, black coffee in her mug. "However, you eliminate the feelings. If you sound angry or upset, they'll know you're vulnerable and they win. Remember that old cop show where the detective asks the witness for 'just the facts?' That's a good strategy to use for people who impose on your good nature."

Nina nodded slowly. It made sense. Yes, she'd stood up to her family the past few days, despite the emotional toll. She'd paid for it not only by feeling guilty but with bad dreams and sleepless nights. "Do you use the technique?"

Astra inclined her head. "As a criminal defense attorney, I have to throttle down at the law firm or I'd totally lose it when one more client tells me that he was in the 'wrong place at the wrong time' and the 'cops are out to get him.' It may be true in some cases, but for many of them it's the complete opposite."

The question slipped out before Nina could stop it. "Would you defend Gary Smith after all he's done?"

"No. His soul is too dark. He can't be redeemed and he lives too close to Corbettstown which is a major nexus for evil. I couldn't be a good advocate for him and that's one of my top priorities as an attorney. I want justice for my clients."

"I thought Beth said he lived in Eagleville."

"He rented a place there, but I don't know if the authorities realize he has a cabin between Eagleville and Corbettstown."

Estelle shifted in her seat. "That's a good place for both of you to avoid. What strategy do you intend to use at the board meeting, Nina? How do you plan to stand up for yourself there?"

"I was hoping to skip it. I've already emailed in my financial reports and I can trust Uncle Omar to pass on those."

Estelle and Astra shared a look before the attorney asked, "Do you want me to represent you? You can provide me with copies of the finances, tell me what's non-negotiable and I'll speak for you as your lawyer."

"Thanks, Astra. I'll think about it." While she didn't want to be considered a coward, Nina also didn't want to see her mother's family in public. Open to the public the foundation meetings often had reporters around who wouldn't hesitate to bring up the assault. Before she could say that, a dark SUV pulled up and parked behind the Lexus in front of the cabin.

Pooka rose from his spot in the grass, stiff-legged and growling a warning. The driver's door opened revealing a stocky, balding man in a black suit. Nina stood, called the young dog and he ran to block the porch stairs. She took a deep breath, murmured his name again, and guided him into the cabin when he joined her. Leaving him inside, she shut the door, then turned to face the stranger approaching the porch, accompanied by a dark-haired, mixed-race woman.

She probably was closer to thirty-five than twenty-five and appeared more muscled than feminine in a dark-gray belted pantsuit. Nina glimpsed a flash of a red blouse and a shoulder holster under the jacket. She tensed as the two came closer. "They're—"

"Law enforcement," Astra spoke behind her. "And this is why my mother wanted me here." She stepped in front of Nina. "Identification, please."

"I'm Special Agent Newsome from the F.B.I. office in Seattle," the man said, stopping at the foot of the stairs, his partner beside him. The two showed their badges to Astra. "This is Agent Endicott. We're investigating what happened to Detective Beth Chambers in the Mount Baker National Forest and we'd like to speak to Ms. Armstrong."

"How would my client know what happened there?" Astra asked in even tones. "She was attacked in one of the barns here on the Armstrong ranch and taken to the hospital while Detective Chambers pursued the assailant."

"We'd like to hear what Ms. Armstrong remembers." This time it was the woman who spoke. "Detective Chambers sent evidence to our crime lab from several scenes. We're interested in what happened to her since she disappeared last April before she got the results."

"Then, you should ask Gary Smith what he did to her," Nina said. "He assaulted me and the Eagleville police have my statement. He probably went after Beth because she was the one person who thought he'd done the same kind of thing before."

"We need to collect any and all information and evidence first." The woman smiled politely, tucking away her badge. "We're interested in solving her disappearance. Will you help us, Ms. Armstrong?"

Nina nodded. "She was my best friend. If she hadn't shown up that afternoon when she did, I'd be dead. What do you want to know?"

7

HER MOTHER ASKED HER TO HAVE DINNER AT THE FAMILY RANCH and remain overnight, but Astra opted to drive back to Seattle. She wouldn't share the fact that she missed Beth Chambers and talking about the homicide detective today cut to the heart. The two of them used to squabble over who was picking up which man at their favorite local watering-hole, Billy-Bob's Cowboy Bar.

Beth was one of the few friends who understood Astra's philosophy that some women talked too much about their sex lives, enumerating previous lovers to new ones. Most guys couldn't handle it. The two of them decided when they found Mr. Right rather than Mr. Make-Do, neither would share what they knew about each other's former bed partners and now, Astra couldn't keep that particular promise or any of the others she'd made to the law enforcement officer she admired.

Yes, her friend was safe in 1888, serving as a new Guardian, but being without her left Astra feeling lonelier than ever. She loved her sisters, but they weren't kindred spirits, not like Beth Chambers who never turned down the opportunity to party with her. Astra took a deep breath as she pulled into the parking garage.

She'd claimed her three dogs as the perfect excuse to return home to the loft apartment. She always took them with her to the ranch when she planned a longer visit. A mix between English bull-mastiff, Bernese Mountain Dog, and Rottweiler with a dash of black wolf-blood, Astra privately thought of the huge, black dogs as 'hell-hounds' although she never called them that where someone might overhear. She saved the endearment for private moments with her pets.

The fledgling witch, Rebekah Gideon, a young veterinary student who served as her apprentice would have fed and taken the trio for a walk through the industrial waterfront to the nearby warehouses, where they enjoyed hunting rats. Still, they'd need more exercise than that. Parking the Lexus, Astra collected her briefcase and headed for the elevators, heels clicking on the cement floor. She heard Rebekah's troubled thoughts before she saw the twenty-something, a curvaceous redhead in hospital scrubs waiting near the private lift. "What's wrong?"

"The dogs disappeared." Rebekah whirled to face her, relief mixed with anxiety in the tense figure. "I promise I took good care of them when I came home after class today before I went to the clinic to volunteer. When I came back this evening, they were gone. Their leashes are still in the hall closet. I should have—"

"This isn't your fault." Astra handed her briefcase to the younger woman. "Anything you did wouldn't change this outcome." She pulled out her cell phone, scrolled through the messages. Nothing. He hadn't called. She went to the contacts, selected one, and pressed the screen. Of course, her ex didn't pick up and it went to message. "Latham, it's Astra. My dogs don't hunt your prey. Return them now, you lying piece of human garbage."

Holding the phone, she waited for him to ring back, knowing he'd be fiercely offended by the insult. He hadn't called by the time she entered the elevator with Rebekah at her side. Astra pressed the button for what would be the penthouse in a regular building. "We'll go to the workroom."

Dread crept across Rebekah's face, landing in her sky-blue

eyes. "I swear I didn't do anything wrong. He says you should punish me when bad things happen—"

"You've always served me faithfully, child, ever since I rescued you. I will never harm you and nobody else will either. "

"The dogs—"

"Someone provoked him and he took them to avenge the affront. That isn't your fault. You couldn't have stopped him."

"What could anyone in Olympia have done to deserve having your dogs set on them?"

"Latham Sellers is a lick-spittle politician. It might be anything from taking his parking space to jumping ahead of him at the espresso stand, to not buying him lunch or dinner, to refusing to support one of his bills." Astra unlocked the door and stepped into the large main room, scanning it for signs of the intruder. She'd taken back his key after their last argument, but he'd given it up too quickly and that should have warned her. He'd undoubtedly made several copies. Once she had her dogs safe and sound, she'd have Rebekah change the locks.

With Rebekah following, Astra crossed to the next room. She paused at the heavy wooden door to dismiss the wards that kept her magick from leaching past the barrier. "He's had time to call and make his excuses. Now, we bring the dogs home."

"You're going to teleport three huge animals from wherever he took them? *Magick* always costs the witch or wizard. Such an effort will use up your powers. How can you defend yourself afterward, even from a wanta-be warlock like Latham?"

"Watch and learn, child. This is why I conserve power so I have the energy required for bigger spells." It wasn't the exact truth. The younger woman, her willing minion was right about the *magickal* toll, but that didn't mean Astra intended to be the one paying it. Thanks to the man who'd traded his heart, soul, and mage-craft for his life long ago, she always had the power she needed.

For a moment, she recalled her younger brother's frequent warnings that her long-time adversary was destined to return in this life and demand recompense for what she'd taken from him. Then, she dismissed it. Orion always opted for what he considered 'honor' – she wasn't so weak-willed. Just because a wizard pledged himself to gain her love, it didn't mean she was bound to him regardless of her family's arrangements, or promises.

Astra shrugged out of her jacket, passing it to Rebekah. "Fetch the candles and I'll begin setting up the circle."

———

On the cabin porch, Nina watched the sun sink lower on the horizon, grateful Astra and her mother stayed until the FBI agents left. Somehow walking through the site of the attack hadn't been so frightening with her therapist and volunteer lawyer at her side. Why hadn't she felt safe in the indoor arena with two law enforcement professionals? They had their badges and pistols, but those weren't enough to protect her from a serial killer.

She leaned forward to stroke Pooka's soft, puppy fur. He heaved a sigh, then settled back into doggie dreams, his head nestled on her foot. She wondered if the F.B.I. agents would find the proof that Gary Smith was a monster as Beth claimed, or if he'd continue to evade justice? Nina shook her head, struggling to dismiss the assault from her mind, reciting the mantra Estelle taught in early sessions and reinforced during each and every visit. *Cancel, cancel. Bad thoughts away. Good memories only today.*

Nina repeated the mantra three times, determined not to invite evil into her house. Peace slowly replaced fear and she relaxed in the handmade, rocking chair. She saw headlights approaching and recognized Orion's truck coming up the driveway. He and Kyle left an hour or so after his mother and older sister. Why did the teenager return now?

She frowned when she saw the horse-trailer hitched to the pickup. What were they thinking? Had Astra discovered an abused animal and sent it here instead of taking it to the Rocking J? Granted, there were two empty stalls in the small barn, but Nina would have to prepare one for a new occupant and feed a second supper to her regulars, or they wouldn't accept the stranger.

She waited until Orion switched off the engine before she and Pooka headed toward the vehicles. "What's going on?"

Kyle strode toward her. "Missus Jamison told me that my job at her ranch ended today and I'm to stay here now."

"There's a bit more to it than that," Orion said, coming toward them. "She felt waves of doom when the three of you were up at the indoor arena. She can't foretell the future, but she feels very strongly that you need more protection."

"Smith?" Nina swallowed the lump of fear that closed her throat. "I have a restraining order."

"And Kyle has a pistol. My mother says that will stop a man more than a piece of paper signed by a judge. The Goddess helps those who help themselves."

The next morning, Pooka brushed past her to face the door, tail wagging. Nina hesitated before she unlocked it. Normally, the puppy waited until she rebuilt her fire in the woodstove and brewed a pot of coffee before they went outside together, but this morning he was eager to go without her. When she opened the door, the half-grown dog bounced past her to greet the man sitting up in the bedroll on the porch.

"What are you doing here?" Nina gazed at Kyle. "We cleared a space for you to sleep in the hayloft."

"Yes, ma'am, but it makes more sense for me to stand guard here." He rubbed the dawn stubble on his jaw. "If someone comes looking for you, he'll head for the house first. Got the coffee going yet?"

"I need to start the fire first."

"Yes, ma'am. I'll feed the horses while you do that."

Before she could say that she'd do it, he was pulling on his boots, gathering up the blankets, and heading for the barn, Pooka gamboling beside him. Halfway to the corral, the puppy turned and streaked back to her, pausing to grab a stick for her to throw.

Nina smiled. Some women might feel controlled by Kyle's

willingness to take over the morning chores, but she didn't. She felt safe for the first time in ages. Somehow, she'd convince him that it wasn't necessary for him to sleep on the porch, but in the meantime, she'd start a fire in the woodstove, put on the coffee and begin cooking breakfast.

When he returned a short time later, he carried a bucket of water. He filled the reservoir on the stove, then glanced at the hand pump in the dry sink. "There should be a gravity-flow system here. Where's the nearest spring?"

"Up the hill behind the barn." Nina flipped the sourdough pancakes on the griddle and then turned the bacon in the other cast-iron skillet. "It probably was safe to drink in the olden days, but now the water in the barn is undoubtedly cleaner."

Kyle nodded. "It'd only take me a couple of days to pipe it over here. Do I have time to shave before breakfast?"

"Sure. There's hot water in the bathroom in the barn."

"And a washstand and mirror on the porch, ma'am. Handier for me to do it at the house." He picked up the teakettle and left the cabin.

Nina followed him to the door and watched as he headed to the far corner near the rail. She'd always wondered about the little cabinet with its tin basin and age-speckled glass. He tipped a small amount of water into the bowl, eyed it carefully, then poured more before bringing back the kettle. She took it from him and lingered as he opened his saddlebags, removing a folded razor. She gaped at it for a moment, then went back to her cooking.

He was a strange man. She couldn't think of anyone else who'd be comfortable using an antique stand, much less a straight-edge razor to shave. Why was he a total throwback to old-time, cowboy days? Had he suffered so much trauma that he opted to live in what he perceived as a simpler lifestyle? What caused a man to go off-grid and did she really care when she'd opted to do the same rather than live with her mother's new family?

After breakfast, she cleaned up the cabin. While she washed the dishes, he refilled the wood box and brought in another bucket of water for the reservoir. They headed for the barn at the same time. He'd watered the horses and fed the hay. Now, he watched and helped with the grain. Once that was done, he began working on the individual paddock fences so she could turn the horses out in the October sunshine.

Instead of starting at the front of the barn with Georgia, she began at the back and groomed Missouri. The retired show horse had excellent manners in the stall. He barely needed the halter she put on him to stand while she brushed him, but she still opted for safety first. A tall, nearly purebred Arabian, the flashy chestnut leaned into the stiff bristles of the body brush. Nina smiled, amused by the cat-like behavior. He was so fussy about his four white socks. He hated getting them dirty and minced around mud puddles out in the corral, snorting when he might have to step in one.

"Want me to fetch a saddle for you, ma'am?"

Nina stopped brushing for a moment and Missouri turned his blazed face to look at her. "You're living here now, Kyle. I won't take offense if you call me by my first name."

"Reckon, I'll have to think on that a while, Miss Nina." He removed his hat, ran a hand through golden-brown hair before replacing the Stetson. "Which saddle do you want?"

"Missouri hates working outside and I don't like pushing him." When Kyle waited, not speaking, Nina took a deep breath. "You think I coddle him too much, don't you?"

"He belongs to you, ma'am. Where I was raised, if a man wants to eat, he should go to work and quit fooling around. I figure it's the same for a horse."

"Good theory." Nina glanced at the horse, then back at the broad-shouldered man in the hallway. "He wears the big brown saddle. The pads are on top of it and there's a snaffle bridle hanging on the horn."

"You could change to a more severe bit if he keeps up the attitude." Kyle didn't wait for an answer but turned and headed for the tackroom.

Missouri nudged Nina and she took the hint, beginning to brush the big red gelding again. "You should count your blessings that I'm the one who rescued you, not a cowboy who thinks you're a step above his pickup. Of course, I've only seen him drive Orion's truck, not one of his own."

8

She dreaded attending the Armstrong foundation monthly meeting but hadn't come up with a strategy to avoid it. After horsy chores and breakfast, she'd gone to the barn to shower, wash her hair, and dress in the slate blouse, slacks, and gray jacket she saved for these functions. Pooka wore his red service dog vest and she attached his leash to the collar ring. Picking up her briefcase, she took a deep breath. *Sooner to it, sooner through it. What doesn't kill me, makes me stronger.*

In the same dark suit he'd worn to the memorial service, Kyle waited for her. He leaned against the passenger side of her pickup. He walked around the truck and opened the driver's door. "Ready when you are, Miss Nina."

Nina paused, took another deep breath. "Did you want to drive? I'll give directions."

"No, ma'am. I haven't been in this neck of the woods long enough to be good with all the traffic you have here."

"All right." Nina pushed the button to move the seat and allow Pooka in the back of the super cab. "Let's do this and get it over with. Next month, I'll arrange for Astra to represent me and I won't have to leave home."

"Reckon, that won't work for long, Miss Nina." Kyle stood, holding the door. "It's like what Will Dawson says, 'Courage is being scared to death and saddling up anyway.'"

"He didn't say it first. He got that from John Wayne, a movie actor."

"Doesn't make it any less true, ma'am."

"I'll think about it." Nina slid the key into the ignition and started the engine. She waited while he closed the door and walked around the pickup to climb in on the passenger side. At the end of the driveway, she braked and gave him time to get out of the rig, close the gates he'd built, and return.

She focused on the drive into Eagleville. She used to enjoy the opportunity to visit with the rest of the Armstrongs, but over the last six months, it'd become more difficult to socialize with each passing day. She flicked a sideways glance at Kyle. "These meetings tend to take up most of the day especially when my mother's family tries to convince Uncle Omar that they need more money."

"He may want to consider putting one of his folks in to manage the spread since you're not around the big barn, ma'am, and don't know what happens every day."

"It'd have to be someone that Deke and Roland couldn't intimidate." Why hadn't the thought occurred to her before? Suggesting it would certainly get the Zacallahs' attention, but that didn't mean they'd avoid her. They might visit more often.

The silence continued the rest of the way into town, but it didn't feel uncomfortable. When she turned in the parking lot, she saw her cousin, Erik, waiting in a close-up slot. Six foot six in his socks, a giant blond, he always dressed western like the stuntman he'd been in his younger days. He didn't work as much in films these days but still managed to do two or three movies a year. He slid the cigarette he held back in the package, tucking it into a blue-plaid, shirt pocket and waved at her.

She nodded and pulled into the spot he'd obviously been saving for her. He opened the driver's door for her when she switched off the engine and slid out of the pickup to face him. He stepped back to allow her space to shift the seat and let out Pooka. Looking up at him, she managed a smile. "What's going on, Erik?"

"Can't I just be a good guy waiting for my favorite cousin, Antonina Arabella Armstrong?"

"You're always good, but you don't usually meet me outside and I'm not your favorite because I sass you too much." Nina locked up the truck, before returning her attention to him. "Usually you're inside doing the *sergeant at arms* thing for Uncle Omar and kicking butt when people start hassling him before the meeting."

A smile softened Erik's rugged features and warmed his gray eyes. "You're a smart cookie." He bent and ruffled Pooka's fur. The pup licked his hand and accepted the treat the man offered. "Who's your friend?"

"Kyle Morgan. Estelle Jamison sent him to watch over me."

"Another smart cookie." Erik nodded a greeting, then shook hands with Kyle when he strode around the Ranger. "Glad you're looking out for her."

"Figure it's best since Smith has her in his sights."

"He's not the only one," Erik said. "With her mother and the Zacallahs, he has more allies than he probably knows. Why didn't you call me when things heated up this summer? I'd have come back earlier. I didn't have to stay until the movie wrapped. You shouldn't have let them drive you out of the house, Nina."

"Wow, you're behind the times, Erik. I moved out three months ago, in the middle of June. I got tired of the constant verbal abuse and when Deke started bitching about Sean Killian giving me Pooka, I couldn't let the Zacallahs hurt another dog. Not that he was a dog then, he only weighed a little over five pounds and was more of a baby furball."

"Well, they're inside pitching a fit about you living with a man and breaking the morality clause. Mom told them to get over themselves, that the clause is old school, and to stop taking it out of context. If the Armstrongs didn't find partners, we wouldn't have anyone to carry on our legacy, much less the foundation."

"Don't they ever get tired of making trouble?" Nina sighed.

"Never mind. It was a rhetorical question. Let me walk Pooka and we'll go inside. Did your parents tell you that I changed my will last spring? Smith's attack was a real *wake-up* call for me and I knew it was time to face my own mortality."

"It's not my business if you got your affairs in order," Erik said, "unless you need me to provide back-up."

"Okay, they didn't tell you." Nina waited while Pooka sniffed around the bushes. "In the event that anything happens to me, you get the ranch. You're one of the few people who sees through my mother's machinations plus you know the front end of a horse from the back end of a cow and I can trust you to look after my four-legged babies."

Erik stopped, stared, and then folded muscular arms. "Nina, nothing is going to happen to you."

"Yeah, that's what I thought too until Gary Smith found me in the indoor arena when I went to check on the evening feeding."

"So, if you're not doing the follow-up on the daily routine in the barns, who is?"

"I have no idea." Nina turned and started toward the main doors of the office building. "I'm taking a giant step backward and staying out of the place where I was attacked. I did notice quite a few empty stalls when I toured with the F.B.I. agents a couple of days ago."

"Not my business either," Kyle said, "but I've been seeing a lot of fancy trailers pulling out of the main driveway. One of the gals came over to tell me yesterday that she'd have the last of her horses moved today."

"Why did she tell you?"

"I was hanging the second gate on Miss Nina's driveway." Kyle pushed back his hat, eying Erik. "Since she doesn't cotton to visitors, they pass messages on to me and I share them with Miss Nina at dinner or supper time."

"Hold it." Erik stepped in front of them. "What brought on the exodus? If they stuck and stayed after you were attacked, why leave now?"

"Reckon, it has to do with the Dawsons si-washing the place."

"The Dawsons? What upset them?"

"The whole kit and caboodle kinda got their tail-feathers in a knot after Bethany's shindig."

"What's he talking about, Nina?"

"My mother and the Zacallahs refused to attend Beth Chamber's memorial service." Nina heaved a sigh, walking around her tall cousin to pause outside the office door. "I told them repeatedly it wasn't a good decision, but they were adamant that she was my customer, not theirs. Since she was adopted by Will Dawson, that made her one of their relations and the extended family took offense. Sean Killian quit and he does all the big barns. He didn't even leave Xanadu Arabians after Audra Dawson was passed over for manager and she went to work for his new wife."

"They have bigger problems than your bodyguard and they're not sharing those." Erik pulled open the heavy glass door. "Let's go talk to Dad. He'll need to put in an Armstrong to save the place or the foundation will end up pouring bucks into the family spread."

"That will cut into the funds used for other endeavors." Nina walked beside Erik toward the large conference room at the end of the hall. With Kyle behind her and Pooka on her other side, she felt safe even when they walked through the big wooden doors and she saw people starting to fill several long tables. The Armstrongs had always been an inclusive family and her relatives came in all races, religions, genders, and shapes. The bottom line was adhering to the same belief of doing for others less fortunate and most importantly doing it with empathy. As Omar often quoted, "there but for the grace of God, go I."

Her mother and Deke stood by her uncle who glanced at her and smiled as she approached. Omar wasn't as tall as his son, more stocky than muscular these days and his once golden hair had faded to a softer blond, but his blue-gray gaze always warmed when he saw her. He held up his hand, stopping the conversation, said a few words to Rhonda, then walked across the room toward Nina.

He reached for her, drew her against him, patting her back the way he did when she was a little girl. "Honey, we've missed you. It may be time for you to move in with your Aunt Sonja and me while I clean house."

Tears burned behind her eyes. "I'm not ready to leave the ranch. I love my cabin and Kyle's there to protect me, Pooka, and the horses."

"I've heard good things from the Jamisons about him." Omar extended his hand to Kyle. "Welcome and thank you for stepping up. Do you have everything you need? I've told the local business folks to give you anything you want for Nina."

"Mostly I pick up supplies at the hardware store, sir, but I'm a fair hand at *making do* with what's on hand."

"Good to know." Omar stepped back, glancing at Erik. "Your momma and sisters have a special place for Nina and her body-guard. Stay with them in case Kyle needs you to watch his back when the dust starts flying."

"Works for me." Erik gestured to where his mother stood supervising the buffet tables and caterers on the other side of the room. Four blonde warrior women, his younger sisters, surrounded her. "Let's go, Nina before she sends over the reinforcements."

Nina smiled and they crossed to the group. Two of her cousins immediately hugged her while a third dropped to her knees and conversed with Pooka, careful not to pet him since he had on his working vest. Inga, the oldest shook hands with Kyle and began talking to him.

"We've been fielding a lot of calls from that woman." Sonja put an arm around Nina's waist. "And I told her gigolo to stop visiting at lunch or supper time because I won't set a place for him."

Nina choked on the hysterical laughter bubbling up inside. "Aunt Sonja, they've been married for twenty-five years. I don't see how you can call him a gigolo."

"If a man lives off a woman, he's not a man to my way of thinking. I informed Rhonda that he's nothing but a lounge lizard again today and I told Erling not to give them one red cent. The whole pack can go find jobs."

Nina winced. Her cousin, the incredible accountant, might claim he was in charge of foundation finances, but he was also the first to say, 'if momma ain't happy, nobody is,' and Sonja ruled the Armstrongs with an iron fist, no velvet glove wanted or required. Once she made a decision, nothing changed her mind. She'd have welcomed Deke and his daughters to the Armstrong clan back in the day but found their treatment of Nina inappropriate and forgiveness wasn't one of Sonja's strengths.

A quick kiss on the cheek and she was off to direct the caterer slicing roast beef about the thickness of the slices. Nina glanced at Kyle. "You were right. I needed to come today."

"Was there ever any doubt?" Inga tilted her head, obviously curious. As the foundation attorney, she wore an air of authority. "If you didn't show up, Dad would have sent the boys to make sure that Deke hadn't done away with you."

"He hasn't come near me in the past three months, not since I moved into the cabin."

"Good." Inga narrowed baby-blue eyes, the shade of the blouse she wore under a gray suit. "I told him it wouldn't be a problem to get a restraining order since I had more than a hundred witnesses to the way he abused you from the time you were a child. I'm glad he believed me."

"A hundred? How did you come up with that number? Did you start tallying the Armstrongs?"

"Don't be silly. We're closer to a couple thousand strong. Besides, the judge would think we were prejudiced against him. Over the years, I've been collecting statements from the Dawsons, the Morgans, the Rileys, the Ortizs, and everybody else Deke's managed to cheat or even annoy. The guy's a master of dirty deeds, all of them immoral if not illegal."

"The Morgans?" Kyle tensed. "Where would I find those folks?"

"Most moved to eastern Washington and Idaho after making millions by selling the Bar M, their long-time home, to the developers twenty years ago. Are you related to them?"

"Maybe. It could be worth looking into," Kyle said. "What happened to the old house?"

"The Morgans insisted the original homesite be saved as a living museum. They arranged for our foundation to supervise the day-to-day operations and my sister, Hilda, runs the place along with its programs. Take a look at Nina's copy of the agenda. This morning, Hilda will provide an update on the upcoming Halloween party for disadvantaged youth. The Morgans were heavily involved in that cause long before the Armstrongs started the foundation."

"Makes sense to me," Kyle said. "Mrs. Audra says, "children create the future," and they have to be helped along."

Inga nodded, then glanced at Nina. "Hilda wants you to bring your camera and take pictures of the kids in their costumes again this year. They're still raving about the photos they got to take home last time. She said something about a giant rabbit and I didn't get that. She never seemed the type to watch old *Jimmy Stewart* movies."

"It was an Easter party and I arranged for Hilda to borrow a costume from one of Erik's friends. He wore it, the kids loved him and he was a great sport when they climbed all over him." Would she be a terrible coward if she refused to participate the way she had before? Undoubtedly, but she dreaded the pity and understanding she'd see on Inga's face more than attending the party here at the foundation. "Well, at least he doesn't have to be Santa yet."

"Yes, but wouldn't he be a kick as the *Great Pumpkin*?"

Nina laughed, wondering at the bewilderment on Kyle's face. Hadn't he ever seen the cartoon? It was on TV so often at this time of the year. "You tell Erik what you have in mind. I'm not."

"First, I have to get Hilda on board. Then, I'll line up my big brother. You get your cameras ready."

PART II

"Never say Whoa on a go-ahead show."

— KYLE MORGAN, TIME TRAVELER, AND
COWBOY WRITER

9

GARY SMITH HAD BEEN WATCHING THE HUGE THREE-STORY HOUSE on the Armstrong place for weeks, but he never saw her. One witness, a yapping, scrawny, brown-haired witch he'd knocked down and smacked with his club, a black nightstick, three times in the head.

She'd still been dazed, hardly stirring when he tore off her jeans, ripped her cotton panties, and had her on the concrete barn aisle. He'd barely pulled up his pants, preparing to use his night-stick to sodomize her. He'd taken the club from his first cop kill and used it on each and every victim in more than one way, but not with her because that damned interfering detective interrupted.

The little do-gooder was the first to survive his attentions. She'd spilled her guts to the police and accused him of the attack while she was still in the hospital. Even if Frank Corbett hadn't started lecturing him the last time he was at his Corbettstown cabin, Gary Smith knew he needed to clean up the mess before leaving the area for good.

It was in his best interest to eliminate this last witness in Liberty Valley although he intended to travel to new killing places. He still hadn't decided between California and Alaska since Beth

Chambers, that witch back in 1888 closed the portal against him and he couldn't return to Junction City in Washington Territory for a while. She'd get busy with her new life and lawman husband and forget to renew the spell. When she did, she'd be the first on his list back there or should he say, 'then'?

It wasn't like the cops in different towns and states talked to each other with all their fancy computers and technology. They hadn't back in the day and they didn't here either. He doubted they realized he was stalking his former victim. He'd read in the paper that her relatives would have their quarterly meeting today and she wouldn't miss that. So, he'd come to the coffee shop across the street from the two-story office building that took up an entire city block and seen the old blue pickup pull in and park in a reserved spot.

He couldn't take her away from the big man who'd waited for her, but at last, he'd found her and as a bonus, she was with the cowboy who'd followed him from the past. Luck was finally on his side. There were too many security cameras for him to sabotage the truck's brakes, or to slash a tire. No, it'd be better to follow her and find out where she stayed. Once he'd taken care of her, he'd deal with the cowboy.

———

Humming an old country song, Nina groomed Colorado, one of the three black ponies she'd dubbed the Three Musketeers. She was too tall and heavy to ride the little liver chestnut, but giving her attention wasn't only required for the animal's good health, it also reminded her of what was expected from a horse. Colorado nuzzled her and Nina stroked the mare's face, straightening the thick, dark forelock over the white blaze. "I promise that someday, your little prince or princess will come."

Pooka lifted his head and with his tail wagging, he raced off toward the entrance. Nina glanced after him and saw Kyle accompanied by a petite brunette and a small, sandy-haired boy. As they neared, she recognized Audra Dawson-Watkins. "Well, hello there."

"Hey, how are you?" Audra rested a hand on the youngster's shoulder. "I managed Silver Lake Pony Ranch for Elinor Talbot-Killian last summer until I married Joe and moved to Pullman in Eastern Washington. I stuck around after the memorial to visit her and the kids. Sean told us about your ponies so I borrowed my cousin, Quaid, when he got home from kindergarten and we thought we'd come to check them out."

Nina blinked. "I haven't found anything for Elinor yet. To be honest, I haven't even looked."

"That's a pony, a big one." Quaid looked up from where he petted Pooka. "What's wrong with her?"

"She has two friends that come with her and she doesn't want to be separated from them, not in the barn or the pasture," Nina said. "That makes it hard to find her a good home."

"Not with us," Audra said. "Elinor isn't in the sales business like my mom or Quaid's, so they'd have a forever home at Snohomish Pony Ranch. She's even willing to put it in writing in the adoption contract."

"I don't have saddles for them or bridles." Nina knew she was grasping at the proverbial straws, but she loved the mischief-making trio. "I don't know how Quaid could ride them."

"Bareback on a witch's bridle like my momma does," Quaid said. "I bet you have baling twine from the hay so I can make one. And it'll be fun for all of us although they have to wear real riding stuff when they teach little kids like my sister."

"Shall I fetch some string, Miss Nina?" Kyle waited as patiently as the other two for the answer. "The boy brought his helmet and carrots. They're out by the corral so the other horses don't get excited."

Nina eyed the three of them, then nodded. "Okay. Let's try it, but if it doesn't work, we'll have to do it with a bridle next time.

Remember to save some carrots for Colorado's buddies. They'll want their share too."

"Sounds fair." Audra stroked Colorado's face. "If you prefer, we could just tie baling twine reins to her nylon halter and that'd provide Quaid with more control, our version of a bitless bridle."

Disappointment slipped across the little boy's face before he nodded. "Okay, but I still think it'd be more fun to have a real witch's bridle and Colorado wants to play too."

Nina had to smile. "Are you like your Aunt Astra? Do you talk to the horses too?"

"Anybody can," Quaid said. "It's not exactly a *magick* spell. They think in pictures and all you have to do is think back at them."

"Hmm, do I want to know what S.O.B. thinks of me?" Kyle scratched California's neck when the Shetland mare came to the front of her stall to share in the conversation. "Maybe not. There are days when I know he's not too fond of me."

"Those are the times when you forget to bring him a biscuit and you act like you're the boss of everything 'stead of being his partner." Quaid glanced toward the strawberry roan at the far end of the barn. "Most days he figures you're doing your best and you just don't know any better."

Audra laughed softly, shaking her head. "It's wiser not to ask a witch or a wizard for an answer, Kyle, if you don't want to hear their truth. It gets uncomfortable."

"Better than folks who never share their opinion." Kyle straightened. "Come on, Quaid. I'll show you where we keep the twine and you can make your bridle."

Nina waited until she and Audra were alone with Colorado. "Do you believe in *magick*, or that your cousins are witches?"

"They're good people so I'll believe whatever they want me to believe." Audra leaned on the stall door. "I know they helped me when my mother had a temper tantrum last summer. They took in Kyle and his horse when they arrived. Aunt Estelle says, 'what goes around, comes around,' so I want good things for them. Don't you?"

"Yes, Estelle is one of the best therapists I've seen and I appreciate the tools she offers. I always feel safer after we talk."

"Same here." Audra glanced further up the barn and spotted the palomino geldings in adjacent stalls. "Aren't those the two horses who won the state gaming championships for years? One of them always took first and the other took second, turn and turnabout forever. Why do you have them?"

"They got old. They have arthritis and can't run like racehorses anymore. It was either me or a one-way ticket to the slaughterhouse in Canada." Nina rested her elbows on the stall door. "Of course, the person who took them would have to be able to get them past the brand inspector at the border since they're losing their sight."

"It happens with some Appaloosas." Audra frowned, then flicked a sideways glance at Nina. "They could still teach youngsters to ride and game at Elinor's. She focuses on patterns rather than speed. Her horses walk more than they trot or canter and the kids groom more than they actually ride. Have you visited her place, seen what she does?"

"I haven't been out much lately. It's difficult to be around strangers."

"Doesn't that make Gary Smith the winner when you give up control of your life?"

The question hung in the air between them. Kyle's return with Quaid, now wearing his equestrian helmet, meant Nina didn't have to answer and she counted her blessings. She helped the boy tie on a baling twine halter. She stepped out of the way when he gathered up the makeshift reins and led Colorado out of the barn to the corral. Two carrots later, Kyle boosted the boy onto her back and then strode over to stand next to Nina at the fence.

Meanwhile, Audra stood in the center of the ring and provided instructions. She'd obviously taught Quaid to ride at some point because he listened and didn't have any difficulties doing what she said. Eyes up, heels down, he had perfect western form even riding bareback. He executed a left turn, guiding the pony out to the rail where she walked around the corral on the left track. After a few circuits, he reversed and walked in the other direction. Then, he moved onto a trot, a slow jog so he moved with her and didn't bounce.

Nina looked at Kyle. "He's a very good rider for his age."

"He went to horse camp at Silver Lake Pony Ranch this summer with Mrs. Audra and Mrs. Elinor. Venus Jamison, his momma, had already taught him a bit and he learned a lot more."

"I'd have to agree." Nina watched as Quaid slowed to a walk, and then signaled Colorado for a show-ring lope. The little mare picked up her right lead and held to a slow pace so the boy didn't lose his balance. "Do you think she'd like a place full of kids?"

"It's your decision, but Mrs. Audra's right about the kind of home they'd give her and the other two. She'd be stuffed full of carrots every day and wouldn't work that hard. Most I ever saw the ponies work last summer was a couple of hours in the morning and a couple in the afternoon."

"I've got to think about it. I want what's best for the ponies and they've had several months to rest. It may be time to let them move to a new home."

Once Colorado cantered on the left track, it was time to stop the ride and enjoy a few carrots, an activity the mare certainly appreciated. She nuzzled Quaid when he walked her back to the stall. He removed the baling twine bridle and fitted it on California by himself. Meanwhile, Arkansas stood at the front of his stall, eagerly waiting his turn. Once both of the black ponies had strutted their proverbial stuff and shown their friend, Colorado wasn't the only fully trained, trustworthy mount, Audra asked if she could ride the semi-retired palominos.

Nina reluctantly agreed, but her trust wasn't misplaced. The other woman stayed at a walk, warming Alabama up slowly. She stopped, backed him, did right and left turns, then tried several serpentines. When he was ready, she used her seat and legs to ask for a jog and the old gelding trotted through several patterns. After carrot-time, it was his younger brother's turn. Audra repeated the same warm-up and riding routine, never losing patience. When she finished, she fed carrots to the horse.

"I'll talk to Elinor and see when she can visit, but I think all five of these would be real assets to the new pony farm. Why don't you and Kyle come to lunch tomorrow, Nina? You can inspect the place and see if it's suitable for your treasures."

"You must figure I'm being really hidebound about letting them go. Everyone in the county knows the Dawsons and Killians have wonderful reputations with horses."

"Why wouldn't I appreciate you being such a responsible horsy rescuer?" Audra stroked Alaska's faded golden neck. "After all your hard work, you need to know they'll be safe at their new home."

Quaid tossed a tennis ball and Pooka raced after it. Alaska snorted at the pair but didn't shift his hooves.

"Can I come too, Cousin Audra? I like hanging out with Jake and the other kids."

"We'll ask your mom."

"Okay." Quaid returned to his game with the puppy.

Nina took a deep breath and then reached for the reins. "I've got a lot to think about so let me put him away."

"Works for me." Audra stepped clear while Kyle opened the gate.

It only took a few minutes to lead the gelding back to his stall. Nina hung the nylon bridle in the tackroom and paused when she heard Audra talking to Kyle outside the barn.

"You haven't told her, have you?"

"Told her what, Mrs. Audra?"

"Why you're really here."

"She knows my brother wanted me to watch over her and keep her safe. It's all she needs to know for now."

"No, it's not. She needs to know about Beth. When do you plan to share that?"

"Did you ever tell Dr. Joe about her?"

"No way. He's not that open-minded. I haven't told anyone what you, Uncle Will, and I know, but Nina is different. You have to tell her the truth. Beth is her best friend and Nina will want to be with her when the first baby comes."

Baby? What baby?

Nina reminded herself that Beth Chambers was dead. She had to be dead. Detective Watkins admitted they hadn't found her body, but he was certain she was gone. Why else would everyone have shown up at a memorial service for her barely two weeks ago?

Nina lingered in the tackroom, contemplating options. Did she want to hide from reality or step up and discover the truth? She took a deep breath and walked out of the barn to confront the pair standing outside. "I heard you. Talk. Is Beth okay? Why didn't she come home?"

Kyle removed his hat, ran a hand through golden brown hair, and replaced the Stetson. "She can't, Miss Nina. It's a bit far-fetched and you're not ready to believe it."

"Don't tell me what to believe." She folded her arms and waited. "I'm thirty-two and I've seen a lot in those years. I can handle whatever truth you want to dish."

Kyle and Audra shared a glance, then she said, "It took me a while to accept his and Uncle Will's story. I understand if you have doubts, but try listening with an open mind. Beth didn't come back because she couldn't. Gary Smith actually ambushed her in Mount Baker National Forest along with Tigger and Luke. She sent Kyle to protect you when Smith returned."

"From where? How did she send anyone if she's dead? Why did you say she's pregnant if she's dead? This doesn't make sense."

"He attacked her, but between the two of them, they opened a time portal to the nineteenth century. They traveled to the olden days in Liberty Valley. He came back to the present and she stayed in 1888 where she has a job to do."

"Okay, you two are nuts." Nina shook her head. "I understand you're grieving for your cousin, Audra, and you want to think she's alive and happy somewhere. I do too. As for you, Kyle, I don't know or even want to know what baggage you have that makes you think Beth is safe and sound."

"Yes, ma'am." Kyle eyed Audra again. "Told you she wasn't ready. I'm going to build fence so we can turn the horses onto some graze. I'll see you tomorrow."

Nina waited until he strode away. She ought to get rid of the guy, but somehow, she still felt safer having him around. "He's delusional and I don't understand why you're pandering to his whims."

"And I can't comprehend why you're so close-minded when you can accept that Quaid comes from a long line of witches and wizards."

"Even if the Jamisons think they're *magickal*, that doesn't hurt anyone, but claiming a dead woman is alive, pregnant and living in pioneer days is just sick."

Audra heaved a sigh. "Let's agree to disagree. I hope you'll still come to lunch tomorrow at Elinor's."

"Of course, I will. I want to see if she has a suitable place for the ponies."

"And the Gold-Dust Twins," Audra said. "I want them back to work too. They deserve a useful retirement and lots of carrots from kids who will respect their abilities in teaching patterns. Be prepared. I'm turning Aunt Marlene and the rest of the Dawsons loose on the county's western game squad who think horses don't have feelings."

"Works for me."

"And do me a favor. Take Kyle to the Morgan museum on the old Bar M. There are displays of antiquarian books he needs to see. Ask your cousin Hilda to pull out the rare first editions."

"Anything else?"

"You bet. She keeps the wooden cameras that belonged to one of the Morgan wives in the back too. Take a look at those and the old family photographs. As Shakespeare wrote, "There are more things in heaven and earth, Horatio, than are dreamt of in your philosophy." You need a wake-up call, Nina."

10

THE NEXT MORNING THE DRIVE FROM EASTERN LIBERTY VALLEY to what had been Sean Killian's bachelor farm in Snohomish took the better part of an hour. Nina couldn't think of anything to spark a conversation and Kyle didn't speak either. However, the silence between them felt oddly comfortable until she remembered what Audra claimed the day before about Kyle being from a different century. Country music from the classic radio station filled the cab of the pickup and Pooka slept between them, occasionally twitching one foot as he dreamed of chasing either cats or rabbits in his dreams.

Spotting the new sign, Snohomish Pony Ranch, Nina signaled to turn into the paved circular drive, passing the three-story log house and heading for the graveled parking lot in front of the huge indoor arena. Spotting an assortment of vehicles, she knew students must be learning to ride. Momentary dread swept through her. She parked next to another truck and switched off the engine.

She couldn't make herself unbuckle the seat belt, much less open the driver's door. She didn't know who was there, but she didn't want to face strangers. Worse would be talking to people who knew her before the assault and revealed their pity. She reached over to pet Pooka. He shifted and licked her hand.

"Would you like to see his mother?" Kyle focused on the large building. "The dogs live on the far side and Sean won't mind if I take you there."

"I'd like that." All at once, she could move. "Should I call and tell him we're here?"

"No need. We'll probably find him in with his critters."

She locked the truck, then walked beside Kyle away from the late model cars and SUVs, Pooka an eager escort, his tail wagging. Her half-grown puppy must recognize the place by its smell.

Kyle opened a door, and they entered a wide barn aisle. The stalls were the kind found in stables. The wooden walls were built of planks four feet high, topped with vertical wrought-iron bars. Heavy sliding doors could have contained huge horses. Instead, they were used to kennel different medium-sized canines that she recognized as Australian Cattle Dogs and Border Collies. She spotted Sean at the far end, his stepdaughter, Lynn beside him.

The two waved at her and Sean came toward them, smiling. He bent down to pet Pooka. "Audra said you'd be here for lunch and to inspect the place. Glad you made it. The arena will empty out shortly and Elinor will show you around."

Nina eyed the tall, dark-haired man in a cowboy shirt and jeans. "Audra seems to think my ponies would be suitable for what Elinor does. I don't know about that, but Quaid Jamison didn't have any trouble riding them yesterday."

"Good to know and Audra has a good sense of what's required for beginning riders. She should after running the Lazy B all those years prior to working at other barns to support her family. Before she heads back to Pullman and Joe, she wants to help Elinor find the last few ponies and horses for this place."

"I'd like that." Lynn sauntered toward them, teen elegance in a Silver Lake Pony Farm sweatshirt and tight blue jeans tucked into elaborately decorated cowgirl boots, golden-brown hair in a neat French braid. "I want back my mare, Gypsy. It wrecks her training when she has to teach beginners. They pull on her mouth too much and never use their legs or seats to cue her to change gaits."

"It doesn't hurt her to do pony rides," Sean said calmly, "and it provides you with the opportunity to clean doggie rooms which is why I pay you. Now, take Nina with you and show her your dog's mom. King is her puppy's big brother and I want to talk to Kyle."

Lynn heaved a dramatic sigh. "It has to be a guy thing. Come on, Nina."

Smiling, Nina followed orders, Pooka pulling a bit on the leash.

———

Kyle waited until the two entered a stall halfway down the barn before he glanced at Sean. "What's on your mind?"

"Audra told us yesterday that she'd been doing research for a project that the two of you were working on and you needed to visit the Bar M museum soon. She wouldn't tell us why. What's the project?"

"I'm a shirt-tail relation of the Morgans," Kyle said. "She wants me to see the place and look for connections."

Sean frowned, his concern still apparent. "I don't understand why Nina has to take you there, why you can't go on your own and Audra isn't talking."

"She's a private person. I overstepped when I shared what she did to support her family, but I didn't know it was shameful. She wasn't selling herself *on the line*, just writing love stories to entertain folks."

Kyle let the silence build, then shrugged and headed for the stall where Nina and Lynn fussed over a golden collie that seemed thrilled with the opportunity to sniff and lick Pooka. Smiling, Nina looked over her shoulder and then returned her attention to the dogs. Slowly, he realized this counted as one of the times he'd seen her relaxed and happy.

When they finished meeting and greeting the critters, the four of them headed for the house, entering through the back door and heading for the kitchen where they found Audra arranging the food buffet style on the granite counters. Trays of sandwiches, sliced fresh fruit, and bowls of salad waited for them. Kyle found himself once again missing the meals that Hannah Ortiz and Ma Sims served up, not that he'd say so, at least not here and now.

After lunch, Clancy Dawson took Nina on a tour of the facility. White board fences separated the fields and she pointed out her aunt's neighboring farm. Then, they strolled through the indoor arena to the row of large stalls that lined one side of the building. Unlike other barns, this one didn't have steel bars between the horses or facing the wide aisle. Those always reminded her of a jail and Clancy must agree, Nina thought, remembering the younger woman's propensity for snarky tees and sweatshirts. Today, Clancy was dressed for work, not in a favorite purple horsy sweatshirt with one equine asking another, 'What are you in for?'

"Each horse or pony has its own paddock for daytime use." Clancy stopped near the second stall where a faded, strawberry roan munched his lunchtime hay, pointing out the back Dutch door. "If it's rainy, windy, or cold, we can close up the barn. You know what winters are like here in Washington State."

"Wow, do I!" Nina eyed the thick plank walls and high wooden ceiling with its fluorescent lights. "Who did Sean get to build this?"

"Ethan designed it." Amusement sparkled in Clancy's violet eyes. "Every time, he thought it was perfect, he showed it to me and I told him how to make it more horsy-appropriate. When he finally let Sean see the plans, he just raved about it. Ethan knows contractors and he found a good one, but he and Sean still took turns supervising the construction. The Ortiz brothers found the wood for them. It came from a barn on the Bar M, the Morgan's old ranch. The developers were going to demolish the structures, but Gavin convinced them it was eco-friendly to repurpose the building."

"Why did Gavin do the talking?"

"He's a college professor and he knows all the buzz-words to accomplish whatever goal he sets. Sean's too outspoken and Ethan likes to list the facts, just the facts."

"So, how did he propose then?"

"Very well." Clancy reached over the four-foot wall to straighten the pony's thick flaxen forelock. "During flood season, my younger sisters, the twin idiots hadn't moved our broodmares and their youngsters out of a pasture with a huge year-round creek. One of the colts got trapped in the rising water and I went in after him."

Nina eyed her. A tall, voluptuous redhead, Clancy oozed sex appeal in tight blue jeans tucked into her boots and a purple T-shirt with white fringe that accentuated her breasts. She didn't look like a champion swimmer, but more like an old-time pin-up girl. "Was the water very deep?"

"Yes. I still don't know how or why he stopped halfway through that creek which is almost the size of a small river during the winter. His dam stood whinnying on the inside bank, but we're not talking about a rocket scientist baby. So, I swam out to him and began guiding him through the water to the herd. The current damn near swept me downstream, but then Ethan showed up. He peeled out of his jacket and boots and dove in to save the day. Well, he saved me and Rainbeau."

"And then what happened?"

"Oh, we had a huge argument about me risking my neck. I was yelling at him and he gives me this look and tells me he can't live without me so I'm not allowed to take unnecessary risks and die in the process."

"Wow, that's romantic."

Clancy laughed. "Not the way he said it. He stated it like it was an obvious fact, one anybody would have learned in math class. Ethan plus Clancy equals happy ever after. So, a few big steamy kisses later and he pulled a jewelry box out of his coat pocket. And we were engaged."

"But why did you call off the wedding last February?"

"Because the twins, my brat sisters decided to raise hell and put props under it. They set me up and I fell for their crap-fest when they lied about Gavin sexually harassing them. I don't want my family at the ceremony now. I want to elope the way that Audra and Joe did, but Ethan's determined we'll have the big shindig."

Nina sighed, shaking her head. "Well, I still think it's romantic that he's doing what my Uncle Omar would and making your little sisters suck eggs, even if they don't admit wrongdoing."

"Wow, I never thought of it like that." Clancy stepped away from the stall. "Well, come on. I'll have students in twenty minutes. I still need to show you the tackroom, the spectator area, the shower for the horses, and the feed room. Hay storage is up in the loft and so is my apartment. I moved up there when the twins raised a ruckus about not being able to live off-campus because nobody else would pay for it and they weren't willing to get jobs."

"What kind of riding are you teaching today?"

"It's a beginner combo. They'll set up what I call grooming stations with their tack and brushes, then bring out their horses and prep them for riding. After that, they ride for an hour at all four walks. If they majorly focus, then we might trot and do some pattern work."

"It doesn't sound too strenuous for the animals."

"It's not. The kids work harder than the horses do and Elinor always insists on two carrots to bridle up, one before the bit goes in and one after. The most difficult part for me is standing back and letting them clean the hooves. That takes forever and sometimes I'd just rather do it myself because it'd be much faster, but it's not my barn so I follow Elinor's rules and remember I'm empowering my students, not enabling them."

A half-hour later, Nina sat in a chair in the spectator room, watching the six students through the windows. Clancy had been right about the agenda and the amount of time it took for each child to groom, then saddle up. Two of the ponies obviously figured it was nap-time, heads down and dozing while they were brushed. A third, the light strawberry roan decided it was too much effort to remain standing. His knees buckled and he plopped into the shavings.

Nina wouldn't have been surprised if he'd started snoring. She heard the door open behind her and glanced over her shoulder in time to see Elinor enter the room. "Doesn't Clancy need your help?"

"Not right now." Elinor crossed to the coffee bar and filled a china cup. "If I go in the arena, I'll start *grandma-ing* up and doing everything for the kids. Bonanza's students know he gets bored when they take forever. They have to *move it* and that's the hardest thing for them to learn."

"So, you're not enabling them either?"

"Nope." Elinor strolled over and sat down in the chair next to Nina's. "Give his rider a couple more minutes and he'll have Bonanza back on his hooves without any abuse."

"Okay."

"Have you come to a decision about your ponies and what Audra calls the 'Gold-Dust Twins'? Are they coming here?"

"I'm leaning that way, but I'm not all the way there yet. I like the big stalls with the turn-outs and I'm glad you don't have automatic waterers. Some horses won't drink out of those. I'm sure having the individual feed schedule on the doors helps your staff keep track of who gets what to eat and Clancy explained that each animal has their own tack and their own brushes."

"Audra taught me that trick last summer during day-camp and it makes keeping track of the inventory much easier. I don't sell my stock because it's so hard to find dependable mounts for beginners and most people don't value good, starter horses and ponies. I'll put that in writing for you."

"Sean told me that you only have drinking-water-safe-hoses in the barn to avoid cancer and you call in Joe's dad whenever you need a veterinarian. Since you're primarily using older animals, what's the end-of-life plan for the horses?"

11

Mid-afternoon, they headed home since they had chores to do and horses to feed. Traffic would only worsen on the winding two-lane highway that took them to eastern Liberty Valley. A car in the opposite lane pulled into hers to pass a slow-moving vehicle and Nina swerved to the shoulder in time to avoid a collision. She hated feeling crowded. Since she always had, she couldn't blame the emotion on the assault last spring. She spotted a historical marker a short distance ahead.

As they neared, she saw the advertised attraction and flicked a sideways glance at Kyle. "It's the Bar M, the Morgan's old home-place. Do you feel like visiting?"

"Sure. What about Pooka? Will he be all right waiting for us in the truck?"

"He has his service vest so we'll take him with us." Nina signaled for the turn and followed the signs to the *living* museum. "Besides, it won't be a problem since I'm supposed to take pictures of kids in their costumes at the Halloween Party and I should confer with my cousin, Hilda, to learn what she wants me to do."

"Makes sense."

"It does to me too." Relief swept through her when she saw the large archway with a sign that read Bar M and the open gates. She parked in front of the huge, three-story log house. "I wonder how many rooms it has."

"No telling. Rad added on every winter, but there were almost twenty when I left."

Nina eyed Kyle. "Your brother?"

"Yes, ma'am." He held up a hand. "I know you don't believe that yet. We won't argue. We'll just go look."

"That works for me." Nina opened her door and slid out of the seat. Pooka yawned, stretched his puppy legs, arching his back and slowly wagged his plumed tail before he followed her. She lingered long enough to adjust his vest, then locked the truck while she waited for Kyle to join her.

She surveyed the large grassy lawn and the flowerbeds. Rose bushes bordered the white wooden fence and she almost heard Beth saying what she wanted some day. *'A home in the boonies with a guy who loves me a hundred percent and gives me lots of babies, but he has to stick around to help raise them. That's non-negotiable. The gardens, white picket fences and the whole bit.'*

Struggling to control the urge to cry, Nina walked up the gravel path toward the wrap-around porch. "Did your brother plant the flowers?"

"No, ma'am. He plowed the vegetable garden every year and sent the men to help hoe and pull weeds. He wasn't much for doing the pretty, but he wanted to eat between his circuit-riding when he went from town to town, settling squabbles. Señora Ortiz did most of the work when it came to planting and such, but Rad had already started the orchard before she arrived. Afore I did too, come to think of it."

It was a good story, Nina thought as she guided Pooka into the pet area to deal with doggie business before they went inside. She didn't want him to disgrace himself indoors, although Hilda was one of the most understanding of the Armstrongs and would just clean up the mess without complaint.

Nina eyed Kyle where he waited patiently near the porch steps.

He was certainly old enough to have served in the military. The scarred cheek was obviously from an injury. Did he have other marks hidden by his clothes? For the first time, she wondered if his stories might derive from some sort of war trauma. Beth suffered from P.T.S.D. after her Army tours in the Middle East. Perhaps, Kyle did too and the similarity between his name and that of a founding family in the county provided some security. Pooka finished piddling and they headed toward the house.

She glanced at the wooden swing in the front corner of the wrap-around porch and the clusters of wooden chairs in what were intended to be conversation groups. Who had started that? The original Morgans or their descendants? The front door opened onto a wide hall and she spotted her cousin ushering a family of visitors in their direction.

Golden blonde hair coiled in a neat bun, wearing a light green dress with leg o'mutton sleeves, Hilda smiled at them. "Hello. I'm so glad you came. If you'd like to wait in the parlor, I'll be back to give you a tour."

Nina almost asked where the room was, but Kyle gestured to the left and she followed him. The formality of the parlor showed it was a far cry from what people would consider a family or living room. A grand piano stood in one corner near the three long windows, artistically draped with swooping gold drapes over thinner gauze sheer curtains. A large mirror over the fireplace reflected the ornate chandelier. Several chairs and a horsehair sofa as well as a few tables completed the furnishings.

Nothing spelled comfort and she winced, looking at Kyle. "I can't imagine hanging out in here at the end of the day."

"It was for company, not family." Kyle chuckled. "If this didn't make visitors leave on time, nothing would. There were other places, more comfortable ones for the family."

"You must be Audra's friend, the one she said knew a great deal about the history of the Bar M and the Morgans." Hilda came into the room. "Sign in on the guest register and I'll take you around. Nina, I put out a display of wooden cameras in the other wing. One of the first Morgan wives was a photographer. Many of her pioneer pictures are in the area libraries and other local museums, but most are here."

"I'd love to see them." Nina crossed to the rolltop desk in the corner near the hallway door and signed her name before she followed her cousin. "Did you and Inga discuss her plan for photos at the Halloween Party?"

"Yes and it sounds wonderful. She's in charge of finding a humongous pumpkin costume for Erik. The party is at foundation headquarters because I expect a full turnout of the kids and despite the size of this house, it won't hold everyone especially since I don't open up all the rooms."

"Why not?" Kyle asked.

"There's too much temptation for theft and vandalism," Hilda said in a matter-of-fact tone, blue eyes calm and serene. "It takes a great deal of time to teach historical appreciation and some of the guests only see the cash value of the antiques and collectibles."

"It's hard to think of household furnishings being worth money," Kyle said. "I don't recall many fancy dishes, jewelry, and such. Everything had to be useful."

"Utilitarian items have their own charm." Nina paused in the doorway to glance up and down the hall. "So do everyday ones. Tell me more about the party, Hilda."

"Captivating Catering, Meteor Jamison's company will handle the refreshments and decorations. She offered to donate everything and Dad refused. It's a newish enterprise and in this economy, it's enough if we pay her costs and she donates the rest. Then, she'll be around to do other functions."

"Omar's a good person, a smart one to think of that." Kyle finished entering his name in the ledger, sauntered toward them. "Meteor and her friends should ask him for advice more often."

"I'll let you tell them that. He loves being the voice of wisdom so he wouldn't take offense if she contacted him outside of the Chamber of Commerce meetings." Hilda led the way into the hallway, then into the next room, a study with bookshelves on the walls. She stopped by a section closest to the desk. "Kyle, this is where we leave you. Audra said for you to pay special attention to these first edition novels. They're written by your namesake. He's considered one of the best regional authors in Washington State. The Morgans say when his most famous book came out about a legendary gunfighter who was actually a woman that masqueraded as a man, it really raised a ruckus."

"Why?" Nina asked. "It was pure fiction, wasn't it?"

"Well, that Kyle Morgan claimed he based it on stories he'd heard in Liberty Valley about one of the more respected families. Although she was almost middle-aged, the founder of the Lazy B threatened to shoot him and leave his carcass for the coyotes. His brother, the marshal, and his sister-in-law intervened to keep the peace."

Kyle laughed. "Somehow, I don't doubt that for a moment."

"The Morgans are good storytellers," Hilda said. "I can't believe anyone actually thought of Trace Burdette as a man. She was one of the most influential women in Liberty Valley until her death in the late 1940s."

"You never saw her swagger through town with her grandpa's pistols on her hips, or called her out on a sunny afternoon."

"Called her out?" Hilda asked. "What does that mean?"

"Challenged her to a gunfight. It wasn't a smart choice." Kyle took one of the volumes off the shelf. "By then, she'd put several men in Boot Hill, the town cemetery, and kept an account with the local undertaker."

Nina gaped at him for a moment. "What did the marshal do about that?"

"He couldn't do much. Outlaws constantly pursued her because she had a price on her head. She usually didn't start any fights with the desperados hunting her, so he took everyone's guns when they came to town to try to keep the peace. Later, his wife was his deputy and she always said, 'it wasn't what you knew, but who' and she was one of Trace's best friends."

Nina bent and petted her half-grown dog to hide the tears that burned behind her eyes. "Beth would agree with that. She was one of the most cynical cops I ever met."

"I don't think so. A true cynic has narrow vision and she still sees the good in people and life." Kyle opened the book, his attention reverting to the words on the page.

Nina knew her friend was gone, but decided to let him keep his illusions. There must be some trauma that drove him to believe he'd traveled through time, leaving Beth behind in the nineteenth century.

"I'm hoping you can explain early photography to me," Hilda said, escorting Nina down the hallway, leading her past several open doors. "I may know a great deal about life in the *olden* days, but some of the technology still astonishes me."

Furnishings in the various rooms provided clues as to their use from the dining room to a sewing room to a back parlor for recreation to a pantry and a scullery off the kitchen. "I'll show you the master suite later," Hilda said, pausing in the kitchen. "It's amazing because it actually has an attached bathroom. Most houses in this period still had outhouses, but Rad Morgan, the marshal who established the ranch was the first person in the area to install indoor plumbing."

"What did you say?" Nina froze in her tracks. "There actually is or was a man named Rad Morgan?"

"You have to love history the way I do to understand that it's basically stories of people living out their lives the best they could. Rad Morgan came west after the Civil War and eventually wound up as the first marshal in Liberty Valley. When he retired, his eldest daughter, Willow-Kylie took up the reins. Well, actually she had one of the first Model Ts in town and she kept it running herself and toured all over Liberty Valley."

Hilda walked to a door on the far side of the kitchen. "This is the wing that was built for his younger brother and his wife. She was the photographer I mentioned. The Morgan brothers were especially close since they were separated as boys after their parents died and when they found each other again, they didn't see much point in living miles apart. Luckily, their wives agreed."

"The house is huge. It certainly has enough room for two families."

"Three if you add in the Ortiz's."

Nina gaped at her cousin, remembering Kyle's story about the biscuits he'd used to make friends with his horse. "Who?"

"Hannah and Gabe Ortiz. He had the first sawmill in the area and she worked as a housekeeper for the marshal. Even after the mill became a profitable enterprise, she preferred living here. Their grown children were the ones who moved out of Liberty Valley and their descendants still run the mill and construction company."

"We have a Hector Ortiz who works for us at the rescue and I know he has relatives in the construction business."

"He's probably related. We'll have to ask Will Dawson." Hilda opened the door to a short hallway that led to a combination dining and living room.

Several cameras sat on a long table, but that wasn't what stopped Nina. She stared at Will Dawson who looked surprisingly comfortable handling the wooden cameras displayed on a long table in the center of the room. Pooka gave a friendly woof and pulled on the leash, always ready to meet a new friend.

"What's going on?" Nina eyed her cousin and Beth's foster father. "This is a real shock."

"It shouldn't be," Will said. "Audra told me she'd arranged for you to visit and asked me to teach you about these cameras. Most folks don't know how they operate anymore, but I learned how to use one when I was a boy."

"Why?" Nina turned her attention to the elaborate wood, brass, and leather contraption in the center of the table. "I'd think you'd want the latest model, not a box style with a bellows."

"Not when my teacher was a real fussbudget about her equipment." Will picked up the camera in front of him. "Let me tell you about this one. It's a Waterbury View Camera and it was manufactured by the Scovill Manufacturing Company in 1888. It was considered a light, compact model that eventually became available in several different sizes. This one is made of mahogany with a rubber bellows."

"Why don't you let me take your puppy for a walk while you two check out the cameras and pictures?" Hilda asked.

"Okay. Bring him back in an hour." Nina handed over the leash and moved closer to Will, fascinated by the explanation of how the camera worked.

———

On the way home, she found herself remembering the sepia photographs Will showed her. Most had been of people dressed in their best clothes standing perfectly still, their faces showing scant expression, but her favorites were of the children. One group stood near a school with a very young teacher. Will told her it was actually part of an orphanage at the Lazy B, the ranch still operated by the Dawson family.

"Thanks for suggesting that visit, Miss Nina. I learned a lot."

"So did I," Nina said. "Will Dawson is going to give me lessons in how to use wooden cameras next week. Can you look after the horses for me and feed them lunch?"

"Yes, ma'am." Kyle scratched behind Pooka's ears and the dog thumped his tail appreciatively. "It'd be my pleasure."

12

When they arrived home, Nina started evening chores by filling the water tubs. Kyle dragged out Minnesota's, dumping it in a dry area of the paddock. He brought back the fifteen-gallon, plastic tub and scrubbed it with baking soda before Nina rinsed it.

She smiled at him. "What do you think about replacing the tub with two water buckets on a shelf outside her stall? Elinor does it with one of her clean water, four-legged fanatics and said it saves time because she no longer needs to scrub that particular water tub each day."

"You're the boss, Miss Nina. It'd take less than an hour to rig up something like that and it could end up saving us time in the morning and afternoon."

"Okay, put the tub back in for temporary and she'll have water while you make the adjustment."

"Yes, ma'am."

She worked her way down the barn aisle, topping the rest of the tubs. When she reached the small liver chestnut, she scratched Colorado's neck, running the hose at the same time. "What do you think, honey? Do you want to try a new home with a bunch of kids who will feed you treats whenever they come to ride?"

No answer from the little mare, just a friendly nudge, and Nina rubbed the pony's neck again. Sean intended to bring over the trailer tomorrow after church and haul the Three Musketeers to his place, then return for the pair that Audra referred to as the Gold-Dust Twins. Nina knew she'd miss the five horses, but a good home with folks who knew how to take care of them wasn't something she wanted to pass up.

She finished watering, then dragged the hose back to the front of the barn and coiled it around the tool cabinet. She glanced at Kyle. "What do you think about the transition? We'll be down to four head by tomorrow afternoon."

"Most everybody needs a job, Miss Nina, and I figure these critters are ready to go back to work after their holiday with you. Of course, you're the one who has to decide since it's your place."

"True, but if I didn't want your opinion, I wouldn't ask for it."

He flashed a grin and she smiled back at him. "I'm going to check supper and I'll be back to feed."

"Sounds fair."

Nina headed for the cabin, Pooka dashing in front of her. He brought over a soggy, yellow tennis ball and dropped it at her feet. She picked it up and winged it back toward the barn. He chased after it, retrieved it, and returned. Another toss and one more chase to find the beloved toy. They played fetch all the way to the back door.

It didn't take long to build up the fire in the woodstove and stir the pot of beans she'd left simmering this morning. She mixed up a cornbread, poured the batter into the small cast iron skillet she used for baking, and put it in the oven. She set the apple pie Audra had given her, a gift from her younger sister, in the warming oven to heat. After she added another chunk of wood to the firebox, Nina was ready to return to the barn.

When she arrived, Kyle had already built the shelf outside of Minnesota's stall and filled the two water buckets. He'd also mucked the stalls and dressed them with fresh shavings. All they needed to do was feed the horses and that didn't take long. He was silent in the barn while they finished up and remained quiet when they strolled back to the house.

Whatever was on his mind didn't affect his appetite. He enjoyed two large bowls of beans and three slabs of cornbread as well as a big piece of Brigid's pie. Nina didn't push or try to instigate a conversation. When they finished eating, she cleaned the small kitchen while Kyle filled the wood box, hauled water, and banked the fire in the stove so it'd heat the cabin all night. Together, the two of them went back to the barn for one last check on the horses. Pooka raced ahead, flushing a rabbit. He happily chased it until the small brown creature disappeared in a tangle of blackberry bushes.

Smiling at the puppy's mischief, Nina glanced up at Kyle. "I had a good day. What about you?"

"It was an interesting one."

She took a step closer to him. "What made it so interesting? Visiting Sean's place, or the Bar M museum?"

"I always reckoned on finding the right gal somewhere, making a home with her, and having a family."

"What's stopping you?"

He stopped, facing her. "It's not gonna be here, Miss Nina. I learned that at the Bar M."

"I don't understand." Dread swept through her. He couldn't leave, not now, not when she was finally starting to trust him and hoping for a future with him. "All you saw were some old books and a house built by a pioneer family."

"Yes, ma'am. And I wrote those books. I didn't do it here like I thought. I did it back in the day in Junction City."

"You're not serious. Okay, so some guy with your name lived back in Liberty Valley in the olden days. He wrote those books."

Silence built up between them and he feathered a thumb over her lips. "You're not ready to hear my story yet. I told Mrs. Audra that a couple of days ago and now I'm telling you. We have time to figure out things."

They were almost the same height when she wore her boots

and she tiptoed up to brush his lips with hers. His mustache tickled her skin, but before she decided if she liked it or not, his hands closed over her shoulders and he gently pushed her aside.

"Not yet, Miss Nina. I'm not a man who settles for a few sweet moments. I want it all."

She stared after him when he strode past her toward the barn. She didn't follow him. Instead, embarrassed and ashamed, she spun and stalked back to the cabin. Pooka paused, looking between them, then ran after her. She sank down on the porch steps, wrapping her arms around his warm body, appreciating the usual puppy swipes of his raspy tongue on her cheek. At least somebody loved her.

What kind of guy turned down a kiss that could have led to a night in her bed? A weird one, she thought. If she'd approached a man in a bar, he'd have been ready to jump her. She remembered Beth saying she was tired of the 'one-night stand' crowd that she and Astra always found at Billy-Bob's Cowboy Bar and Grill.

The evening classes at the community college hadn't filled the void caused by Beth's post-traumatic stress. Neither had horseback riding, although she claimed to enjoy her lessons with Nina, so they'd started shopping for a horse. After she bought Tigger from Xanadu Arabians, Beth began competing in endurance trail contests.

She dated a few cops, but they weren't ready for anything serious and she gave them up too. She wanted a forever kind of love with a 'real' man. Nina had agreed with her at the time, privately wondering if it was a fantasy brought on by too much wine. Were there any men left who truly desired lifetime commitments, rather than 'lust in the dust' encounters?

Despite everything Audra claimed about Beth living elsewhere, Nina knew her friend was dead and gone, her body lost in the National Forest so they couldn't give her a proper burial. Maybe, she ought to join Kyle in his dream world and pretend her best friend was happily married to Kyle's older brother and the two of them would have lots of children.

No! It was madness.

Nina hugged Pooka one more time, then stood. "Come on, big guy. Let's hit the hay. Tomorrow, we'll have company. I want to groom the ponies and the Gold-Dust twins and make them shine even if I can't bathe them before they go to their new home."

———

The next afternoon Sean Killian brought a borrowed, big stock trailer to haul the ponies and the old palomino geldings at the same time. To Pooka's obvious delight, Lynn and her younger brother, Jake, had come along and they took turns throwing his toys so the puppy could play fetch until his tongue literally hung out. While he rested between bouts of his favorite game, the youngsters helped load the Three Musketeers. Nina apologized again for not having saddles or bridles for them or the Gold-Dust Twins.

"No worries," Jake told her, grinning as he petted Colorado's dark neck. "We've collected tons of equipment over the years and we're bound to have properly fitting tack for them. Clancy will do what Audra calls *fashion police* and make sure their new blankets and new bridles make them pop."

"I don't get it. Why do they need to pop when they're horses?"

"Because my grandpa used to say, we sell the sizzle, not the steak." Lynn led California close enough to join the conversation. "Lightning really hates boys and he's gray, so he dazzles when we dress him up in pink and purple which attracts the little girls. This way he gets tons of carrots and doesn't have to tolerate riders that he detests, and nobody falls off, breaking Mom and Audra's anti-splat rule."

Nina smiled, loving the explanation. "Well, their halters and lead ropes probably won't make them pop either, so are you going to find them new ones?"

"Oh, yeah." Jake straightened Colorado's thick, black forelock. "And they'll be nylon ones so Mom can wash them when the kids drag them in the dirt. She loves the big washer that Sean has in his barn and Lynn's crazy about the shower stall for Gypsy."

"It's the *Taj Mahal* of barns," Lynn agreed. "Mom had some qualms after last summer when Clancy wanted to move into the manager's apartment, but Brigid promised to kick butt if Clancy got all *princessy* and refused to do the dirty work."

After loading the second palomino gelding, Sean strolled over to join them. "Are you two telling Nina so many stories she'll want back her rescues?"

"Oh, no." Nina laughed. "I've known Clancy Dawson for years and she is a bit of a diva. I remember when we were kids, she always used to manipulate Ethan into doing her chores at the Lazy B and when he visited the club on our camping trips in the mountains."

"He never complained, but she's grown up a lot since Audra married Joe." Sean winked, humor shining in his gray eyes. "The two of them have been crazy about each other for years, but they had to wait forever until her family didn't need her. I'm glad they finally got together."

"Me too." Nina didn't add that being more mature would undoubtedly help Clancy in her relationship with his older brother. The focus reverted to the ponies and it didn't take long to load the trio.

A tear streaked down her cheek as she watched the trailer pull out. Granted, this would be a great home for her equine mischief-makers and the Gold-Dust Twins, but she always hated seeing her babies move on to new pastures.

She took a deep breath and went into the barn, Pooka tagging at her heel. She found Kyle cleaning the empty stalls. "There's no point in keeping your horse at the far end by himself, so when you finish, move him up next to Missouri's stall. It will put the two geldings on one side of the barn and the two mares on the other."

"Yes, ma'am. I figured on asking you." He eyed her for a long moment, then rested the fork against the wall. "Are you all right, Miss Nina?"

"I'm fine." She held up her hand when he started toward her. "Don't. You already made me feel like a slut when I kissed you last night. So, just don't. I need some time and space."

She didn't allow him to answer but spun and walked to the tackroom. She'd groom and saddle Missouri, then take the retired show horse out for a ride across country and see what he remembered from Kyle riding him in the corral, pastures, and on the trails for the past few days. She might not be able to outrun her turbulent emotions, but she was willing to try.

———

It didn't take long to muck the empty stalls, so he went on to clean the adjacent paddocks and mend two broken fences. Not for the first time he wished Rad was here. His older brother never hesitated to give advice regardless of whether it was wanted or not.

Kyle grimaced. He'd seen the fear in Miss Nina's eyes when he came here little more than a week ago. He hadn't blamed her for being wary after what Smith did to her, but she still castigated herself for the attack. Why else would she call herself names? A slut?

What would his older brother do in such a pickle? Even though he was badly wounded and it meant he'd be alone in a cave with Detective Bethany Chambers, Rad Morgan hadn't hesitated to send for help. He'd even told Kyle to bring back a dress for her so he could marry the girl if he didn't succumb to the bullet that penetrated his lung. Now, Kyle wondered if the two kissed when they were alone for more than a week. Sparks had certainly flown between them that night and it reminded him of what folks often said. The first baby can come anytime, but the second takes nine months.

———

The well-maintained trails between the cabin and the main buildings on the ranch didn't have any branches or logs in the way so she urged Missouri into a collected trot. Even the gold and red autumn leaves had been swept off to the sides, leaving pristine dirt paths. She wouldn't ride cross-country all the way to the indoor arena. She didn't want to see any of the Zacallahs or her mother. The big Arabian didn't spook at the birds, the squirrels, or the occasional rabbits flushed by Pooka. When they reached a grassy meadow, she squeezed her legs and asked for a slow canter. He flicked his ears and responded.

A cool breeze brushed her cheeks and she caught the sound of the river flowing over rocks, but she smelled something else. Smoke. She reined Missouri to a stop, looking around the area for a fire, listening for the crackle of wood blazing. Who'd smoke a cigarette here? All of the help knew better. Even Deke and Roland didn't break fire safety rules. They'd had a hot dry summer and it might be early October, but the fall rains hadn't started yet. Even a small campfire could set the woods ablaze. She reached in her vest pocket and removed her cell phone.

She wouldn't call for help until she knew for sure there was a problem. She swung onto the left-hand trail, following the faint scent. It cooled off at night, but she didn't recall seeing any lightning strikes or hearing thunder rumble in the foothills. Pooka stayed with her, his quest for rabbits momentarily abated.

The smell grew stronger and she took a deep breath, tasting smoke on her tongue. She glanced down at her phone, grateful she had a signal, and called the main house. Her mother answered.

"It's me, Nina. I'm on the Appaloosa trail and somebody's trespassed and started a fire."

"Do you have your truck, or are you on foot?"

"I'm on one of the horses."

"How close can you get? Are you able to give me more details?"

"I'll try." Nina touched a reluctant Missouri with her heels and rode further into the woods. Ahead of them, she saw a brush fire eating grass and working its way toward her. It was too big for her to put out by throwing dirt or using the scant amount in her water bottle. "Hang on, I'm sending you a picture."

"And I'm already sending Deke and the boys from the barn on the ATVs," Rhonda Zacallah said. "If it gets any worse, haul butt out of there, Antonina. The trails are too far off the beaten track for the fire department to be any use, but I'll call them. They can protect the main barns and this house. I'll have one of the auxiliary trucks go to your cabin."

Nina nodded, then realized her mother couldn't see her. "All right. Thanks."

She waited and watched until she heard the roar of motors. Missouri danced underneath her, pawing and rearing. The fire hadn't scared him all that much which came as a surprise. However, the sound of approaching vehicles obviously did.

She tightened her hold on the reins, making the large Arabian remain somewhat still until she spotted Hector Ortiz in one of the farm pickups with a big water tank in the bed of the truck. She pointed toward the brush fire and he gave a quick toot on the horn. Leaving the men to handle the blaze, she turned Missouri toward home.

She let him trot part of the way before she slowed him to a walk. She wouldn't teach him that bolting back to the barn and his stall was any sort of an option. It was too much of a hazard, not only for him but also for any rider in his horsy future. Pooka caught up with them, dashed ahead on the Andalusian trail, and happily started a bunny rabbit quest again.

She rode into the corral a short time later, not surprised when she saw Kyle talking to the waiting fire-fighters. Pooka barked a greeting, and then waited outside the ring, oddly careful to remain a safe distance from the strangers. Kyle gestured for the leader, a huge dark-haired man to join him and they walked toward her. She remained in the saddle, refusing to dismount since she'd be shorter than both men and too vulnerable.

"This is Jed Corbett." Kyle introduced the giant in black fire-fighting gear. "If you tell him where you saw the fire, Miss Nina, he'll take his crew there."

"It's across country," Nina said, "and there are only trails. A lot of them are pretty narrow, just wide enough for two horses to ride side by side, not big enough for vehicles."

"We're volunteers and we work for Corbett Logging. We can get there if you point the way, ma'am."

She nodded, pointing past the corral to the woods and the trails that honeycombed the ranch. "All right. All of the trails are named after breeds of horses and they have wooden signs. The main one is the Quarter Horse. Follow that for approximately a mile and it branches onto the Andalusian. Turn left onto the Appaloosa and you should find my stepfather with his crew."

"Works for us." Jed swung around and jogged toward his large four by four.

She waited until they were out of sight before she swung out of the saddle. "I don't know what you did with Missouri, but he's never ridden better across country. He was totally steady when we found the brush fire and I wouldn't have blamed him for spooking."

"I would have." Kyle stroked the horse's blaze. "I'll put him up for you, Miss Nina."

"Why? I can take care of my own horse."

"Yes, ma'am, but then dinner will be really late."

Nina felt laughter bubbling up inside her and passed him the reins. "I should have known. Okay, I'm on that mission."

13

THE NEXT DAY, WHILE SHE CLEANED UP AFTER LUNCH, SHE started a stew. The beef, onions, and spices would simmer for a few hours in a pot on the woodstove and when she returned, she'd add the rest of the vegetables. She closed and locked the cabin door behind her, then strolled toward the barn, Pooka racing in front of her. She found Kyle repairing the manger in Alabama's old stall. The younger of the Gold-Dust twins always redecorated his room when he became bored, taking down walls, or smacking the boards on the manger with his hooves. She hoped the children at Elinor's kept him entertained.

"I'm going to ride out and see what damage the fire caused to the trails." Nina took the tennis ball from Pooka and tossed it down the aisle. Tail wagging, the pup raced after his toy. "Do you want to come?"

"Yes, ma'am." Kyle finished nailing the board into place. "Be interesting to see if we can find the cause."

Nina nodded agreement and headed for the tackroom to collect Missouri's gear. Halfway to his stall, Kyle met her and lifted the saddle and pads from her arms. He carried the western tack the rest of the way. She should give him the lecture about being strong enough to look out for herself but decided not to bother. He was stronger than she was, so let him pack her old forty-pound Western saddle.

She returned to the tackroom and gathered up a handful of carrots as well as the grooming kit. On the way to the Arabian's stall, she shared out the treats with the mares, then passed on a couple to S.O.B. The poor horse still needed a better name, but crunched down on the veggies, not complaining because they weren't homemade biscuits. She fed the last three carrots to Missouri. He nuzzled her and she petted him, then got started on grooming.

A short time later, they rode out of the corral, across the pasture, and into the surrounding evergreens. Nina flicked a sideways glance at Kyle. "So, what *magick* spell did you cast on Missouri? This is the best he's ever been outside of the ring."

"No *magick*." Kyle pushed back his cowboy hat with a thumb and eyed her. "That's more what Miss Venus does when she's training. I just settled his hash so he'd be a decent lady's horse for you. If he's rarin' to go and can't go for rarin', how would you or some other gal be able to ride him proper in town?"

"What do you mean by 'proper'? There's too much traffic to take him off the ranch." She frowned thoughtfully, recalling his fantasy of being from the nineteenth century. Back then, women rode sidesaddle, but she hadn't participated in costume classes in years, not since the equine rescue took up so much of her time that she didn't show the horses. "I can't imagine wearing anything but jeans when I ride. Did the women where you come from wear dresses, or pants when they took out their horses?"

"Miss Prescott orders in riding habits for those who want to buy 'em at the mercantile, but most women make their own for coming to town. Rad refused to lock 'em up for wearing pants in Junction City, but it's not the same in Snohomish City or Seattle."

"I haven't heard you say anything before about dressing up when we went into Eagleville for the foundation meeting last week and I didn't wear a skirt then. What changed?"

He shrugged a wide shoulder. "Reckon, I'd thought I'd have to accept the way things were here with women wearing all sorts of clothes, but after visiting the Bar M, I know I'm not staying beyond next September when Bethany opens the gate."

"What gate?"

"The one to take me home."

Nina drew a deep breath, then slowly exhaled, deciding not to discuss his delusions about her best friend being alive. "You taught Missouri to be trustworthy beyond the corral before we went to the Morgan place. What was that about?"

"I wanted you to be safe on him and it doesn't hurt him to know his job as a lady's horse."

"And your horse?" She glanced at the strawberry roan walking calmly beside her gelding. "He looks like a quiet ride. Is he a lady's horse too?"

"What?"

"Just wondering. He's got a nice walk, but he's not spooky. What would happen if I rode him?"

"Nothing. He's a solid, good, hard-working horse." Kyle narrowed his gaze. "Are you poking fun at me, Miss Nina?"

"Well, you did ask for it. Nowadays, a man usually doesn't say a woman's horse needs special treatment."

"He doesn't and he shouldn't get it. He does need to be 'dead broke' for her, else when she's riding sideways on him and he jumps, or bolts, or flies off the handle, she'll break her neck."

"Again, I'm not riding Missouri or any other horse sidesaddle across the country."

"We'll see."

Nina heaved a sigh and turned the big chestnut onto the Andalusian trail. She flicked a sideways glance at Kyle as he rode next to her. Even in jeans, a plaid work shirt, and boots, he was a good-looking guy. What made him think he was from an earlier time? It must be some sort of trauma, but she hesitated to ask if he was a veteran. With an all-volunteer military, not every man enlisted, especially when the country had been at war for such a long time.

She heard men's voices and chainsaws before they reached the point where this track intersected with the Appaloosa trail. However, it didn't sound as if the crew was dropping any trees, so it should be safe enough to continue their journey. As they neared, she recognized Hector Ortiz and a few of the others cleaning up the area. She spotted Jed Corbett further down the track and waved to Hector. "What's going on?"

"Stayed to clear back the brush and cut up the dead wood to prevent any more fires," Hector said, approaching her and Kyle. "Mr. Zacallah asked us to help the lieutenant and a couple of his folks so they could find the point of origin and make sure there weren't any hotspots."

Nina nodded, then turned her horse to walk further along the path, scanning the swath of grass and brush burned by the fire. The long black patch was about ten feet wide, paralleling the trail for approximately thirty feet, yet oddly enough it hadn't crossed into the giant cedars. She shook her head, baffled. It couldn't be a lightning strike and her stepfather didn't allow smokers in the barns or on the property, especially during what had become the dry seasons of summer and early autumn.

When they reached the firefighters, Kyle swung his horse toward Jed. "Reckon you see the same thing I do, Corbett. Somebody set this blaze."

"What?" Nina reined Missouri to a halt, gaping at him and then turning her horse to face the dark-haired fireman. "He's paranoid."

"No, he's right." Jed frowned, before gesturing to where the blackened grass stopped. "That's where it started and it burned in your direction. Whoever did it probably thought the first person here would try to put out the fire and then call for help."

"How could I?" Nina leaned forward to pet Missouri's red neck. "I didn't have a shovel, and only one water bottle. All I could do was use my cell and make like E.T. and "phone home." I'm glad my mother was actually around and that my stepfather had a crew working on a Sunday, or things would have been much worse."

"Especially if the fire hit those trees," Kyle said, gesturing to the old-growth evergreens they'd ridden through on the way here. "If the wind was right, it'd have burned through the woods to your barn and cabin."

"And if the wind came from the other direction, it'd have taken out the rest of the buildings and that huge house." Jed held up a plastic bag containing part of a cigar. "Does your stepfather allow camping on the property? Could it have been a transient?"

"Of course not." Nina glanced over her shoulder at the ranch hands. "Most of the employees live off-site, so it wasn't any of them. My uncle would have to give permission for a group to camp here and he wouldn't at this time of the year. Deke, my stepfather, knows better than to break Uncle Omar's rules."

Jed turned, studying the area again. "Well, someone stayed back here. We found a few empty beer cans, more cigar butts, a crumpled cigarette pack, and even a place where he had a tent."

"How do you know it was a man?" Nina tensed in the saddle, then forced herself to relax before she upset the horse. "It could have been a woman or even teenagers."

"No, it was only one man." Jed pointed to a beefy, dark-haired firefighter examining the ground. "My cousin, Junior Corbett, has a sense for these things. He found where the guy did his business."

Kyle swung off the strawberry roan and passed the reins to Nina, taking a moment to adjust his gun belt. "Show me the campsite. I want a look-see. Might be someone I trailed afore."

"Who?" Nina demanded.

"You know who, Miss Nina, and so do I. Gary Smith."

"But, I have a restraining order against him."

"Yes, ma'am, and I have a gun. Like I told you when I came to stay, I'll trust that more than a piece of paper."

———

Kyle strode through the grove of cedars, coming to a stop as they neared a campsite with a small fire ring surrounded by stones. He looked where Jed Corbett pointed. "Is that where he had a tent?"

"Yes and I'm not sure why. It's not really cold enough for one and we've barely had any rain. Even the dew isn't that heavy in the morning."

"He may not like sleeping under the stars, or he might have wanted to keep his things dry." Kyle went to the far side of the clearing, studying the ground. Bright gold and red leaves covered too much of the dirt which made little sense because there weren't any maples nearby and thankfully, they hadn't seen much wind during the past few days since that could have set the forest ablaze.

He dropped to one knee, gently brushing a few aside long enough to see the sweep of a cedar bough used like a broom to try to disguise tire tracks. The treads weren't far enough apart for a car or truck, not even the small one Nina drove. "What kind of rig left these?"

"Probably an ATV," Jed Corbett said. "Makes sense. Whoever it was had to be able to move their belongings."

"And Miss Nina." Kyle rose to his feet, back-tracked the vehicle to a trail branching off the one they'd ridden, and came to a halt when his gaze narrowed on a piece of gray tape. "Smith would have taken her along with him if he had the chance."

Jed stepped cautiously around him, advancing on the tape. "Why?"

"She survived his attack and talked to the police and the F.B.I. agents who came to see her. He needs to get rid of her before she testifies in his trial."

"That'd do it." Wearing gloves, Jed carefully picked up the scrap of tape and put it in an evidence bag. "I'll turn in what we've found to the lab and there will be more investigations. Hopefully, we'll get some fingerprints. Since arson is a crime, you'll undoubtedly be hearing from the prosecutor's office too."

"We'll be waiting." Kyle swung around and stalked back to his horse, leaving the dark-haired giant behind. Once he'd mounted up, he turned S.O.B. onto the trail, waiting while Pooka darted ahead to lead the way. "Reckon, we've seen what we came to see, ma'am. Let's head home."

She hesitated for a moment, then reined Missouri to follow him. "What did you find?"

"Pretty much what Corbett said, evidence someone was hunting you."

"He didn't say that."

"No, ma'am. He didn't, but he doesn't know what we do. Gary Smith is after you and he's way too close to where you live, but he'll have to come through me first. We need to go to town tomorrow and buy a lady's gun for you."

"That's impossible."

Kyle stopped his horse cross-wise on the trail. "Miss Nina, you may not like guns. Most ladies don't and that's all right, but you don't live in a place where the law can keep you safe and I'm only one man. If Smith gets by me, you need to defend yourself."

"I can't buy a gun, not legally." Defiance filled her face and she lifted her chin, narrowing lovely hazel eyes, the mixture of green, brown, and gold that reminded him of autumn bronze leaves. "I probably should have told you I'm a convicted criminal, but I figured somebody else had."

"I don't believe it." He watched tears shimmer for an instant before she blinked hard enough to stop them. "Reckon, you can tell me about it later when you trust me. Meantime, if you can't or won't buy a gun, I'll teach you to shoot mine and I'll use my rifle."

Nina took a deep breath and then squeezed her legs, urging Missouri to follow Kyle and his horse toward home. When had the cabin become her home? Taking her animals along, she'd initially moved there to escape the Zacallah drama. At first, the silence in the small one-room cabin overwhelmed her nearly as much as cooking on a woodstove, but she'd grown to love the place. It'd become even more of a sanctuary since Kyle Morgan arrived.

She gazed at the broad-shouldered man riding in front of her. What made him so special? He always treated her with so much courtesy and respect, more than she remembered receiving from the men she'd dated over the years, through college and afterward. Of course, her stepfather tried grand-standing about the Armstrong ranch whenever he met one of them and her step-sisters did their best to drive them away. Their maneuvers always proved success-ful, undoubtedly because she didn't fight back.

Nina frowned. Was she to blame too? Maybe she hadn't cared enough to stand up for herself. That changed after Smith's attack. She'd refused to accommodate Deke's and his daughters' policy of *blame the victim*, no longer *going along to get along*, and even if she'd moved to the original Armstrong cabin, Nina viewed that as a win, not a loss. Kudos to her, she hadn't left the ranch.

Back at the corral, she dismounted and dropped her reins on the ground. Missouri stood like a rock, more credit to Kyle's training. Previously, the Arabian gelding would have strolled around the ring, socializing with the other horses, but today his behavior made it easy to unsaddle him. She unfastened the breast collar and cinch, tying up the latigo, and then stepped around to the right side to hook up the rest of the equipment. Kyle arrived in time to pluck off the saddle and pads, carrying them to the tack room.

Nina gathered up the reins and led her horse into the barn. "I'll check supper, but then I want to ride Georgia and Minnesota before night chores. They haven't been getting their fair share of attention. Next time we go on the trails, I'll take one of them."

"You could ride Missouri and pony one of 'em while I led the other." Kyle lingered outside of the stall, scratching the Arabian's blaze when the gelding nudged him. "You need a horse who can outrun Smith if he comes on us unawares, Miss Nina. Those mares are willing, but they're not as long-legged as this fella."

Nina waited until the former show horse spit out the bit before she gave him one final pet and left the stall, latching the door behind her. "I'll think about it."

"Think about this too." Kyle stepped closer, framing her face with his hands and brushing his mouth over hers.

She stared up into his face, so near to hers. "I thought you didn't want—"

"You figured wrong. I didn't want to overstep the bounds."

"It's not overstepping if I invite you."

"I'm learning that, but I won't settle, Miss Nina. Afore you agree, know it's for always, not just a sweet moment or two."

She smiled, stepping closer to him and sliding her hands around his neck. "You talk too much, Mr. Morgan." And she kissed him.

14

WHILE THEY WATCHED THE SUNSET FROM HER PORCH THE NIGHT before, they shared a few kisses. Nina remembered the sweet innocence of those moments as she drove home from the Bar M and the photography class with Will Dawson. She glanced at Pooka sleeping in the passenger seat. "There's time," she murmured. "I feel like we have lots of time, all of us."

The steering wheel jerked in her hands and she heard a sudden thumping. Crap! There went the right rear tire. Grateful, she'd adhered to the low speed limit on the narrow, winding highway, she slowed even more. She didn't have to worry about flipping the Ranger into the big drainage ditch and thank heaven, the few October rains hadn't filled it yet. It'd be a different story if they were in the midst of what she privately thought of as the monsoon season with gray clouds socking in and rain-filled months from November to March.

She aimed for the paved shoulder, braking to a halt beside the road. She switched off the engine, pulling out the keys and snapping them onto a loop on her jeans. When Pooka stood up on his seat and barked, ready to get out, she shook her head. "No, buddy. You stay here. Stay."

She looked over her shoulder, made sure there wasn't any

oncoming traffic and opened her door. Thanks to Uncle Omar, she knew how to change a flat, but she wondered why it happened. Since she hated jacking up a vehicle and wrestling with old tires, she bought new ones every four or five years instead of waiting until they actually wore out. She heaved a sigh. "Well, sooner to it, sooner through it."

She'd just assembled the jack when a large four-by-four pickup pulled up behind her rig. She tensed, her hand tightening on the lug wrench, and took a step closer to the Ford Ranger, ready to run around the cab to the driver's side. Then, she recognized the huge, dark-haired man behind the wheel of the other truck.

At six-foot-six, he stood more than a foot taller than she was. Thick coal-black hair curled around his ruggedly handsome face. Today, he wore faded chopped-off blue jeans, a flannel red plaid shirt that jarred with the bright orange suspenders, and corked boots. Jed Corbett sauntered toward her pickup, his dark gaze on the right rear tire. "Looks like you have a problem. Let me change that for you."

"I can handle it." She clutched the lug wrench even more tightly, hoping she didn't show her apprehension. "Why would you offer to help?"

"Well, I could say that my momma raised me to be a gentleman, but that wouldn't be true since she died when I was born." He stopped, resting his hand on the tailgate of the Ranger. "My uncle brought me up and he's not politically correct at the best of times. He figures there's women's work and there's men's work. Changing a flat tire is what a man does."

"And what do women do? Make cookies?"

"Only if they're chocolate chip or peanut butter." Jed remained where he was, still watching, but not approaching her. "The best ones are the kind that combine both and have those huge chocolate kisses."

"Is that a hint? You've got the wrong woman. I'm still learning to bake using a woodstove."

"More of a suggestion. I admit I have a hell of a sweet tooth and when I load up on cookies and other desserts, I stay out of the bars which keeps me out of brawls and the Gray-Bar hotel." He grinned at her, his dark eyes amused. "I'll fetch my tools and get started. You may want to take your dog for a walk. Most puppies don't like me."

"Why not?"

"That's a story for another day. We don't have time for it now and you may not believe it anyway. Stay close so you can take off when I finish."

She nodded but waited until he turned back to his rig before she lowered the lug wrench and placed it near the jack. She unlocked the passenger door, opened it, and snagged the leash so Pooka didn't escape the confines of the cab. Plumed tail between his back legs, he stood stock-still, stiff-legged between her and the man, growling.

"Let's go for a potty run." She remained on the shoulder to avoid oncoming traffic. She tugged on the line, and walked up the road, towing the reluctant dog behind her for a few steps until he decided he no longer needed to protect her. She let him sniff the weeds bordering the ditch until he chose the perfect spot to piddle. When she looked back toward the Ranger, she saw a cop car positioned behind Jed Corbett's full-size rig and the officer helping with the tire.

It didn't take long with two men working to switch to the spare and she headed back toward her rig. As she neared, she saw the distinctive emblem for the Corbettstown Police Department, a five-pointed star with a wolf's head in the middle and lettering around the side proclaiming they protected and served. She nodded a greeting to the young, dark-haired man in the dark brown uniform. "Thank you."

"No worries, ma'am. Jed will drop the tire at the repair shop in Eagleville for you since it's closer to your place."

"I appreciate that." Nina guided Pooka back into the cab and closed the door on the annoyed collie mix. He promptly planted his front feet on the seat and barked out the back window at the two men. "I'm sorry. I don't know what's gotten into him."

Jed shared a look with the deputy. "Most dogs don't like me."

"Must be the alpha in you." The officer chuckled. "Maybe he thinks he should be the boss of the pack instead."

"I'm not an alpha."

"Not yet, but your day will come. I'll radio in and have dispatch call your uncle and let him know you'll be late for dinner."

Nina watched the cop return to his vehicle while Jed finished tightening the lug nuts on the spare. "Did you see anything that made the regular tire lose air? I didn't drive over a screw or a nail, did I?"

"Looked like the valve stem might be loose, but I'll give the shop your number and they can call with a proper diagnosis."

"Okay." She waited until he stepped back, shifting the flat tire out of the way before she went around to the driver's side and slid into the pickup cab. She started the engine, driving cautiously toward home. As she passed the next turn off the highway, she glimpsed a white RV parked beside the road. It was an odd place to camp. Apparently, the police officer thought so too because he signaled for a right turn and headed that way. In a moment, she glimpsed Jed Corbett repeating the same maneuver.

Relief swept through her when she saw the large black and white carved sign, reading 'Armstrong Horse Ranch', and the smaller letters at the bottom, 'Home of Armstrong Horse Rescue,' a short time later. She saw Orion Jamison's pickup in front of her cabin, but the sandy-haired teen wasn't in sight.

She removed the collar from Pooka's neck, then opened the truck door. "Let's go find the menfolk and see what they're doing."

With a woof of agreement, tail wagging, he bounded off in the direction of the barn. Nina laughed and followed him. She found him on the far side of the building where Kyle, Orion, and Hector Ortiz worked on a pasture fence. Pooka dropped his tennis ball near Kyle and he promptly threw it.

Nina paused for a moment and watched him. Why did she find him so attractive? He wasn't a big man, barely three inches taller than her own five feet, four. His brown hair curled down his neck, longer than hers. His smiles tended to warm the dark brown eyes and her dog adored him. So did her horses, even Georgia who tended to be ultra-snooty.

Kyle winged the ball across the grassy field and Pooka tore off in eager pursuit. "How was your visit with Will? Learn lots?"

"It was good." Nina crossed to him and glanced at the pasture. "What's the plan?"

"Grazing for the horses." He gestured to the rectangular pen with its three completed fence lines and the one under construction. He'd used the materials from the woods around them to create solid post-and-rail barriers. On his visits during the past few days, Orion had brought in his chain saw and they'd cleared the evergreen groves of alder and maple saplings. The two men dropped the smaller, crooked, ungainly cedars that blocked sunlight from reaching other trees, cutting them into posts. "I know they have paddocks, but horses are herd animals that want to roam."

"They're social creatures and they'll enjoy the outside time together." She took a deep breath and stepped closer to him. She smiled when Pooka dashed to Hector, dropping the soggy tennis ball at the man's feet and barking encouragement until the catch rider followed puppy orders and threw the toy.

It delighted her to see the young collie happily playing. "I had a flat tire on the way home and it really upset him when Jed Corbett came along and changed it. I'm glad my dog's back to normal."

"I'm glad too." Kyle reached in his shirt pocket and removed an old-style flip cell phone. "Give me your number and next time call me. I'll come help you."

"I don't remember seeing that before. When did you get it?"

"Today. Orion brought it. He said it was Astra's idea for me to take a step into the *now* and then I'd be available if you needed me."

"Good idea." Nina pulled out her own phone and programmed in his number, then added her own to his contact list. "I'm going to put some potatoes in the oven before I ride Georgia. At supper tonight, I'll tell you all about what Will taught me and the pictures I took with the Waterbury View Camera."

"I can't wait to hear."

"And I can't wait to tell you all about it." She tiptoed up to kiss him, a quick, light touch.

The next day, after the photography class with Will Dawson, she drove into Eagleville. She parked in front of a two-story Victorian house, smiling at the bright mural of various, fantastic animals that included unicorns, centaurs, and winged horses frolicking on the structure as well as huge letters spelling out Captivating Catering. Who'd have thought Meteor Jamison could be so artistic?

Leaving Pooka to wait in the Ranger, Nina strolled up the sidewalk. Bells chimed when she opened the door and walked into the reception area. Classic country music played back in the large, industrial kitchen. Nina glanced around for Brigid Dawson, the baker famous in Liberty Valley for her cakes and desserts. "Hello? Brigid, are you here?"

Carrying a large silver tray filled with several dozen cookies, a strawberry-blonde, statuesque woman wearing an apron over a clinging blue t-shirt and jeans glided across the room. "Hey, Nina. Thanks for the order. I love making traditional *Peanut Butter Blossoms* and I hate waiting until Christmas."

"They look amazing, Brigid." Nina admired the chocolate candies on top of the small brown cookies, then snitched one of them off the tray and savored the flavor of crunchy peanut butter, allowing the chocolate to melt on her tongue. "Yum. I have to get these to the tire shop to pay back Jed Corbett for rescuing me yesterday, so please tell me you have a box."

"And gift wrap and ribbons." Brigid laughed, her green eyes amused. "We'll make them look all girly."

Bells chimed again and Nina saw Meteor Jamison come through a different door, glimpsing a flight of stairs behind the younger woman. She was a smaller, plumper version of Astra, her red-haired sister. Nina nodded a greeting. "Hi, how are you? Thanks again for helping me out."

"No worries." Meteor grabbed an apron off a hook by the back wall. "Brigid told me about your adventure and I stopped by the repair shop during my lunch to take a look at the tire. Someone attacked you, my dear. My sisters and I will visit your home and ward your truck."

"I appreciate the thought, but it's not necessary."

"My mother disagrees and we do what she says, rather than face her consequences." Meteor picked up one of the cookies. "Let's send some of these home with Nina too. You have plenty, Brigid, enough to share with the community."

"I told you when I started, cookies are my thing." Brigid put the tray on the island counter. "I have more."

"Of course she does." Meteor shook her head, laughing. "Well, go get them my little, kitchen witchling."

"I wouldn't call her little when she's taller than both of us," Nina said. "I only asked about the peanut butter and chocolate ones."

"Well, she also made snickerdoodles, chocolate chip, and oatmeal raisin ones. If you hadn't told her they were for the macho guys at the tire shop, she'd have done fancy sugar cookies with different colors of frosting and tons of sprinkles."

"I should definitely get her on board for the Halloween party that my cousin Hilda hosts for disadvantaged youth. Kids and cookies go together. However, I need a box of what Brigid calls *Peanut Butter Blossoms* for Jed Corbett. He was kind enough to stop and change my tire yesterday and that was after putting out a fire in the woods over the weekend."

"Like I said, you have an enemy." Meteor held up her hand. "I'm not saying it's Jed. He's all brawn with very little brain and runs on his libido, a total slut puppy. He's fought with almost all the men in Corbettstown and screwed most of the women. Now, he's expanding his activities to Eagleville."

"Ooh, that's just gross." Nina wrinkled her nose in disgust, shaking her head. "My dog doesn't like him either."

"Well, he's a good judge of character then." Meteor opened a cabinet door on the island and began removing an assortment of boxes and tissue paper. "Just be careful who you trust, Nina. I don't know who is out to get you, but watch your back."

"Always. I learned that lesson when I was a kid in boarding school."

Surprisingly, when she arrived with the cookies, she found Kyle and Orion at the tire shop, totally engrossed in a conversation with the manager, a gray-haired friend of her uncle's, not one of the salesmen. The three stood between racks of tires aligned in several rows.

Nina approached the trio. "What's going on?"

"We're just confabulating." Kyle eyed her and the boxes she held. "You need a new tire, Miss Nina. The one that Jed dropped off had too much damage."

"What kind of damage? I was careful when I pulled off the highway."

"It wasn't anything that happened once you had the flat," the manager said. "You must have driven over several nails or even broken glass because you had three puncture holes and a bad valve stem. You're lucky you made it as far as you did and Jed Corbett was on his way home from work."

"That doesn't make any sense." Nina shared a look with Kyle. "I drove straight from the ranch to the Bar M and back. Most of the parking lot at the museum is paved and I didn't drive on the gravel section."

"I don't know why it happened. I just know it did and even with a tube, the tire probably won't hold air. I wouldn't trust it. Omar called in and said to replace it. He wants us to check the rest of them too."

"How did my uncle hear about this?" Nina heaved a sigh. "I didn't tell him."

Orion shrugged. "Who knows? Eagleville isn't that big and neither is Liberty Valley. People talk. If you'll give me your keys, I'll have the tire jockeys move your truck."

"First, I have to do something with these cookies and then I have to get Pooka so he doesn't have doggie lunch. He freaked out yesterday when Jed was changing the tire."

"I'll bring you Pooka," Orion said. "He likes me and it's a pack thing. Jed isn't part of yours, so the pup had to protect you from strangers."

"Well, that explains everything." Nina started toward the counter and the young guy waiting at the computer. "How are you part of my pack, Orion?"

"Oh, I'm not. My sisters and I are just in charge of protection on the psychic plane, since Kyle handles the physical one."

15

SHE GLANCED AT THE WIND-UP CLOCK ON THE TABLE BY THE daybed. Eleven o'clock at night and all really wasn't well. Despite having a busy day, she couldn't sleep. Pooka had no such problems. He snored softly on the foot of the bed, feet paddling as he chased a rabbit in his dreams. She eased out from under the covers, pausing to slide into her fleecy, dark-green robe and tying the belt before she crossed the room.

When she opened the door, she spotted Kyle sitting on the top stair. "What's going on? Why are you awake?"

"Cogitating while I look at the stars." He shifted slightly so she could sit beside him. "It's a clear night, at least in this part of the woods."

She glanced up at the night sky, the moon partially hidden by a few clouds and the stars glittering against the darkness. "Aren't they the same where you come from?"

"They're not quite as bright here and I always hear rigs on the highway. Sometimes, if the wind is right, I even smell them."

She eased closer so her arm pressed against his. "Is that good or bad?"

"It's just a fact." He turned, his breath warm on her face, his lips a whisper away. "I don't think this is one of your better ideas, Miss Nina."

"Not if you're going to call me that." She laughed softly, then kissed him. "Take me to bed, Kyle Morgan. Here and now."

"I have more honor than that."

"I'm glad one of us does." She unfastened the belt on her robe, shrugged a little so it slipped from her shoulders. "How do I change your mind?"

His breath caught. "I think you already are."

"Good." She fitted her mouth to his, letting her tongue dart inside for an instant.

———

When the kiss ended, he was almost ready to surrender even if it wasn't right. Instead, he stood and held out his hand. She took it, gripping his fingers and rose to her feet. Her robe puddled onto the floor at the top of the stairs. He left it, leading her not to his bedroll, but to the chair in the opposite front corner. He sat down and pulled her onto his knees.

She laughed again. "I thought—"

"Wrong. You're only the boss of this spread, not of me."

"Want to bet?" She feathered a finger over his mustache. "Kiss me."

A skimpy, sleeveless flowered nightshirt revealed most of her arms and legs. His mouth went dry. He threaded a hand in the cap of chocolate brown hair. "You're lovely in the moonlight."

She tipped her head back, smiled up at him. "Kiss me."

"Have I ever told you that you're the prettiest woman I've ever seen?" He framed her face with his hands, stroked her cheekbones with his thumbs.

"Stop talking and kiss me." She slid her fingers through his hair.

He chuckled. Then, he did. He kissed her. The first kiss led to a second, a third. Finally, he lifted his lips from hers. He trailed slow kisses over her cheekbones, to her nose, up to her eyelashes, her brows.

His lips explored the column of her throat. He pushed away one thin lacy strap of the nightshirt until it fell partway down her arm. She moaned when he kissed the top of her breast. He slid one hand in the loose neck opening, found her nipple, and coaxed it to life.

She wriggled closer. "Take me to bed."

"Not yet, Miss Nina. I can wait and so will you." He slid the nightshirt down to her waist. Now, he could cup her breast. He rubbed his thumb over the nipple again and felt it peak into his palm. Lowering his head, he slowly worked his way toward her nipple and drew it into his mouth.

She arched her back as he sucked. He knew she'd said he could have her tonight, but it wasn't time yet. He captured the other nipple between his thumb and finger, rubbing it. Her soft sighs and whispered moans nearly made him loco. She tangled her fingers in his hair to hold his mouth there.

He smiled against her skin. Then, he caught the bottom of her nightshirt, pulled it up. His fingers smoothed up her calf to her knee and finally her thigh.

"Please, Kyle." She wriggled nearer, her bottom pressing against him. "Let's do it all. I can't take much more."

"I've barely started with you." He blew on the nipple, took a moment to tease it with his tongue. Then, he put his hand on the soft brown curls between her legs.

"Oh, my Gawd." She rose to meet him.

"Slowly." He kissed her. "Nice and slow."

Then, he slid his fingers through the hair, working his way down until he found what he wanted. She gasped when he touched the small nubbin, moaned when he rubbed it gently and he kissed her, swallowing her cries as he pleasured her. His hips moved against hers and she pressed ever closer, emitting a low scream of delight.

This time, he slid a finger inside her, following it with a second one and allowing his thumb to continue its motion. When they finally went to bed together, they'd have each other all night long. The idea thrilled him. He lifted his mouth from hers and leisurely explored her throat, working a new path to her breasts with long, slow kisses. She arched upward as he sucked on one nipple and then the other. Her hips ground back and forth against his hand as he moved his fingers, a prelude of what would happen when he really had her.

He stopped a moment before she was satisfied. "Say you want me, only me."

"You know I do."

"I want to hear the words."

She tightened her grip on his shoulders. "Finish it, Kyle."

"I will when you say it." He adjusted his fingers, sliding them in and out of her. "First, that you want me, then that you love me."

"Damn you." She thrust her hands into his hair, yanked hard. "It's sex, only sex. That's all I want."

"Don't lie, not to me and not to yourself." He paused, watched her hazel eyes. When the ecstasy faded, he started again. He brought her to the pinnacle and stopped. "Say the words, Miss Nina. I double-dog dare you."

"What if I say I hate you, Kyle Morgan?" She nipped his ear. "Will that make you happy? Finish it."

He smiled, kissed her quickly. "Give me what I want or I'll keep this up until you're begging."

She pressed into him, sliding her arms around his neck. "Begging sounds easier."

"It's not." His fingers slid into her and he began the motion that made her crazy. It took another three times before she surrendered.

"I want you, Kyle Morgan. I'll always want you."

"Say it again," he ordered as his hand stroked her.

She obeyed, chanting the words over and over as the waves of pleasure took her. When she collapsed against him, he smiled down at her.

"I'll remember this tomorrow when you balk and refuse to let me teach you how to shoot a pistol." He curved his hand over the brown curls below her stomach. "I can't wait until I have my mouth on you."

She quivered against him, staring into his face. "Neither can I."

He chuckled, kissed one of her breasts until he slowly sucked on her nipple. He lifted his head. "Now, you'll know what I'm really thinking when I say, Miss Nina."

"You've called me that since the day we met."

"And I'm not going to stop." He trailed a path to her other breast and nipple. "From here-on, I'll have you at night, every night."

"You can stop talking and have me now."

"I want my woman hot, wild, and screaming for me."

"That could happen if you'd just get down to business."

"Nope, not yet. I may have come real close, but you're not desperate enough." He slid one finger into the wet tightness between her legs. "But, you will be."

"Not again. Not if you won't finish it."

"Haven't you learned anything about me yet?" He eased a second finger inside her, let his thumb rock into the small nubbin of flesh nested in the bronze curls. He knew how to please her and it wouldn't take as long this time to make her cry out in joy. "I'll give you what you want, Miss Nina and we both know you'll like it. Say the words again."

And she did. The words escaped between gasps and moans as she called his name, hips bucking against his hand when she came. Afterward, she closed her eyes for a moment, before she looked up into his face. "I never expected—"

"You should have. I want you to be happy."

"I'd be happier if we made love all night long."

"Soon, but not tonight." He lowered his head, brushed his mouth over hers. "You're mine, Miss Nina. Say that too."

A blush seeped into her face as she obviously recalled what

he'd told her earlier about always desiring her. "You want all of me."

"And I'll have it." He smiled down at her. "I'm your man for now and always. Are you my woman?"

She took a deep breath. "All right. You win, Kyle Morgan. For now, I'm yours."

"That will do, but you'll eventually agree to always."

"Maybe."

He eased her off his lap, swung her up into his arms, and carried her to the door of the cabin. "I'll wait for that night."

"Don't you want me now?"

"Of course I do." He twisted the knob, opened the door, and lowered her feet to the floor. "First, you promise me I can have you for the rest of our lives, and then I'll take you. Meantime, I'll keep sleeping on the porch. It's easier to control myself outside."

She glared at him. "You'll wait forever."

"I don't think so, Miss Nina." He shook his head, amused at the bewildered disappointment on her face, hoping his own regret didn't show. "You're too riled up to keep me waiting for more than a day or two."

———

She didn't have a photography class the next day so she spent the morning working with the horses while he built the fence with Orion Jamison and Hector Ortiz. She hadn't thought Kyle Morgan would be that much different from other men she'd known. She'd lost her virginity in college to a sweet boy who read her poetry and was nearly as inexperienced as she was.

She'd dated over the past few years when she had time away from the horse rescue. Granted, she hadn't picked up guys like Beth and Astra did on Friday and Saturday nights, but there'd been a few men over the years, although none wanted a full-time commitment and most weren't as good in bed as the men in Destynee LaFleur's erotic romances.

Nina couldn't think of a single one who'd have spent almost three hours with her while they kissed, touched, and necked on the porch, but never gone all the way. Okay, that was too many euphemisms. Sex had always just been sex, a fun exercise until the trauma with Smith. She'd been afraid she'd never want a man again. She wanted Kyle, but she definitely wasn't looking for more than a good time.

A red Ford Expedition stopped in front of the cabin and Nina went to meet Meteor Jamison and her sister. Pooka dashed in front of her, coming to a stop near Venus, the youngest of the triplets. He dropped his favorite, soggy tennis ball at her feet and she obediently threw it for him. The half-grown pup tore off after it, always ready for someone new to play with him.

Meteor waved a greeting. "Hi there. I made pizzas for lunch, three huge ones since I know my brother is here and he never shares."

"Wow, how kind of you." Nina walked beside them toward the porch. "What's the occasion? My next appointment to see your mother isn't until next week."

"We're here to *ward* the cabin and your truck." Venus threw the ball again. "Where are the guys working? I'll go get them and we can eat first."

"Behind the barn." Nina waited until the younger woman sauntered away, accompanied by Pooka. "What do you mean by 'warding'?"

"White-lighting your rig." Meteor opened the back door and handed over three large cartons that smelled like heaven. "It will provide protection from most adversaries, if not all of them. Someone truly evil will still be able to trap you, but you won't have to be wary of everyone, or simple mischief-makers."

"Okay, I'll keep that in mind."

Supper that night was leftover pizza, green salad, and sodas. Afterward, they went through their usual evening routine. She cleaned the small kitchen while Kyle filled the wood-box, hauled water, and banked the fire in the stove so it'd heat the one-room cabin all night. Together, the two of them went back to the barn for one last check on the horses. He held out his hand to take hers while they walked back to the cabin.

Excitement rocketed through her when they climbed the stairs and entered the kitchen, leaving Pooka on the porch. "What's next?"

He stopped and looked down at her. "I spent most of the day reckoning on how long it'd take to get you out of your pants."

"That depends on what we do afterward." She stepped closer and unfastened two of his shirt buttons, then kissed the hollow of his throat. "I have a few ideas. What about you?"

"I do too." He cupped her breasts, his thumbs rubbing her nipples through the western blouse she wore. "Reading Mrs. Audra's books provided a real education."

"I didn't know she was a writer."

"Most folks know her pen name, Destynee LaFleur but haven't put two and two together. Bethany told me who Mrs. Audra was before I came here so she could teach me how to build a story."

She felt her nipples tighten against her bra and wondered how long it'd been since that happened. Last night didn't count since she had been wearing her nightie when she went to seduce him. "Are you planning to write those kind of books?"

"No, Miss Nina. I'll tell my own tales, not someone else's." He paused, his hands sliding down to her waist and he lifted her up. She wrapped her legs around his hips, pressing into him. She finished unbuttoning his shirt and allowed her fingers to trail over his chest.

His mouth closed over her nipple, his tongue rubbing the cloth against it. She moaned as both nipples tightened even more. "Oh, my Gawd. Come on, Kyle. Let me take off my shirt. Please."

He carried her over to the kitchen table, his hands clasping her bottom. "In a moment. First, I'm getting you out of those pants."

"I can undress myself."

"I'll give you three minutes and then I'll do it." His hands cupped her breasts, thumbs rubbing her nipples. "Hurry up, Miss Nina."

"I am." Her fingers fumbled with the buttons on her jeans, barely managing to undo them. "Are you taking me to bed tonight?"

"Only if you agree to marry me."

"I'm not ready for that."

"Then, I'll try to change your mind. Now, about those pants…"

She undid the last button. "I have to stand up to take them off the rest of the way."

"You're out of time, Miss Nina."

She stood on trembling legs, pushed off the blue jeans and her panties. They'd barely hit the floor, then he had her sitting on the table again. He pushed her knees apart. One of his large hands was between her legs, two fingers sliding deep inside her where she was already wet and wanting. His thumb rocked into her. She moved with him, unable to remain still. Clinging to him, nipping at his ear, his neck, her nails dug into his back.

Meanwhile, somehow he managed to unsnap her shirt, undo the front closure of her bra. His mouth claimed one nipple, sucking hard while he rolled the other one between his fingers. She heard herself moaning, gasping, crying out his name as he continued tormenting her on their journey to the stars, becoming part of the universe. Finally, she felt as if she'd exploded in a million pieces, collapsing on the table.

When sanity returned, she became aware that he sat in a chair between her legs. She rose on her elbows, gaping at him. "What are you doing?"

"I told you last night. I'm going to have you again, this time with my mouth."

16

DRIVING HOME AFTER THE PHOTOGRAPHY CLASS WITH WILL Dawson, she paid attention to other vehicles on the road. She glanced quickly in the rearview mirror but didn't see anyone stalking her. Three cars quite a ways back, followed by an old white RV, none close enough to be tailing her. She took a deep breath, relaxed her vigilance, and allowed herself to enjoy the maple trees dressed in fall colors bordering the highway.

Sometimes, a grass fire in the woods in the dry season and a flat tire were simply that—occasional flukes. Bad things happened and nobody hunted her. She hadn't seen a trace of Gary Smith in six months. He must be adhering to the restrictions imposed by the protective order. For a moment, she wished she could buy a pistol, but she didn't want to end up in jail. As Inga Armstrong, the foundation lawyer pointed out, it was better to respect the letter of the law if a person didn't want to deal with the consequences.

Her cousin was a civil, not a criminal attorney. For a moment, Nina wondered what Astra Jamison would advise. The woman had left a business card when she visited two weeks ago. Was it appropriate to call and seek an answer to the question because it'd been so long since she pleaded guilty to the charge of felony trespass for driving on a closed highway when she was twenty?

Yes, I'm a convicted felon, but the crime didn't endanger anyone else and I've been on the straight and narrow for twelve years. I haven't even had a traffic ticket. Could Astra remind the court I was the victim of a violent assault last April and I'd like to protect myself.

No answer came to mind when she parked at the grocery store. She guided Pooka to the grassy pet area for a quick potty break before they headed into the store. It didn't take long to buy the few items they needed and a bag of ice. Her favorite gourmet ice cream was on sale so she picked up a pint of butter pecan. If they ate it before dinner, it wouldn't have time to melt. Would Kyle love it as much as she did?

She trembled for a moment recalling his kisses, his touch, and then focused on pushing the cart toward the check-stand. It wasn't as if she'd never had sex before. *I've just never had that many orgasms even when I had sex with a guy and none of them wanted anything more than the proverbial one-night stand. The word 'commitment' sent them running for the door.*

Kyle Morgan was different. Now, she had to decide if she could take the risk of forever with a man she'd known less than a month. She still hadn't made a decision when she arrived home.

She grimaced when she saw the late model, two-seater ATV in front of the cabin. Her mother waited on the porch, Leah beside her in the second chair. Both women wore expensive jeans, clinging shirts under their jackets. Nina grabbed her groceries, so the dog wouldn't be tempted by the food or make mischief with the ice. She rolled the window down an inch, far enough to provide air, but not so low, he'd try to escape, then locked Pooka in the cab.

"What's the occasion?" Nina walked to the porch, scanning both dark-haired women. "I don't remember asking for company."

"I need to talk to you about that man you're living with," Rhonda Zacallah said, "and Leah came to give a younger person's perspective."

"Hello, it's the new millennium and statistics show that

marriage isn't as popular these days. More couples live together than ever before." Nina glanced around the porch, grateful Kyle kept his bedroll in the barn during the day. The ice couldn't wait, so she unlocked the door and went inside. She put the sack of groceries on the table, hoping she didn't blush as she recalled sitting on it while he drove her crazy with his lips, and tongue.

She took a moment to check the stove and added two more pieces of wood. While the other women watched and waited, she pulled out the ice chest. Surprising her, Leah rose from the chair and helped carry it down the steps so Nina could pull the plug at the bottom and let the ice water drain onto the grass.

"Is she serious?" Nina glanced at her stepsister. "The two of you came to advise me about Kyle staying here to protect me from Smith?"

"Nobody's seen him around so that story won't hold up and the Armstrongs are talking about your new man. Aunt Sonja told Mom that they should get together to design the wedding invitations and plan the reception."

"Oh, my Gawd." Nina struggled not to laugh. Trust her aunt to poke, prod, and try to provoke a confrontation since she really despised Rhonda and her new family. "What did my mother do? Ask Uncle Omar or the foundation for more money for some toy that your father suddenly fancies and the ranch doesn't need?"

"That doesn't have anything to do with you getting engaged and not telling us." Leah narrowed her dark eyes, ignoring the embarrassed flush that crept into her cheeks. "Why didn't you think about notifying your family before the announcement came out in the local paper?"

"Because I'm not related to you, your sisters, or your father, and my mother honestly doesn't give a rat's backside what I do."

Nina paused, silently contemplating the situation. She climbed the steps with the drained ice chest and lingered for a moment on the porch. "Wow, wait a minute. I forgot. Because of mistakes I've made in the past, I can't take charge of my trust until my 35th birthday unless I'm married. Once I do, the entire ranch is mine and I no longer have to answer to the foundation, the board of directors, or Uncle Omar for any of my decisions."

Utter silence from her mother and stepsister which wasn't unusual when she said something they didn't like. Nina shook her head and pointed to the ATV. "You can go now. You came. You shared your opinions. When I marry, I'll provide enough notice so all of you have time to pack."

"How can you say such a thing?" Tears trickled down Rhonda's face. "You're my daughter and I love you. What will it take for you to move back where you belong?"

"For you and the Zacallahs to get out of my house. I've told you all summer that I'm done and I mean it. I'm finished with all of you."

———

Smoke coiled from the chimney as he headed from the barn to the house. He saw Nina playing fetch with her dog, the pup happily chasing his favorite, soggy ball. When Pooka spotted him, he raced toward Kyle, tail fiercely wagging. The yellow ball landed at his feet and he winged it in the direction of the stable. A fierce bark and the collie-mix raced in hot pursuit of the toy.

Kyle chuckled and strode across the lawn to greet Nina. "How was your class?"

"Good. I'm getting the hang of it." She brushed her lips over his. "Hilda and I talked about the Halloween party too. It's actually two weeks from tomorrow, Saturday the twenty-seventh since Halloween lands on a weekday this year, the following Wednesday."

"Makes sense." He traced her lips with his thumb. "What did your ma want?"

"She freaked because my aunt tormented her about me getting married."

"I didn't know you'd made any such plans. I'm first in line when you're ready to get hitched."

"Good to know, but I'm not getting married. At least not yet." She tilted her head to one side. "I bought some ice cream. Let's eat it before it melts and I'll tell you my sad story about why I can't legally have a gun."

"All right. I'd like to hear it. Once you've shared that nonsense, I'll teach you to shoot my pistol. I want you to be ready to protect yourself."

"I'd like nothing better, but I'm not willing to go to jail."

"I won't let that happen, Miss Nina."

"It may come as a surprise, Kyle Morgan, but you're not in charge of the world." She stepped back, turned, and strolled into the house.

While he waited for her to return, he threw the puppy's ball several times. They could sit in the two chairs on the porch, but he wasn't amazed when she opted for the staircase instead. He tossed the ball again, then crossed to sit next to her on the third step, low enough that they could take turns pitching the pup's toy.

He eyed the carton. "Yester-year Ice Cream. It's not common to hear that name around these parts."

"It's produced locally. The Dawsons started it ages ago when the health food craze really took off and people wanted ice-cream made with all natural ingredients." She handed him a spoon, then peeled off the top. "I know the Armstrongs invested and I'm sure some of the other long-time families in Liberty Valley did."

Their shoulders bumped as he dug into the treat. Sweet flavors of cream, sugar, vanilla, and butter melted on his tongue. It reminded him of the last social he'd attended in Junction City and the ice cream served to the entire town. He couldn't tell her about the Fourth of July celebration yet, so he took another spoonful being sure to snag a pair of pecans this time. "Thought you had a story to tell."

"I guess it's time." She leaned closer, sucking the last of the goodness on her spoon. "This place isn't on a river, so we don't worry too much about flooding during the rainy season, but other people and places aren't so lucky."

"What does that have to do with shooting a gun?"

"I'm getting there, Kyle Morgan. It's my story so let me tell it my way."

"Yes, ma'am."

"Even in college, I knew this place was mine so I took classes that would help me operate the rescue. Twelve years ago, I was home for Thanksgiving break and the November rains were terrible. The rivers swelled and the water flooded homes, barns, everywhere, but we were still safe here."

"Others weren't."

"No, and Marlene Dawson called about some horses stuck in a low-lying field adjacent to the Destiny River at the eastern edge of Liberty Valley. I took the stock trailer and went to save them."

"Were they your horses?"

"Not yet." She took another spoonful of ice cream. "Clouds piled up, rain slashing across the windshield and wind whipping so hard, I didn't know if I could keep the trailer on the highway. When I got closer, the state patrol had already been there and put up signs closing the road because the ditches were full and there was water on the pavement."

"Reckon, you were smart and turned around and went home. You knew those lawmen had already taken care of the critters and the folks who lived down there, or they wouldn't have closed the road."

"Are you serious?" She stared at him, her bronze eyes narrowing.

He chuckled, leaned over to kiss her. "No, Miss Nina. I was joshing you. I know my woman. You got out of your rig, moved those signs, and went to see for yourself those horses were safe and sound."

"That's right. It terrified me since a good mile of the highway had at least a foot of water rushing across it, but I made it to the pasture, although I thought I'd lose the trailer a time or two when it fishtailed and we'd end up in the river." She scraped up more of the ice cream. "The herd had already huddled up to the pasture gate, scared half to death. The water was belly deep on the ponies and knee-high on the horses. It took some finagling, but I backed up the trailer to the gate and opened it in such a way they had to get in the trailer. I didn't bother tying them."

"How many did you find?"

"Fifteen and three of them were pregnant mares. Luckily, none were as big as Missouri and none were draft mixes. Turned out the bunch belonged to a church camp who pasture boarded them up in Liberty Valley every winter. The deacon in charge of the program would have a volunteer run up hay every few days. In the spring, they'd load up however many survived the winter and take them back for the next summer when they'd be ridden by the kids who came to the camp. When the deacon wanted replacement stock, the church advertised for donations and picked up a few more head."

"You must have had a big trailer."

"It's the old twenty-four foot stock trailer parked up by the indoor arena." She stared off in the distance for a moment, then shook her head. "Anyway, I headed up the road, got through the floodwaters to high ground, moved the signs, drove through, and was putting the signs back again when the cops arrived."

"Were they happy you'd rescued those horses?"

She laughed, a short, sharp sound that grated. "Come on, Kyle. You're smarter than that. Of course, they weren't. The cop in charge had a fit since I moved their damned signs and drove on a closed road, so he ticketed me for felony trespassing. The only reason they didn't haul me off to jail was because they'd have had to deal with fifteen animals and they didn't want the responsibility. Later, I learned my loving stepfather, Deke, reported the trailer stolen."

"Weren't you in trouble for taking the horses since they weren't yours?" Kyle put his arm around her shoulders. "They still hang rustlers, don't they?"

"That was part of the charges against me, felony trespassing for moving the signs, driving on a closed highway, more felonies for the fifteen counts of horse stealing, and even more for taking the stock trailer." Tears glinted for a moment before she blinked hard. "The Armstrong foundation came to my rescue and my cousin, Inga, did her best to defend me."

"Did the church folks get back their horses?"

"No. My stalls were already filled with rescued horses so when I picked them up, I took them to the Lazy B and Darlene Dawson since she had room in one of her barns for the herd. She arranged for a vet check on all of them. Between what Doctor Art charged and the board bill, it ran into thousands of dollars so the deacon opted to sign the horses over to her. She found good homes for some of them and still uses the rest in her camp program. By the time I went to court, that issue was resolved."

"I'll bet the Dawsons weren't happy with what happened."

"They blamed themselves because they asked me for help. Marlene went to the church and told them she couldn't end their horse program, but they'd do better if they arranged for a reputable barn to contract and provide services for the kids. They agreed since it'd be a publicity nightmare if she involved her friends in the media."

"And the trailer?"

"It belonged to the foundation. The prosecutor dropped that charge as well and Uncle Omar told Deke if he ever used the law to go after me again, he'd be homeless."

"So, all that was left was driving on a flooded highway."

"Yes, and I couldn't get out of that one. I pled guilty and received a suspended sentence. As long as I don't do it again, there won't be any jail time, but I am a convicted felon. That means I can't vote, can't get a gun permit, can't go camping or hunting with friends, nor can I visit anyone at their house if their guns are on the property at the time."

"Pretty harsh judgment for someone having the intestinal fortitude not to leave fifteen souls to die, eighteen if we count the unborn foals." He whistled softly. "That means you'd be in serious trouble if the law learned I'm here and have a gun to protect you."

She nodded. "It's a calculated risk, one I'm willing to take.

Being tortured, raped, and murdered by Gary Smith isn't high on my bucket list."

"Not on mine either." Kyle tipped up her chin and kissed her. "Comes down to it, I'll take you home with me. We'll leave these silly folks and their crazy justice behind."

"You make it sound very tempting." She turned her face against his shoulder, heaved a sigh. "What about Pooka and the horses?"

"They'd come too. Trust me. I'll take care of all of you."

Another sigh. "Wow, I wish it was as easy as you make it sound, but when I run from my troubles, I have to take myself along and we can't travel to Liberty Valley of yesterday or yesteryear."

"Not yet." He tightened his hold on her. "I'll have to line up help for that. Reckon, I best talk to Astra Jamison and her sisters."

PART III

"My day starts when your day ends."

— BETHANY CHAMBERS-MORGAN,
HOMICIDE DETECTIVE

17

ANOTHER SLEEPLESS NIGHT AND OF COURSE READING ONE OF HER favorite Destynee LaFleur erotic romances wouldn't put anyone to sleep. Nina lay in the darkness contemplating whether she wanted to light the kerosene lamp and pick up from where she'd left off in the story about two werewolves from warring packs. She didn't. Instead, she eased out of bed so she wouldn't disturb her puppy.

She left her robe behind, heading for the door and Kyle. When she stepped out on the porch, she saw him in his bedroll, leaning against the cabin wall. He glanced at her, then held out a hand and she crossed to sit next to him.

She kissed his cheek, her lips lingering for a moment on the scar. "It's your turn to tell a story. What happened to your face?"

"I was passed from pillar to post when I was a boy. The last place I lived, the folks had a son a bit older than me and he wasn't partial to company, especially when his pa took a shine to me."

"What do you mean by that? Did he—"

"Oh, it was nothing bad, Miss Nina, not on his part or mine. He liked having someone willing to work in the barns and fields who didn't have to be stood over. He was a fair sort. If I did my chores, he didn't wallop me and he made sure his wife gave me an equal share at meals. It didn't anger him if I fell asleep when she was reading the Bible after supper. They didn't have a lot, so I wore their son's cast-offs, but she made me a new shirt for Christmas and baked a cake for my birthday that year. They bought me a pocket knife too."

"It's your story and I'm not pushing the pace. Something happened to wreck that home. What?"

"Their boy took after me during evening chores one night. He said if he ruined my pretty face, his folks wouldn't cotton to me anymore. In the tussle, he tore my cheek with a hay hook."

"Oh my Gawd!" She drew back, hearing the sincerity in his tone. "Where was your case-worker? Didn't the doctor report it? What about the cops? They must have taken a report. That's assault."

"No doctor. His ma tended me and thought up a tale for the neighbors who might see me. His pa threatened to beat me if I said differently. I lit out that night."

"Of course, you did." She kissed Kyle's scarred cheek again. "They betrayed you."

"What do you mean? They were his folks, not mine."

"No, but they'd treated you as if you mattered until it came down to a choice between the two of you. They picked their son and turned against you. It's similar to what my mother did when my father died and she brought in Deke Zacallah. She stopped loving me and chose his daughters instead."

"Reckon, that's why we're both looking for family, but I found Rad and he made room for me in his life and on his spread."

She brushed Kyle's lips with hers, choosing not to bring up the fact that sometimes she thought he lived in a fantasy world. He had the right to use whatever coping tactics worked for him. "Well, there's room for you here too."

"I'm glad about that, Miss Nina." He stroked her knee, pushing her short nightgown upwards.

She shuddered when he touched the curls between her legs. She gripped his shoulders when his finger slipped inside her.

"Hot, wet and so tight." His thumb started its magic, rubbing the small, sensitive bit of flesh. "Kiss me."

How could he be calm when she caught fire at his touch? She turned her head and their mouths met, clung. Her tongue enticed his into a passionate duel. Meanwhile, he continued the rhythm with his hand, and her excitement built. She moaned his name.

He smiled and his mustache tickled her skin. "Wait until I have my mouth on you."

"Not again. I thought I'd die last time when you did that."

"My hands, my mouth, and finally my body."

He pulled her onto his lap and she gasped for air. "Aren't we sharing your blankets, Kyle?"

"We will." He pushed the straps of her nightgown off her shoulders. "Let's get rid of this and then I'll kiss you as much as both of us want."

She rose to her feet for a moment, long enough to lose her nightie, then sank back onto his lap. She laced her arms around his neck, feeling the bulge in his long johns against her. "Big talk, Kyle Morgan."

"I'm not rushing." He kissed the hollow of her throat. "I'll taste you everywhere first."

She squirmed on his hard thighs, felt the dampness increase between her legs. She caught her breath when he explored her breast with his mouth. "Now, you're just teasing me."

"You're right." He drew on her nipple, sucked gently, then harder. Slowly he shifted, so they lay side by side. They kissed, one long kiss fading into the next.

He lifted his head and smiled at her, before sliding downward. "Now, I'll keep my promise."

"Which one?"

He cupped her bottom and brushed his lips up one thigh, then the other. She wasn't sure when he got her legs over his shoulders, but she gasped when his mouth claimed her.

His tongue delved deep, two, or was it three strokes? His lips sought a certain spot and he tugged on the nub of flesh. He lapped at her with his tongue, before he settled in earnest on her. She bucked against him, pushing up into the kiss and his mouth. Her hips writhed and she matched the pattern he set. How could she resist him? She exploded in delight.

"Keep going. Take me." She gaped at him when he shook his head. "No? Why not?"

"I'm not done kissing you." He lowered his head and licked the small bit of flesh.

She moaned as his mouth found her. His tongue drove into her. She found herself rising, falling, meeting each movement of his tongue. When she returned from the whirlpool of madness, she looked at him, staring into his face. He was still between her legs as if he intended to take her with his lips a third time.

"You have to stop." She struggled to breathe normally. "Please. I can't take much more."

His smile widened. "Yes, you can and I told you I like the way you taste."

She arched against his mouth as he started again. Thought fled as he licked, sucked, and finally took her with his tongue.

He was naked when she opened her eyes a lifetime later. He lay beside her in the blankets, his hand stroking her hair.

She let her fingers stray over his broad chest, teasing the hard buttons of his nipples, seeing the concern on his face. "What's wrong?"

"I'm afraid I'll hurt you when I have you for real now." He kissed her forehead. "I've wanted you ever since we met."

She rolled on top of him. "Let's take it slow, then."

"We can do that."

"And I'm scared too." She kissed him. "I hadn't been with anyone for three years before I was attacked last spring. What if I can't do this?"

"You'll be fine and so will I." He held her tight, then kissed her. "You choose what we do next, Miss Nina."

"And I know what you're thinking when you call me that. Meantime, it's my turn to drive you crazy." Sitting on his lap, she leaned forward and nibbled her way down his neck, nipped at his ears and he groaned. Kisses interspersed with soft touches as she explored his chest.

He parted her legs with one hard thigh. "Are you ready?"

"Yes." She felt him probe with his body this time, and he eased slowly inside her. Oh yeah, she was more than ready for him and they both knew it.

He shifted, pushed deeper, gripping her hips. "Do you want to start now?"

"You know it." She rose, fell against him. "Or do you want to take charge?"

"Believe me, I will." He moved under her, guiding her through a series of long, leisurely strokes.

He kissed her as they moved together. Suddenly, she realized he'd changed the pattern of his thrusts. Some were so deep, she thought she'd break in half, others were shallow as he teased and tormented her. Then, his pace increased and so did hers until she reached the heights. He was still hard, buried inside her.

He began to move again. She met him, motion for motion. They ascended, higher and higher. Each thrust took them further and further. Astonished, she suddenly knew she moved as he directed. She really was his woman.

She struggled to stop, to alter their movements. Instead, she discovered she could only go with him. He smiled, drawing her closer and his lips claimed hers. His tongue plunged into her mouth as he drove her past the stars. Their hips met, clashed and they achieved fulfillment in an explosive moment. Completely spent for the moment, she lay on top of him.

He pulled her next to him and ran his fingers through her hair. "So, are you going to make an honest man of me, Miss Nina?"

"I haven't decided yet." She trailed a finger over his mustache. "I've never bought a horse after just one ride."

"Well, let me rest up and we'll go again."

She sighed and cuddled close to him, burying her face against his shoulder. "Promises, promises."

He chuckled. "Next time, I'll have you with my mouth until you beg to marry me."

"Not happening, Kyle Morgan. I've never begged a man, not in bed or anywhere else."

"Oh, I'm changing that rule. Wait and see."

The next day a smile crept to her lips every time she remembered the night spent with him in his bedroll on her front porch. They hadn't slept much, but it didn't matter when she recalled his kisses, his touches, and the varied ways they'd made love. He was happy doing it side by side or with her on top, letting her decide where she was most comfortable.

She finished grooming and saddling Missouri. When she led him out to the small corral, she saw Kyle working with Orion and Hector on the rectangular pasture fence while Pooka happily rotated between the men with his second favorite toy, a heavy-duty flying disc. She led the big red Arabian around the corral in both directions, allowing him the opportunity to check out the surroundings. Then, she swung into the saddle and warmed him up at the walk, circling the small ring.

She reined him to a halt when Kyle approached. "That fence looks good. Do you think we can turn out the horses tonight? They'd love the grass and it'd save on hay."

"We'll hang the gates in the next couple of hours and it will be done. We haven't had a frost yet, so the grass still has nutrition. Don't want them to founder, so let's bring them in at dark and give them a light feeding."

She nodded. "That makes sense."

"Will Dawson sent a couple of pack saddles over with Orion. Thought we could try them on the mares tomorrow and teach them to pony out on the trails."

"That'd be new and different plus we'd have all of them out of their stalls for a few hours each day."

"And the training would mean they're ready if we have to hightail it."

"I wasn't going to say that." She lifted her chin. "I've never run away from my problems."

"Sometimes, we don't have a choice. Rad used to quote Tacitus, the Roman historian all the time. 'He that fights and runs away, may turn and fight another day; but he that is in battle slain, will never rise to fight again.' Reckon, I'll let my older brother's wisdom guide me to keep us safe."

"You've said before that he wanted Smith dead."

"He does, but he'd be the first to say, if possible, to let the man have a trial first. I promised Bethany that I'd look after you. I'm doing my best, but having Smith prowl around the place makes me itchy."

"We haven't seen him." Nina opted to avoid mentioning her best friend. There were more important things to worry about than Kyle's fantasies and Gary Smith stalking her was one of them. "He could be playing it smart and following the rules."

Kyle considered the idea, then removed his Stetson, ran a hand through his shoulder-length golden brown hair, and replaced the hat. "Reckon, you can think so, Miss Nina, but nonetheless, I'll keep my eyes peeled for him."

"You do that." Nina swung the horse to the right and picked up a slow jog.

That evening they enjoyed watching the four horses graze together in the new pasture. To Nina's amazement, the equines got along well, neither Missouri nor S.O.B. fighting with each other over the mares. "It looks like we can leave them while we have supper and put them in before dark. Maybe in a few days, if the weather is good, they can stay out all night."

"Makes sense to me." He picked up the yellow tennis ball, throwing it toward the yard for Pooka to give chase. "Of course, when the winds blow cold and it snows, they'll need shelter."

"And that's when we'll keep them in the barn twenty-four-seven." She glanced up at him. "Isn't that what you and your brother did?"

"Some stock we kept close in, but the rest took cover in the trees and we hauled out hay for them. We chopped ice in the ponds so they could drink safely and not break any legs."

"I remember my dad telling me stories about my grandparents having to do that before the foothills were logged and now, there's nothing to hold the snowpack so it melts off very quickly which is why we have more floods."

"But not here. The Armstrongs were careful about where they homesteaded, choosing land away from the rivers."

"Exactly." She took his hand as they walked toward the cabin. "Tell me something, Kyle Morgan. Do I get to have my wicked way with you tonight or are you going to be honorable and sleep on the porch?"

"That's up to you." He stopped, tipped up her chin, and brushed his mouth over hers. "I think I'd enjoy seeing your wicked ways, Miss Nina."

"Oh, I have more than 'seeing' in mind."

"I hoped you'd say that."

18

They'd developed a routine.

Between the photography classes with Will Dawson, preparing for the Halloween Party at the Armstrong foundation with her cousins, trail riding with Kyle so they could train the horses to work together, and spending every night in his arms, the last few days had flown but she'd never enjoyed her life more. Today, they had places to go.

Nina finished cleaning the kitchen while Kyle brought in one last armload of firewood. She glanced over her shoulder. "I'm going to take a shower before we go. Want to wash my back?"

"Reckon, I can be talked into it, Miss Nina."

She giggled, collecting the stack of towels she'd placed on a waiting kitchen chair. "Let's go then."

Pooka raced ahead of them toward the barn and the utility room. He stopped outside the door. He loved splashing and playing in the creeks, but hated baths. Nina laughed, before leading the way inside. "Stay here, buddy."

Since she had clean clothes fresh from the dryer, she put the towels on the counter, kicked off her flip-flops, and peeled off her t-shirt. She crooked a finger at Kyle. "Your turn. You'll want to be naked if you intend to get wet."

He chuckled. "I was busy watching you."

"I know, but time's a-wastin', cowboy." She headed for the shower, turned on the water, and tested the temperature before she finished undressing. Nude, she stepped under the warm spray. "Are you coming?"

"Yup and so will you." He followed her under the warm water.

Between kisses, they slowly bathed each other. She even shampooed his hair, amazed at how thick it felt even when it was soaking wet. It took less time for him to wash hers. Warm water rinsed them.

He stepped closer, tipped up her chin so their gazes met. "Have you ever loved in here?"

"No." She moistened her lips. "We need to finish and get ready to go."

"We have time for this." He clasped her waist. "We'll make time."

She gasped when he lifted her against the tiled wall, then shifted his position so she could wrap her legs around his lean hips. He slid inside her. She gripped his shoulders, nipped his ear. "How did you know I had this in mind?"

"Because it's the same thing that's on mine whenever I see you." He began to move, rocking into her, each thrust as deep as the one before. "And I'll make sure you like it."

———

In Eagleville, she found her cousin Erik waiting in a close-up slot in front of the foundation headquarters. Six-foot-six in his socks, a giant blond, he still wore his favorite faded jeans, a plaid western shirt, and boots. She parked in the spot he'd obviously saved for her, then slid out of the driver's seat, followed by Pooka in his service vest. "Good morning. Where's your costume?"

"Remind me to pay you back for this stunt." He rumpled her short hair. "You're a brat, my favorite one, but definitely a brat. I saw that giant pumpkin suit. It's scary."

"No, what's going to be freaky is when you sit in the pumpkin patch that Hilda and I put together." Nina tiptoed up to kiss his cheek. "Come on. You know you love being the star of the show and at Christmas, you get to be Santa."

"I'm just grateful you don't dress me up like a turkey at Thanksgiving." He slung an arm around her shoulders and nodded at Kyle. "So, what did my cousin and sister decide you have to do at the party?"

"I'm protecting Miss Nina." Kyle shifted the camera bags. "Everything else comes second or third."

"I like your job better than mine." Erik escorted them into the building to the area set up for photos. "Hilda arranged for plenty of printer paper so you can send the photos home with the kids today. We'll do two sessions, one this morning and then another in the afternoon, but you'll be done about three or four unless you intend to stay for the haunted house."

"I fully admit to being a wimp, but count me out." Nina waved a greeting at her aunt. "I haven't seen any monsters lately, but that doesn't mean they don't exist."

"It's why you have your bodyguard and I'll always have your back."

"I count on it." Nina winced when she saw her mother coming toward her. "Oh, my Gawd, what is she doing here?"

Erik chuckled. "You sound just like Mama. Send Rhonda back to her when you're done being social. Mama has a list of crappy jobs that still need doing."

"Thanks, I'll keep that in mind." Nina took a deep breath. "Go put on your costume. Kyle and Pooka can help me set up."

"Be right back." Erik strolled away after giving a meaningful look at Rhonda Zacallah.

Nina began to assemble the tripod while she waited for the first volley. Pooka curled his lip, growling softly, and pressed closer. She tightened a bolt, then petted the half-grown dog. "Hi, I didn't expect you here today."

"This is a traditional foundation event. Where else would we be?" Rhonda glanced at Kyle. "I'm surprised you're still here."

"Where else would I be, ma'am?" Kyle unzipped a bag. "I take care of Miss Nina."

"She has a family to do that."

"Yes, and most of them are here." Smiling at him, Nina took the digital camera he offered. "The rest will be along before the party starts in an hour."

"I meant me, Deke, and your sisters."

"I don't have any sisters." Nina checked the battery, replaced it, and removed the memory card. "You've mixed me up with one of your other daughters."

That earned another glare but before Rhonda spoke, Aunt Sonja arrived in a floor-length white toga. She was definitely a goddess from the silvery blonde hair cascading down her back to the gold low-heeled sandals. Elaborate cosmetics emphasized her light blue eyes.

"You look amazing. I have to take your picture." Nina gestured to the throne waiting for Erik. "Go sit down, Aunt Sonja."

"In a minute, honey." Sonja turned a regal gaze on Rhonda. "The caterer needs more room in the walk-in fridge. Go clear shelves and don't leave the kitchen until Meteor Jamison and her crew have everything organized."

"I left Gretchen there to help."

"I didn't put her in charge of the kitchen. I put you." Sonja's adamant tone didn't change. "Don't argue with me, Rhonda. You won't win and you will be looking for somewhere to live after Erling finishes auditing your finances."

Rhonda spun and stalked away. With a swirl of her robes and a satisfied smile bordering on a smirk, Sonja kissed Nina's cheek. "I'm ready for my close-up pics, my dear."

"Wow, you kick butt, Auntie."

"It's my job, don't you know?" She glanced at the elaborately decorated throne. "I think you should park your puppy by me for my Halloween shots."

"That's doable."

Nina discovered she enjoyed the party more than she'd originally thought possible. Erik played a very convincing *Great Pumpkin* and Kyle stayed close enough that she didn't have to worry about her mother, or the Zacallah women sabotaging the photo sessions with all their drama. When she finished taking the last of the pictures, Nina retreated to the office with the memory cards and began printing off the photographs. Kyle took Pooka outside for a quick potty run, promising they'd return and deliver the finished copies to a table near the pumpkin patch for the kids to collect them.

The door opened and she glanced across the room at her mother and stepfather. "This isn't a good time." Nina clicked the mouse on the next frame. "I have a lot of work to do before the kids leave."

"You've been avoiding your mom all day." Deke Zacallah folded his arms, an older, gray-haired man in a dark suit, happily playing the patriarch. "You need to get rid of that man you're shacking up with or we will."

Nina heaved a sigh, focusing on the next row of photos. "I'm thirty-two years old. I choose who lives on my ranch and who doesn't. Kyle came to protect me from Gary Smith. Until he stands trial for attacking me and murdering Beth Chambers and is safely locked up, Kyle's job isn't over. He's not going anywhere, but you two are." She pointed to the door. "Don't let it hit you on your backsides."

Anger darkened Deke's deep brown eyes and he took a step toward her. "Who do you think you are?"

"The woman who owns the place where you live." Nina picked up the camera. "And if you try knocking me around again, I'll video this assault and your sorry butt will be in jail before supper time. I'm not a heartbroken seven-year-old, not anymore."

"How dare you talk like that to your father?"

"How dare you?" Nina stood, aiming the camera as if it were a weapon, and glared back at Rhonda. "How dare you call yourself my mother when you encouraged him to beat the crap out of me? I loved you and you turned against me because he was better in the sack than my *real* father. If I hadn't called in Uncle Omar to protect me, you'd have let your new man kill me. He wasn't your husband yet and you let him use me like a punching bag."

Rhonda paled for a moment before bright red splotches filled her cheeks. "Watch your mouth, young lady. You're too old to be spreading lies like that."

"Kiss my—"

The office door opened and Kyle entered, accompanied not only by Pooka but also by Astra Jamison. A peaked black hat on her strawberry blonde hair, she wore a sexy witch's costume, a short dress revealing black fishnet stockings that ended in spike-heeled, knee-high gleaming black boots.

The lawyer swept an icy night-blue gaze over the three of them, then pointed her silver-star tipped wand at the exit. "*Out, demon spawn. No room for you here at night or dawn. Be gone and torment a different pawn.*"

Nina felt the tension seep from her body, relaxing as her mother and stepfather, silently, reluctantly obeyed the attorney's decree. Kyle closed the door after them and unsnapped the clip on Pooka's leash. The pup trotted across the room and nudged Nina's hand. She petted him, heaving a sigh. "Wow, am I glad to see all of you."

Astra crossed to the desk and sat in one of the visitor's chairs, crossing one fishnet stockinged leg over the other. "I actually didn't plan on getting rid of them. My mother asked me to invite you and Kyle to dinner at the Rocking J after the party. If you don't come, we'll all be eating leftovers for the next couple of weeks since Meteor always makes far too much food for these events."

Nina barely managed to smile and noticed Kyle's nod of agreement. "Thanks, we'd like that. We'll head over as soon as I finish printing these pictures."

"And we'll be happy to help distribute them." Astra twirled her wand. "I should get points for not turning those two idiots into frogs, or something more creepy-crawly."

Nina felt laughter bubbling up inside her. "Aren't you a *good* witch?"

"Goodness is vastly overrated and I greatly prefer naughty." Astra winked suggestively. "I haven't heard many complaints."

Kyle chuckled. "Then there must have been some."

"Yes, but not from anyone who matters in eons." She heaved a sigh. "I'm not counting my mother since she always lectures me about my choices having consequences."

Tuesday, as she drove home from the Bar M, Nina remembered the party and the evening spent at the Rocking J. The entire Jamison family made her and Kyle feel welcome while Quaid and his younger sister frolicked with Pooka as soon as Nina removed his service vest. He'd adored having two youngsters who'd happily play fetch with him until he collapsed in a puppy pile and then received as many tummy rubs as he could handle.

The only shadow came when she overheard Estelle lecturing Astra about casting a *geas* at the Armstrong party and that she should remember something called the *three-fold* rule. Astra hadn't seemed concerned, remarking that she'd handle any dire results but she believed in defending innocents, not letting them suffer needlessly. It seemed to be an old quarrel, yet it didn't spoil the evening unlike what happened in the Zacallah house when someone always slammed out in a huff, usually blaming Nina for the upset.

Sunday, she and Kyle went to the Killian stable to see the Gold-Dust twins and the Three horsy Musketeers. The five equines eagerly munched the organic carrots that Nina brought, then ate more when students of varying sizes arrived. The ponies participated in one class, enjoying being groomed and saddled before they were ridden by little beginners at a walk.

In the next session, the two old palomino geldings had their turn. Their gaming class focused on different patterns, all completed at one of the four walks and then at a slow jog. Clancy Dawson stressed 'correct routines' first, followed by 'speed'. She never disqualified the riders but added in time penalties for errors. After the classes, all the former rescues had more goodbye carrots before the children departed.

What had originally been intended to be a short visit turned into an all-afternoon excursion. Grateful they'd turned their own horses into the new paddock, Nina didn't feel too guilty when they arrived home in time to do evening chores. She'd spent Monday in Eagleville working on her report for the foundation and emailing it to the board, then rewarded herself with a quick stop at Captivating Catering for doggie and horsy cookies as well as frosted Halloween cupcakes for her and Kyle. Since Pooka had his service vest, they'd finished off the day by going to the grocery.

That meant she could spend Tuesday with Will Dawson practicing her photography. Pooka snoozed beside her in the passenger seat, obviously recuperating from all the activities this past weekend. *I have my life back and it's wonderful*. Humming along with the country song on the radio, she turned into the driveway and headed for the cabin.

Smoke curled from the chimney. Whether Kyle Morgan claimed to be from another century or not truly didn't matter. He had his own issues, but he always kept the home fires burning in more than one sense. She parked and headed inside, Pooka at her heel. She added wood to the fire in the stove, surprised it was down to coals. Had Kyle's new project kept him away from the house longer than he planned? Or was one of the horses sick?

She took a moment to stir the beef stew she'd started that morning. At some point, he'd added the vegetables. She replaced the lid and decided to go to the barn and help with the evening chores. She could tell him about the pictures she'd developed today and he'd share what he and Orion Jamison accomplished.

They'd intended to lay out a new pasture for the horses and cut posts and rails for a new fence.

Pooka dashed in circles around her, dropping his favorite yellow tennis ball at her feet. Laughing, she hurled it across the yard and he raced in pursuit. "Find Kyle."

The half-grown dog cocked his head, ball in his mouth and she repeated the command. "Find Kyle."

The tri-colored collie mix bolted toward the barn and she followed him through the gate, closing it behind her. She glanced down the row of empty stalls, noticing they'd already been cleaned and the water tubs filled. Hay waited in the mangers. Pooka whined and she petted the pup. "Find Kyle."

She heard a sound in the tackroom, started to turn. A shadow shifted and she flung her hand in the air. Too little, too late. Pain exploded in her head. Darkness claimed her.

19

KYLE SAT IN THE SMALL ROOM AT THE POLICE STATION AND waited. Not for the first time since he'd been brought here, he wished he had a pocket watch like the one Bethany bought for his older brother, but clocks had never been important to him, not when he gauged the hours by the position of the sun. This room didn't have a single outside window, yet he knew he'd been here for quite some time, hours upon hours. That meant Nina would be headed home soon and she'd never been more vulnerable.

He remembered what Orion told him when the police arrived at the ranch that morning, interrupting their work on the new pasture. "Tell them you want a lawyer. Keep saying it until Astra gets there. They can't do anything if you insist on having an attorney."

One of the officers ordered Orion to shut his mouth and the boy backed away, hands in the air. He'd repeated the advice, then mouthed it when Kyle was locked in the back of the black and white vehicle.

The door opened and Kyle saw the burly blond man who'd attended Bethany's memorial. He didn't wear a uniform like the other officers, but a tan jacket over a white shirt and a striped tie.

Light brown pants touched shiny black shoes. A real city boy, Kyle judged, but the man had a pistol in the shoulder holster he carried.

"John Watkins. Let's talk, Morgan."

"Where's my lawyer?" Kyle leaned back in the chair. "I've nothing to say until she gets here. I'll wait for her."

"If you haven't done anything wrong, you don't need an attorney."

"Still waiting for her."

"Tell me about your gun. Where'd you get an antique like that?"

Kyle folded his arms and didn't answer. He'd bought the 1873 single-action Army revolver with his first wages when he worked in the Dakotas, shortly after he started West to find his brother. He kept the .45 Colt in good condition and discovered when he and Rad met up that his lawman brother used a similar six-gun.

John Watkins glared at him, then turned and slammed out of the room. It was supposed to intimidate him, but Kyle wasn't impressed. Rad could have given the man lessons in interrogation tactics. Wishing they hadn't taken his phone and he had some way to contact Nina, Kyle stood and paced the room.

He'd walked the floor eight times, ten steps from corner to corner when the door opened again and Watkins returned, accompanied by Astra Jamison in a dark suit, knee-length skirt swaying as she walked, spike heels tapping on the floor. She gestured to the table and Kyle drew out a chair for her. Once she was seated, he sat next to her. "Is Nina—?"

"Later." Astra placed her briefcase on the table and opened it, removing a file folder containing several pages. "I have Mister Morgan's paperwork here including an affidavit from Omar Armstrong. Kyle is a licensed private investigator hired by the Armstrong foundation to protect Nina Armstrong. As such, he may carry a weapon around her regardless of whether she's a felon or not."

"Why didn't he say so?"

"Probably because your office has shown a sincere lack of

interest in pursuing Gary Smith as her assailant, although you suspected he murdered one of your own. You didn't even have officers cruise by Armstrong Horse Rescue after he was released on bond when you knew Nina Armstrong was the only living witness to his crimes. You also knew the judge hadn't even ordered him to wear an ankle bracelet to monitor his whereabouts."

Remaining silent, Kyle watched her hammer the detective for the next several minutes. Watkins slowly looked through the sheaf of papers. When he tried to return them to her, Astra shook her head. "Those are copies for your office. I have other cases, life and death ones. I don't have time to waste with harassment fomented by the Zacallah clan because they're upset about the Armstrong foundation suing them for malfeasance."

"This department doesn't work for the Zacallah family."

"You could have fooled me." Astra stood, straightening her jacket. "Let's go, Kyle."

"They have my gun, my phone, and my wallet."

"Detective Watkins will fetch everything for you." Astra walked to the door and paused, while the law enforcement officer hastily opened it. Kyle followed her out of the room. "Come along. We have places to go and things to do tonight."

Kyle froze for an instant, then strode to catch up with her. "They brought me here this morning. What time is it?"

"Almost six. I was in court when Orion called and this was the earliest I could get here."

"It's not your fault. Do you have Will Dawson's number or Hilda's at the Bar M?"

"We'll call from my car." Astra led the way to the entry, stopping at the counter. "Wait until we get there before you say anything else."

"But, Nina—"

"Wait." Astra took a step closer. "There isn't any privacy here and they don't care about her safety. It's our concern, not theirs."

Watkins arrived in time to hear her last comment, passing an envelope and the six-gun to Kyle. "If you think she's in some kind of jeopardy, say so."

"Why?" Astra demanded, taking the manila envelope from Kyle and gesturing for him to buckle on his gun belt. "You'll just keep us here, wasting more of our time while Smith hacks her to pieces."

"Let's go." Kyle took the envelope, removed the leather wallet, putting it in his pocket, and then opened the flip phone. "I have to find her."

"If she's in trouble, call me."

Astra looked the detective up and down, scorn obvious. "I don't think so. Instead, I'll just file a suit against your department for colluding in her murder." She took Kyle's arm and guided him to the outside door, muttering under her breath. "What goes around, comes around. Let their evil return three-fold—"

As they crossed the parking lot to her car in the gathering gloom of dusk, Kyle waited for a signal. He pressed buttons to connect him with Will Dawson. "Smith has her, doesn't he?"

———

Head pounding, she struggled back to consciousness. Something liquid trickled slowly down her cheek and she tried to lift a hand to wipe it away. She couldn't. She heard a clink and slowly realized her wrists were fastened behind her back. Metal bit into skin. Handcuffs, she thought. Cold, she was so cold and the floor felt so hard.

She finally managed to open her eyes and realized she lay on concrete. Florescent bulbs burned overhead, light reflecting off white walls. She must be in a basement. Where? Why?

Her right thigh throbbed and she saw a dark stain on her jeans, but oddly enough it seeped from the back of her leg, not the front. Her pants hadn't been removed and she knew she hadn't been raped. Whoever abducted her spared her that much, at least so far.

Her right side ached and she felt twinges from cracked ribs, followed by sudden stabs of pain from the broken ones when she propped up on an elbow. Last spring, Smith kicked her several times when she fought back during the attack, hurting her worse than any rescued horse.

She shifted enough to gaze around the room. It wasn't very large and she shivered when she glimpsed the large drain under a metal exam table taking up the center. Cabinets lined two walls and she saw the gleam of medical instruments through one of the glass doors. At the far end of the room, she spotted a closed door, undoubtedly locked.

Dread swept through her when she heard footsteps and recognized the sound of someone coming down a flight of stairs. She debated playing possum as Kyle called it, and decided against it. She fought to rise. Her right leg screamed in protest, buckling under her before she was even halfway to her feet. She sank back down, settled for sitting up instead, and stretched her legs out in front of her.

She glared at the thin, gray-haired man in the doorway. "Gary Smith. I should have known it'd be you."

"Think you're so smart, don't you?" He smiled, but it didn't touch empty brown eyes. "I'll be back to deal with you. Got to get rid of your truck first."

She shuddered but refused to give him the satisfaction of seeing any fear. "Where's my dog?"

"Took off running across the field into the woods. He wasn't hurting me, so I didn't do anything to him."

"Thank you." She saw the impact the polite words made, but he hastily suppressed the surprise on his face. "And my horses?"

"In the pasture. I didn't do that. Your cowboy had turned them out before the cops picked him up."

She nodded, wincing. "How did you manage that?"

"Wasn't me. I just took advantage of the situation."

When he started to close the door, she forced a weak smile. "Aren't you worried I'll escape while you're gone?"

"Not hardly. Not when I cut your hamstring muscle an hour ago."

The door slammed and she was left alone, agony lancing through her right leg, head still pounding, shoulders aching, wrists burning. She glanced around again. For the first time, she realized she'd been left in what he undoubtedly considered his killing room, a place with the aura of a laboratory where a pathologist performed autopsies.

But, I'm not dead. Not yet.

"Where are we going?" Kyle looked out the windshield at the main street of Eagleville. "We're not leaving town? This isn't the way to the Armstrong place."

"We're meeting my sisters at Meteor's. Orion already went to pick up your horses and gear. You and Nina aren't safe here, not when her family is willing to turn her over to Smith. You have somewhere better to take her, don't you?"

"I don't know how to get there. Bethany said she couldn't open the gateway until next September and that's almost a year away."

"The *Guardian* may be dependent on certain dates and phases of the moon, but we're witches. The Goddess grants us other powers. We'll open the *Time Portal* from this end and send a message to the *Other Side, the Land of the Dead* once we see you and Nina on your way."

"But, they're not dead."

"Not to you." Astra signaled for a turn into a parking lot by a large building painted with pictures of fanciful creatures. "Not to us, but to most people around here and hopefully to Gary Smith, they are because we're sending you and Nina to Washington Territory in 1888."

Astra parked her vehicle and gestured for him to open the door. She slid from the car and turned her attention to the small man waiting for them. "I didn't see anyone following us, but that doesn't mean anything since *The Bard* is married to Watkins' cousin."

"I'll take the lawmen around and about for most of the night. I'll be back at dawn."

Astra nodded. "Thanks. By then, our business should be finished. Kyle and Nina will be on their way to sanctuary."

Kyle followed her through the back door and up a flight of stairs into a large apartment. He saw Venus standing at a table, her attention on a map and a pendant spinning on its chain in her hand. "What are you doing?"

"Scrying for enemy activity." The tall redhead turned a violet gaze on him. The youngest of the three sisters, she wore dark clothes that clung to her curves and carried a sheathed sword. "I found the cabin Astra told us about and Meteor went to see if Smith lurks there."

"That's not safe." Kyle swung around, starting for the door. "He'll kill her too."

"Stop." The tone held an order impossible to disobey. "Do you think I'd send my sister into danger? He won't see her and she should be back soon from her spying."

Astra crossed to the kitchen counter where an assortment of sandwiches, a pot of soup, and salads waited. "Kyle, come eat. It's going to be a long night. Did you prepare this meal, Venus? Or did Meteor?"

"No, she called in her witchling to cook and prepare warding potions. Is your fledging going to join us? Rebekah is a gifted healer, isn't she?"

"Yes, but I left her home to look after my familiars. The dogs need her, and I didn't want to listen to her lectures about magick always having a price."

Kyle slowly turned and gazed at the two sisters. "You're both—"

"All three of us are witches." Meteor came in from the balcony, tying the belt of a long, silk robe around her waist. "We generally don't publicize the fact, but you already know the

Guardian. She opened the portal for you to come here and defend the innocent. The *Bard* taught you to spin tales."

"What did you see?" Astra continued to fill bowls with a hearty beef soup. "Is she there?"

"Her truck was, but Smith drove it away. I didn't see her on the main floor when I looked in the windows."

"He needs to establish an alibi." Astra shifted her attention to the sandwiches, serving them. "How far away is the place?"

"Five minutes as an eagle flies, probably fifteen by road. Eat while I dress and we'll take the van. I've used it for *magick* trips before so it'll be easy to cloak." Meteor left the room, bare feet silent on the hardwood floor. "I can still hear you. I won't take you anywhere until all of you eat something."

Venus heaved a sigh and put down the pendant. "She's such a mommy. Come along, Kyle. She can out-stubborn all of us."

———

After she managed to wipe some of the liquid from her face onto her shoulder, Nina took a deep breath. *Okay, so I'm injured, but I won't die without a fight. I survived last spring. I'll do it again.* Brave words, but how would she do it? That was the question.

All right, first things first, Antonina Arabella Armstrong, she told herself. She needed her hands in front of her so she could locate the key or something to pick the locks on the handcuffs. Even if she didn't find a crutch or cane and had to lean on a counter or that evil table, she'd cause more damage if she had more mobility. *I may end up one of his victims, but I won't make it easy for him.*

Another deep breath and then she brought up her legs as high as she could. Her right leg protested and her stomach lurched. For a moment, she thought she'd lose her lunch, but she forced back the nausea. Tears streaked down her cheeks, and she ignored them. *Keep breathing, big deep breaths, and don't stop.* She pushed down her arms so the handcuffs were below her feet and finally pulled the cuffs up to the front of her body.

Gasping for air, she straightened her legs. The right one continued to swell, but she couldn't do much about the bruising right now. First, she had to escape from the madman who intended to kill her. It was easier to lift her shoulders and wipe her face on the sweatshirt. Why was she still bleeding? She remembered Beth, a former Army medic had told her that head injuries were always messy.

Nina focused on the handcuffs. She'd hoped she could slide them off her wrists, but Smith had obviously encountered that problem before with previous victims and he'd used ratcheted ones. She needed a key or a stiff piece of wire. Time to start hunting.

Yes, her right leg throbbed and ached. The agony might slow her down, but it wouldn't stop her. *I'm not dying, not here and not today.*

20

THE MOON PLAYED HIDE AND SEEK IN THE CLOUDS AS METEOR drove through the darkness. On her phone, Astra texted her brother providing directions toward a future meeting place. Venus leaned back in the passenger seat, eyes closed, clearly taking the opportunity to doze.

Kyle shook his head, not quite believing that he intended to take three women into a battle that might escalate into a gunfight. "What if Nina can't ride?"

"Astra will *Heal* any injuries." Meteor didn't take her attention off the highway. "That's *Her* gift."

"What if she's—?" Kyle stopped, unwilling to say the word.

"She's not dead. I'd know if she crossed into *Summerland*, or *Liminfovia—the Time In Between* and as long as there's a breath of life, I can bring her back." Astra's attention remained on the phone. "As my sisters say, let it be."

"Think of the future." Opening her eyes, Venus glanced over her shoulder. "Stop blaming yourself and own what is yours to own, Kyle Morgan. You came to protect her. Do your duty and let those who do harm bear the consequences of their choices."

"I'll strengthen the *geas* against her mother which will protect

Nina from the woman and her new family." Astra narrowed dark blue eyes. "You should know I lied to Detective Watkins about the suit against them. Your departure may provide the impetus for Omar Armstrong to take action. It was all I could do to get a letter from him saying he hired you to protect Nina. He believes in the letter of the law, rather than justice."

Meteor turned into a tree-lined driveway. "Our mother doesn't approve of your view of justice either, Astra."

"Which is why we didn't share tonight's work with her and she babysits the little ones." Venus barely waited for the vehicle to coast to a stop before drawing her sword. "Now, we defend an innocent."

Kyle hastily followed her toward the A-frame cabin, but the woman melted into the night. He climbed the steps, twisted the knob but the door didn't give. He backed up a step, kicked the lock, the door flying open and he saw Venus already inside. "How did you—?"

She gestured to the open window behind her. "Slightly more tactful, Morgan, but I do understand your frustration."

He glanced around the empty main floor, all one room with a bath partitioned off in a corner. He climbed the stairs to the loft, but she wasn't there, not in the king-sized bed or on the carpet. Back downstairs, Astra came out of the bathroom, shaking her head. "Where is she?"

Meteor stood in the kitchen. She pointed to a door so deeply inset into the wall, it was nearly impossible to see. Another gesture and it swung wide, revealing a set of concrete stairs.

"The pantry and storage."

"I'll guard your backs." Sword glittering in her hand, Venus stood between them and the outside entrance. "Go."

Kyle didn't wait any longer. Drawing his pistol, he hurried down the stairs. He spotted shelves of canned goods, cases of bottled water, and a narrow bunk against one wall. A sturdy wooden wall divided the room in half and he saw a key in the latch of the door. He turned the key, pushed open the door, and barely managed to avoid a glass jar hurled at him. It crashed onto the cement floor behind him, shattering into pieces releasing a sharp medicinal odor.

"Remind me not to ruffle your feathers, Miss Nina."

"You came? You really came."

"Of course, I did. I had to find you so I could keep you safe, didn't I?" He holstered the Colt, strode to her, taking in the blood-soaked right leg, the steel handcuffs binding her wrists, the bruised face, and the cuts on her forehead. Enraged, he controlled his fury and swept her into his arms, carrying her to the door. "I'll take you home."

"No. They called the police on you."

"I know. My home." He felt sobs shake her body. "We'll go to my home."

Burying her face in the hollow of his shoulder, she cried harder. "Pooka ran away."

"We'll find him first and take him with us." Kyle headed for the stairs. "I promise."

"He's been found." Meteor patted Nina's back. "Orion has him and your horses safe. He's meeting us soon. Now, Kyle will take you to the van and we'll get out of here."

"After you aid me and Venus in rendering my kind of justice, Sister."

"Of course," Meteor said, nodding at Astra. "Once we're on the road, you'll heal Nina so she can escape with Kyle."

"Definitely."

———

Nina felt his hand stroke her hair, the kisses he dropped on top of her head. "Smith hurt me, but he didn't rape me, not this time. I can't walk. He said he cut my hamstring muscle. I can barely stand."

"I'll need her clothes and those cuffs." Astra came to the back of the van. "There are bandages and a change in the duffel bag. Kyle, I want some of your blood too."

"Why?" Nina asked. "What are you doing?"

"Staging a crime scene for the police." Astra held out a paper cup. "We call it the *Law of Contagion*. They'll find enough evidence to prove Smith killed both of you."

"But, there won't be any bodies." Nina rested her head in the hollow of Kyle's shoulder. "You'll be framing him and I'll be in more trouble when the cops will find us."

"No, they won't." Astra handed the cup to her. "Kyle knows how and where to hide you."

"All right." Nina let him help her to a position where she could sit in the doorway of the van. She took a deep breath, eying first him and then the other woman before passing the cup to Kyle. "After this, help me change, and then, let's get out of here."

"Sounds like a winner to me." Kyle stepped away long enough to cut his wrist and allow it to drip blood into the cup.

"Let me remove those handcuffs while we wait."

"Do you have the key?"

"It's not needful." Gripping the cuffs, Astra murmured softly. In moments, the locks sprang open and she gently removed them from Nina's wrists. "I'll add these to the evidence I'm leaving for the police."

"All right."

Kyle returned and held out the cup to Astra. She set the container aside, rested her hands on the injury, and stopped the bleeding. In a few moments, Nina noticed that only a faint scratch remained.

It was time to do her part. She pulled off her sweatshirt. The blood she'd wiped on her shoulder and sleeve had soaked through to the t-shirt so she added it to the pile. Her bra followed. She unfastened her jeans and Kyle helped her slide them off her hips. It took both of them to work the pants over her swollen thigh.

She gasped, bit her lip, and finally covered her mouth with the back of one hand so her screams wouldn't be heard. The blue jeans ended up on the pile along with her socks and panties. She kept the lace-up boots. The wound on the back of her leg still seeped and he unfolded a large bandage, securing it in place.

"Use this to provide compression." Astra handed him a roll of brightly colored elastic tape. She gathered up their belongings. "I'll be back shortly."

The three women hadn't returned by the time she was dressed. Nina struggled to ignore the dread sweeping through her. How much longer would it take? She wanted out of here, right now. She wanted the comfort of Pooka's warm, wriggly body and his puppy kisses. She pressed closer to Kyle and stared across the dark yard.

Astra and her sisters stood by the porch, their voices rising and falling together. Nina didn't hear what they said. Suddenly, Venus pointed a sword at the cabin. A bolt of lightning flew from the blade. It struck the wooden building and flames erupted. The trio turned and hustled toward the van, splitting up so Meteor headed for the driver's side, Venus to the passenger door and Astra to the rear of the vehicle.

"Okay, let's move it." Astra gestured to the back of the van. "The fire department will be here soon."

"Where are we going?" Nina cuddled next to Kyle, relishing the warmth of his body. "Why did the police come after you? Smith said he had nothing to do with your arrest, that he just took advantage of the situation."

"He was arrested for carrying a weapon without the proper permit. If you'd been home, he'd have faced more trouble because you have a felony conviction. Luckily, my younger brother was there so he contacted me and Kyle was smart enough to refuse to talk."

"Only because Orion told me to wait for you."

"He's brilliant in his own way." Astra dampened a white washcloth and knelt in front of Nina, beginning to clean the side of her face, gently stroking her hair. "You've got a nasty bump on your head. He must have come up behind you and hit you with something, probably the club I put in the basement."

"Won't that catch on fire too?"

"No, I made sure of it. When they put out the blaze, the fire department will find the torture chamber and call in law enforcement, including the feds. The investigators will discover Smith killed both you and Kyle."

"That means Smith will be arrested for something he didn't do," Nina said.

"My kind of justice." Astra smiled, her dark blue eyes sparkling with amusement. "What goes around, comes around, but sometimes the Goddess needs a bit of help."

She hummed softly while she continued cleaning the head wound. Feeling safe for the first time in hours, Nina allowed herself to doze in Kyle's arms. Slowly, she sank into sleep. When she woke, she lay on an air mattress in the back of the van under a thick fleece blanket. Pooka pressed next to her, snoring softly while he paddled with his paws.

"Chasing rabbits again?" She buried her fingers in his white, furry ruff. "Such a silly doggie, my silly doggie."

"You're awake?" Kyle stood in the open doorway of the van, all cowboy in jeans, a flannel shirt, and a heavy denim jacket. "Meteor cooked breakfast. Come fill your belly before we ride into the hills."

"I can't ride. I can barely move my leg."

"Astra took care of that while you slept."

Nina gaped at him, then shifted slightly. Nothing happened. Nothing hurt. She eased the blanket aside and studied her legs. Somehow, her right leg was the same size as her left one. "What did she do?"

"Her kind of *magick*. She made you better."

Nina touched her thigh, let her fingers rove to the back of her leg where she'd been stabbed the night before. No blood, no wound – it was a miracle. How was it even possible? She eased out of the bedding, slid toward him, and stood. *It's amazing. I can stand. I can walk.*

She smiled up at him. "Where are we?"

"Meteor brought us to one of her friends. She says we're camping in their driveway. When you're ready, we'll ride into what Orion calls, the Mount Baker National Forest and I know the trails to take us home."

"Okay. That works so what's for breakfast?"

"Pancakes, eggs, bacon, sausage, coffee. Whatever you want, Miss Nina. Whatever you want."

———

While she ate and visited with the Jamison women, Kyle checked the horses. Orion had tacked all four of them. The two geldings wore their usual saddles and bridles. The mares had the pack saddles and equipment. Kyle took the bedroll from the van and tied the blankets into place on Georgia. "I appreciate everything you did yesterday and the words of wisdom."

"I'll miss your friendship." Orion stroked the bay mare's neck. "This is the right thing for you and Nina to do. Three go to Liberty Valley of yesterday and three come forward."

"Smith is going to follow us?"

"I don't know that. I think he'll be busy here dealing with the mischief my sisters make for him, but somehow I know there are three of you traveling today."

"And those who come forward? Who are they?"

"Wizards." Orion glanced over his shoulder, lowering his voice. "Don't tell my sisters. Astra made trouble for one of them, played *magick* mud-pies with his life and he seeks retribution, but he won't harm her. My mother arranged their binding eons ago. He'll insist Astra keep the witch promises she made to him instead of continuing to ignore her vows."

"She's been extremely helpful to Miss Nina and me. You won't let this stranger harm Astra, will you?"

"Of course not. She's my big sister."

Pooka darted back and forth between the two of them and the women at the campfire. Nina finished eating and bent to offer her leftovers to the pup. He dropped down into the dirt and proceeded to finish off the food, licking the plate clean.

After she hugged the other three women one more time, Nina buttoned her jacket and walked toward Kyle. "I guess I'm ready to go. Are you? Are they?"

"Yes." He led Missouri closer and held the horse while she gathered up the reins and swung into the saddle without her usual grace. He still saw the residue of pain from the injuries on her pale features. Dark circles under the hazel eyes revealed her exhaustion.

Leading S.O.B., Kyle crossed to Astra. "She looks worn to a frazzle. How long should I let her ride today?"

"Over the ridge, through the *Portal,* and into the *Time In Between.* Then, let her rest. She'll continue to heal for the next three days. By Saturday, she should be herself once more."

Astra stepped nearer and kissed his cheek. "You've been a blessing here, Kyle Morgan. Live well in your own place and era."

He nodded. "I'll do my best."

"Be happy." Meteor hugged him. "Both of you deserve so much and your days will be bright together."

"So will your nights." Venus gripped his arm. "Be sure to take care of yourself so you can guard her, your children, and your family."

He glanced at the three sisters and nodded in agreement. "All of you made this trip successful. I'd say you were my blessing. Thank you again."

———

They'd ridden for hours through the forest, giant alders and maples giving way to pines, cedars, and firs. Leading Minnesota, the gray

Arabian mare from his gelding, Kyle didn't hesitate when it came to choosing one trail after another into the high country. Tall in the western saddle, his broad shoulders never bowed and his back remained straight. If he was as tired as she'd begun to feel, he certainly didn't show it. Neither did Pooka who romped around their horses, then trotted ahead of Kyle's horse for a short distance, before returning to trail after Missouri.

Nina dropped her stirrups and stretched her legs, pointing her toes at the ground, then dropping her heels. If she wasn't ponying Georgia on a lead-line behind her, she knew she'd take time to stand up and sit down a few times on the retired show horse she rode and perform other exercises. She eased her feet into the stirrups again. "How far are we going?"

"Another few miles. We'll stop before dusk so we can make camp."

"Sounds good. I can't wait."

The sun sank in the sky and it grew darker under the trees. Suddenly, a ridge rose before them. Huge granite boulders lined the path while smaller fragments covered the trail. A light sprinkling of dirt covered the slick gray stone, and a tiny evergreen clung precariously to the side of the hill. Fog shrouded the top of the ridge, hiding the steepest part of the ascent.

Kyle reined his horse to a halt, turning to face her. "We're getting closer to home. It's on the other side of this hill, but we won't make it tonight."

"Are we staying here?"

He shook his head. "No, Miss Nina. It'd be safer to cross over now and then ride the rest of the way tomorrow."

She eyed the rocky path. "Well, as Will Dawson says, 'sooner to it, sooner through it.' Let's mosey, cowboy."

Kyle smiled, warmth landing in his dark brown eyes. "I think we should probably go a bit faster than that."

"Are you serious?"

"Moseying is slower than molasses in January. We want to be

at the Bar M, the Morgan homeplace before the snow flies. Let's ride."

She stiffened in the saddle. "The cops will look for us there especially since I've been taking photography classes with Will Dawson."

"Not in this time, not when we've ridden through the gateway to the past."

21

Corbett's Town, Washington Territory
~ Wednesday, October 31ˢᵗ, 1888

SUNRISE PAINTED THE DARK SKY WITH FINGERS OF RED LIGHT. Rain on the horizon, the last thing Hugh O'Donnell wanted. Of course, it was cold enough to snow, but he hoped it didn't. He intended to be in Junction City by nightfall. From there, they'd take the next steamboat to Snohomish City, and then he'd decide whether to return to Texas or head east to Montana.

He'd wanted to leave immediately after the funeral yesterday, but it wasn't possible when dusk fell early on these late fall days. He couldn't bear to be in the same place with the same people who killed the woman he loved without wreaking vengeance, but she hadn't wanted that. On her deathbed, she'd asked him to save her son, to take the seven-year-old to safety with her sisters if he couldn't raise him to be an honorable man.

She'd said nobody would stop them because she'd told her husband's entire family that her former affianced, he, Hugh O'Donnell, a drifting, forty-dollar-a-month cowhand was the father of young Edwin, not the rich timber baron she married. Still, it'd be wise to leave town quickly before Tom Corbett returned from his business trip.

While the Corbett women and the minister chastised Mary for her supposed sins, she simply smiled at Hugh. She'd whispered that the greater crime would be to leave Edwin to his father. Tom Corbett had beat her, thrown her down the stairs in their fancy home, and abandoned her to die in agony. Her baby came two months early and Mary had begun to bleed. Since his best friend, Rowdy Tall-deer was a skilled healer, Hugh brought him in to see her, but it was too late. Nothing Rowdy did saved her.

They'd overstayed their welcome in town. That was clear before three wanta-be toughs confronted the half-breed in the saloon last night. The fight ended with two men badly injured and unconscious, but the third died on the sawdust floor. The town marshal refused to arrest Rowdy, saying men who looked for trouble had no business calling on the law to handle what they couldn't and the mayor, the patriarch of the extended Corbett clan agreed. He'd urged them to leave as soon as possible. Had he wanted them somewhere secluded so there wouldn't be any witnesses to an ambush? Did he intend to kill all three of them, even a child?

Hugh turned in the saddle to check their back trail. A chill went through him. He hadn't seen anyone in hours, but couldn't shake the feeling of pursuit. Who or what followed them? He glanced at Rowdy, a lean, dark-haired man in well-worn buckskins who led the way, Edwin's paint pony behind him. Did the older man sense it too? They weren't alone in the forest. Should they have waited until Hugh had the opportunity to face Tom Corbett?

Anger swept through Hugh again. He eyed the towheaded boy who rode the brown and white pinto mare. Edwin must be safe before Hugh orphaned him for once and for all. Despite his puny size, the boy was a fair rider and he hadn't had a coughing spell in the past two days. That was lucky since Rowdy refused to give

Edwin any of the bitter tonics the doctor provided to ease his breathing.

Rowdy said he didn't know what was in the medicine, but he didn't trust the man who'd moved Mary back to her bed before bandaging her broken bones. If she'd had appropriate care right away, the outcome would have been different. She'd probably have survived both the beating and being thrown down the long flight of stairs, although she could still have lost the baby boy who hadn't taken a single breath.

Hugh reined his buckskin stallion to a halt and listened. The breeze rustled evergreen boughs. A nearby creek chuckled over rocks. An indignant squirrel chattered. Something more sounded. What? A mist swirled past the giant cedars. Vapor cloaked the trees in soft, cool shrouds. Gray fog thickened, became a curtain separating him from Edwin and Rowdy.

———

Rowdy tasted snow in the wind. Should they camp early or push on to the next town? He heard the cry of an owl as it hunted and stiffened in the saddle. That wasn't a good omen. Those birds sought prey at night, not in the middle of the afternoon. He glanced over his shoulder, saw the small blond boy, but no sign of his saddle partner and opted for the nickname he used for the other man. "Where's Holt?"

Edwin blinked at the question, then swung his pony to stand across the trail. "Uncle Hugh? Where are you?" His voice carried in the sudden silence. He lowered it to almost a whisper. "He was right behind me, Rowdy. Honest."

"I believe you." Rowdy rode past the boy to retrace their steps. Hugh wouldn't leave the child he'd called his son for the past three days. The youngster always spoke with respect to Hugh but didn't admit their blood tie. Rowdy had to respect Edwin for honoring truth along with his mother's wishes.

"Stay behind me, boy." Rowdy drew his Winchester from the

scabbard. "If this is a trap, you escape. This trail will take you to Burdette's town and the marshal's lady, the new *Guardian* will put you on the next steamboat to Snohomish City. The captain on the boat will look after you until your mama's sisters arrive. You'll know them by their jewelry. They'll protect and treat you well. They'll show themselves to you, but not to me or Hugh."

The owl screeched again. When the cry died, Edwin said, "Why haven't I met them before now? Mama only spoke of them a few times. She said they couldn't come to Corbett's Town, that there was too much evil and blood *magick* for two good witches to suffer silently. How will I know them?"

"Two women with hair like fire and *magick* in their bearing." Rowdy allowed the memory to seep into him like whisky. "Your mama's enchanted necklace, the one she gave you to wear will call to theirs."

"What do I tell them about you and Uncle Hugh?"

"We died well. We thought of them at the last. We'll find them in our next lives. They better be waitin' if they know what's good for them."

"Sounds kinda rude, Rowdy. I don't want them walloping me as soon as I meet them. Can I wait to say that part?"

The owl's cry came again and saved Rowdy from an answer. Three cries of an owl in daylight meant it wasn't the shapeshifting Corbetts or their *relkinam* on the prowl, hunting them. It was someone else, one of the three queens of the *Trecesalty*, perhaps. He'd take care. He wouldn't let his hopes lead them into danger. He replaced the rifle, rested a hand on the butt of his pistol. Slowly, he led the way down the trail, retracing their steps.

No tracks appeared for nearly a hundred yards. Then, he spotted the distinctive hoofprints of the buckskin. Hugh had ridden off the trail into a grove of cedars. Wisps of fog tangled in the trees.

"Stay close, Edwin."

"I will. It's downright spooky."

An eagle dove from the top of one of the evergreens. The bird flew toward Rowdy. Its wings almost brushed the hat from his head. A long, black feather fluttered. It twisted, twirled in the air, and then landed on his right hand.

He lifted his fingers from the gun, caught the gift. As soon as he touched the feather, he knew. "Lead the way, Sister. We'll follow."

The bird circled above them, then flew through the trees. He was grateful to have the chance to follow Hugh on one more adventure, Rowdy thought. Somehow, he doubted things would be easy. His bride, chosen by the regent of a foreign power tried to poison him on their wedding night. When that failed, she arranged for her lover to murder him more than once. Last night's ambush in the saloon hadn't ended as those two planned. The shapeshifter pack should have ripped him to shreds, eating him alive and quarreling over his bones. The only reason they didn't succeed this time was Hugh. He kept the fight fair, limiting it to the first three attackers.

As he and Edwin rode the new trail, Rowdy glanced behind them to see the trees shifting position. The opening vanished. The giant evergreens stood as sentinels, witnesses and the wind swirled. Remnants of dirt, pinecones, cedar needles, and broken branches covered the tracks, followed by snowflakes. In moments, no sign of the three who rode through the mists into *Liminfovia* – the *Time In Between* remained.

———

Corbett's Town, Washington Territory
~ Wednesday, October 31st, 1888

Tom Corbett studied the tracks again. They stopped in the mud before a cluster of huge evergreens. The men who'd stolen his son disappeared with him several hours ago.

"Let's ride." His uncle dismounted and came to stand next to him. "We can catch up with the others and make Junction City by dark. It's the nearest place to catch a steamboat. They know that too."

"I came through there yesterday and they'd have to wait a week for the next boat." Tom turned his anger on the older man. "What happened while I was away? How did my wife and baby die? How could you give away my son?"

"Like everyone told you, on her deathbed, she swore you weren't his father. She claimed she'd been with Hugh O'Donnell and he sired the boy. She passed him off as yours to get our money. What did you want me to do? Let her bring more disgrace on us?"

"Are you serious? You called Creed a shame to us until you discovered he intended to use the church's power for your ends. We don't have a single person in the pack who hasn't committed at least one mortal sin except for the children and their innocence is always short-lived. You could have sent word to me in Portland by a raven or *magick*. You insisted I go to Oregon even when I told you Mary was too close to her time and I didn't want to leave her."

"She wasn't due for two months and it was pack business. I didn't dare send anyone less in stature to the meeting. Now, stop your whining. It doesn't become a Corbett."

Tom glared at the man, then scowled at the dirt and the tracks again, pushing his way past the branches into a grove of cedars. "I don't understand why she lied. She knows Edwin's always been sickly. He can't go a week without seeing Doc. Why did Mary do this? She must have had a good reason. What could it be? You—"

He heard the click of the gun and swung around to stare at his uncle. "What are—?"

Too late, Tom scrabbled for his pistol. A bullet slammed into his chest. His knees buckled. He tasted blood, the metallic silver of it, and knew. "You did it. You killed Mary and our son."

"And you." His uncle stood over him, rage in the pale gray eyes. "If you two would just stay dead, would stop finding each other in every new life, would stop breeding brats, I wouldn't have to do this time after time. Four damn lives. You never learn. It's your own fault."

"Next time—" Tom struggled to rise, to attack his murderer, but his legs wouldn't support him. "Next time, I'll kill you first."

"No, you won't." His uncle laughed, rage changing to amusement. "You always say that at the end, but I kill you the right way so you can't shape-change and heal. When you return, you won't have any memories of how this life ended. As for your little whore, she thinks you're the villain, not me. She won't forgive you again."

"Mary loves me. She'll always love me."

"Not anymore. Not after *you* killed her babies."

A second silver bullet struck his chest and Tom knew the next one, the last one would tear his skull apart. In the final moments while he waited to die, he prayed Edwin was safe with Hugh O'Donnell. *Take good care of my boy for his mama and me, please.*

———

Hugh eyed Edwin's sleeping form. How long would the boy keep them in this campsite? He'd dozed off in the saddle today. His horse slowed and walked easy in an effort to look after him. Obviously, he had his parents' *magick* with critters. Hugh turned, strode to where their horses grazed.

"They're fine." Rowdy poked at the campfire with a branch, breaking up the coals. "Let them eat, Holt. We'll travel faster in the daylight. Decide how you'll protect us from those who mean us harm, especially witches."

An eerie silence filled the woods around them. Hugh hadn't heard birds or small creatures during their ride this afternoon. Yet, it wasn't the first time he'd felt the ominous quiet. "You're right, Rowdy. I'd forgotten. How many lives has it been since we were here?"

"Cogitate and the answers will come to you."

The buckskin stomped and whinnied at the edge of the clearing. Something or someone bothered the stallion. Hugh's hand

JOSIE MALONE

went to his pistol as he headed toward the horses. Being left afoot was nigh on murder and a man could die here as well as anywhere else.

"Hello, the camp?" A man called. "Got room for company?"

Hugh paused, as a young dog frisked forward, tail wagging, obviously expecting to be petted. "Who wants to know?"

"Kyle Morgan."

Hugh ruffled the dog's fur, glancing toward the trail and the two riders. "Any relation to the marshal in Junction City?"

"My older brother." Kyle stopped his strawberry roan beside his companion's mount, a big blaze-faced sorrel. "We're headed home to get hitched right and proper."

———

Nina forced open her eyes. She'd struggled to remain awake for the past two hours ever since they'd ridden over that crazy hill and further into the National Forest. This was the first decent camping spot they'd seen and of course, it was already claimed. She didn't blame Kyle for saying they were engaged. He probably intended to keep her safe.

Pooka was already making friends with the two men, one a tall, ruggedly handsome blond in his mid-thirties and the other who was older and part Native American. He'd tied his long black hair speckled with gray in a ponytail with a leather thong. He wore a suede shirt, brown pants, and low-heeled boots. Wiry, lean, and muscular with lethal grace, he walked toward her. He smiled up at her and a new strength slid through her, replacing the exhaustion that made her sway in the saddle.

He took Georgia's lead line and passed it to his companion. "My saddle partner, Hugh will look after your stock, ma'am. I call him, Holt most of the time, 'cause when he grabs a-holt of things, they move. Why don't you let me take care of you? I've got coffee and stew on the fire. You'll feel better after you eat something."

"Rowdy's a fair to middling camp cook." Hugh gripped the rein close to the bit. "I'll bring your bedroll right soon."

From the corner of her eye, Nina barely saw Kyle's nod of approval. She eased out of the saddle, swinging her right leg over the cantle. Her thigh throbbed and she wondered if she'd even be able to stand. She didn't dismount correctly, but clung to the horn and slowly started down, freeing her left foot from the stirrup, grateful when Rowdy grasped her arm and kept her from falling.

He guided her to a big convenient rock near the fire and she promptly sat down before her knees buckled. He filled a tin cup with coffee and she clutched it in gloved hands. "Thank you."

"You're welcome." He reached out, touched the side of her head. "Who hit you? The marshal's brother?"

"No! Of course not. He saved me."

"From the man who hit you." Rowdy stepped back, picked up a tin plate. "After you eat, I'll tend your injuries."

"Astra already did. I'm fine."

"I don't know anyone named Astra, but whoever that is only started the work. I'll finish it."

———

Hugh added a log to the fire, glancing at Rowdy. He'd healed the young woman who now slept while her affianced husband sipped coffee. "Who attacked her?"

"Gary Smith. He's headed for jail again when the police arrest him." Kyle leaned back against his saddle. "Astra said she'd try to make sure he stayed there a while, but first she and her sisters arranged for us to head home."

"From where?" Rowdy asked. "Most folks don't find their way to *Liminfovia*."

"What's that?" Kyle asked. "Or should I say, 'where's that'?"

"It's a *magick* place," Hugh explained. "Betwixt Time, Life and Death. Men end up here when they anger witches. It takes days, weeks, or even years to escape."

"I've never angered any witches," Kyle said. "The ones I know have always been plumb helpful. This must be the place that Astra calls the *Time In Between*. I ended up here before when Bethany opened the gateway for me to go to her world from mine, and today, the Jamison women arranged for us to go through the portal so I could take Nina home with me."

Hugh eyed Rowdy, then Kyle. "How many witches and where are they?"

"It's more like *when*, not where. They're still in Liberty Valley, but it's the future, more than a hundred years from this time."

"Reckon, we'll go look for that gate of yours and head through it in the morning," Hugh said. "We have some scores to settle with a pair of witches."

"It'll wait, Holt." Rowdy stirred up the fire and added another log. "They'll keep a day or so until Miss Nina is ready to ride."

"Astra said Nina would need to rest for a couple of days once we reached the *Time In Between*. I can look after her."

"You'll help, but I'm a *Healer*, born and bred. I don't forsake my duty. I'll stay until she's fit as a fiddle."

22

Liminfovia ~ the Time In Between
~ Thursday, November 1ˢᵗ, 1888

SHE SMELLED WOOD SMOKE, BUT THIS BED WAS MUCH HARDER than hers. She knew she wasn't home, although she recognized the feel of the thick fleece blanket covering her. She felt the warm shape of Pooka pressed next to her and slowly opened her eyes as memory returned. She and Kyle had ridden deep into Mount Baker National Forest yesterday, crossed a strange hill, then kept going through groves of giant, first-growth evergreens until they found a campsite.

It'd already been claimed by two men, but they'd made room for her and Kyle. She opened her eyes and glanced around the small clearing. Mist still clung to the surrounding trees and she saw four other bedrolls spread around the campfire, but she was obviously the only one still sleeping, well other than her snoring puppy. No wonder the bed seemed hard – since she was lying on the ground. Sitting up, she eased out of the blankets.

Rowdy, the older man from the night before returned her gaze.

He smiled and filled a tin cup with coffee. "Afternoon, ma'am. Holt went fishing with your man and young Edwin. If they catch something, we'll have it for supper. If not, we'll have to break into our provisions and yours."

"I don't know what we brought." She rolled her shoulders, surprised they didn't ache. When she reached for the cup, she noticed the scrapes on her wrists from the handcuffs were barely visible. "Orion Jamison had already packed the panniers when we joined him."

"We?" Rowdy topped off his own cup and sat down on a convenient rock. "You and Kyle Morgan?"

"And Orion's sisters. They came with Kyle to rescue me." Nina frowned into the dark depths of the strong, black coffee. "I was a mess when they found me in this torture chamber. Smith said he severed my right hamstring muscle and it still oozed blood when Astra had Kyle bandage it."

"What was she doing? Why didn't she *Heal* you immediately?"

"It was strange." Nina sipped the coffee. "She was weird. She talked about this contagious law and took away my bloody clothes and made Kyle give her a cup of his blood."

"Dark *magick*." Rowdy drank some of his coffee. "I hope she's prepared to pay the cost for misusing the *Law of Contagion* instead of just reading its elements for the Goddess."

"There shouldn't be a cost for Astra. She's a good person. She spoke up for me with the federal agents when they came to interrogate me. She saved Kyle from the police when they arrested him for protecting me from Smith. Then, she did some sort of *Healing* to fix me so I could ride well enough to escape into the hills with Kyle yesterday."

"What else?" Turning back to the fire, Rowdy lifted a cast iron lid and removed two biscuits from a matching kettle. "Something else weighs on you."

"I didn't expect Venus, she's Astra's youngest sister, to set fire to Smith's cabin. Venus just pointed a sword at the building. A bolt of lightning flew from it and flames whooshed up in less than a heartbeat."

"The marshal's brother didn't say anything about *war-magick* last night or this morning." Rowdy put the biscuits on a plate. "Did he see it?"

Nina tilted her head to one side as she considered the question, then shook her head. "No, I don't think so. He was busy taking care of me."

"All right."

She drank more coffee while she watched him prepare a meal obviously intended for her. "Do you really know Kyle's brother?"

"We haven't been formally introduced, but I know of him. He married the new *Guardian* this past spring and that news flew on the wind to folk like us."

Nina eyed the plate he handed her. Two biscuits swimming in a pool of syrup, slabs of thick-sliced bacon, and a large spoonful of brown beans. Suddenly hungry, she dug into the breakfast. He refilled his coffee cup and sat down across from her. "Who are folk like you? Or should I say, *what* are you?"

"Wizards, witches, and others who do *magick*." He smiled. "You don't believe me, but that's fine. You'll come to terms with it soon enough."

"I don't know what I believe anymore. Kyle claimed my best friend sent him to guard me against Gary Smith and everybody knows he killed her. That was my fault too."

"How?"

"If she hadn't come to see me, she never would have foiled his attack last spring, and then she wouldn't have chased him into the forest where he—"

"After you eat, I'll finish the healing I started last night. Guilt cripples us as much as physical injury, Miss Nina. You're only responsible for the choices you make, not those that others do. Let them own what is theirs to own."

"You sound like Astra's mom, Estelle Jamison, my counselor. She preaches that credo too."

"A wise woman." Rowdy chuckled. "I'll bet she wishes her daughters listen to her the way you do."

Nina giggled. "Last time I visited their house for Sunday dinner, I overheard her lecturing Astra about her choices and actions."

"And I expect the words fell like snowflakes melting on this campfire."

"Exactly and you weren't even there."

"Ah, but she won't be the first young witchling determined to make the world answer to her brand of justice. The *Wheel of Truth* turns and we learn life lessons as we grow older and wiser."

Without speaking, Nina focused on the food. When they first met, it'd been easy to conclude Kyle Morgan must be a former soldier suffering from Post-Traumatic Stress like Beth Chambers. Now, the mystery deepened. If he'd been injured in a battle in America's latest war, he might have read western novels and watched old movies in the hospital until he honestly believed he'd come from a simpler time. That was before she'd joined him on a ride deep into the National Forest.

Today, she was in the middle of a strange adventure. How on earth had Astra healed broken and cracked ribs, a concussion, and an injured hamstring muscle in such a short time so Nina could walk, much less ride for hours? Granted, she'd been exhausted when she fell into her blankets last night after barely managing to drink some coffee and eat a few bites of stew, but she remembered Rowdy kneeling beside her in the middle of the night.

He'd given her some sort of herbal tea more than once. She'd dozed off to his gravelly voice chanting in an unknown language and dimly seen an odd light emanating from his hands as he moved them above her, lingering above each of the areas where she'd been injured. She couldn't finish everything, so when Pooka yawned himself awake, she passed off the last of the bacon and beans to the young dog while she drank the rest of the coffee.

Rowdy handed her a stout stick. "Reckon, you'll need to take a walk before I start tending your injuries again."

She nodded and rose to her feet. "This is one of the reasons I usually don't go camping. I'll be back in a few minutes."

"Holler if you need help."

———

With Pooka as an escort, he'd taken the four horses to water at the nearby stream shortly after mid-morning. Hugh, Rowdy, and Edwin had ridden out in the dawn, heading for the gateway to the future. Kyle staked the mares to graze, glancing at the two geldings who continued to munch the knee-high grass. "Let's go see how Miss Nina feels."

She still slept, but Rowdy had claimed she was on the mend and would be ready to ride the next day. Kyle poured a cup of coffee and sat down on a large rock. Pooka lay next to him, chewing on a stick. They were safe here and he hoped the other men would find what they sought in the future.

Nina stirred, slowly waking. Eventually, she sat up and looked at him, then at the campsite. "Where are they?"

"Headed to the place we left behind, Liberty Valley in 2018." Kyle filled another cup of coffee and passed it to her. "Rowdy said you only needed sleep and then you'd be back to yourself by dawn tomorrow."

She pushed a hand through the cap of chocolate brown hair, narrowing hazel eyes. "I'd feel a hundred percent if we were somewhere I could take a shower."

"I can't provide that, but there's a hot spring with a pool a short distance away."

"Really?"

"I'll never lie to you, Miss Nina. Do you want to eat or bathe first?"

"Definitely a bath." She shoved the blankets aside and reached for her boots. "I think I'm going to love camping with you. I'll take clean clothes and wash these while we're there. Bring yours too."

"Sounds like you have more in mind than a bath."

"No reason why not." She laced up the second boot, then stood and stretched, rolling her shoulders. "I may not be ready to leave here yet, but I sure feel better than I did when we started riding a couple of days ago. Rowdy and Astra should bottle their healing *magick*. They could certainly teach lessons to the doctors I had last spring. Those ones would have been cutting and sewing me up and it'd have taken months for me to recuperate."

"Time we don't have if we want to make it to the Bar M before the weather turns against us."

———

They rode out of the campsite early the next morning. Tail wagging, Pooka darted ahead of Kyle. They were off on a new adventure, Nina thought, and she was finally ready to face what came next. She petted Missouri's neck and rubbed Georgia's face when the little bay mare nudged her leg.

The narrow trail wound through more giant evergreens. Occasionally, she glimpsed the bluish-purple sky slowly filling with clouds. A cold breeze brushed her face and she tasted snow. She shivered in her denim jacket, grateful for the knit cap and gloves she wore. When Kyle glanced over his shoulder at her, she waved cheerfully at him.

He reined up for a moment and allowed her to ride closer. "Reckon, we won't make Junction City tonight or the Bar M, but we'll probably get to the Lazy B before dark."

"Will Darlene Dawson and her daughters welcome us or turn us over to the police?"

"They won't be there for more than a hundred years, Miss Nina. I figure on asking Gruber if we can stay overnight at the line cabin. If we go visit the Burdette family, we'll end up staying for days."

Nina heaved a sigh. She'd decided to go along with his stories, but she knew better than to believe they'd traveled through *Time*.

Sooner or later, he'd have to come to terms with the facts. Yes, they could hide in the National Forest from Gary Smith for a few days, or weeks, or even months. However, they'd eventually run out of supplies and have to return to civilization. She wouldn't be the one to disillusion a wounded, former soldier.

They didn't stop for lunch, opting to eat biscuit and bacon sandwiches in the saddle and washing them down with cold water. Regardless of the western t.v. shows or cowboy movies she'd seen featuring the Old West and people galloping for miles, Kyle kept the horses to a ground-eating walk. When they reached occasional clearings, she noticed the sky grew grayer and the temperature continued to drop.

By mid-afternoon, it started to snow, needle flakes piling up on branches, and then on the ground, accumulating into three inches or more. As the next two hours passed, the sky darkened. The snow increased, the wind blowing it into her face. The trail widened until she would have had enough room to drive her pickup. Not for the first time she wished she had the truck and its heater to warm her bones.

Kyle gestured for her to ride up beside him. "We're close to the Lazy B. We'll be there shortly. Best to stay the night if we can and push on in the daylight."

"I can't wait."

Approximately, a half hour or so later, she saw lights flicker through the gloom. It wasn't quite dark yet, thanks to the snow on the ground. Oddly enough, huge logs lined the right side of the dirt track, providing some kind of barrier. She didn't remember seeing that kind of fence on the Dawson place and decided she must not have come from this direction before. Pooka remained near them as they approached a wooden swing gate.

A tall, dark-haired man in rugged outdoor clothes, cradling a rifle stood sentry. "Well, young Morgan, sure and it's been a while since you rode this way. Where you heading?"

"Town, but we won't make it tonight, Mac." Kyle stopped his horse. "Got room for company?"

"Wait here and I'll signal Burdette at the main house."

He stepped back and Nina flicked a sideways glance at Kyle. "Doesn't he mean the Dawsons? They—"

"No, Miss Nina. Nowadays, Trace Burdette still owns the Lazy B."

Before the dark-haired Irishman returned, a gray-haired man in a heavy coat, pants, and boots came to the gate and opened it. "Get down and come inside. There's coffee on the stove."

"Thanks, Gruber." Kyle led the way inside, turning his horse away when S.O.B. tried to bite the stranger. "This is Detective Morgan's best friend, Nina Armstrong. She's come to visit awhile."

"Thought you said Smith killed her."

"He tried." Nina met the older man's gray gaze. "He failed. I'm tougher than I look."

"Yes, ma'am. I wager you are." He closed the gate behind them.

Mac met them at the corral near the small cabin. "Burdette sent word for you to stay with us. She'll be up with Prescott in the morning to do the pretty unless the snow gets worse."

"Do you think it will?" Nina watched her half-grown puppy sniff the man's hand, then allow Mac to pet him. "It seems early for snow."

"It's already November, ma'am and we expected it afore now."

Kyle passed his reins and Minnesota's lead line to Gruber, then stepped close enough to hold Missouri's bit while Nina dismounted. "I'll be in after I take care of the stock. You go warm up. It's been a long day and a tough ride."

For a moment, she considered arguing that she could do her share and look after the horses too, but a sudden wave of exhaustion swamped her. She nodded, took a deep breath, and headed inside. She carefully closed the door and scanned the cabin. One oil lamp sat on the table and another was on the shelf by a window.

The small room was about half the size of her place on the

Armstrong ranch. A wood-burning cookstove provided heat and she saw the coffee pot, along with a large kettle sitting on top. Four narrow bunks lined two of the walls. Clothes hung from pegs on a third wall. Canned food lined the shelves on the wall next to the door and she spotted a blue enamel cup.

She filled it and put the cup on the table near the stove. She shrugged out of her coat, peeled off her stocking cap and gloves, then hung the coat where it could dry. She sat down and let the cup warm her hands.

The door opened along with a gust of cold air. Gruber kicked it closed behind him and carried an armload of wood over to the stove. "Young Morgan says you haven't eaten since morning."

"We had sandwiches while we rode but that was hours ago." Nina eyed him, wondering about the matching scars on his cheeks. What caused those? She chose to be polite and not ask for the moment. "Why do you call Kyle that? Young Morgan?"

"Because he's younger than his brother, the marshal." Gruber stoked the fire, then proceeded to remove the lid from a pot on the stove and check the contents. "I made *Eintopf.* Mac says it's like the stew his mother cooked in Ireland, but it's good on a cold day. Rabbit from his snares, meat broth, vegetables, potatoes, and since we both like them, I added dumplings."

Nina stood and went after the enamel bowls on the shelf. "It sounds wonderful. I haven't had that since I studied in Germany years ago. I'm warm now. I'll help dish up."

Gruber stroked his mustache. "What did you study?"

"It was the summer exchange program with my boarding school, so I went for ten years. We had classes in literature, mathematics, music, and science as well as classic horsemanship, jumping, and dressage."

"Sprechen Sie Deutsch?"

"Ja, ich spreche Deutsch."

23

Kyle heard Nina's and Gruber's voices rising and falling in conversation when Mac opened the line-cabin door. It surprised Kyle that they spoke in German since she'd never said she knew other languages. Pooka scooted hastily under the table, undoubtedly figuring 'discretion was the better part of valor' and Kyle smiled, appreciating the pup's sense. He carried in the panniers from the pack saddles and put them by the far wall, then took the bedrolls from Mac, placing those on the two empty bunks.

After the meal, Kyle headed outside with the other two men. He carried in water while Mac brought in more wood and Gruber checked on the horses. Nina cleaned up, washing the dishes at the dry sink, just like she did in her own cabin. Kyle opened one of their containers and removed Pooka's metal dish, then added dry food from the bag Orion included in their supplies.

Nina had scraped the leftovers from their four plates onto one and now she stirred the bits of stew and dumplings into the kibble for the dog, then took the bowl from Kyle. "I'll feed him, but I appreciate you doing it the last few days while I was under the weather."

"I'll do anything for you." He brushed a kiss over her lips. "It's good to see you back to yourself, not worn to a frazzle."

"It's good to be normal again." She dropped to one knee and gave the dish to the pup. "Why do I think we won't be sharing the same bunk tonight?"

"Because it's a case of 'when in Rome, do as the Romans do,' and you already knew that."

"Yes." She stepped close to him, sliding her arms around his neck, and kissed him. "Thank you for rescuing me from Gary Smith again. I'm sorry you didn't get to kill him the way you wanted."

"Not as sorry as I am, but taking you to safety was more important." Kyle stroked her hair, then tipped up her chin and admired the golden glints in her hazel eyes. "We'll let the law have him for now, Miss Nina."

"That works for me."

He held her until he heard footsteps on the porch, then reluctantly released her. She went back to the dishes. He found the broom and swept the floor while he waited for the dog to finish eating. When he returned from walking Pooka, he found Gruber reading a German newspaper near the stove while Mac and Nina played chess.

———

She woke to the rattle of stove lids and knew someone built up the fire in the woodstove.

When she opened her eyes, she saw Heinrich Gruber stirring something in a large bowl. She pushed the blankets aside, disturbing Pooka who yawned at her. She sat up on the bottom bunk. She drew on her boots and laced the first one. "I can cook breakfast in a few minutes."

"It's just sourdough hotcakes, side pork, and coffee."

"Doesn't sound too difficult." She took her coat off a peg, snapped her fingers for Pooka to follow her and the two of them went out the door. Kyle had escorted her to the outhouse the night before and she headed that way first. It'd amused her to actually find scraps of newspaper there to be used as toilet paper, but she hadn't mentioned she'd heard the pioneers used old store catalogs.

She came to a stop when she saw two riders stop in front of the cabin. She stared at the larger of the two horses, a light palomino Appaloosa with a blazed face, two white socks, and a white rump decorated with peacock-style spots. "Wonder?" She took one step, then a second, and ran toward the seventeen-hand stallion. "Wonder? Wonder? Wonder!"

The stud neighed, then pulled the reins out of his rider's hands and trotted through the snow to meet her. He nosed her pockets and she laughed, rubbing his cheek, then his forehead and straightened the white forelock. "I'm so sorry, buddy. I don't have any carrots."

"I have a biscuit you can give him, but don't tell Mac. My housekeeper sent them along for the men."

The low amused voice came from the other woman who approached. They were about the same size, but the stranger probably was a couple of inches taller. She wore a heavy black duster over dark clothes and packed two pearl-handled pistols on slender hips. High cheekbones, long black braids, brilliant green eyes, but she was obviously part Native American. "I'm Trace Burdette. Welcome to the Lazy B."

"She's actually Trace Burdette Prescott." A blond man followed her. Good humor shone on his beard-stubbled, handsome face and reached his smiling sky-blue eyes. "I'm her husband, Zeb Prescott. We've been married a full year and she still forgets her name."

"Zebadiah talks too much so I suppose we should be grateful he thinks he's charming." Trace collected the reins and tugged gently on the horse's head. "Come along, Emancipation."

"Why do you call him that? His name is Wonder."

"You can call him whatever you want, but I named him Emancipation when Marshal Morgan gave him to me as a baby after a cougar killed his mother. I heard you rescued him from Gary Smith and I appreciate that." She petted the horse's neck with a gloved hand. "He's sired most of the young-uns in my remuda over the years. I'd be happy to give you one of his colts when he's ready to be weaned, or a saddle-broke mare or stud, but I can't bear to part with my first Appy."

"I understand." Nina rubbed the Appaloosa's blaze again. "I always name my horses after different American states. He was the first one I didn't. He's something special, but I already have three other horses. I'm just glad he's safe and healthy."

"The offer stands whether you change your mind tomorrow, next month, or next year."

"And Trace is real fussy about who gets her horses." Zebadiah Prescott stood still, but seemed too alert, too ready for action, reminding Nina of one of Beth Chamber's soldier friends. He petted Pooka who leaned against him, running his fingers through the young dog's white ruff. "Did we make it here in time for breakfast?"

Nina felt heat rush into her face. "O.M.G., I forgot. I told Heinrich I'd be right back and start cooking."

"Don't do that," Trace led her horse over to the hitch-rail. "You've got to 'begin as you mean to go on, Nina Armstrong, and go on as you began' like that preacher in England, Charles H. Spurgeon said. If you cook for these fellas, they'll never let you away from the stove."

Nina blinked. "How do you know my name?"

"Detective Morgan told me."

Two hours later, they prepared to leave the Lazy B and continue their journey to the Bar M. Nina tucked a gift of home-made doughnuts wrapped up in brown paper into her saddlebags, promising to give them to Detective Morgan. It confused her when Kyle told Heinrich she was a friend of the detective when as far as she knew they'd never met. Another unanswered question popped into her mind. Why did some people refer to Kyle's older brother as a marshal while others called the man a detective?

The idea she'd met a woman calling herself, Trace Burdette still puzzled Nina. Had they ridden into some sort of 'looney-bin' where everyone masqueraded as the original settlers of Liberty Valley? She supposed she should count her proverbial blessings and be grateful they'd successfully escaped from Gary Smith.

The horses kicked up snow under their hooves, but the sky was a bright blue despite the puffy white clouds. The sun shone, but it was still cold and most of the snow hadn't melted. She flicked a sideways glance at Kyle who rode next to her. His hat dipped low and she barely glimpsed his brown eyes. "How long will it take us to reach the Bar M?"

"We'll be there tomorrow afternoon if the weather stays warm."

She shivered in her denim jacket, grateful for her knit stocking hat and gloves. "You're calling this warm?"

"As Mac would say, it's November and it usually starts snowing in mid-October around here."

"I'll keep that in mind."

The narrow track, almost a one-lane road wound through the evergreens as the hours passed. Missouri picked up a slow trot, catching up to Kyle when he stopped his gelding on a small hill. He pointed to a cluster of buildings in the distance. "Junction City."

Nina gazed at what seemed to be a small settlement. The main dirt street stretched more than a half-mile and other roads branched off to the left and right. Most of the structures appeared to be single-story, built out of wood, and covered with cedar shakes. To the far left, she saw the glimmer of a river and a boat dock. "Does somebody have their own sailboat?"

"Trace Burdette owns most of the town and has supplies shipped up from Snohomish City a couple of times a month." Kyle frowned thoughtfully. "Probably won't see another shipment before spring unless the river doesn't freeze. I'm sure Trace had Miss Susanne stock up at the mercantile so nobody will go wanting or hungry."

"Why do you call Trace by her first name?"

"Most folks do but it's not disrespectful." Kyle started walking

S.O.B. down the rise. "Rad said she'd been here since she was a tyke and everyone was in the habit of calling her that or by her last name even before Zeb Prescott returned to Liberty Valley. He was the first one who pointed out she was a woman and married her straight away."

"Didn't anyone else know?"

"According to Miss Susanne, everybody in Liberty Valley pretends they knew, but they didn't. Some fellas in the saloon told me Burdette had shot my brother, so I confronted her. I didn't have a clue she was a woman. If I had, I wouldn't have called her out."

"What does that mean in plain English, Kyle?"

"It means I was stupid enough to challenge her to a gunfight the first day I arrived. She and Zeb Prescott would have 'kicked my butt' as your folks would say, except I was ambushed before they could give me the comeuppance I richly deserved. When I was wounded, she arranged for the doctor to treat me and offered to pay the bill."

"And why are you telling me this?"

"Because if I don't, someone else will. My brother casts a big shadow and folks find me wanting in these parts."

"Then, they're the stupid ones." Nina rode up beside him, switched her reins so she could take his hand. "I'll bet they wouldn't have come into Smith's torture chamber and saved me. You're my hero, my guy and I'll tell anyone so."

He squeezed her fingers for a moment. "Any luck at all, someday you'll marry me."

"That could happen." She rose in her stirrups long enough to kiss his cheek, feeling the prickle of beard stubble against her lips. "I'm not ready yet, but it doesn't mean I won't be some day. I need more time."

"And I'll give you that time."

She heard tinny music from an out-of-tune piano as they passed the first large building and Kyle told her it was the one and only saloon. They kept riding down the street until he stopped in front of a stone house, created from river rock and cement. He dismounted, wrapped the reins around the hitch-rail, then came to stand next to Missouri.

Stiff from the day of riding, she swung out of the saddle. At least, she wasn't in the kind of pain she'd been when they started this excursion. "So, what's this?"

"The town jail. It used to be the Madisons' home, but after Zeb's stepfather died, his mother and sisters moved out to the Lazy B. Trace and the mayor convinced the town council that it'd be the perfect place for a marshal's office."

"Why is it made out of rock when everything else is built out of wood?"

"Rad told me Reverend Madison was afraid of fire and if the summer is really dry, everyone has to be careful."

She nodded. That made sense. With Pooka in front of them, they crossed the boardwalk and entered the main room, Kyle closing the heavy wooden door behind them. It was obviously an office with a desk and chair off to one side, an old-style kitchen with cupboards, a woodstove for heat, a table, and chairs. The collie pup trotted off and happily curled up on the rag rug near the stove, proceeding to lick his snow-white paws clean.

An adjacent alcove held a bed and a smaller table with an oil lamp. Clothing, mostly men's, hung from hooks nearby. She saw three cell doors to her right. "So, that's where the bad folks go?"

"Mostly the loggers when they've been drinking and brawling." Kyle chuckled. "We don't have many outlaws around here. Once upon a time, those were the Madison girls' bedrooms."

Nina glanced around the room again, her gaze narrowing on the Wanted posters tacked to the wall near the desk. Before she asked, the door opened behind them and she saw an older man staring at her. He must be in his late fifties or early sixties. Six-foot, rail-thin in a black suit, a deputy's star on his jacket, he wore two pistols with extra ammunition on the gun belts. He carried a rifle in one hand. Gray hair hung to his shoulders and his coal-black eyes were cold, but somehow, he didn't scare her, not the way Gary Smith had.

He looked past her and his gaze suddenly warmed as a smile crossed his face. "Well, I'll be hornswoggled. You're home."

"I'm back, all right." Kyle waited while the man hung the rifle in the rack, then the two shook hands, gripping tight. "How are things around here, Cal?"

"Busy as always when one of Connor's crews is in the Cedar Stump." Cal drawled. "Prince Beauchamp is trying to stay on Detective Morgan's good side and it ain't easy since the marshal rode out alone on his circuit a couple of weeks ago. Who's this?"

A faint red crept into Kyle's cheeks. "Sorry, my manners got away from me. Miss Nina Armstrong, this is Cal Cabot, Rad's deputy who pretty much runs everything in town. Cal, this is my affianced, Nina Armstrong."

"It's a pleasure, ma'am." Cal smiled at her. "Welcome to Junction City. Hope you like the place and the folks."

"I'm sure I will." Nina took a deep breath. "Did I see coffee on the stove?"

"Yes, ma'am. It's not particularly strong since Detective Morgan made it this morning, but reckon it might be drinkable by now."

Amusement filled Kyle's voice. "I hope you didn't criticize it earlier, Cal."

"I didn't dare, not when the detective's stomping around, cussing up a storm." Cal went over to the counter, removed cups, and proceeded to fill them. "Come and set a spell."

The door banged open and a dark-haired boy in work clothes and corked boots staggered inside, reeking of alcohol. "I ain't done nothing wrong. I can work and fight and drink."

A German Shepherd nosed him, baring gleaming white teeth. The dog growled when the young logger continued to complain. "How come you didn't arrest them other guys?"

"Because they weren't stupid enough to look for trouble." The door slammed and a curvaceous, red-haired woman in a dark blue coat and ankle-length divided skirt shoved the boy toward the first cell. "You come to my town, raise hell and put props under it, plan to pay the piper."

"It's not fair."

Nina stood stock still, gaping at the other woman. "You're alive." She barely heard her own voice, the whisper. "Beth, you're alive."

"It ain't my fault. I didn't sass *you*, Detective Morgan. It was the whisky talking."

"Tell me something I don't know." The cell door banged and the lock turned. "You barf in that cell, sonny buck, and you'll be scrubbing the floor because I sure as sugar won't."

"I told you to behave yourself in the Cedar Stump, Steve Green and you just didn't listen." Cal shook his head, gray hair rustling around his shoulders. "Detective Morgan is downright peevish since the marshal left to ride around Liberty Valley without her. Now, she'll be insisting someone take word to your pa to come and fetch you 'cuz you're not old enough to do a man's job. Only thing worse would be if she sends a rider out to the Lazy B and lets Burdette know you're too young to get hitched to that orphan gal you want to marry."

"I can live with that." Beth spun, shooting a green-eyed glare at the old man. "Why did you go off and leave me at the Stump, Cal?"

"Because you and the dog wanted to chew on somebody and nobody was gonna give you the pleasure with me hanging about."

"Makes sense to me." Kyle strode across the room. "Why did Rad go alone?"

"Because he's a pigheaded, caveman jerk who thinks pregnant women can't do anything." Beth looked him up and down. "I don't believe this. I told you I couldn't bring you home—"

"Until next September. I had help on the other side." Kyle drew her into a quick hug. "I brought you a present."

"Really? And it better damned well not be more baby crap. You'd think nobody had ever expected a kid before. Another set of hand-sewn cloth diapers and I'm going to hurl. What is it?"

"Me." Nina took one step forward, then another and another until she reached the two of them. She lifted her hand, gently touched Beth's shoulder, feeling the solid warmth. "He brought me. And you're here. You're really here."

"Of course, I am. Where else would I be?"

PART IV

"When a man thinks he's as ornery as cactus, he oughta try ordering around someone else's dog. It's a downright, humbling experience."

— RAD MORGAN, LAWMAN, AND RANCHER

24

KYLE WATCHED THE TWO WOMEN HUG AS IF THEY HADN'T SEEN each other for a hundred years, rather than a few months. Well, that was actually fairly close to the truth. He glanced past them to Cal. "I could use some help putting up our horses. Where would be best? Connor's place, the town or the hotel livery?"

"Connor has empty stalls and it's part of the marshal's pay so we'll go there." Cal stepped around the embracing women, heading for the door. "We'll bring in your gear first."

"Sounds fair."

When he returned with her belongings from Missouri, the big red gelding, Beth and Nina sat at the table. Nina had a cup of coffee and Beth glowered at her tea. The two dogs had apparently decided to share the rug near the woodstove, so peace reigned throughout the town jail.

Nina rose to her feet and came to take the saddlebags. "When we stopped at the Lazy B, Trace sent a package of homemade doughnuts from her housekeeper. She said they were for Detective Morgan."

"That's me." Beth heaved a sigh. "I miss visiting them."

"Why don't we go there?" Nina sipped her coffee. "It'd only

take a day by horseback since you don't have your Jeep and I don't have my pickup."

"Because this is my first baby." Beth gestured to the door. "Go away, Kyle. I'm about to share 'girly' stuff with my friend and you'll be embarrassed to hear it."

"We're headed for Connor's barn as soon as we bring in the panniers. I'll put them and the bedrolls in the two empty cells for now. Don't arrest anybody else until we head out to the Bar M."

"I'll think about it, but it's not exactly my choice. If people act stupid, I have to put them somewhere."

Kyle chuckled and went back to the horses. Once the mares had been stripped of the extra gear, he led Minnesota and S.O.B. toward the mayor's large house and even better the barn behind it. Cal followed with the other two horses. When each of them had a stall, Kyle began unsaddling. "Appreciate the help."

"I appreciate you showing up today with the detective's friend. She doesn't say anything sentimental, but I know she misses your brother something fierce. They haven't been hitched that long."

"Just over six months." Kyle hefted his saddle onto the stall wall. "Kind of surprises me that Rad rode out. Wasn't there anyone else to send?"

"Not really. All the other marshals have bigger cities to watch over and only Rad has all of Liberty Valley." Cal removed the pack saddle from Georgia, neatly avoiding the mare's teeth when she nipped at him. "He told me he'd give some of the towns a lick and a promise, but this is the last circuit he can make before the heavy snow hits and he couldn't do less than his job."

"I'm sure Bethany told him other ladies ride when they're expecting."

"Yes, but they don't faint in the middle of the mercantile in front of the marshal." Cal moved onto Missouri and began untacking the big, blaze-faced sorrel gelding. "Will Green brought in a crock of what he called sauerkraut, from his womenfolk for Miss Susanne to send out to the Lazy B for Heinrich Gruber.

When Detective Morgan caught a whiff of that fermented cabbage, she was down for the count. Doc Jenkins and Rad agreed she should take care. Of course, neither of them thought to consult the detective about that decision."

"Most folks in these parts figure Rad Morgan has more sand than a desert." Kyle moved onto taking care of the dainty gray Arabian mare. "Reckon he proved it when he laid down the law to the detective."

"Got to go along with that. He might not be strong on brains, but he doesn't lack guts."

———

The coffee was stronger than what she made, but it warmed her from the inside out, Nina thought, wrapping her hands around the enamel cup. "So, when is the baby due?"

"Sometime in late February or early March." Beth made a face as she sipped her tea. "I had most of my period in June, so I wasn't sure, especially when I was still spotting in July, August, and September. I thought I was when Kyle left, but my cycle has always been wonky. It's not like I could run to the corner drugstore for a pregnancy test and there's no way Susanne carries those at the mercantile."

"You could ask her to order in some, couldn't you?"

"And have her think I'm totally nuts?" Beth shook her head. "Although I started heaving when I smelled coffee, I figured it was because of the way Rad ruins it. He never throws out the grounds. He just adds a little fresh to it and brews it strong enough to float a horseshoe."

Nina suppressed the urge to laugh. "Then, it's funny the two of you ended up together when you're such a fanatic about grinding your own beans and using distelled water to brew it. You're the one who always ran a tab at the local espresso stand and could drink three or four triple-shot mochas a day."

"Add those to the list of things I miss. They rank right up there with pizza."

"We used to make pizzas at your condo back home. I bet we could do it here." Nina paused, deciding not to make waves until she knew more about the situation. "So, tell me how you ended up with a bunch of folks who think they're living in the old West and are re-enacting roles from those days."

"They aren't and we are." Beth frowned thoughtfully. "It's a long story. Let's start with something simple. Did you and Kyle cross a crazy-looking ridge the first day?"

"Yes. It was kind of creepy."

"Tell me about it." Beth untied the string on the brown paper package, revealing an assortment of deep-fried doughnuts dusted in powdered sugar. "I was following Gary Smith through the National Forest and when I reached that hill, he bushwhacked me."

"But, you're okay. You're sitting right here talking to me."

"Yeah, but I didn't walk away from that ambush, not straight off." Beth flicked a cautious glance toward the cells, then lowered her voice to a whisper. "He killed Luke first. Then he shot Tigger who reared and went over on top of me. I died there, crushed beneath my horse."

"No, you didn't." Concerned about her friend's sanity, Nina leaned across the table to take her hands. "Beth, you're sitting right here. You're with me."

"Only because I prayed for another chance to stop Smith on a night when there was a full moon, a red moon and it was Friday, April 13th, a day when the Goddess rules. She saved me." Beth kept her tone soft as she eased away from Nina's grip. "They call me, the *Guardian*. I have some pretty strange powers. The main one is I can pretty much *heal* anyone and any animal as long as they're not dead."

"Rowdy Tall-Deer mentioned the marshal marrying someone he called, the *Guardian*. He said 'the news flew on the wind to witches, wizards, and other *magickal* folks.' He was somewhat odd, but he was nice."

"Who is Rowdy?" Beth savored a bite of the first doughnut and pushed the package toward Nina. "I'll share. I never heard of him."

"We ran into him and his friend that night when we were looking for a campsite after crossing the ridge. He was a *healer* like you say you are."

"Why did you need him?"

"Smith." Nina picked up a doughnut of her own and bit into the homemade treat. After she chewed and swallowed a bite, she said, "He abducted me. He intended to torture and kill me, but Kyle and the Jamison triplets rescued me. I was a mess that night. Smith told me he severed the hamstring muscle in the back of my right thigh. I had cracked and broken ribs, a concussion, cuts, and bruises."

"You look fine now."

"Thanks to Astra Jamison. I don't know how she did it, but she *healed* me so I could ride. When we ran into Rowdy, he said he had to finish what she started and he did. Beth, I spent nearly the entire month of May in the hospital and had multiple surgeries after Smith attacked me the first time. Most of the summer, I did physical therapy. I wasn't hurt as badly then as I was last Tuesday."

"If they hadn't intervened, you'd be dead." Beth ate a second doughnut. "That's why you could come here. It's the same reason I did. I'm considered dead in our world, but I'm alive here and now."

"That's what Astra said she intended to do." Nina froze in the chair, recalling the scene at Gary Smith's cabin. "She staged a crime scene for the police. They'll find enough evidence to prove Smith killed both me and Kyle."

"Sounds just like her. She's my kind of attorney. She twists the law so the end result is real justice. The innocents are saved and the guilty suffer." Beth drank her tea. "When she rescued horses, she'd send me evidence to go after their abusers. If we couldn't nail them for what they'd done to the animals, she'd find another way. I admire her, but I didn't know she was a *healer*."

"She says she and her sisters are witches."

"Did they open the portal for you and Kyle to return home?"

"Well, they arranged for us to come here."

"Then, I'd go along with what they told you. They undoubtedly are witches. I thought Kyle would have to wait until next September for me to bring him back."

Nina gaped at her best friend. "Is that what you meant when you said you had powers? Can you bend *Time*?"

"I wouldn't say I bend it. I tend to think of it like a yellow onion, the kind that has several layers. If the conditions are right, I just open doors from one place to another." Beth munched the last of her doughnut, then tied up the remaining ones in the package. "Come on. Let's cook some supper. I feel better, but I need to eat a regular meal before I walk around town. You can come with me on my rounds and we'll swing by the mercantile and get you some suitable clothes."

"I don't need anything."

"You need to fit into civilization since you found it and me." Beth rose to her feet. "Most folks will accept you wearing pants to travel here. You can wear them again when we head out to the Bar M, the Morgan ranch after Rad gets back. Until then, you have to adhere to the customs in Podunk, U.S.A."

"I thought this was Junction City."

"Same difference."

Two hours later, Nina found herself strolling down the boardwalk to a long, two-story building that Beth called the general store. When he'd heard they intended to go shopping, Kyle told Nina to put whatever she needed on the Bar M account. He'd take Pooka with him when he went back to check the horses one more time and then he'd go with Cal to make sure the local loggers behaved appropriately in the saloon.

Once inside the store, Nina scanned the merchandise. Kegs and barrels of sugar, molasses, cornmeal, buckwheat flour, and regular flour sat around the room including the stereotypical cracker and pickle ones. Crocks of honey, jars of butter, containers of vinegar, bottles of baking soda lined one shelf. Bags of potatoes, cabbage, squash, turnips, and onions nearly took up another corner. Baskets of pumpkins, apples, and eggs showed to advantage in the nearby bay window at the front of the store.

In the left-hand corner, Nina saw a selection of ladies hats and a ready-made scarlet walking dress. Along that wall, bolts of bright calico lined another counter. Pants, shirts, overalls, and other clothes as well as pairs of boots filled the shelves. Beyond them, was an assortment of household items like various sizes of crocks, wooden tubs, steel knives and forks, pewter spoons, dishes, pails, and brooms.

Beth smiled at the tall, sturdy blond woman behind the long counter at the back of the room, tallying an order. Cans of coffee, teas, spices, and tinned food were organized neatly on more shelves behind her. "Hello, Susanne. This is my best friend, Nina Armstrong. Kyle brought her to visit me until I have the baby. Nina, this is Susanne Prescott. If she doesn't have what we're looking for, she can get it."

Nina smiled politely. "Are you related to Zeb? I met him and Trace at the Lazy B this morning."

"He's my younger brother." Susanne set aside her papers. "How are they? I haven't seen them in a coon's age, not since—"

"Oh, go ahead and say it. Not since I embarrassed myself by doing a face-plant in the middle of the store when I smelled that rotten cabbage last month."

Susanne grinned. "Neither of us may care for sauerkraut, Detective, but Trace told me that Mr. Gruber would be thrilled to have it for his birthday."

"Personally, I'd rather have a chocolate cake."

"Me too." Nina agreed. "If I can get the ingredients, I'll make you one since I missed your birthday in September."

"You make the list and I'll order in the supplies for you."

"That would be wonderful." Nina followed Beth over to the shelves of clothes. "What do you want to buy?"

"I'm fine, but you need some skirts, shirtwaists, undergarments, the works. Kyle should have given you time to pack for yourself so you'd have your own clothing."

"I told you already. He rescued me from Gary Smith and we came to find you right away. Orion filled the panniers and I still haven't had time to go through them so I don't know what all he sent."

"Men." Disgust filled Beth's voice. "Add being unable to pack what's important to the list of things they can't do."

Susanne laughed and came around the counter to join them. "Let me help. Welcome to Liberty Valley, Nina. I'm glad you're here. We're having a quilting bee to make baby blankets for Detective Morgan at Mayor Riley's next week. I hope you'll join us."

"I'd love to."

"You're the only one."

"Quit being so grumpy." Deciding to play the 'go along to get along' card and pretend she actually believed she was in a pioneer settlement, rather than some enclave of re-enactors or even survivalists, Nina bumped Beth's arm gently. "Unless you plan to sew everything yourself, you should be glad to have friends who want to share your upcoming joy, especially since they're willing to put their time, energy, and needles to good use."

"Oh, I'm so glad you're here." Susanne's blue eyes widened. "You have to come with me to my sister's tomorrow. We're baking cookies and tea cakes for the party and Detective Morgan has been too busy to help."

"She'll help if she wants to eat them."

"It's not nice to pick on me when I'm in 'a delicate situation' as Rad says, even if I barely have a 'baby bump' yet." Beth began to sort through a stack of divided skirts. "Since Kyle's here, he can help Cal for a couple of days while we prepare for my party and because you're with me, Nina, I won't be so scared of having this baby."

"There's nothing to be scared of." Nina slid an arm around her friend's thickening waist. "I've got your back and when I'm in your situation, I know you'll have mine."

"Definitely." Beth heaved a sigh and leaned against her. "I didn't know how much I missed you until Kyle brought you home."

25

NINA WOKE TO THE SOUND OF A CONVERSATION IN THE MAIN ROOM of the town jail, the early dawn light creeping through the small glass window of the cell, which was currently her bedroom. Two days before, Beth turned over the young, now sober, logger to his boss, and the mayor promised to make sure his men didn't create a ruckus in town. Prior to his release, the logger had cleaned the cell, changing the bedding and scrubbing the floor.

Everyone in town seemed to be walking on tenterhooks because Cal and Kyle hadn't found any lawbreakers. The two men took turns sleeping in the bunk in the second cell and the third remained empty in case they needed it for a prisoner. Kyle offered to escort Beth to the Bar M, but she adamantly refused to go anywhere at this time. She insisted on waiting for her husband to return to Junction City, although she rarely said anything complimentary about him or her new town.

Even when they'd gone to visit Susanne's younger sister at her home behind the newspaper office, Beth had been super sarcastic about the upcoming party. Other than the first day at the general store, she hadn't admitted to being apprehensive about her pregnancy or the future. Not for the first time, Nina wondered if there was a way to take her friend to an area hospital and a real doctor.

She lay in the narrow bunk in the cell under her fleece blanket, Pooka snoring softly beside her. She recognized Kyle and Cal's tones, but there was another man talking to them and she didn't know the stranger. None of the men seemed upset and she wondered who'd come to visit the local law-keepers. Well, she wouldn't find out lying here and playing possum as Kyle put it. She missed the comfort of sleeping in his arms, something else she didn't share.

She eased out of the bunk, leaving her puppy snoozing in the middle of the bed. She wasn't about to investigate in her sweat-pants and a long-sleeved t-shirt. She kept her own underwear, a bra, and panties under the sleeveless camisole, lace-trimmed, knee-length drawers, and petticoat layering those under the dark red, old-time dress Beth bought for Nina at the mercantile. It buttoned from the top of the rounded neckline to her waist. The full skirt fell to her ankles, disguising the low-heeled riding boots she'd brought with her. Highly-gathered sleeves had decorated five-button cuffs and best of all, two pockets in the side seams of the skirt held little necessities.

"Go along to get along, Antonina Arabella Armstrong." She might not know exactly where she was in the middle of Mount Baker National Forest, but so far everyone had been kinder to her than she'd actually expected. Best of all, she had Beth Chambers back in her life, and although there hadn't been time or space to yell at her friend for scaring the proverbial whiz out of her, at least Nina no longer had to blame herself for the older woman's death. Pushing aside the blanket hung over the opening so she would have privacy, Nina entered the main room.

Kyle turned when he heard her footsteps. Smiling, he brought her a cup of hot morning coffee. He gestured to the tall, black-haired man wearing a gray shirt and dark pants, a gun belt with two pistols around his narrow hips. He stood on the far side of the room, in front of the curtained-off alcove, holding a blue enamel mug. "Miss Nina, this is my brother, Marshal Rad Morgan. He rode in a couple of hours ago."

"Not that he came here first and let us know he was all right," Beth said, from behind him. By the sound of clothes rustling, she must be getting dressed. "Oh no, not Mister Macho. I mean, Marshal Macho. He had to circulate all over town and let everyone else know the biggest stud in the duck pond was back among us."

"You're in a sod-pawing, horn-tossing mood, Missus Morgan." Amusement slid across Rad's rugged features and landed in navy blue eyes. "I hope folks made you welcome, Miss Nina, especially my sweet bride."

"Spit in the wind and call it a shower, Morgan."

Cal finished his coffee and put the cup on the counter by the dry sink. "Reckon, I'll mosey over and see what Doc Jenkins found out about that body you brought the undertaker, Marshal. Kyle, now would be a good time for you and Miss Nina to look after the horses at the mayor's place. If you time it right, Miss Riley will be pulling biscuits out of the oven and she'll invite you to join her pa for breakfast."

"What body?" Wearing a white shirtwaist blouse and heavy gold divided skirt, Beth joined them and continued pinning up her strawberry-blonde hair. She side-stepped Rad to eye Cal, then turned her attention back on her husband. "Who died? Did someone hurt—?"

"I just found the fellow and he'd already been dead a couple of days. Never even pulled his gun so somebody he trusted shot him. I didn't know the man, but I'm not done talking to folks to learn his name before we bury him." Rad cupped her cheek for a quick moment. "Put on your boots, fetch your coat and we'll go see him."

"Was he by himself? Who shot him?" Beth looked him up and down. "Where was the killer? He didn't stay to attack you?"

"I'm fine." Rad raised his cup to his lips. "Stop fretting, Missus Morgan."

"I'll fret if I want to." Skirt swishing, she spun around and stalked back behind the gingham curtain. "It's part of being partners, Morgan. It's also part of marriage. You should have thought of that before your charming proposal."

Cal shook his head. "Reckon, I'll go take a look around town and see about getting breakfast at the hotel. This seems like family business."

"Thanks for looking after her while I was gone, Cal." Rad nodded at the older man. "I know it wasn't easy."

"Still here. Still listening. Save the malarkey for someone dumb enough to believe it, Radolf Morgan."

Cal chuckled, adjusted his gun belt, picked up his rifle, and started for the door. "You're gonna need all the charm you can find to smooth those ruffled feathers. Good luck, Marshal."

"Charm?" Kyle choked on a swallow of coffee, as the door closed behind the deputy. "You, Rad?"

"Be quiet, Kyle." More rustling ensued in the alcove. "You always get in trouble when you talk."

"You'll become accustomed to them." Rad chuckled and winked at Nina. "They've been squabbling since they met."

"We'd have gotten along a lot better if he hadn't wasted time when I sent him for help last April." Her trained police dog at her heel, Beth came out of the small side-room, buttoning a jacket over her shoulder holster. "Nine freaking days in a cave while he lolly-gagged all over Liberty Valley. And if you think you were Mister Sweetness and Light with a sucking chest wound, Morgan, you're wrong."

Nina stared at the couple, first at the tall, broad-shouldered man who stood like a former soldier, before she focused on her best friend. "Beth, if he was shot in the lung, why is he here? I didn't see a hospital. How could he possibly live?"

"What do you think I did in the *sandbox*, Nina? Sleep behind a sand dune?"

"No, I know. You were an Army medic and you did several combat tours. I saw you off the last time and hung out with your dad while you were in the Middle East."

"Yes, but you don't understand they trained me to treat

catastrophic injuries like those kinds of gunshot wounds. Even without Med-Evac support and no way to get him to a hospital from the middle of nowhere, with the Goddess on my side, I did all right. I may not have had all the resources I wanted, but I still saved his life. Granted, some days I wonder why especially when he rides off without back-up. He knows he needs me to watch his six so nobody hurts him."

"You just keep sassing me, woman." Rad turned and placed his mug next to Cal's. "I've been hoping you'd settle down a mite now that I'm home for the winter."

"Good luck with that." Kyle grinned at his older brother.

"Murder victims are my business." Beth glared at the two men, then swung around and paced to the outside door. "Nina, go with Kyle and look after the horses. Cal's right about Kate's cooking. She's amazing and she's very sociable. You'll want to be friends with her since she's hostessing that silly quilting bee for the baby on Friday."

"And we'll head home to the Bar M on Saturday or Sunday." Rad strode after Beth. "Do whatever needs doing while we're in town, Missus Morgan, because we'll be staying at the ranch until Christmas."

"You may want to reconsider that idea, Marshal Macho. Father Daniel is coming on the last steamboat of the season next week and he'll be holding Mass at the hotel." Beth waited while he opened the door for her and Luke. "Trace and Zeb are bringing the children from the Lazy B and you'll be eating with Luke and Nina's dog if Michael and the girls don't come home with us, because I will certainly tell Hannah it was your decision and doing, not mine."

"Anything else I need to know, Missus Morgan?"

"If I think of something, I'll tell you."

Once the door closed after the pair, Nina shook her head. "Wow, the sparks certainly fly between them. What do you suppose that's about?"

"Too much company and not enough privacy." Kyle lifted his

coat from the peg. "While we're there for breakfast, I'll talk to Connor Riley about making sure his crews continue to behave themselves and suggest to Rad that he take a room at the hotel for him and Bethany."

Nina felt a blush scorch into her cheeks. "You mean all that snarkiness is because he didn't take care of business when he arrived?"

"How could he?" Kyle chuckled, shrugging into his coat. "There's far too many of us here for any monkeyshines."

"I never even thought of that." She glanced over her shoulder at the sound of puppy toenails clicking on the floor and smiled when Pooka joined them. "I don't blame you for hiding out. It was a good idea."

When Kyle stopped in front of her, she lifted her chin enough to meet his gaze. "Hmm, we haven't had any privacy for three days. Maybe, you'd better kiss me before I forget you know how."

"Good idea, Miss Nina." He drew her into his arms and lowered his head. "Since there aren't any computers in Liberty Valley nowadays, I don't have to worry you'll be complaining on the Internet. I still don't want you taking out an advertisement in the newspaper that I'm no kind of a man."

She laughed, brushed her lips over his. "Then, give me a good reason why I shouldn't."

Later that morning, she left Kyle and Pooka to go to the saloon and hire grave-diggers, a task she didn't want to share. Instead, she returned to the jail where she found Beth packing her clothes neatly into a carpetbag, Luke lying near the woodstove to keep a watchful eye on her. "What's going on? I thought you didn't want to go to the ranch yet."

"We're not. We're moving to the hotel. Rad will be back in an hour to take us there, so you'd better get your things together."

"I'm not going anywhere. I just settled into the guestroom here and I like it."

"I've got a news-flash for you, Nina. Whether you believe it or not, we've crossed the proverbial stream and we're in 1888. You can't stay with two men by yourself unless you want everyone to think you're a total sleaze. Rad's arranged for you to have a room at the hotel Trace owns. I told him the dogs are going with us and luckily Trace has enough of her own, not to freak out if we take them with us for protection."

Nina folded her arms and took a deep breath. "I know you think we're in some kind of time warp and I'm not exactly sure what I believe about this place. After what happened with Smith, I didn't know if I'd ever have sex again. Kyle and I are together and I like sleeping with him."

"I'm not stupid. I saw it as soon as you arrived and I'm glad for both of you." Beth neatly folded a shawl and tucked it into an empty space. "If he hadn't been shot, I probably would have jumped Rad in that silly cave. But, he was hurt and I didn't."

"You love him."

"No surprise there. I've always looked after myself. I never had a man wait on me. He saddles and unsaddles Tigger for me. He opens and closes doors, carries anything he thinks is too heavy for me." A smile tugged at Beth's lips. "I know I'm sarcastic and I don't suffer fools gladly, but I don't have to play games with Rad."

"Like what?"

"Oh, like that crap-fest about being nice and polite, so he'll love me. I can say exactly what I think and he's good with it. We definitely don't do the 'I'll be less so he can be more' game the way I did with other guys when I dated in the past. Granted, Rad has some issues when he thinks criminals don't treat me respectfully, but they don't have the Miranda warning here."

"But, you still adhere to your own code of morality." Nina realized her tone made it a statement, not a question. "So, what happens if Kyle comes to the hotel?"

"He'd better be discreet if you two don't want to end up married when Father Daniel gets here."

"I'm not Catholic."

"Neither are most of the folks who will be attending Mass. Church services are entertainment in Liberty Valley. So is the quilting bee for the baby. Did Kate talk to you about the Christmas program the children are presenting at the town school?"

"Yes. Kyle told her that I'd take photographs of it." Nina heaved a sigh. "When we went back to the barn and groomed the horses, I tried to explain to him that I couldn't since I didn't have my digital camera or access to a computer or a printer like we had at the Halloween Party. He told me Orion Jamison already took care of the problem."

"How?"

"I was taking lessons on how to use an antique wooden camera at the Bar M before we came here. Your dad gave that Waterbury View Camera and glass plates to Orion and they're packed in one of the panniers. I still need to order the chemicals and I'm not sure how to get them."

"Tell Susanne and she'll add them to the list she sends down on the steamboat. It won't be back until spring, but weather permitting, Captain Jensen will be running pack trains from Snohomish City."

"And what do I do for a darkroom?"

"We have plenty of space at the Bar M. Kyle can create a room for you and Rad will help. It will give him something to do because he has issues when he can't ride out to work on the ranch or patrol the settlements. He says when the past crowds in on him, he adds on a room or two. Soon, the place will be as big as Winchester Mystery House."

26

THANKS TO RAD MORGAN, SHE HAD ONE OF THE MOST EXPENSIVE rooms at the hotel. It was elaborately furnished with a large brass bed, a bureau, a wardrobe, and a fireplace. There was even an adjoining bathroom, but she shared it with him and Beth who told her to be grateful there was a flush toilet. They didn't have such luxuries at the Bar M, at least not yet.

A knock on the door roused Pooka from his nap in front of the fireplace and Nina followed the pup to the door. He wagged his tail so it didn't come as much of a surprise to see Kyle standing in the hall, looking all cowboy in his hat and a long yellow slicker. When she stepped back, he entered, pausing to pet the collie mix, and took a moment to add a log to the fire.

She closed the hall door and smiled at him. "Hey there. What are you doing here?"

"I figured I'd mosey over and go with you when you took your dog for a last walk tonight and you could tell me all about the party at Kate Riley's today."

"Let me get my cape and I'm ready." She choked back a laugh when he took the ankle-length garment from her and settled it around her shoulders. She adjusted it to cover her dress. "Wow, do I feel like I'm in a movie."

He grinned appreciatively and lifted the hood to cover her hair. "You look as lovely as any of the gals I saw on TV."

"Thank you, kind sir." She took his arm and they headed out of the hotel.

Moonlight reflected off the snow and she breathed in the cold air. They walked toward the river and then angled across the street to stroll eastward along the bank, frozen snow crunching under their boots. Pooka dashed in front of them, jumping into the occasional drifts and startled a rabbit once. Nina heaved a sigh, pressing closer to Kyle's side. "I don't know what to do to help Beth."

"Why do you need to help her?"

"At the party, I listened to a lot of gossip from the older women who'd had babies." When he stiffened beside her, she elbowed him. "You asked. Now, don't wimp out on me. It made me remember what Darlene Dawson told me about restricting riding for her pregnant customers. Even if their doctors didn't express concerns, Darlene said bad falls off horses could result in miscarriages."

"I think Bethany rides well enough to stay on her horse."

"Yes, but that creates another problem. As an experienced rider, she's in the habit of sitting deep in the saddle, pushing down on her seat and legs. She already told me she's having some issues." Nina took a deep breath, then wished she hadn't. It was so cold the inside of her nostrils felt like they'd freeze. "Pretty sure you don't want to hear about those problems. So, what do I do? How do I keep her from riding out to the Bar M next week?"

"You don't." Kyle stopped and pulled her into his arms. "You talk to Rad and let him put his foot down. He's her husband. He can borrow Kate's buggy or a wagon from Connor and drive Bethany to the ranch."

"She'll be majorly pissed at me when she finds out who interfered."

"Probably, but won't she be more heartbroken if she loses her baby?"

Nina nodded. She reached up to rest her hand on his beard-stubbled cheek. "Thank you. I'm glad you brought me here." She brushed her lips over his. "So, how do you stay with me tonight and not have all hell break loose? I know you told some people that we're engaged, but I'm not ready for that kind of a commitment yet."

"I'm not pushing you, Miss Nina." He tipped up her chin. "All we have to do is be discreet. I'll leave before folks are awake. I'll meet you and Rad in the dining room for breakfast and you can tell him what you want him to do."

"Okay, I can live with that."

They walked a little further and then swung back toward the hotel. As they neared the large three-story building, Nina frowned when she saw a shadowy figure of a tall man standing by the front doors. "Who is that? Does someone want to see you?"

"It's too cold out here for anyone but us." Kyle guided her toward the wide porch. "Why? Who did you see?"

"Nobody now." Nina blinked hard and stared into the darkness, but it was just her, Kyle, and Pooka who stood in front of her, growling softly. "I guess it must have been my imagination."

"Well, let's go to bed and you can use your imagination on me."

"Sounds like fun." She giggled and took his hand. "It's been days since we were together and I have lots of wild, crazy ideas to fill tonight."

"I can't wait."

———

Pooka raced ahead of him, found a stick, and brought it back for Kyle to throw. He winged it further down the track beside the river and the pup ran after it. Early morning sunlight glinted through the gray clouds. A big black and brown shepherd trotted by him then rushed to play with Pooka. Kyle slowed his pace and looked quickly over his shoulder, recognizing his brother walking toward him. "Doesn't Bethany usually walk her own dog?"

"I told her I'd do it today so she could go back to sleep." Rad shrugged deeper into his heavy jacket. "You must have arrived early at the hotel. I didn't hear you in the hall or knocking on the door."

Kyle eyed his brother and saw barely suppressed amusement. "I'm going to marry her."

"I figured as much. When?"

"Well, it won't be next week during Father Daniel's visit, but Connor Riley is the local justice of the peace. He married you and Bethany. As soon as Nina agrees, he can do the same for us."

"Makes sense to me."

They walked on in companionable silence for a while longer, then swung around to head back to the hotel. Before they reached the hitch-rail in front of the building, Kyle said, "Miss Nina needs a gun and someone to teach her how and when to use it. Will you do the honors?"

"Why don't you?"

"Because she got in trouble with the law back where she comes from and she won't let me."

"What kind of trouble? Does Bethany know?"

"I'm not sure if she does or not. They have strange crimes on the other side of the ridge. Miss Nina was arrested for saving a herd of horses from drowning in a flood."

"That makes no sense."

"They didn't belong to her and she went on private property to rescue them."

"Better than leaving livestock to die. The owner should have given her a couple of them as a reward if he didn't have the cash to pay her."

"Instead, he was the one who planned to testify against her."

"Some folks aren't worth the powder it'd take to blow them to hell." Rad opened the main door and they entered the lobby of the hotel. "I'll take her shopping at the mercantile for a pistol and teach her to use it when we're at the ranch. What are you worried about? Or should I say, who?"

"Gary Smith. He wasn't locked up when we left. If he comes after us again and I'm not there, I want her to be able to defend herself."

Rad nodded and then gestured toward the stairs. "I'm taking Luke back to Bethany and we'll meet you and Miss Nina in the dining room for breakfast."

"Fair enough. She's worried about Bethany and the baby so you'll probably hear about that too."

"I'll listen."

"Can't ask for more than that."

———

When she entered the restaurant, Nina saw Rad Morgan sitting alone at a table in the corner. He stood politely when he spotted her and she noticed the three-piece gray suit, a definite change from the rugged outdoors clothes he'd worn the previous two days. He must have business in town. Taking a deep breath, she went to join him. "Where's Beth?"

"Asleep." Rad pulled out a gold pocket watch, checked the time, and then replaced it in his vest pocket. "She wore herself out while I was gone. Kyle will be along in a while. There was a dust-up over to the saloon and he went to help Cal."

"Why didn't you go too?"

"Figured if Bethany woke up, I could head her off at the pass and see she ate something before she ran amuck rendering justice." He raised his hand, signaling the waitress. "Menu's pretty simple here. It's ham and eggs, hotcakes, fried potatoes, coffee. That do you?"

"It sounds wonderful." Nina waited until she had a cup of coffee, he'd given their order to the young woman and they were alone again. "Kyle says one of your friends will loan you a buggy or a wagon to take Beth to the Bar M."

"And why would I ask for one?" Rad eyed her over his cup. "She hasn't broken any bones. She can ride her horse. Lord knows he needs the work after eating his head off for the last three weeks."

"Tigger's a handful at the best of times. Carrying Beth when she's expecting a child isn't one of them. If she comes off him, she could lose the baby."

Rad lowered his cup, rubbed his jaw. "Miss Nina, I'm not one for beating the bushes unless I'm hunting a scalawag. My wife is a dang good rider and she says you were one of her teachers. Just say what worries you."

"All right, but remember I'm from the same place she is and I'm not good at 'double-speak,' so this isn't intended to be offensive."

"And I won't take offense."

"Fine." Nina quickly described her concerns and saw the words make an impact.

A muscle twitched in Rad's jaw and his dark blue eyes narrowed. "I'll talk to Doc Jenkins and he'll agree Bethany should stop riding until spring. I'll borrow a rig from Connor Riley. Then, I'll tell her the way things are."

"I don't understand. Why are you involving the doctor?"

"Because you're her friend and she'll want an ally when she complains about me."

Nina shook her head, smiling at him. "You're a smart man. Thank you. I hate arguing with her, but she doesn't scare me. I want what's best for her."

"You're welcome." Rad waited while the waitress returned with two loaded plates. Once their coffee cups were refilled and she'd left again, he said, "Kyle tells me that you need to learn to shoot and I promised to teach you. There's a lot of varmints in these parts and not all of them have four legs."

Nina gazed down at the large slab of ham and the mountain of scrambled eggs. "I have a felony conviction. It's against the law for me to pack a gun."

"Not Morgan's law. Kyle says you met Trace Burdette-Prescott. She packs two pearl-handled Colts and she owns Junction City. She'd be the first to say you need to be able to defend yourself."

"More like the third." Deciding not to let the food go to waste, Nina picked up her fork. "First, was your baby bro, Kyle. Second, was you. I'm sure Beth would agree I should be able to protect myself in case Gary Smith turns up here. Trace didn't make it to town yesterday for the party, so she'd be the fourth to give me her blessing."

Rad nodded, slicing into the ham on his plate. "Since he skipped out on his trial last time he was here and all but killed the town lawyer, Smith better pray you and Kyle get to him first. Everyone in these parts knows Smith stole Trace's prize stallion and almost killed you when you tried to save Emancipation. If the Lazy B crew finds him, the fella will be guest of honor at a necktie party."

Nina nearly said it was nice to know where she rated, right after that particular horse, but opted to stay silent. Sarcasm wouldn't go over well and she'd already won what she wanted from Beth's husband. Her best friend might be annoyed, but she and her baby would be safe.

After breakfast, Nina went upstairs with a plate of leftovers and some kitchen scraps to feed Pooka. Once the young dog ate, she collected her hooded cloak and decided to stop next door to check on Beth before going to the mercantile.

Sitting in a chair at a table in the center of the room, Beth poured a second cup of tea and smiled at Nina. "Good morning. Come join me."

"Okay." Nina crossed the room and drew out the other chair. She spotted Luke lying near the fireplace and Pooka promptly joined his doggie friend on the rag rug. "How are you feeling?"

"I'm good." Warmly dressed in a tightly fitting, high-necked, dark-blue wool sweater as a short bodice to a matching full skirt, Beth appeared much healthier. She wasn't as pale or washed out as she'd been. She'd already put butter and honey on a biscuit and picked up the waiting half. "I've been super bitchy and worried about Rad while he was gone. I'm sorry I took it out on you when I'm so glad you're here."

"No worries." Nina sipped the hot raspberry tea. "So, where do you buy this kind of tea? I didn't see it at the general store."

"Lizbeth over at the parlor house has her major-domo make it up for me. Since he cooks dinner and supper here, he had the maid bring it up for me."

"What's a parlor house?"

"Rad explains it as a fancy house or brothel." Beth took another bite of her biscuit, chewed, and swallowed. "Prostitution is legal in Junction City. The feds say the age of consent for girls is ten years old. Washington Territory is a little better, but not much. The legislature says it's fourteen. I don't allow pedophilia here. It's Morgan's law."

"And you're the Morgan who enforces it."

"You've got it." Beth continued to drink tea around bites of the biscuits. "You heard me tell Rad we're waiting for the girls to get here. They're sisters and it took some doing to convince the little one we wanted them both. We adopted the pair this past summer after Kyle left. Michael is Hannah Ortiz's, our housekeeper's son. They've been visiting the orphanage and their friends at the Lazy B since Trace Burdette pretty much raised our youngest and Michael for years."

"I'll look forward to meeting them."

"They're good kids and I'm not just saying that because they're ours, but it's a bit twisted. Gary Smith actually rescued the girls from an abusive situation. When he learned Sorrel, the older one was being molested by her uncle, Smith saved her. She told him that her younger sister, Becky would be victimized and he went back for her too."

"No way." Nina gaped at her friend. "He's scum."

"Yes, but the girls conned him. They were super polite to him, so he didn't realize how spunky they are, much less what survival instincts they have. When we arrested him, he asked Rad to keep them safe."

"If you arrested him, how did he escape?"

"He attacked his lawyer during a consultation and almost killed him. That provided enough of a distraction for him to get away and cross over the ridge to the future."

"And Kyle followed him."

"Kyle volunteered to go. I asked him to look after you. When he was gone, I learned Rad had too. He even gave Kyle a couple of Destynee LaFleur's erotic romances." Beth slathered butter on another biscuit. "I hope he put them to good use."

Heat scorched into Nina's face. "Shut up, Beth, or I'll be sorry he brought me here."

"No, you won't." Beth giggled. "I'm not. I'm glad Rad took the time to read them."

27

THE DOOR OPENED AND RAD ENTERED, FOLLOWED BY A TALLER, dark-haired giant of a man Nina recognized as Jed Corbett. Oddly enough, he didn't wear the logging attire he'd worn to rescue her when she had a flat tire on the way back from the Lazy B, but a black three-piece suit with a white shirt and narrow dark tie.

The lawman stepped around the dogs to add a log to the fire, and then came across to the table. Nina frowned when he didn't introduce his companion. Instead, Rad placed two gray bullets on the table. "Didn't you forget something or should I say, someone?"

"What are you talking about, Nina?" Beth eyed her impatiently, then turned her attention to the ammunition. "Are these from the victim you found, Morgan?"

"Doc pulled them out during the autopsy. The other one fragmented." Rad poked at one of the rounds. "They're strange. I've made bullets for years, but these are silver. Not lead, coated in silver, but totally silver. You'd need a forge and a very hot fire to melt the metal. The closest place a blacksmith could do it is out at the Lazy B and Lars would spend the silver, not waste it when Miss Susanne sells boxes of cartridges at the mercantile."

"Excuse me." Nina glowered at the two of them, then glanced

at Jed Corbett who still stood silently near the door. "Actually, excuse you. Why haven't you introduced him to Beth?"

"Introduced who?" Rad looked around the room, obviously not seeing the stranger who waited politely. "What's wrong, Miss Nina?"

"Introduce him. The guy who came with you."

"I came by myself." Turning, Rad scanned the room, his hand on the butt of a pistol. "Who do you see?"

"Jed Corbett. I should know him. He's the guy I bought cookies for when he changed the tire on my pickup."

"What's a pickup?" Jed approached the table, curiosity filling his handsome features. "You see me, ma'am?"

"Of course, I see you. You're standing right there." Nina frowned impatiently, not amazed when Pooka came to stand between them, hair erect on his neck, growling. "And my dog still doesn't like you."

Beth leaned forward in her chair, lifting a hand to stop Rad from speaking. "Nina, this is going to be weird, but I've always been straight up with you. Neither of us see what you and Pooka obviously do. Who is here with us?"

"Tom Corbett, ma'am. I followed the marshal when he left the undertaker and my body."

"What?" Nina glared at him. "Are you claiming to be some sort of ghost?"

"Well, since my uncle murdered me, reckon I am." Tom held out his hand. "I fade in and out. When the marshal brought me to town, I followed along, hoping the *Guardian* might help me save my son. Didn't figure on finding a *Seer*."

"Who is here?" Beth repeated. "If you're seeing ghosts, Nina, tell me about it."

"He's not a ghost and this is some kind of sick joke."

"Okay, then just tell me what he wants so he can pass over."

"He wants the *Guardian* to save his kid."

"My boy, Edwin. My uncle killed my wife and my son will be next."

Nina heaved a sigh. "Okay, I'll play along with you people. He wants us to rescue his son before his uncle murders him too."

"All right," Beth agreed immediately. "Where do I look?"

"No, wait a minute." Nina took a deep breath and held up her hand. "When Kyle and I came here, the first night we camped with two riders and a boy. I remember Rowdy telling me that Kyle went fishing with his friend and Edwin, while Rowdy stayed in camp to heal me."

"From what?" Rad asked. "You look fine as frog's hair to me."

"Smith knocked me around when he abducted me and Rowdy finished healing the damage. Never mind, it's not important right now." Nina turned her attention back to their guest who still didn't appear the least bit insubstantial to her. He was nothing like the ghosts that she'd seen in movies. Granted, they were played by actors, but it seemed normal to expect something more surreal than a man that others didn't see.

"Your son is with two good men and Kyle said they were headed somewhere safe. Your uncle won't find them."

Relief swept over Tom's face. "That's fine, then."

"Okay, we're done." Nina gaped at the spot where he'd stood, watching him fade away. "He's leaving."

"Hold up there," Rad said. "Why did your uncle use silver bullets to kill you?"

"Only thing that works on a shifter." Tom Corbett reappeared. "I'd have healed and gone after him if he used store-bought cartridges, even silver-coated ones."

Nina stirred in her chair, remembering the Destynee LaFleur books she enjoyed so much. "Are you saying you're a werewolf?"

"I'm a shifter. I'm not limited when I change. Sounds like we met in a different place and time, *Seer*, if I helped you and you made me cookies."

"I didn't make them. I bought them from the local caterer and Meteor warned me you were a total slut-puppy, that you'd slept with every woman in Corbettstown, and I should be careful not to let you charm me."

"Well, that was tacky," Beth said. "I was called to back-up the other deputies one night after a barroom brawl in Eagleville. I arrested Jed for being drunk and disorderly. He was perfectly polite to me even after he'd busted a pool cue over some guy's head and thrown a political hack through a plate-glass window. Didn't resist at all when I put him in my rig."

"Do I want to know what a slut-puppy is?" Rad asked.

"Probably the equivalent around here would be someone who spends way too much time with the girls upstairs at Prince's saloon since Lizbeth wouldn't welcome such a rowdy client."

"It's not true, not for me. I was married when we moved to my uncle's settlement and I never strayed. It'd break my wife's heart." Tom Corbett began to fade. "I don't know if I like the man you thought I was, *Seer*, if he's that sort."

Nina stared at the empty spot where he'd stood. Pooka pressed against her leg, tail wagging and she petted the pup. "He's gone."

"Do you think he crossed over?" Beth asked, adding more tea to her cup. "Or is he still hanging out here?"

"I have no idea." Nina stroked Pooka's white ruff. "I'm sorry I was so rude. I honestly thought the two of you were ignoring him for some purpose."

Beth propped her chin on a fist. "So, when did you start 'seeing' dead people?"

"I never have before." Nina laughed, recognizing the reference to an old film both of them watched during a horror movie festival at a local cinema the previous year. "That was totally bizarre and he didn't look at all like ghosts from Hollywood. He was totally solid."

"Did he have two bloody wounds in his chest and part of his skull missing like the guy at the undertaker's?"

"How gross." Nina wrinkled her nose in disgust. "No, he was perfectly normal and I really thought it was Jed Corbett, all dressed up. The last time I saw him was after work in faded chopped-off blue jeans, a flannel red plaid shirt that jarred with the bright orange suspenders and corked boots. He's not my type, but he's good-looking enough, I guess."

"You guess?" Beth sipped her tea. "Girl, you didn't get away from your horse rescue enough if you can only guess. The guy is pure sex on the hoof."

Rad cleared his throat. "You're married, Missus Morgan."

"Yeah, but I wasn't then." Beth winked at Nina. "I'd never date someone I had to testify against in court. You didn't have that problem."

"Stop being such a twit. I'd already met Kyle by then and Jed Corbett is nothing in comparison. Besides, my dog didn't like him."

"Well, I can't argue with that." Beth reached across the table to take Rad's hand and he squeezed hers. "There's something special about these Morgan men. Unfortunately, they know it."

———

That evening, Kyle knocked lightly on the hotel room door when he returned with Pooka. Nina opened the door and gestured for him to come inside. She'd changed from the dress she'd worn all day to her nightclothes, covering them with the dark-green robe he'd seen her wear at her own cabin.

He reached into his coat pocket and drew out two small glasses, then the flask of brandy. "Beth told me you had a shock today so I stopped by Lizbeth's for some higher-class liquor than what Prince buys and brews."

"Thanks, I think." Nina took the glasses and brandy to the table in the center of the room. "Did Beth tell you what I saw in her room?"

"She left it for you to share with me." Kyle picked up the poker and shifted the logs so they burned brighter in the fireplace, then added more wood to the blaze, before adjusting the metal screen so they'd be safe from any sparks. Pooka lay down and proceeded to wash his wet, white paws. "What was it?"

"A ghost." Nina sat down at the table. "I thought it was Jed Corbett. The guy looked just like him, but he said his name was Tom Corbett. He claimed he was murdered and he wanted Beth to find his missing son, Edwin, and protect him. That was the name of the boy you went fishing with when we found Rowdy and his friend. Or do I have it wrong?"

"No, you're right." Kyle removed his coat and hung it in the wardrobe before he joined her, sitting in the other chair. He opened the brandy, pouring a measure into each glass. "They rode off to find the way into 2018. They should be there by now."

"How do we send them a warning to look out for Tom Corbett's killer?"

"We can't." Kyle waited while she sipped the alcohol. "I know you're suspicious, Miss Nina. You don't believe we've crossed through *Time* and we're in Liberty Valley of yesterday, do you?"

"I don't know what I believe anymore, Kyle. I never expected to be able to see a ghost and I'm sure I did this morning. He called me a *Seer* and from what I've read in Destynee LaFleur's books, that's someone who interacts with the dead. I never could do that before."

"Are you sure about that? I've seen the *magick* you create with your photographs. You capture the essence of people, places, and things."

She finished the brandy, put down the glass, and leaned over to kiss his cheek. "That's the sweetest compliment I've ever had."

He grasped her wrist and pulled her to sit on his lap. "I can do better."

"Really?" She shifted a little and eased her head into the hollow of his shoulder. "I think you'd better show me."

He pushed open the robe, stroked her knee, let his hand trail up her thigh under the skimpy nightgown she'd worn their first night. "I can do that, but you'll have to be quiet and not disturb the neighbors."

"Oh, I think I can manage that." She nipped his ear. "Can you?"

"Yes, but I'll have to leave earlier than this morning. I need to sleep at the jail tonight, or Cal will come looking for me."

"Well, I reckon you'd better get busy, cowboy."

She gasped when he found the nest of dark curls and slid a finger inside, following it with a second one. "Kyle!"

"Quieter than that, Miss Nina."

He kissed her, swallowing her moans while he moved his fingers in and out, then allowed his thumb to join the dance, rocking against the small bud. He hoped he'd have enough control to wait and take her to bed, but he wasn't sure that was possible. Not when she squirmed on his lap in rhythm with his hand, her tongue dueling with his as they kissed. It'd be a wild night.

———

In the morning, she looked out the window and saw more snow falling, but she still needed to take Pooka for a walk after she dressed. She started with a 'combination', a utilitarian, cotton undergarment consisting of a camisole bodice attached to drawers. At least nothing would itch, she thought. That was a downfall of wool clothing. Crossing to the wardrobe, she chose a brown, ankle-length divided skirt, teaming it with a matching wool jersey, a snugly fitting, high-necked, brown sweater with tight sleeves.

She sat in a chair at the table to pull on a pair of her own socks and then her low-heeled waterproof barn boots which thankfully looked enough like what other women wore that nobody would either notice or say anything. Heat scorched into her cheeks as she recalled Kyle boosting her onto the table the night before.

He'd driven her so crazy with his mouth and tongue that she barely managed to save the bottle of brandy before it hit the floor. One of the glasses hadn't been so lucky, but thankfully it hadn't broken since it landed on the hooked rug and rolled under the other chair.

She shrugged into the long heavy coat that reminded her of Trace Burdette-Prescott's duster. Calling Pooka, they headed out the door and down the stairs. Small snowflakes dotted Nina's cheeks and gloved hands. The half-grown pup bounced along ahead of her, happily darting in and out of snowdrifts.

She wasn't the first person walking along the riverbank. She saw another woman ahead of her. The stranger wasn't dressed for the cold weather. She wore a light blue flowered dress with a drooping set of deep folds down the back that caused the skirt to hang straight from the hips. The overskirt swooped up and revealed the matching under-skirt. The back was gathered in several low-hanging puffs, but there wasn't a bustle. Her red hair was neatly confined in a bun under an ivory and blue hat decked out with artificial flowers, feathers, lace, and beads. A few loose red tendrils escaped, teasing her forehead and neck.

Nina stopped for a moment when she realized snow didn't land on the other woman, not on her clothes, or hair, or even her lace-up ankle boots. In fact, she actually stayed a few inches above the ground. Something about her features and the blue eyes reminded Nina of Meteor Jamison, yet it wasn't the caterer who waited to talk to her.

"Who are you?" Nina approached the other woman. "You obviously know who I am."

"I'm Mary Corbett, or at least I was." She unfurled a blue and white fan, waving it gently. "You're the *Seer*. I couldn't see you at the hotel, not when my husband was lurking about, not when he killed me."

"Wait a second. He said his uncle murdered both of you and asked us, the *Guardian* and me to protect your son."

"From him and that pack of killers in Corbett's Town."

"If I do, will that help you cross over?"

"When I'm ready to go to *Summerland*, I will. For now, I think I'll visit a while until you promise to keep my son safe from all the Corbetts."

28

ALTHOUGH IT'D SNOWED THROUGH THE PAST WEEK, THE RIVER hadn't frozen and the steamboat from Snohomish City arrived late that afternoon. The hotel filled up with guests, not only from the boat but also from surrounding farms and ranches. Nina could have sworn Cal almost rolled his eyes when children from the Lazy B settled into the jail cells. Father Daniel planned to conduct Mass Wednesday morning and after that, Rad said they were leaving for the Bar M.

Meanwhile, the priest would lead a funeral service for Tom Corbett. It surprised Nina when most of the townspeople turned out for the somber ceremony walking after the horse-drawn hearse, following it to the graveyard. It seemed like proof of what Beth said about limited entertainment in Junction City. Father Daniel admitted he personally hadn't known the man who died, but still managed to deliver a heartfelt eulogy.

Nina spotted Tom Corbett's spirit standing near two women in dark mourning garb. They'd arrived on the boat and when she approached them, she realized why they looked so familiar. The younger, taller one bore a striking resemblance to Venus Jamison, but she wasn't paying attention to the coffin, or the priest. Instead, clutching her handbag, she gazed off in the distance to the rolling hills where a pack of large dogs clustered.

No, they weren't dogs, Nina realized, they were wolves. She eased past Beth and her adopted daughters, advancing on the guests. "Good afternoon. Thank you for coming."

"We wanted to be sure the reprobate was dead and gone, *Seer*." The older one, a woman in her early thirties was a petite strawberry-blonde with dark blue eyes that almost matched her black dress. Her stiff posture radiated tension and her voice crackled with barely suppressed rage. "He killed our sister again."

"For the love of the Lady and the Lord, Astrid, stop blaming me." Tom Corbett sounded as if this was an old argument, one that lasted eons, not merely a week since his death. "I've always loved your sister and she loved me. I never hurt her, never even touched her in anger."

"He keeps saying he didn't harm her." Nina deliberately lowered her voice so only the three of them would hear the conversation, four if she counted the ghost. "He told me when he arrived that his uncle murdered them."

"He never takes responsibility for anything, *Seer*." This time, the younger woman spoke. "His pack comes to witness this rite. You should watch your younglings before they bear them off for meat."

"Unfortunately, Kallisto tells the truth about my relatives." Tom folded his arms, eyeing both women sadly. "I just wish they'd accepted me as her husband and visited Mary. Maybe, they'd have saved her."

"It takes time and that's the one thing none of us control." Nina glanced at the wolves creeping closer. "Shouldn't they be afraid of humans?"

"Real ones are." Kallisto opened her purse and removed a pistol. "These are shifters who've obviously been sent for prey."

Before Nina could say anything, Trace Burdette neared. She hadn't dressed up for the funeral. She pushed the heavy black duster out of the way, revealing dark clothes and the pearl-handled pistols on slender hips. Narrowing emerald green eyes, she pulled the Colts from their holsters. "I don't like the look of those critters."

"Neither do I." Kallisto measured her with a warrior's calm. "Unless you have silver bullets, you won't kill them."

"I'll settle for frightening them away today."

The two women paced away and Nina saw Zeb Prescott follow them, rifle in hand. She turned her attention to Astrid. "What prevented you from seeing your sister?"

"I angered the Goddess and her punishment was separating me from both of my sisters. I only found Kallisto a few years ago. I didn't know where Mary was until last month."

"I'm sorry." Nina took the older woman's arm. "I know how devastated I was when I lost track of Beth for six months. Your agony must have been overwhelming."

"That's a good word for it, *Seer*."

It didn't surprise Nina when Kyle didn't join her that evening after walking Pooka. He said he had to help Cal maintain order in town since the populace had more than doubled. In addition, he and some of the other men planned to patrol the streets in case the wolves returned. She poured herself a shot of brandy and sat down at the table wishing she could watch TV, or a movie on her laptop, but she didn't have that luxury in the middle of Junction City, or as Beth called it, Podunk, USA.

Someone tapped on the door and she answered it, finding Beth in the hallway. "Hey, what are you doing here?"

"Being bored out of my mind. Rad took Luke and went to check on the girls. I promised to keep an eye on you and the other guests in the hotel until he gets back. Then, I'll jump him. Meanwhile, do you want to come mosey the halls with me?"

"Sounds like more fun than sitting here trying to think of something to do." Carefully leaving Pooka in the room, Nina closed the door. "So, did you meet the Hunter women? They remind me of Astra and Venus Jamison."

"I noticed." Beth took a deep breath, closing her eyes for a moment. When she opened them, she had a strange faraway look, seeming oddly remote. "They will be two of the Jamison triplets when the *Wheel of Truth* turns and they come around again. However, they still have a great deal to learn in this life and we will be their teachers."

After attending Mass in the large hotel ballroom the next morning, Nina finished packing. She changed her clothes, layering up her jeans and sweater over her combination long underwear, then adding one of the larger heavy divided skirts. She opted for a wool jersey, her denim jacket, and the duster. She'd just pulled on her waterproof boots when she heard a knock on the door and Pooka leaped up, tail wagging to answer.

Laughing, Nina followed the pup. She opened the door and found Kyle waiting, a dark-haired boy standing behind him. She smiled at him, wishing they could kiss, but she knew better. "Hello there."

"We came for your things. Rad has a wagon waiting. Since we never shod the mares, they won't slip in the snow. The girls are excited about riding them out to the Bar M."

"How can they when we don't have tack for them?"

"Miss Prescott and I worked out a deal on saddles and bridles she had in the mercantile. She took the pack saddles and she's sending for those chemicals you want as boot." Kyle picked up the pannier that held her photography equipment. "Michael, get that other one. Miss Nina, have you made sure you have all your belongings?"

"Yes, I have and yes, I do." She followed him out into the hall, escorted by her dog.

Before they reached the staircase, Beth hurried toward her, eyes shining in wonder and excitement filling her face. "Nina, come see what Rad did. It's absolutely breathtaking. He's so romantic, the best husband ever. It's going to be so much fun going to the ranch."

"See what?"

Beth grabbed her arm, hugging it. "A sleigh. A two-horse

sleigh. He borrowed a team from Mayor Riley and they have bells on their harnesses and everything."

"It's not really a sleigh." Michael Burdette came toward them, a dark-haired, green-eyed young version of Trace. "It's the mayor's working buckboard and the marshal took off the wheels and put on runners because of the snow. I don't see anything romantical about that."

"It sounds like a sleigh to me." Nina slipped an arm around her friend's waist. "Come show me where you'll be riding."

"On the seat upfront because Rad ordered so much from Susanne Prescott for Thanksgiving and it all arrived on the steamboat. We even have two turkeys, but thank goodness they're not live ones. I'd have a hard time eating them once I got to know them."

"Are we really having Thanksgiving dinner?"

"Of course, we are." Michael led the way down the stairs. "I'll bet my mother's been baking up cornbread for the stuffing for the past three days."

Nina lowered her voice to a whisper. "I didn't know they celebrated Thanksgiving here."

"President Lincoln issued the proclamation for a national festival during the Civil War," Kyle said. "Of course, we'll honor the day as we should. Rad will lead the prayers just like Mayor Riley does on Sundays when we don't have a preacher."

"It's going to be so much fun." Beth beamed at Nina. "I've invited everyone who would otherwise be alone. Prince Beauchamp will be hosting a dinner at the saloon and he said he and the loggers will police the town so Cal can ride out to join us."

The loaded wagon led the way out of town almost as if they were in a parade. Wrapped in a long coat and two blankets, Beth happily nestled close to Rad's side. Eleven-year-old Sorrel, a red-haired girl about the same size as Michael rode Minnesota, the dainty gray Arabian mare and her younger sister, a petite blonde waved to all her friends from Georgia's back.

Nina barely managed to suppress a smile as she turned her

gelding next to Kyle's. He led Rad's black Appaloosa mare. "I'm amazed at the way your brother pulled this off. How did he know Beth would be so thrilled with a sleigh ride?"

"I don't reckon he did." Kyle reined S.O.B. a little closer to Missouri. "We always take off the wheels on our rigs during the winter so they won't break in the snow. We don't want the horses hurting themselves trying to move the wagons when they're stuck in deep ruts or drifts."

"Well, I'm certainly not sharing any of that with Beth." Nina tightened her hold on the lead-line to Tigger's halter and brought the gray Arabian stallion up beside her horse. "We'll let your big brother be the hero all the way home."

"He'll enjoy it."

"Now, tell me why Michael looks so much like Trace. I didn't think she and Zeb had any children of their own and Beth said his mother lives at the Bar M."

"Trace is his older half-sister. She took care of Michael for years when his mother couldn't. She's married to Gabe Ortiz now and he's actually Michael's half-brother as well as his stepfather. Things get a mite confusing in Liberty Valley."

"You're telling me." Nina thought of the two Hunter women and the way Beth had said they were the ancestors of the witches who'd sent them here. "I hope it doesn't take much longer for me to get used to the people and the place."

It took most of the day to reach the Bar M. Nina stiffened in the saddle when she saw the huge log house. It was still three stories and it had a wide front porch, but it didn't wrap around the structure, at least not yet. She stared at the building, knowing it was the same house she'd visited when she took photography classes with Will Dawson.

A tall, dark-haired, Hispanic man in his late twenties approached, a smile on his handsome face. "So you made it home, Kyle." The two gripped hands, then he nodded to Nina. "I'm Gabe Ortiz. Welcome to the Bar M."

"Thank you." Nina studied him, seeing a resemblance to the

catch rider who'd worked at the Armstrong stable. With another nod, Gabe took Tigger's lead-rope and led the stallion off toward the barn. "He's related to Hector, isn't he?"

"Probably a ways back." Kyle pushed back his hat. "Gonna be a while though. He and Señora Ortiz aren't expecting any young-uns yet."

"Okay, good to know." Nina swung out of the saddle and leaned against her horse for a moment, allowing the stiffness to work out of her body. "Then, I won't say anything about what's to come."

That earned her one of his sexy, warm smiles as intimate as a kiss. In a few moments, more men arrived and their horses were led off to the barn. Kyle walked beside her to the house where she met Michael's mother, Hannah, a pretty dark-haired woman. She greeted Kyle with a surprisingly quick hug and a promise to make extra biscuits for his horse.

As soon as she joined them, Beth hugged the housekeeper too. "I'll take Nina off to my room for a bit so you and the girls can organize a place for her."

Hannah tucked a flyaway black strand of hair into place before wiping her hands on the bib apron she wore over a flowered blue dress. "I made *empanadas* with the apples we dried in September, Detective Morgan. I'll have Sorrel bring you some and a pot of coffee."

"Tea would be better," Nina said. "Coffee's bad for the baby."

"And it also nauseates me."

Pleasure shone in Hannah's face and she quickly hugged Beth. "I told you I thought you were *enceinte* when you and the marshal left."

"Yes, but I wasn't sure yet." Taking Nina's arm, Beth led the way to her room. "Shall I give you the tour now or is it okay if we wait a bit?"

"I've seen this house before." Nina glanced quickly over her shoulder to be sure nobody else would hear. "I came to take photography lessons with your dad. It's way bigger in the future than it is now. There's two more wings."

"I told you already. Rad likes to expand the place during the winter." Beth walked further down the hall and opened a door into a large room.

Nina slowly looked around. The plank walls gleamed a soft gray under what must be a coat of whitewash. A hooked rug stretched across the wooden floor. A large wooden wardrobe stood in the left corner while a matching bureau and a washstand with a china pitcher and bowl filled the remainder of that wall. A mirror taller than most men stood in the right corner.

"I haven't seen hardly any roads worth the name." Nina pointed to the fragile-looking glass. "How on earth did that get here?"

"By steamboat a couple of years ago."

"Wow. That's amazing." Nina continued to scan the room and gaped at the four-poster bed in the center of the room. It'd obviously been built somewhere local, if not at the ranch from pieces of cedar like the table and chairs on the right wall. The furniture still smelled like the woods. She gaped at the pillows piled against the headboard and the bright patchwork quilt on the large bed. "So, will my room be anything like this?"

"It won't be as big." Beth crossed to the fireplace and held out her hands to warm them. "Heat rises, so the second and third floors are fairly comfortable, but the kids will be close. Kyle sleeps downstairs."

"I know. There can't be any hanky-panky unless I marry the guy."

"You got that right."

A tap on the door heralded Sorrel's arrival with a tray of delicious-smelling pastries. She carefully placed it on the table. "The marshal's gone off to check on the stock in the barns and Missus Hannah says to leave room for supper. She's made chili with beans like you taught her and cornbread. There are more *empanadas* and *conchas* too for afterward."

"We can't wait." Beth patted her adopted daughter's shoulder. "I think Nina would like a room next to yours and Becky's."

"I'm headed upstairs to help." Grass-green eyes sparkling, Sorrel grinned at Nina. "You should know when Becky has bad dreams, she climbs into bed with me. Since she's determined to make you like her so you'll share Georgia with her, you may find her cuddled up with you too."

"Sounds fair." Nina felt a smile coming to her lips. "I should warn you that Georgia's wanted a little girl to bring her treats for a long time. I think one or two of Señora Ortiz's biscuits might do the trick."

"I'll tell Becky."

29

"MISS NINA, I GOTTA GO."

Nina roused enough to see Becky in a long nightgown standing next to the bed, shifting from one foot to the other, a shawl wrapped around her shoulders. "Okay, honey. I'll take you to the outhouse."

After three days and nights on the ranch, Nina knew not to keep the eight-year-old waiting. She eased out from under Pooka, rolled to her feet, grabbed the dark-green robe on the foot of the bed, and shoved her feet into the waiting boots. She stopped by the bureau and lit the lamp, then used it to light their way. "Let's go, sweetie."

Becky led the way down the stairs to the first floor. When they reached the hall, Nina realized they weren't the only ones awake in the middle of the night. Light shone from the oil lamps in the kitchen and Nina saw Beth sitting at the table, Luke curled up nearby. "We're heading out back. Why are you up?"

"I was hungry." Beth dipped a spoon in the bowl in front of her. "Thought I'd have some of what my dad called johnnycake pudding. Want me to make up some for each of you?"

Becky paused to draw on her boots before she pulled Nina toward the back door. "What's in it?"

"Crumbled cornbread, honey, and warm milk. It's really good."

"We'll take your word for it, but we don't want any." Nina opened the door, guiding the child to the porch. Luke rose and joined them just before she shut the door, leaving the heat from the woodstove inside.

"Do all ladies in the family way eat strange things, Miss Nina?"

"Pretty much." They crunched through the moonlit frozen snow toward the privy. "I think Detective Morgan is making up for lost time because some foods made her sick for a while."

"She said that was because the marshal's coffee was so bad, but she still puked when Señora Ortiz made it at breakfast time. All our new mama could drink was her special raspberry tea."

"I'm not surprised."

When they returned to the house a short time later, they found Beth stirring something in a pot on the stove. Smelling the aroma of chocolate and milk, Nina said. "Is that Mexican hot chocolate? I really enjoyed eating everything you learned to make in the class."

"It comes in handy around here. I taught Hannah some of the recipes and her husband just loves *empanadas*." Beth kept her attention on the liquid in the pan. "I can't leave this so do you want to make toast?"

"Sure." Using a cloth Nina picked up the teakettle from the woodstove. "Let me wash my hands and I'm on it. Becky, do you want to join us for a snack, or do you want to go back to bed right away?"

"Are you making your special cinn-mon toast?"

"Definitely."

"Then, I wanna be with you and Mama."

The three of them were settled around the table munching away when Rad arrived. He shook his head, poured himself a cup of coffee, and sat down next to Beth. "Bad dreams again?"

"Not this morning." She dunked her toast in the hot chocolate, then took a bite. "I was hungry."

"About time." He smiled at her, smoothed back a strand of red hair that fell on her cheek. "You haven't been eating enough to keep a flea alive."

"That's going to change. I'll get fat since I'm eating for two, me and your kid." She lifted her cup, sipped it, and then lowered it. "I also had to take a walk. You need to install indoor plumbing here."

"It's a ranch house, Missus Morgan, not a fancy hotel."

"Yeah, well in a couple more months when this baby drops lower, I'll be heading to the outhouse a lot. So, you have that much time to build an inside bathroom. I'll settle for one now, but I'll want more as time goes by."

Nina hid a smile at the bewilderment on Rad's face. He hadn't refused yet and she figured she wouldn't tell him he'd be building the most elaborate house in Washington Territory before long. "Wait a minute. I thought you said he'd help Kyle build me a darkroom so I could develop the photographs I'm supposed to take at the Christmas program."

"He will." Beth finished her toast and reached for the last slice on the plate in the middle of the table. "Any questions?"

"What 'bout our ice house so's we can have more ice cream?" Becky asked. "Our new pa is s'posed to build that too now it's cold. He promised me and Sorry when you folks 'dopted us."

"An ice house?" Nina cocked her head to the side. "How does that work?"

"It won't take much work." Rad leaned back in his chair, amusement creeping into his navy eyes. "Gabe and I designed it already. We'll use a few of the small evergreens, cut them into logs for the walls. He's already split out shakes for the roof and there are plenty of shavings from his mill. The ponds haven't frozen yet. When they do, we'll cut blocks of ice and take them to the new ice house."

"Hannah is very excited about it." Beth took the last bite of toast, then finished off her hot chocolate. "She says it'll be better than the spring house she uses now to keep meat, butter, and milk cold."

"I'm amazed you haven't thought to have the marshal make her an icebox, Beth." Nina rose and collected the empty cups, carrying them to the sink. "You said he made the furniture in your bedroom and a craftsman like that should be able to create an icebox to give to Señora Ortiz for Christmas. Then, she wouldn't have to go to the spring house for cold food. She could just go to the pantry."

Becky yawned. "What's an icebox, Miss Nina?"

"It's rather like your ice house. It's a small cabinet with shelves for food like milk, eggs, cheese, and butter. In the bottom, there's a place for a chunk of ice."

Rad rubbed his beard-stubbled jaw thoughtfully. "What keeps the ice from melting?"

"Oh, it melts, but there's a tray for the water and then all you need is a man to take it out and dump it when it gets full. He also adds another chunk of ice when it's required."

"Kind of like an ice chest, except it's made out of wood and stands upright," Beth said. "Rad could do that. Now, I'm going outside again. Becky, do you want to come with me?"

The little girl tilted her head, considering the question, then nodded. "What about you, Miss Nina?"

"Oh, certainly. Let's have a potty party."

Becky giggled. "You're like Mama. You say the silliest things, Miss Nina."

"Good to know."

Hours later, after breakfast, Nina bundled up to go help Kyle load hay in the buckboard and take it out to the horses wintering in the pasture. Using the other wagon, Rad would take another load to the few cattle he raised.

Beth caught up with her and Pooka at the back door. "Hold up, Nina. We need to talk."

"About what?"

Beth took her arm. "Let's go to the parlor and we'll have some privacy."

"We haven't used it before now."

"We haven't had company, but it's where I'm putting the Christmas tree when we cut one next week after Thanksgiving."

"Okay. It's not like you'll be working and keeping us safe from crazy shoppers on Black Friday weekend."

"Another blessing from the Goddess."

When they entered the room, Nina spotted the differences between what she'd seen when she and Kyle came the first time. The formality still showed it was a far cry from what people would consider a family or living room. To keep the room warmer, heavy drapes blocked the long windows. A large mirror over the fireplace reflected the chandelier. Several chairs and a horse-hair sofa as well as a few tables completed the furnishings.

Beth followed her gaze. "What are you looking for?"

"The grand piano."

"No way. The poor thing would die on the trip here. If the steamboat didn't kill it, the wagon ride from Junction City to the ranch would."

"The Bar M had one when Kyle and I visited in 2018."

"Well, that gives us plenty of time to get one."

"True. So, what's on your mind?"

"Hannah asked me when you'd need the rags we use here for menstruation and I told her I didn't know, that I'd ask you." Beth narrowed her eyes, more of a detective than ever. "Your cycle was always regular, unlike mine. You knew the exact day it would start and slapped the snot out of any boy-horse in the barn who gave you crap during that time. Did things change after Smith attacked you in April?"

"No." Nina mentally calculated the days. "O.M.G., Beth, I had my last period just before your memorial at the end of September. I haven't had one in almost six weeks, not since I started sleeping with Kyle the first part of October. Do you think I'm pregnant?"

"Hello, what's wrong with you, girl? Yes, you're P.G. unless you two were taking some precautions you didn't tell me about."

"I feel super stupid. There was so much drama going on at the rescue that I completely spaced on getting my birth control prescription refilled."

"Join the club." Beth shrugged. "We've been up the hill and over the ridge. Now, we deal with the situation. It looks like your baby will be born sometime in July."

Nina elbowed her best friend. "Well, you did say there was something special about the Morgan men."

"Yeah, and I also said, unfortunately they know it."

When Nina joined him, Kyle had almost filled the bed of the buckboard with hay from a stack in the closest field. She picked up the second pitchfork and jumped in to help him. With the two of them working, it didn't take much longer to finish the task. They put the forks in the wagon and she climbed up beside him. He started the team in the direction of the horse herd, Pooka running next to them.

"Took longer than usual for you to come outside, Miss Nina."

"Yes, Beth wanted to talk to me." Nina took a deep breath. "She's playing detective and told me something I should have figured out for myself. I think I'm pregnant."

He pulled back on the lines, stopping the young horses. "Say that again."

"I didn't do anything to stop conception and you didn't either." She lifted her chin and met his brown gaze. "I haven't menstruated once since we started sleeping together."

"We don't do much sleeping." He wrapped the lines around the brake for a moment, turning to face her. He leaned close enough to kiss her. "After Thanksgiving, let's drive into town and see the mayor. Connor Riley is the local Justice of the Peace and can marry us like he did Rad and Bethany."

"Are you proposing because I'm pregnant?"

"No, Miss Nina. I've wanted to marry you since before we met."

"How is that even possible?"

"Bethany showed me your picture with Trace Burdette's horse

on the camera Smith stole. As soon as I saw you, I knew you were the one."

"You're such a romantical man, as Michael would say." Nina traced his mustache with her finger. "I reckon you'd best start driving, cowboy. And yes, I'll marry you."

He picked up the lines, clucked his tongue, and started the team. "If you'd rather, we can arrange for Connor to come to the ranch to do the ceremony so Bethany and Rad can be there."

"If the snow continues to pile up, it'd be better to have a party when the weather breaks. I don't want to wait to marry you, not when people will be counting on their fingers when they learn about the baby. Like Beth says, everything around here is considered entertainment." Nina shifted closer to him. "Are you sure you're okay with this?"

"I'm more than okay." He kissed her cheek. "Now, what Orion said when we left makes sense."

"What was that?"

"On the day we rode out, he said, 'Three go to Liberty Valley of yesterday and three come forward.' I worried he meant Smith might follow us, but Orion told me that he figured his sisters would make enough mischief to keep Smith occupied."

"So, you, me, and the baby makes three going, but who were the other three?"

"I figure it was Rowdy Tall-Deer, Holt O'Donnell, and Edwin. They rode off looking for the ridge and a future with the Jamison women. They must have found it."

"I hope so."

———

A baby, his baby.

Before the end of the month, he'd be a married man with a family of his own. His boyhood dream would finally come true.

Kyle marveled at the idea as they drove out to the pasture where the nervous Appaloosa herd crowded up close to the gate.

That was strange. Normally, they grazed throughout the thirty-acre field and only came up when they saw him start pitching out hay. He passed the lines to Nina, his soon-to-be wife. "Something's spooked 'em. Keep an eye out and your dog close."

"Be careful."

He nodded and took his rifle, walking down the split-rail fence. Pooka growled, then barked, but didn't leave the wagon. Kyle leaned his carbine against a post long enough to climb through the fence, then trudged through the churned-up snow until he saw the pond. It wasn't cold enough to freeze so that meant none of the yearlings had been driven out on the ice, a trick of an old lame cougar who roamed the hills.

He still saw tracks, but not those of a cat. Rather, the paw-prints were reminiscent of a dog's and Kyle spotted several sets. He glanced toward the grove of cedar trees bordering the pasture and saw a large wolf looking back at him. He raised his rifle to his shoulder, took aim, and fired. He didn't miss. The shot struck the gray animal in the chest, but it didn't fall, didn't die, didn't even writhe in anguish.

Instead, it merely backed a couple of steps. Two more melted out of the evergreens and stood next to the one he thought he'd mortally wounded. Then, the three turned and walked away as if the threat he posed was less than nothing. He strode toward the place where the first one had stood, seeing a small patch of blood as if the critter barely suffered a scratch. He didn't follow them into the woods where they might be waiting to attack.

He turned and went back to the wagon. "Let's feed these cayuses. I'll talk to Rad, but I don't think we have another field that's closer to the house."

"Shouldn't those wolves have run from you especially when you shot at one?"

He inclined his head in acceptance. His affianced was a smart woman. "Yes, they should have, but there's something strange about them. They're not afraid of people or guns. When I open the gate, bring in the wagon."

"All right, but watch those horses. They're going to try to race past me."

Kyle unlatched the gate, using it to block the herd as she drove through. Between him, the dog, and her skill with the team, they didn't lose a single one from the remuda. When she stopped for a moment, he climbed up in the back and began pitching out hay right away. She made a circle in the field, staying away from the pond and the trees the horses would normally use for shelter in rough weather. Although the Appaloosas began to eat, the older geldings remained on edge while they munched hay. They stood guard between the mares and the young stock.

Standing next to him, Nina frowned at the horses. "I wish I'd brought that box of silver cartridges with us, the ones Kallisto insisted on giving me. I wonder what would have happened if you'd shot that alpha with one of those rounds."

"He should have dropped when I nailed him."

"Should have, would have, could have." Nina drew a scarf up over her head. "Let's come back with another load of hay. I'll bring those bullets and the pistol Rad bought me at the mercantile. We'll kick some wolf butt."

"You haven't shot that Colt yet."

"No, but I was on my high school's rifle team all four years. I can hit my target."

"You are one surprise after another, Miss Nina." He caught her shoulders, pulled her close for a kiss. "Lock up your pup when you get the cartridges. We don't want Pooka giving chase to those wolves. They'll rip him to shreds."

30

WHILE KYLE LOADED UP THE BUCKBOARD WITH MORE HAY, NINA took Pooka to the house where she found Beth helping Hannah Ortiz and the girls make mincemeat for pies. This time Nina invited Beth into the parlor to discuss the wolf issue. "It's weird. They're not afraid of us."

"I think Astrid Hunter was right when she warned us they'd be stalking you and me." Beth folded her arms, considering options. "I'll talk to Rad about setting up some targets and we'll have everyone practice shooting after dinner."

"It'll be dark by then."

"Remember, around here they refer to lunch as dinner."

"I forgot." Nina scrunched her fingers in Pooka's ruff. "I'm leaving him here with you. Don't let him out to follow us. He could get hurt."

"Trust me. I've got your six." Beth returned to the kitchen.

Nina went upstairs to her bedroom. She opened the saddlebags and removed the box of cartridges as well as the pistol. Then, it was time to rejoin Kyle. When she headed for the back door, she saw Pooka happily gnawing on a bone under the table and discreetly left the house. She crossed the yard and climbed up in the wagon.

Their first stop was the nearby paddock where S.O.B. and her horses grazed. They unloaded half the hay, and then drove toward the pasture where the twenty head of Appaloosas still ate their daily ration of fodder.

"You certainly received a well-rounded education at that boarding school, Miss Nina. I heard you speaking German when we visited Gruber at the Lazy B and now you're telling me you're some sort of marksman. Do you want to send our children somewhere like that?"

"Of course not." She moved closer to him, relishing the warmth of his solid body. "It wasn't like I had a choice when it came to studying. I was seven when my mother shipped me off because she loved Deke Zacallah and his daughters more than she did me. Our kids will stay with us."

"So, what all did you learn?"

"Beyond the usual academics, the curriculum covered everything from gourmet cooking to photography to fencing to self-defense to classical equestrian horsemanship."

"What sort of fencing? Why would they teach girls to dig post-holes and split rails?"

"Not that kind of fencing, cowboy." She giggled, resting her head on his broad shoulder. "We learned to fight with blunted swords and competed in tournaments with other schools. I liked shooting at targets better so I joined the rifle team."

"How many languages do you speak?"

"German, French, Spanish, Japanese and some Italian. It was either go to the foreign language rooms or practice playing a musical instrument and that got old in a hurry."

"So, when we get a piano at the Bar M, you can teach all the children to play."

"No, that so isn't my thing. We'll make Beth do music and singing."

"I didn't know she knew how."

"When she left the Army after her enlistment ended, she still struggled with Post-Traumatic Stress Disorder or P.T.S.D., so she used to take all kinds of night classes, not just cooking ones. She plays the piano and the organ. She'd just started violin lessons but she wasn't very good yet. Of course, she also studied art and learned to paint portraits."

"That explains why she draws pictures on the Wanted posters at the marshal's office in town." Kyle brought the team to a stop at the gate and passed her the lines. "Watch for those wolves."

"Believe me, I am."

———

Throughout the next two days, they didn't see any sign of the shifters. Rad set up targets by the woodshed and all of them practiced shooting, but not with the silver rounds. They saved those for times when they went to feed the livestock. During one of their late-night conversations, Nina brought up the necessity of making more silver ammunition. Beth agreed and wrote a letter to Trace since the nearest forge was at the Lazy B. Because two of the men would be off to visit family over the holiday, they'd drop the letter at the mercantile as well as taking Nina's note to the hotel for the Hunter women.

On Tuesday, Nina collected the rifle she'd borrowed from Rad and the carton of special cartridges before she went to meet Kyle. She left Pooka with the girls who were helping make pies for the holiday. By now, they'd developed a routine. Beth and Rad would take one buckboard to feed the cattle while Nina and Kyle used the other to feed the horses. On the way to the Appaloosa pasture, she loaded both rifles with silver bullets.

"Do you think they'll be roaming around, Miss Nina?"

"Better safe than sorry." She scanned the area as they approached the horses that remained wary. Luckily, they hadn't lost any of them to the predators which seemed totally strange. What did the wolves eat since they weren't going after the livestock?

Kyle opened the gate and she drove the wagon inside. He

closed it behind them and climbed into the bed, ready to spread hay. She began making their usual circle around the field. With the drop in temperature, the pond froze near the edges. The next step was to break the ice so the horses would be able to drink.

She parked the wagon. Carrying one of the rifles, she went to loosen the check-reins so the team could lower their heads and water. However, the big red lead mare didn't even attempt to quench her thirst. She tossed her head, ears pricked. Nina turned and saw the alpha wolf lurking in the shadow of the trees, focusing on Kyle, creeping closer. "Behind you."

He glanced over his shoulder, then nodded at her. "Do it."

She took a deep breath, raised the rifle, and pointed it at the animal. He didn't stop, just hunkered down, ready to leap on the man, her man. Kyle signaled her, then dove out of the line of fire. She aimed and pulled the trigger.

The first bullet hit the wolf mid-chest. He howled in pain, falling onto the snow-covered ground, hard. She advanced on the animal, shot again. The second round followed the first and the third sliced across his skull. He rolled in agony, blood spurting from the wounds. As she watched, his fur melted away. Skin emerged, first in patches. Bones shifted and the wolf's body slowly changed to that of a well-muscled, dark-haired man. He lay naked in the snow, more blood spilling underneath him as he bled out.

Nina kept the rifle pointed at him and walked away from the wagon toward him. Two bullets had torn into his chest and she knew he'd be gone in moments. "Why are you here?"

"He's dead, Miss Nina." Kyle strode to stand beside her. "He can't tell you."

"He hasn't left yet." She eyed the shifter, watching his spirit rise. "Answer me."

"We were sent." The wraith spoke haltingly. "Help me, *Seer*."

She shook her head. "Who sent you?"

"The alpha of the pack."

"I thought you were the alpha."

"Only of this hunting party. He rules the town. Corbett's Town." The wolf-man began to fade. "Please, *Seer*. Send me to *Summerland*. Please. Don't give me back to him. Don't let him shred my soul again."

"Very well." Somehow, she knew what to do. She stepped between him and the evergreens, blocking him from the sight of the other wolves, and then raised her hand, pointing to the overcast sky. "Go to the rest you have earned, *Truth-speaker*. Wait for Tom Corbett to arrive in *Summerland*. Serve him from this day forward instead of the one who sent you to die."

"Thank you, *Seer*. I will." The spirit vanished.

Kyle put an arm around her waist. "What do we do with his body?"

"Take it to Junction City and have him buried in consecrated ground with suitable prayers."

"Father Daniel left on the steamboat last week."

"I'll ask the Hunter women to speak the words to protect his body. I've already saved his soul."

––––––

Supper over, Kyle went to the barn in search of Rad who'd agreed to build a coffin for their unwelcome visitor. His brother had already chosen the rough-cut boards he intended to use and laid them, side by side, on the sawhorses. Kyle glanced at the corpse, washed and dressed for burial in old clothes that Señora Ortiz claimed were too good for the rag-bag, even if they were too far gone for most folks to wear.

Rad sorted through an assortment of handmade nails. "What's on your mind?"

"When I think I know all about her, I keep learning new things about Miss Nina."

"Sounds about right. Did you meet as soon as you left here?"

"No, not until the end of September. You married Bethany last April and you two had barely known each other two weeks."

"I'm sure you'll get to the point sooner or later. I'd prefer sooner."

"Do you know everything about her?"

"Knew what I needed to know." Rad picked up a hammer and turned back to his project. "Come hold this board in place."

"Bethany doesn't act like other women in town."

"No. If I wanted one of them, I'd have married years ago."

"But, you didn't court anyone else."

"None of them were Bethany Rose Chambers. She was mine the night we met. She found me dang near dead and wouldn't ride off and leave me, even when I told her to go so whoever shot me wouldn't kill her. Instead, she patched me up and took me to the nearest safe place."

"She healed you. Doc Jenkins says he couldn't have done it."

"No, but he's not Goddess blessed. She's strong, smart, and doesn't have an ounce of *give-up* in her. She makes me smile. She's right for me like Miss Nina is right for you."

"She shot him when he went for me." Kyle jerked his head toward the dead shifter. "Never hesitated, just blew him to doll-rags."

"A man has to admire a woman who does what needs doing."

"He was a goner, but she talked to him anyway. I couldn't hear him say anything, but it seemed like they conversed. She agreed to send him somewhere special and safe."

"Why does that surprise you when Bethany told you Nina saw the ghost of that murdered man in town?"

"Reckon I didn't comprehend she chatted to them."

"Well, you know now. Fetch me the next board."

Late that evening, he heard voices in the kitchen, the rise, and fall of conversation. It was after midnight, but several hours until dawn. Pulling on his pants and shirt, he went to join the group in the other room. Wearing her dark-green wrapper, Nina stood at the stove, toasting bread while Bethany sliced cheese into a cast-iron skillet, her dog, Luke sleeping in a corner. Rad filled three cups with hot chocolate, adding a fourth at the sound of Kyle's soft footsteps.

"What's going on? Why are you folks up so early?"

"I had to take a walk." Bethany carried the pan over to the stove, standing next to Nina. "And when I do, I'm always ready to visit the spring house and come back with the means to create a snack."

"Becky needed to go to the privy." Nina flashed a smile over her shoulder at him. "When we returned, she headed back to bed since I wasn't making anything sweet tonight. Sometimes, she'll stay up with us if we're having cinnamon toast."

"You'll have to make that for me sometime." Kyle carried the crock of butter and knives as well as four small plates to the table. "What else shall we talk about tonight?"

"Our plans when we go to town next week." Nina flipped the bread on the top of the stove. "We're seeing Mayor Riley and getting married."

"I thought you would." Beth hugged her friend. "I'd come stand up with you, but it's better if Rad and I stay home to watch out in case those wolves return."

"Makes sense," Kyle said. "While we're in town, I want Miss Nina to invite the Hunter women here so we can make plans to eliminate the entire pack." When she joined him at the table, he pulled out a chair for Nina. "We don't know what those critters eat, but I don't figure killing one will be enough to stop them."

"At Tom Corbett's funeral, I remember Kallisto saying they hunted younglings and the shifters would pack them off as prey. She meant our children, not just the ones at the Bar M, but those who live in Liberty Valley."

Beth shuddered, her hand protectively going to cover the baby she carried. "We'll have to keep the girls and Michael close to the house until we know they're safe."

"We will." Rad rested his hands on her shoulders, drawing her back against him. "Kyle, when you're in town, you'll need to pass the word to Prince and Cal so they can let folks know we have a rogue pack stalking the area. Tell Paul to put an article in the paper."

"If I mention it takes silver bullets to kill them, everyone will think we're loco."

"You don't say that." Rad narrowed navy-blue eyes. "You just warn our neighbors so they'll be packing rifles and regular bullets. When you wounded that wolf the first time, the rest withdrew for a couple of days. That's all we need, a respite while we come up with a plan to destroy them and their town."

Beth wrapped a towel around the handle of the pan and carried it over to put it on the trivet in the middle of the table. "You have to do it in the next few weeks, early enough that Nina can go with you and I'll guard the ranch."

"She'll stay with you." Kyle eyed Nina, seeing the defiance on her face. "I mean it. I don't want you riding into trouble."

"Get over yourself, Kyle Morgan. I have to be there to send the ones who ask to *Summerland*, their version of Heaven. I'm the *Seer*. It's my responsibility. I'll arrange for Astrid to hold down the fort with Beth."

"I'd rather have you here."

Rad pulled out a chair for Beth. "And I'd rather stay with my wife and my child, Kyle, but Miss Nina is right. We have to saddle up and the three of us will go with Kallisto Hunter and the posse to take on the pack."

"Now, let's talk about something more cheerful." Beth picked up one of the knives and started spreading melted cheese on a slice of toast. "Have you two designed a wing to add onto the house? I don't want Nina living miles away from me any more than Rad wants you on the other side of the moon, Kyle."

"No, we haven't." Kyle watched a smile light up Nina's face. "Let's get started tonight. We've come home and we don't want to live anywhere else."

An hour later, their discussion came to an end when Beth yawned, almost falling asleep in the chair. Rad stood, lifted her into his arms. "We'll leave the two of you to tidy up and see you both in the morning."

"No worries." Nina rose to her feet as they left the room, Luke padding behind them. "We've got this."

It didn't take long to wash up their few dishes and to put away what remained of the food. He banked the fire in the woodstove, then swung around to face her. "Do I get to kiss you goodnight before you go upstairs?"

She smiled and advanced on him, pressing her body against his. "I think it's my turn to slide out early. Take me to bed, Kyle. Your bed."

He brushed his mouth over hers. "We won't sleep."

"Good. I didn't have sleeping in mind."

"You'll have to be quiet." He stopped at the table, turned down the lamp until the light faded. "You can't wake the neighbors."

"I'll try if you don't make me crazy."

"Let's go, woman." He chuckled, picked her up, one arm around her shoulders, and the other under her knees. "I don't know what part of you I want to kiss first, but I'm ready to start."

31

WHEN THEY ARRIVED IN JUNCTION CITY, KYLE DROVE THE
mayor's buckboard to the Rileys' barn after a brief stop at the
undertaker's to leave the coffin containing the shifter. They'd look
after his horses as well as their own since they planned to ride back
to the Bar M after a short honeymoon. While he unhitched the
team of imported Welsh Cobs, Nina took care of Missouri and
S.O.B. Once all four horses were in the stalls, watered and fed, the
two of them headed for the hotel to check into a room and have a
late dinner or an early supper before Kyle tracked down Connor
Riley to perform their wedding.

Prior to leaving the Bar M, Beth had pointed out if they were
married before dark, they could stay in the same room without
shocking everyone in town. If they had to wait until the following
day, he'd have to sleep in one of the cells at the jail. Beth hadn't
said anything more about Nina and Kyle expecting a baby and
even now, Nina wasn't sure if Rad suspected there'd be another
addition to the Morgan family next summer.

After they ate, Nina and Pooka walked with Kyle through
town. She wanted to find a new hat to go with the scarlet day dress
she planned to wear for the ceremony. He left her at the mercan-

tile, the pup dashing ahead of him. When she opened the door, she saw Susanne Prescott waiting on a customer at the back counter.

Nina stopped and stared at the sunset-haired woman standing in the corner, dreaming over the new red velvet walking dress, and recognized Astra Jamison. *Not dead. She's not dead. She can't be dead.*

Nina hurried across the room, gaping at the lawyer's shadowy form. Instead of wearing her usual professional attire, she wore jeans and a fleece-lined denim jacket over a red turtleneck and sweatshirt. Oddly enough, she also had on dangly gold earrings, matching gold bracelets, and an elaborate necklace that simply didn't go with the casual garb.

"What are you doing here, Astra? What happened to you? Are you—?"

"Chill out, Nina." Astra swung around, amusement sparkling in the deep blue of her eyes. "I'm visiting, that's all. I'll go back when my body is healed."

"From what? Who hurt you? Gary Smith?"

"No, not him. You don't know the guy who tried to kill me, but I'll deal with him when I get back unless my new mate claims the privilege." Astra glanced around the store. "You're the first person in town that knows I'm here. Where's Kyle? Where's Beth? I miss her so much. I wanted to see her."

"Kyle's going to the mayor's house." Suddenly realizing others might hear her talking to an ethereal woman that only she could see and believe she'd lost her mind, Nina lowered her voice to a whisper. "Beth's out at the Bar M ranch. Kyle is arranging for us to get married."

"Awesome. Can I come to the wedding?"

"Of course. We'd love to have you join us. Now, help me choose a hat."

It didn't take long to find a red toque, a very small bonnet without a crown and with wide ribbons, trimmed out in small feathers and artificial flowers. The two of them left the general store and walked toward the mayor's large home. Nina took a deep breath of the winter air. "So, Rowdy and Hugh found you?"

"Yes, they arrived the day after you left."

"Tell me the truth. Did we really come to Liberty Valley in 1888?"

"Of course. Haven't you realized where you are by now?"

"I guess I didn't want to believe it. I wanted to think we were in some kind of settlement created by former soldiers who'd opted to hide from society and when things calmed down, I could return home."

"Well, that's a creative explanation, but why didn't you listen to me? I said we were sending you and Kyle to safety. What could be safer than this place and time?"

"Excuse you. There's a bunch of vicious shifters who intend to eat the local children."

"I know, but you'll organize a posse, wipe them out and burn their town to the ground. Then, you'll find suitable homes for their innocent pups."

"How do you know that when the operation is still in the planning stages, Astra?"

"It's local history. You're living it, but where I come from, you've already handled it." Astra petted the spectral black dog that escorted her. "If I'd known everything that was going to happen before you left, I'd have told you, but I didn't have all my memories until Rowdy and I met."

"So, the two of you clicked?"

"That's one way to say it." Astra laughed. "My mother arranged a match between us ages ago because she thought meshing our powers would make us stronger. It may sound strange to you, but it's the way witches in my coven get married. The Elders always choose our mates to ensure each generation has more magick than the ones before."

"Did she do the same thing for your sisters?"

"Yes, but the liaison she created for Meteor hasn't worked. Her mate keeps killing her."

"Wait a second." Nina flicked a sideways glance at the younger woman. "Are you talking about Tom and Mary Corbett? I've seen both of them haunting this place. He says his uncle murdered both of them and begged me to promise to protect their son, Edwin."

"Rowdy and Hugh brought him to the future with them." Astra took a moment to obviously consider the idea. "When did you start seeing the dead?"

"Last week, a few days after we arrived. Kyle says I always saw the essence of people and it's what makes me a good photographer, but I never talked to ghosts until I got here. Why did that happen?"

"It must have occurred because you came so close to dying when Gary Smith abducted you. If we hadn't rescued you when we did, you'd have bled out on *Samhain* eve."

"But, I lived. You and Rowdy healed me."

"That's probably the other part of it. We not only walk the paths among the stars, but we also rule the night, Death, and the crossroads. We must have inadvertently given you the power to speak to ghosts. Do you want me to try and take it away?"

"Could you?"

"Perhaps if you haven't used it yet, or been called by name by the dying."

"When he went after Kyle, I killed a shifter and he called me, *Seer* when he asked me to send him to *Summerland.* I did."

"I'm sorry, but you're committed to the work of the Goddess now. How could you kill a shifter? It takes silver—"

"I know. Silver ammo. I got a box from Kallisto Hunter. As the *Guardian,* Beth knows things and she says Kallisto will be your sister, Venus in her next life and she has lessons to learn from us here and now."

"Audra Dawson-Watkins is the *Bard.* You and Beth will end up working with Audra so leave her the material she needs since she lives more than a hundred years from now and her outcome means she won't be traveling here."

"Beth and I will take care of it." They crossed the snow-covered street and stepped up on the next boardwalk. "Do you have any more advice for me?"

"I'm not sure." Astra shrugged. "I'll be around a few days. I'll let you know. Where's my younger 'sister-to-be' staying? I want to see her."

"She and Astrid have rooms at the hotel."

"That must be me in this life. I know she'll see me when I visit."

"Do you want me to tell her that you're here?"

"No way. I'll do it."

———

The wedding had gone off without a hitch although the mayor offered to hold it the next day when he did church services at the hotel so more folks could attend. At some point, he'd have to come to terms with the rough frontier humor in Junction City, but Kyle wasn't ready to laugh with the people who lived here yet. Bethany must have taken Cal aside at Thanksgiving and shared their plans because the deputy had rounded up Doctor Jenkins, Susanne Prescott, her sister Ursula and Ursula's husband, Paul Levine to stand as witnesses along with Kate Riley and her beau, Tim O'Neill.

Kate must have suspected their plans even earlier because she'd baked a wedding cake and those fruitcakes usually needed weeks or months to age. She'd frosted it with boiled icing and decorated it with sugar flowers. Nina carried boxed slices for them to have later on their first anniversary. She tucked her other gloved hand in the crook of his elbow as they walked to the hotel. Pooka darted and danced in front of them playing in the snow as if he had a doggie companion who shared his joy in the day.

Kyle gestured to the puppy, enjoying his antics when he rolled in a drift of powdery snow. "Looks like you'll have to find a towel to dry him off when we get to our room."

"Undoubtedly. He really likes having Freya here to romp with him."

"What?"

"Freya, one of Astra Jamison's dogs. She's very good with puppies."

"After working at the Rocking J, I know Freya. Are you telling me Astra Jamison died and came here?"

"She's not dead. She's just visiting while her body recovers from an attack, but I didn't get all the details."

"Do it now."

Nina heaved a sigh. "Are you going to be one of those macho husbands who thinks he can order his wife around? Didn't you notice that Mayor Riley left out the word, *obey* in the vows? I promised to love, honor and cherish you for the rest of our lives and you promised to do the same for me. It shocked everyone but Doctor Jenkins. He said it was a Morgan tradition because it was the same vows that Beth and Rad shared."

"Antonina Arabella Armstrong-Morgan, ask her now. If she needs our help, we have to give it."

Another sigh and he could have sworn she rolled her eyes like he'd seen Sean Killian's step-daughter do when she decided her parents were too old to be believed.

"Well, you heard him." Nina gazed at the empty place next to her on the boardwalk. "What happened to you?"

She listened intently, then nodded. "Okay, here goes. She was told about an injured F.B.I. agent. She went with her apprentice witch and new mate, which I guess is like a husband…" She heaved another sigh. "Astra, if he's not your husband, then what is he? And how do I explain him to Kyle?"

"I didn't know she was affianced, much less that she planned to marry. Who's the lucky fella?"

Silence for a moment and then Nina shook her head. "Astra says he wouldn't call it luck, but a *magick* bonding. It's Rowdy Tall-Deer, the man who finished healing me when we arrived. Their pledges aren't what we'd think of as marriage vows because they exist beyond this lifetime and don't end with either of their deaths."

"Sounds like an eternal love to me."

"Yes, but you're the romantic in our new family. At any rate, she and Freya came here for a visit since she walks among the stars. It sounds like some form of astral projection."

"What's that?"

"When Destynee LaFleur writes about it, she says it means Astra leaves her body behind and her soul goes wherever it wants for a while. She needed a break from her reality and decided to visit us."

"There's more to it than that."

"She says you're a smart guy, but not to worry." Nina smiled and hugged his arm. "She has other people to visit here so she'll leave us alone when we get to the hotel. She certainly doesn't plan to intrude on our wedding night."

"Thank you, ma'am."

Nina laughed. "Of course, if you ever call her, *ma'am* again, all bets are off."

He'd taken Pooka for a last walk, promising her privacy to change her clothes. Because they'd had such great sex when she wore the short, spring nightie, she'd made sure to bring it for their wedding night. She shivered, feeling her nipples tighten against the thin cotton, and pulled on the dark-green bathrobe. The fireplace didn't do much to heat the room, but once they got in the large bed, she wouldn't have reason to complain.

She took time to pull back the coverlet and blankets on the bed, revealing the sheets so they wouldn't have to wait too long when he finally arrived. Then, she crossed back to the table and poured two glasses of brandy, debating whether she should have alcohol, and decided one small, last drink on her wedding night wouldn't hurt the baby. It wasn't as if she'd get wasted on a regular basis for the next seven and half months. She sat down to wait.

The door opened and she turned with a smile as he entered. Pooka trotted over to flop near the fireplace, emitting a doggie sigh. She rose and went to kiss Kyle, brushing his lips with hers. "What happens if I say it took you long enough?"

"Blame your dog." Kyle removed his hat, then his coat. "He found a bunny to chase, but he didn't catch it."

She smiled and kissed him again. "How long will it take for me to get you out of the rest of your clothes?"

"I'll do it. You can sit and wait for me, Missus Morgan."

"Ooh, a strip-tease." She returned to her chair and picked up the glass with the minuscule amount of brandy, prepared to watch him disrobe. "Wow, what a treat."

He chuckled, then proceeded to remove his boots and placed them along with hers out in the hall to be polished. After locking the door, he turned, still unbuttoning his shirt. He shrugged out of it, hanging it neatly in the wardrobe. His pants followed. When he was down to what he called a 'union suit', he came to join her at the table.

He pulled his chair close and parted the robe to stroke her knee, pushing the short nightgown upwards. "I'm glad you wore this tonight."

"I thought you would be."

She caught her breath when he slowly explored her thigh, working toward the curls between her legs. She squirmed closer, aching for him to touch her, really touch her. But, he didn't. Instead, he eased back and picked up the glass of brandy.

"I thought—"

He winked at her. "I know what you thought, Missus Morgan, but I can wait for a while."

"You're a very bad man, Kyle Morgan." She rose, untying the belt, and pushed off the robe so it pooled onto the floor. She eased onto his lap, rocking against the bulge in his long underwear.

"After all the times you said you wanted to marry me, I figured you'd be a good husband."

"Whatever gave you that idea?"

"Silly me."

He lowered his head and his mouth tormented hers. She tasted brandy on his tongue and moaned when two fingers slid inside her. "Oh, my Gawd."

"No, it's me." His thumb rubbed the small nub of flesh. "Your husband. The man who will take you all night long. Kiss me, Antonina."

She turned her head and their mouths met, clung. Her tongue enticed his into a passionate duel. Meanwhile, he continued the rhythm with his hand, and her excitement built.

He smiled and his mustache tickled her skin. "I'm going to have my mouth on you next time."

"Promises, promises."

"This is one I'll keep until you beg me to stop." He kissed the hollow of her throat, the side of her neck, her ear. "I'm tasting every inch of you tonight. We've barely been together at the ranch and I've missed having you in my bed."

She squirmed on his hard thighs, felt the dampness increase between her legs. She gasped when he pushed down the strap of her nightgown and explored her breast with his mouth. He drew on her nipple, sucked gently, then harder. They kissed, one long kiss fading into the next.

He lifted his head and smiled at her. "Now, I'll keep my promise."

"Which one?"

"You already know."

Amazingly, he managed to stand up even with her across his lap and carried her over to the bed. He lowered her onto the sheets. He cupped her bottom and brushed his lips up one thigh, then the other. She wasn't sure when he got her legs over his shoulders, but she gasped when his mouth claimed her.

His tongue delved deep, two, or was it three strokes? His lips sought a certain spot and he tugged on the nub of flesh. He lapped at her with his tongue, before he settled in earnest on her. She bucked against him, pushing up into the kiss and his mouth. Her hips writhed and she matched the pattern he set. How could she resist him? She exploded in delight.

"I'm ready. Take me." She gaped at him when he shook his head. "No? Why not?"

"That wasn't begging, Missus Morgan." He lowered his head and licked the small bit of flesh. "I told you what I wanted."

She moaned as his mouth found her. His tongue drove into her. She found herself rising, falling, meeting each movement of his tongue until she flew among the stars. When she regained control, she stared at him still between her legs as if he intended to take her with his lips a third time.

"You have to stop." She struggled to breathe normally. "Please, Kyle."

His smile widened. "You haven't given me what I want yet."

She arched against his mouth as he started again. Thought fled as he licked, sucked, and finally took her with his tongue. She heard herself crying his name, then begging him to take her, really take her. He was naked when she opened her eyes a lifetime later. He lay beside her in the blankets, his hand stroking her hair.

She let her fingers stray over his broad chest, teasing the hard buttons of his nipples, seeing the concern on his face. "What's wrong?"

"We've always done it side by side and with you on top." He kissed her forehead. "Do you trust me enough to let me be on top tonight?"

"I don't know, but I'm willing to try with you, only you."

"I'll go slow and if you change your mind, tell me."

"I can do that." She kissed him, nibbled her way down his neck, nipped at his ears until he groaned. She explored his chest and sucked on one of his nipples.

He shifted until he was on top of her, supporting most of his weight on his elbows. He parted her legs with one hard thigh. "Are you ready?"

"Yes." She felt him probe with his body this time. He slid slowly inside her. Oh yeah, she was more than ready for him and they both knew it.

He pushed deeper, gripping her hips. "Is this all right?"

"You know it." She rose against him, hips meeting in a series of long, leisurely strokes.

He kissed her as they moved together. Suddenly, she realized he'd changed the pattern of his thrusts. Some were so deep, she thought she'd break in half, others were shallow as he teased and tormented her. Then, his pace increased and so did hers until she reached the heights. He was still hard, buried inside her. He started again. She met him, motion for motion. They ascended, higher and higher. Each thrust took them further and further. He smiled, drawing her closer and his lips claimed hers. His tongue plunged into her mouth as he drove her past the stars. Their hips met, clashed and they achieved fulfillment in an explosive moment.

He rolled to the side and pulled her next to him, running his fingers through her hair. "How are you?"

"I'm good." She trailed a finger over his mustache. "I never thought I'd be able to do it like that again."

"We'll do it your way again, but I'm glad you let me choose the way I wanted it tonight."

32

THEY'D BARELY MADE IT DOWNSTAIRS FOR SUNDAY SERVICES THE previous day and contemplated skipping them entirely, but before leaving the Bar M, Nina had promised they'd maintain some decorum and adhere to the expected social norms. They'd had dinner with the Rileys at the hotel, then claimed they had to look after their horses to escape a supper invitation. This morning, Kyle intended to hire grave-diggers at the saloon after he took care of their horses. Meanwhile, Nina took Pooka for a stroll along the river bank. It didn't take long for Astra and her dog to join them.

"Did you find the Hunters?" Nina watched the dogs romp ahead of them. "Were you able to talk to them?"

"Yes, I found them, but I swear Astrid is the most stubborn witch alive. She barely listens to me before she starts lecturing."

"Wow, I wonder where she gets that from, or should I say I wonder where you got that from?"

"Shut up, Nina."

The request lacked heat and Nina laughed, enjoying the camaraderie. "Yeah, right. I will when you do."

Ahead of them, she saw the spirit of Mary Corbett and eyed Astra. "Have you two talked yet?"

"No, this is the first time I've seen her. Hopefully, she's more amenable to what I have to say than our sisters."

"Good luck with that."

"Will you leave me alone with her?"

"Of course." Calling Pooka, Nina turned back toward the hotel. The half-grown puppy raced ahead of her, diving into the occasional snowbank to find a rabbit to chase.

That afternoon when she visited the mercantile, she found Astra fantasizing about the red velvet dress again. Nina left the attorney to it and went to give Susanne the shopping order from Beth. The Bar M was well supplied with staples for the winter, but her friend wanted more tea, a few spices, and the gifts she'd ordered for Christmas which had arrived on the steamboat but hadn't been unpacked when they left town before Thanksgiving. Luckily, almost everything had arrived including the two wax dolls with real hair and glass eyes, elaborately dressed in gowns that could be removed.

"I'm not sure how you're going to get everything to the ranch." Susanne gestured to the wooden crate she was in the process of filling. "You may have to borrow Mayor Riley's buckboard and team again."

"I'll talk to Kyle about it. Perhaps, we could just rent a pack-horse from the livery and buy back one set of those panniers he traded to you. I'm having tea with the Hunters this afternoon and inviting them to the Bar M. I don't know how much of their belongings they'll want to bring along."

"I'll lend the panniers to you. It's not like anyone will want to buy them before next spring anyway, especially since so many of the trails in Liberty Valley are closed by snow."

"Did someone take the note from Beth to Trace at the Lazy B?"

"I sent it with the Swensons when they came for supplies before Thanksgiving."

After a few more minutes of conversation, Nina left the general store and headed back to the hotel for her meeting with Astrid and

Kallisto Hunter. She found the two women in the dining room where they'd already been seated and a waitress was serving tea, small sandwiches, and cookies.

Nina joined them at the table, accepting a cup from Astrid. "Did you get my note about the wolves out at the ranch?"

"Yes, but they're not *real* wolves." Kallisto sipped her tea. "I told you that at Tom Corbett's funeral."

"I know." Nina lowered her voice. "I shot one with the bullets you gave me when he went after Kyle. We brought the body with us and I need one of you to say prayers over him this afternoon."

"I'll do that." Astrid picked up a tiny ham sandwich. "What happened to his soul, *Seer*?"

"I sent it onto *Summerland* with the provision that he help Jed Corbett in the future."

"Who?" A storm brewing in her violet eyes, Kallisto glared at Nina. "None of the Corbetts are worth the silver it'd take to blow them to pieces."

"Jed helped me out a couple of times when I was in danger before coming here. He's a decent guy, but I'm afraid that the same person who killed Tom Corbett may hunt Jed in the future."

"You've been listening to the woman I'll become in that time, haven't you?" Astrid picked up the teapot and refilled their cups. "She tends to issue orders."

"She and her sisters opened a portal so Kyle and I could come here before I was murdered in that time. Of course, I'll pay attention to what Astra tells me. Do you walk among the stars too, Astrid?"

"That's not one of my powers, at least not yet. It may come with time."

"It will." Nina selected a small cheese sandwich. "Meantime, I have a lot to teach you throughout the rest of my life and the rest of yours. We need to make plans, so I'd like you to join us at the Bar M, the Morgan ranch for Christmas."

"I hope those plans include destroying that pack of rogue shifters," Kallisto said.

"Definitely."

"Then, I'm happy to visit. When do you want to leave?"

"The day after tomorrow."

"Wednesday is fine. I'll rent horses for us at the livery." Kallisto glanced at her sister. "You haven't said anything, Astrid. Are you agreeable?"

"You've spoken for both of us. I'll start packing."

They held the funeral for the shifter in the late afternoon with few people in attendance, the undertaker, grave-diggers, Kyle, and the Hunter sisters. Nina noticed the spirit of Tom Corbett, still attired in his black suit, and Astra Jamison, accompanied by her dog arrived before the mayor opened his Bible and read the customary prayers.

When he finished, Kyle stepped up beside Nina. "The women-folk want some privacy to say a few more words. If you'll join me at the gate, I bought a bottle of whisky from Prince and we can share a drink."

The idea went over well and all of the men, except Tom Corbett, joined him in a solemn procession to the far side of the graveyard. Astrid Hunter stepped forward, facing the coffin, holding a thick white candle that remained lit despite the occasional gust of wind. Her sister flanked her and Astra stepped up on the other side.

After a moment of silence, Astrid spoke. "The Goddess sent us here to experience life in all our forms. In death, we return to her and the Summerland where we experience peace."

Silence reigned for a moment before Astrid glanced at Nina. "*Seer*, did you learn his name?"

"No. I forgot to ask before I sent his spirit away."

"I saw his body at the undertaker's, " Tom said, "He was my cousin. We called him Junior, but his 'real' name was Frederick after his father. He's mated, but doesn't have any children yet."

Astra nodded, then repeated the information to Astrid who continued the ritual. "Frederick Corbett, by the element of Earth, you ran as a wolf and a man in the physical world. By the element of Air, you learned as a boy, a pup to serve your pack, your alpha, and communicated with all you loved. By the element of Fire, your passions inspired you to choose your mate who grieves your loss. By the element of Water, you brought your dreams to life. By Earth, by Air, by Fire, by Water, we send you onto *Summerland* to await your next visit to this realm."

She stood the lit candle on the coffin, then turned to Nina. "Do you want to provide your memories of him, *Seer*?"

"I only knew him at the end of his life when he sought redemption and asked me to save his spirit."

"I'll speak for him since we grew up together if you'll share my words, *Seer*."

Nina inclined her head in agreement. "I'll be happy to, Tom."

The ritual ended with a final blessing before Astrid extinguished the flame, then passed the still warm candle to Nina. Escorted by the living and the dead, she went to join Kyle. "We've finished saying goodbye. Mr. Levine, will you please make a marker for Frederick Corbett's grave?"

After the undertaker agreed, Nina tucked her hand in the crook of Kyle's arm and walked with him toward town. "Thank you for your help. I'm sure they'd have been shocked by what Astrid said and did."

"Indubitably." Kyle drew her closer, then glanced at the others. "Would you like to join us for supper at the hotel?"

"I'd love to," Astra said, "but I don't think his invite includes either you or me, Tom."

"Who are you?" Tom eyed her curiously. "You look like them, but you're not Astrid or Kallisto Hunter."

"I'll be one of them in my next life and you'll meet me there where you'll be known as Jed Corbett. For today and in this time, I'm just visiting."

"I must have made a favorable impression in that life since both you and the *Seer* like me."

"I wouldn't go that far, but you did your best to save me from the man who tried to kill me." Astra turned off toward the mercantile and the dress in the window. "Go to *Summerland*, Tom Corbett."

"I will when I'm ready."

Nina smiled, shaking her head when he vanished. "He's a charmer in a hundred or so years from now too. He made the *Guardian* laugh when she met him there and arrested him for disturbing the peace."

"He must not have killed our sister in the future." Kallisto glared at Nina. "His actions are unforgivable."

"Tom claims his uncle framed him for your sister's death, attacking her when she was alone. On his return home, Tom confronted his uncle and the man murdered him." Nina held up the candle to stop Kallisto's protest. "Open your mind and consider the possibilities before you tell me again what you think of your brother-in-law. If he's a decent person in the future, couldn't he be one here? Isn't it possible that he is the victim of foul play too?"

"You believe his story, don't you, *Seer*?" Astrid took a deep breath. "We'll try to accept that and him, but it won't be easy. We loved our sister."

"I know and I've only spoken to her once, but I really liked the woman she becomes in the future. She came with Kyle to rescue me from the man who abducted and meant to kill me."

"Do you mean Meteor Jamison?" Kyle stopped her before they crossed the street, allowing a team with a wagon to pass. "Or are you talking about one of her sisters since all three of them helped me deal with Smith?"

"I mean Meteor, the same woman who brought pizzas for lunch."

"She made me lots of cookies and pies when I worked at the Rocking J. That woman can cook."

"You'd better praise my desserts as much when we have a place of our own, Kyle Morgan."

"Oh, I will, Missus Morgan. I don't want you getting your dander up and sending me outside to sleep in the barn again."

Heat burned into her cheeks and she elbowed him in the ribs. "You're such a jerk."

"That doesn't sound very wifely. I'll let you make amends later."

"You wish."

He chuckled and guided her across the street. "Nope, I know."

———

She'd roused briefly when he left to walk Pooka the next morning, then slept until his return. He'd pulled the covers away and she awakened as he pushed up her nightshirt, kneeling on the bed. He slid between her thighs, lifting her legs over his shoulders. His mouth claimed her, his tongue lapping at the soft folds before he slipped it inside her and started a new pattern. Still drowsy, she'd risen and fallen, arching against the long, slow torment of the intimate kiss. When he drew the small bud between his lips, he sucked until she came apart.

He hadn't stopped. He'd taken her a second time with his mouth before he stood and undressed. Once he was naked, he'd climbed back into bed. They'd really made love, first with her on top and then with him. Afterward, they'd shared a bath before he left to arrange for a packhorse. He told her that he'd also make the rounds of Junction City with Cal but intended to be back for lunch, or rather dinner in the dining room.

That gave her time to start packing for their return to the Lazy B on Wednesday. Pooka stirred and yipped. Nina glanced at the opening door, expecting to see Kyle. Instead, Astra entered followed by Rowdy Tall-Deer, both insubstantial figures. "This is a surprise."

"You're telling me." Astra gestured to the door and it closed behind them. "He came to tell me it was time to return home."

"And we're leaving as soon as she warns you." Rowdy folded his arms, his long black hair speckled with gray tied in a ponytail with a leather thong. He wore the same kind of clothes she'd seen him in before, a suede shirt, brown pants, and low-heeled boots. "Folks will be missing us."

"All right." Nina folded a shirt-waist blouse and tucked it into the carpetbag. "What did you want to tell me?"

"First, I sent off Tom and Mary Corbett to *Summerland* so you won't be seeing them again. Second, my demon-father is trying to open a portal for Gary Smith to come here. Keep an eye out for him."

"For both of them, Jarvesel and Smith." Rowdy's tone remained detached and utterly calm. "Smith can't die in this time or he'd never have brought the *Guardian*, or you to Liberty Valley of yesteryear, and the *Bard* would have no stories to share of us and our deeds."

"Strange, but that actually makes total sense." Nina eyed the pair. "Will I see you again?"

"Possibly, but there aren't any guarantees." Astra smiled at her. "Do your best in your new home and be happy, Nina Armstrong-Morgan. Take lots of photographs. We'll see those in the future."

———

They left Junction City immediately after breakfast on Wednesday since it'd take most of the day to reach the Bar M. Leading the pack-horse he'd rented from the livery, Kyle looked at the three women riding in front of him. Like Nina, Kallisto had opted for a divided skirt, but her sister rode side-saddle in a dark blue habit. He didn't hear their conversation, but it didn't matter. They were undoubtedly discussing topics his wife would share with him later.

His wife. He marveled at the concept once more. It'd taken too long, but at last, he had a family. He watched Pooka guide the way to the Bar M. The pup seemed to love their new home as much as his owner. Kyle gazed ahead at Nina's straight back under the heavy duster. He couldn't see her short dark brown hair covered by a knit cap, but perhaps she'd let it grow as long as his when she felt safe.

He remembered the warning she said she'd received from Astra Jamison yesterday before the witch left for the future. Gary Smith might show up in this time and they'd have to deal with the man if he did. Granted, they probably wouldn't be able to kill him, but at least they could see Smith stood trial and was imprisoned for his crimes.

As the hours passed, the temperature dropped and snowflakes brushed his face. It was late afternoon when they arrived at the ranch. Nina stopped her horse in front of the house.

Before she dismounted, the door opened and Señora Ortiz rushed out on the wide porch. "Did you find them?"

"Find who?" Kyle urged S.O.B. closer. "What's happened?"

"I sent the children to collect eggs for me this morning and they disappeared. Everyone's looking for them."

33

NINA TURNED HER HORSE FURTHER INTO THE YARD AND RODE closer to the dark-haired woman standing on the porch. "When did you realize they were gone?"

"After dinner." Hannah Ortiz pulled a shawl closer around her shoulders. "The girls helped me with the dishes and Michael filled the wood-box. They've spent so much time around the house these past few days. They were stir-crazy and I didn't see the harm in letting the three of them go to the hen-house near the barn."

"How old are they?" Kallisto and Astrid shared a glance. "Did any of them have a rifle or pistol?"

"Of course not." Hannah twisted her hands. "I know Michael learned to shoot when he lived at the Lazy B, but there isn't any need for that here, not when I keep him close."

"Becky's eight and Michael turned eleven a couple of months ago. Sorrel's almost twelve." Nina frowned thoughtfully, glancing around the snow-covered buildings, but she didn't see any unusual tracks, just boot-prints of varying sizes. "Kyle, why don't you put the packhorse in the barn? Hannah, do you have something that belongs to one of the kids? A shirt or a dress or a nightgown?"

"What are you thinking?" Kyle reined his strawberry roan close for a moment. "I know you have an idea."

"When you first came to work at my place, we taught Pooka to find you and I'm betting he can find the girls. He plays with them often enough."

"Brilliant notion. I'll be right back."

When he'd ridden off toward the barn and Hannah Ortiz had hurried into the house, Nina eyed Astrid. "I'm betting if something or someone killed any of the children, I'd see their spirits. Is that right?"

"You're right. As the *Seer*, it's your job to send the dead where they need to go."

"That's what I thought." Nina swung out of the saddle and passed the reins to Astrid. "Kallisto, you'll need to reload our rifles with silver ammo. I don't know where the children are, but I suspect they haven't returned home because they're trapped by some of those wolves."

"That makes sense." It was the other woman's turn to dismount. She removed the rifle from the scabbard on the saddle. "I'll do mine first, then yours and Astrid's. Mister Morgan can take care of his when he rejoins us."

The front door opened and Hannah hustled toward Nina, holding out two garments and a dirty sock. "I did laundry on Monday so these are the ones the girls were wearing this week. Michael changes his socks every day."

"Fair enough." Nina called the dog and petted him when he came to stand in front of her, tail wagging. "Okay, Pooka. Time to play." She held out the smallest nightie to him and he sniffed it. "Find Becky."

Pooka cocked his tri-colored head and she repeated her action, letting him smell the article of clothing. "Find Becky."

The young dog scurried around the yard, tracking a scent, then trotted off toward the barns. She tucked the other nightshirt and Michael's sock in the saddlebags. Picking up Missouri's reins, Nina followed her pet. He moseyed around the hen-house by the barn, then by the cabin Hannah shared with her husband and son.

When Pooka paused to scratch an itch, Nina approached him. She held out the small nightgown again. "Find Becky."

The dog yipped, then tore off toward the pastures. She put her left foot in the stirrup and vaulted back into the saddle. Collecting on the reins, she squeezed her legs and sent the retired show-horse into a slow canter after the collie. She heard hoofbeats and glanced over her shoulder, not surprised to see Kyle riding behind her, followed by the Hunter women.

He caught up within a few strides. "Where do you think they went?"

"I'm not sure, but Pooka seems to know."

They passed the field where her horses had originally grazed with other stock kept close in for riding. Pooka kept going down the track and they followed the dog. Nina eyed Kyle. "I think he's taking us to the pasture where Rad keeps the Appaloosas. He planned to put Georgia and Minnesota in with them while we were gone."

"I hadn't recalled that, but you're right."

They neared the next paddock and Pooka advanced on the gate, barking wildly. Nina pushed her Arabian to a gallop. She saw the herd of horses running toward them, several wolves behind the brightly colored Appys. She vaulted out of the saddle, quickly sliding her rifle out of the scabbard. She dropped the reins on the ground and Missouri froze, a credit to Kyle's training. She steadied the rifle on the fence rail, picked her target, a large male wolf streaking toward Georgia, and pulled the trigger. The bullet struck the animal in the chest and he tumbled into the snow. The small bay filly whinnied and raced in her direction, followed by her former stablemate, then the rest of the horses.

Nina aimed at another wolf, fired, and watched it fall. She suddenly grew aware that Kyle stood next to her, shooting at the pack. A third wolf stumbled into a fourth, each wounded and barely able to walk. Kallisto didn't hesitate to shoot at them and neither did her sister.

"Enough." Astrid lowered her Winchester as the remaining

wolves turned and bolted into the evergreens. "Let them go for the time being. We'll hunt the rest later."

"Works for me." Nina leaned down to pet her pup who sat next to her. "Now, where are those children? Pooka, find Becky."

The dog whined, then ducked under the bottom rail. Nina passed her carbine to Kyle while she went between the middle and lowest poles. She took his rifle and held both of them when he followed her. Meantime, Astrid collected the reins of the waiting horses and held them so her sister could join the quest.

Several of the horses came to greet them and Nina paused to pet her two mares before she went after the collie. He headed toward the pond before he swerved to the left and three giant logs in a pile, obviously left to dry, prior to being split into posts and more rails. He stopped, tail between his legs, and whimpered.

Nina caught up with her pup and rumpled his white ruff. "Becky, Sorrel, Michael, where are you?"

"Here." Michael stood up behind the logs, holding a hefty wooden club. "We're here, Miss Nina."

She advanced on him, then saw the two girls behind him, petite, blonde Becky hugging a white wolf. Blood dripped from several bite marks on the animal's body. "What on earth are you doing, child?"

"She ran off to visit Georgia." Michael sounded disgusted. "And Sorry and I came to find her, only there were a bunch of mean wolves. These two drove us in here and they fought the rest."

"Where's the other one?"

"Here." Red-haired, green-eyed Sorrel waved to Nina from the wooden sanctuary. "And she's hurt bad. I think she's gonna die."

"Okay." Nina took a deep breath and went into the makeshift fort. She saw the smaller black and gray wolf lying in the snow, blood pooling from the injury in the throat, more gashes in the animal's chest and legs. "Sorrel, go with Kallisto and get my saddlebags. We'll do our best to bandage them up and take them to your mama. She told me she can heal people. I'll bet she can heal these two wolves as well."

"Detective Morgan healed Trace's stallion," Michael said. "If anyone can make that wolf better, she can."

"Astrid has the healing touch too." Kallisto urged the girls from behind the logs toward the pasture. "I'll send her your way. Mister Morgan, keep an eye out in case those others return. They're not going to be happy because these two betrayed the orders of the pack leader."

Kyle nodded agreement, then passed Nina's rifle to Michael. "Your ma said that Trace taught you to shoot. I figure you can help me stand guard."

The boy checked the weapon, heaving a sigh of relief. "I'd really like it if you'd tell her I'm eleven now and not a baby."

"I'll do my best, but I'm not losing out on Señora Ortiz's biscuits. My horse would never speak to me again."

Nina suppressed a smile, then turned to the darker wolf and stroked her head. "Thank you for saving them."

"I don't hunt or eat children, not my own, or those of witches, or humans." A woman's shape drifted in and out of the animal's body. "You sent my mate to Summerland, *Seer*. If I die, send me to join him."

"I will." Nina smoothed the black fur. "Like your husband, you have to promise to help Jed Corbett in the future when you come around again. He was known as Tom Corbett here."

"I promise." Breath rattled in her throat. "So will my pack sister when her time comes."

"Good to know." Nina glanced at the white wolf who limped toward them. "We owe you too. You're welcome at the Bar M for as long as you want to stay."

———

Kyle closed the bedroom door behind Beth. "How are they?"

"Sleeping. I've done my best with Ruby. She was a mess, but

Petrina only had a few serious injuries. Astrid and Kallisto are looking after them tonight." Beth started for the stairs. "Any idea about what I do with my girls? Becky shouldn't have run off like that, but Sorrel and Michael should have come to get us."

"Most folks would wallop them."

"I'm not most folks." Beth led the way toward the kitchen and Kyle followed his sister by marriage. "I had too many beatings growing up and I didn't learn a damned thing from them except to run and hide from sons of bitches. When I couldn't escape, I fought back. Rad said you and I have a lot in common because you were raised by strangers too."

"That's true. He told me once that Trace Burdette-Prescott's grandpa used to say if 'you give a child or a critter a lesson in meanness, don't be surprised when they learn it.' I won't whip any of my sons or daughters."

"Nina had her share of poundings from her stepfather before she went off to boarding school. She won't strike a child either."

Kyle saw the entire family gathering around the table in the kitchen, Señora Ortiz washing up after supper. He went to join his new wife, putting an arm around her waist, and glanced at his older brother. "Reckon this is your business and Bethany's, so Nina and I are going to leave you to it."

"Any suggestions?" Rad studied the three children sitting at the table. "I'll admit to being plumb out of my depth with young law-breakers."

"Beth said Trace Burdette-Prescott raised Becky and Michael." Nina pressed close to Kyle's side. "What would she do if you broke the rules at the Lazy B?"

"Lots of extra chores," Michael said immediately. "And if she was really mad, she'd take away your horse, like she took Frog away from me until she decided I was old enough to handle him, but at least she didn't sell him. Not like her grandpa did to her horse in Arizona when she was bad."

"Don't take Georgia." Tears filled Becky's light blue eyes and rained down her cheeks. "I'm sorry I was naughty. Really I am. I just missed her so much."

"She'd have missed you more if Ruby and Petrina hadn't risked their lives to save you." Pausing to pick up an oil lamp from the counter, Kyle turned Nina toward his room, Pooka following them. "We'll see you in the morning and you can tell us what you and Bethany decided, Rad."

"Sounds fair to us."

Once in their room, he stepped away from Nina and went to add wood to the blaze in the fireplace. "Well, that was an adventure. I'm glad Gabe took the ranch hands to bring back the bodies. None of them spoke to you, did they?"

She shook her head. "Their spirits must have followed the pack home to Corbett's Town. We need to go there as soon as we have enough ammunition. We've been lucky so far, but they're not going to stop, are they?"

"No, they're not." He unbuttoned his shirt and hung it in the wardrobe. "Let's call it a night, Missus Morgan."

———

Nina eased out of Kyle's embrace and the four-poster bed. She lingered to cover him up, before sliding into her robe. Pooka snoozed by the fireplace and she left them to sleep. The large room was a mirror image of the one that Beth shared with her husband, easily big enough for a married couple. Like other rooms in the house, the plank walls glistened a soft gray under a coat of white-wash. A hooked rug stretched across the wooden floor. A large wooden wardrobe stood in one corner with a matching bureau and a washstand along the same wall.

She saw lamplight in the kitchen and headed there to put on her boots for the late-night trip to the outhouse. Beth sat at the table along with Kallisto and Astrid Hunter. The three of them enjoyed tea and toast while a tall, slender woman with ash-blonde hair had joined them. She wasn't having a light snack but ate a thick roast beef sandwich.

Nina eyed the stranger. "Who are you? When did you get here?"

"I'm Petrina Corbett and your husband carried me here on his horse, *Seer*."

"He brought a wolf—" Nina stopped speaking. "Well, that was stupid. You're a shifter, aren't you? How's your friend?"

"Sleeping and healing. Thanks to the *Guardian*, she'll live."

"And thanks to both of you, so will my daughters." Beth rose to her feet. "Do you want a cup of tea, Nina?"

"I'd love one, but first I need to take the proverbial walk. When is your husband installing indoor plumbing?"

"Soon, very soon."

When she returned to the house, she found Petrina drawing a diagram of Corbett's Town, describing the inhabitants and the pack structure. Kallisto asked questions about who'd lead the attack against them and which of the wolves would be most formidable.

Petrina shuddered, clenching her fists until her knuckles whitened. Blue eyes filled with terror. "Frederick Corbett is the alpha, and he thinks he's tough, but the enforcer, Grayson Mallory, is actually the most dangerous in the pack."

"Which one will come after you and Ruby when the others report what you did?" Nina leaned forward to cover Petrina's hands with hers in an attempt to offer comfort. "The alpha or the enforcer?"

"Grayson." A tear slid down the pale cheek. "He'll kill me for betraying him, but he didn't know I overheard his orders to take the *Guardian's* children and bring them to him for meat."

"So, he dies first." Beth refilled their cups. "The only question is which of you gets him, ladies."

"Me." Astrid shared a look with her younger sister. "We've been hunting him for a long time, *Guardian*. If we don't take him in this life, we'll destroy him in the next."

34

WHEN SHE WENT TO THE KITCHEN FOR BREAKFAST, SHE FOUND Beth finishing her meal while the two girls in matching blue dresses and white pinafore aprons washed dishes and Michael filled the wood-box by the stove. Nina glanced at Beth. "So, what punishment did they receive?"

"We opted for something they'd get at the Lazy B." Beth gestured to an empty chair at the table. "More chores, but I also added in essays."

"I don't see why Michael and I are in trouble when we only went after Becky." Sorrel glared over her shoulder at Beth and continued scrubbing plates. "It's not fair."

"And that's how I know it's appropriate." Beth winked at Nina. "Becky has to write a letter explaining why you shouldn't sell Georgia."

"What?" It was her turn to glower at her best friend. "We've talked about this. I was going to—"

"And now you're not." Beth sipped tea. "Nothing changes until you receive a letter from Becky detailing how and why she's old enough to have Georgia as her own horse instead of you selling the mare to someone in Junction City as a Christmas present for their good little girl."

"Michael has to write one to Trace about Frog explaining why he should keep the horse rather than having Gabe and I return him to her." Hannah put a plate with ham, scrambled eggs, and fried potatoes in front of Nina. "After that, he has to write a second one explaining why he's old enough to have a rifle and Gabe will decide whether or not to get him one of his own."

"It's not fair when Trace let me have one at the Lazy B." Michael stomped toward the door. "And she'd have skinned Becky alive so's me and Sorry won't be in trouble."

"No, she wouldn't." Becky sniffled hard but hardly managed to control her sobs. "Trace loves me and she said I could always come home to the Lazy B if I wanted 'stead of living here if the marshal and 'tective got mad at me."

"Well, you're my sister and you're not going anywhere. I'm staying here at the Bar M and you're staying with me." Sorrel passed her a plate to dry. "We both know there are worse things than extry chores and writing letters, Becky, even if our new mama won't tolerate misspelled words and bad grammar."

"There you go." Barely hiding her amusement, Beth raised her teacup to salute Nina. "Too bad Destynee LaFleur can't hear that."

After she ate, Nina pulled on her boots and jacket, then left the house to find Kyle. He was in the barn hitching up the team to take out hay to the horses. The ranch hands would feed the cattle while Rad and Gabe built coffins for the two dead shifters. Although, badly wounded the other two had fled with the rest of the wolves.

Astrid Hunter had brought out old clothes for the bodies. Petrina Corbett stood nearby and murmured something that Nina didn't overhear. She approached the other two women. "What's the plan for today?"

"I have their names." Astrid rested a hand on Petrina's arm. "We'll send those with them to the undertaker. We're going back inside to look after Ruby and then Kallisto will go with you to feed your stock so you have another person to keep watch."

"That works." Nina went to join Kyle, pausing to rub Pooka's shoulder when the collie pup frisked up to meet her. She took the lines Kyle handed her and led the horse out to the buckboard. He followed with the second gelding.

"It's busy around here this morning." He hooked the horse to the wagon. "Did you talk to Bethany about the young-uns?"

"Yes." Nina heaved a sigh. "I sure hope Becky gets the letter done in time to have Georgia for Christmas."

"If Sorrel finishes hers, she gets Minnesota." Kyle hitched up the second horse. "They're certainly feeling the pain from disobeying the rules and we didn't have to strike any of them."

"Not my thing." Nina climbed up on the bench seat. "I don't think it's yours either."

"No." He drove toward the front of the house so they could wait for Kallisto Hunter to join them. "I'm not the sort of man who wallops children."

"I wouldn't have married you if you were." She slid closer to him and kissed him. "I love you just the way you are."

"And I love you." He put an arm around her for a moment. "You've given me the future and the family I didn't know I'd ever have."

"The same holds true for me." She rested her head on his broad shoulder. There were unanswered questions, unresolved problems, but nothing they couldn't handle together. "We're home, Kyle Morgan and we have a good life ahead of us."

"I knew that would come to pass on the day I met you."

EPILOGUE

Eagleville, Washington
~ Wednesday, November 28th, 2018

METEOR JAMISON PARKED HER VAN IN FRONT OF CAPTIVATING Catering. *It's time to go back to work.* She unlocked the back door and walked inside, switching on the overhead fluorescent lights, then her favorite classic country music station. When she opened the cooler, she saw tall, upright carts with trays of cookies waiting to be baked.

Obviously, her apprentice had spent time here in the industrial, super-sized kitchen over the weekend instead of shopping holiday sales, or celebrating with her family, or saving a federal agent from angry shifters. Meteor wondered why. What had happened to send the other woman to create dozens of cookies?

When Brigid returned to work, the question would be answered. For now, Meteor closed the walk-in refrigerator door and crossed the room to turn on the ovens. Two hours later, the bells at the front of the store jangled and Meteor walked up to the showcases to look after the customers. However, it wasn't anyone wanting cookies, or to order a cake, or to arrange an event. This time it was Hilda and Erik Armstrong.

Meteor took a deep breath, hoping her dread didn't show. She hated hurting others, but Kyle and Nina simply weren't safe in this day and time, not when the Corbett wolves saw them as prey. The couple had a better chance of survival in Liberty Valley of yesteryear. "Hi. Have you heard anything?"

"Not from law enforcement or the detectives we've hired." Erik stood six-foot-six in his socks. As usual, the giant blond man dressed in western cowboy garb like the stunt man he'd been in his younger days. "Hilda found a trunk at the Bar M that Nina left for you and your sisters. Where do you want it?"

"Upstairs in my apartment." Meteor walked around the end of the counter to hug the tall blonde woman. "I'm so sorry. I know you miss them. I wish there was something I could do to help you."

"It's all right." Hilda smiled, faint amusement slipping into her face. "I know this will sound absolutely strange and my big brother thinks I'm ready for the looney bin—."

"I haven't said that."

"I see it in your eyes when I talk about them." Hilda lifted her chin. "Nina came to the Bar M for weeks to take photography classes with Will Dawson. She never was in the storage area where I keep the vintage clothes."

"Just because you didn't see her doesn't mean she wasn't there."

"She wasn't." Hilda gestured to the steamer trunk. "I know that even if no one in my family ever believes me. If they have me locked up in an insane asylum, I expect you and your sisters to rescue me, Meteor Jamison."

"We will." Meteor glanced at the trunk. "What did you find?"

"I didn't remember seeing it before, but I must have. When I opened it, I found a red walking dress, button-up shoes, and a 'fascinator' style hat. They were very carefully wrapped with a tag addressed to Astra. There's an ornate dagger in a sheath for Venus and for you, an assortment of recipes in a bundle of sheet music for a spinet piano."

"How did she know I had one?" Meteor glanced at Erik. "Your cousin was never upstairs in my apartment and I don't recall mentioning my piano to her."

"I don't know." Hilda's smile widened. "I think I'll opt for Shakespeare and Nina's favorite quote, 'There are more things in heaven and earth, Horatio, than are dreamt of in your philosophy.' She left that in a note for me in another place she never went to when she came to the Bar M."

"Really?" Erik glowered at his sister. "Where was that?"

"The closed-off wing of the house where the original Kyle Morgan, his wife, Antonina, and their children lived."

While Erik and Hilda squabbled about their cousin, Meteor led the way upstairs. They might not entirely believe it, but now she knew she and her sisters had been right to save the young couple. They'd obviously lived a full life in Liberty Valley. Nina had left them a message letting them know *magick* worked and they'd used it appropriately, at least this time.

THE END

———

Turn the page for a preview of the sixth book in the *Liberty Valley* series, *A Time in Between!*

———

Keep up with Josie Malone and subscribe to her newsletter!
https://sendfox.com/josiemaloneauthor

———

Don't miss out on your next favorite book!

Join the Satin Romance mailing list
www.satinromance.com/mail.html

A TIME IN BETWEEN

"Where no matter what, soulmates find each other."

ONE

Everett, Washington ~ Wednesday, October 31st, 2018

HEREDITARY WITCH, VENUS JAMISON PACED THE HOSPITAL WAITING room, clutching the medallion she'd worn day and night for the last seven years, the thin gold chain biting into the back of her neck. "Whatever I do comes back thrice-fold so I can't fight the Corbetts with their own weapons, but if it weren't for the *Rule of Three*, I'd wreak vengeance."

"Stop it, Venus. I've told you too many times that we serve the Goddess and the Light. We won't be less than what we are. Your brother was drunk and had no business driving. I just pray he lives." Petite and plump, Elder Witch, Estelle Jamison slumped into a chair in the hospital waiting room. Gray-streaked red hair curled around her face, then fell halfway down her back. Dark blue eyes filled with tears. "How could Orion take such a risk? Why didn't he stay at his friend's and return home tomorrow or call one of us for a ride?"

"It's my fault, Mother." Venus hurried across the room, knelt in front of the chair, and wrapped her arms around the older woman.

"I should have read the omens better. I thought it'd be safe for him to hang out with his buddies at a Halloween party."

"I didn't know they drank. Orion loves flying. Why would he jeopardize his chances of attending the Air Force Academy?"

"He wouldn't."

Venus knew their age-old enemies practiced demonic rites. If she'd recognized the lack of warning as one, she'd have kept Orion home on the ranch. However, she'd thought the people in Corbettstown were too busy dealing with the federal investigators and the county law enforcement officers after the disappearance of Nina Armstrong and her fiancé, Kyle Morgan in a blood-soaked cabin, on the outskirts of the community.

Everyone suspected the young couple must be dead either in an attack or in the fire set by the attempted murderer, although their bodies hadn't yet been discovered. Nor would they be. Early this morning, Venus and her sisters sent the pair to safety in Liberty Valley of yester-year, and no one would look for them there. Meanwhile, having law enforcement hunt for Nina and Kyle should have distracted the town mayor and his pack enforcer, the police chief so they couldn't attack any of the Jamisons, or the members of their coven.

Despite what Detective Watkins told her, Venus knew her half-brother's accident wasn't the result of too much alcohol and teen hijinks. Orion never touched the wine they used during their own ceremonies – he drank fruit juice instead. He insisted nothing affect his responses as a new pilot.

Footsteps on the tile floor alerted Venus. She glanced at the doorway in time to see her older sisters. The three of them were triplets, but not identical, despite their red-hair and blue eyes. She was taller than Meteor, her middle sister, but both were more curvaceous than their oldest sibling, Astra. Estelle never spoke of their father, claiming he had nothing to do with them. Still, Venus wondered what he was like. Had he been a wizard? Did any of their *magickal* talents derive from him? Or was it like their mother

328

said? Everything came from her family, the Jamisons. How could that be?

Tonight, Meteor wore a lemon-yellow wig with purple streaks. Light blue eyes revealed a willingness to fight. Skin-tight black pants clung to her curves, and a matching crop-top revealed a gold ring in her navel. Knee-high, low-heeled boots completed the ensemble, undoubtedly part of the costume she needed to tend bar at one of the parties she and her college friends would be catering tonight.

Where was her sister's amulet? The pendant focused power and they'd need all they could summon even if it was near a Sabbat and the Lady and Lord would be listening. The answer came in the next moment. Meteor had the vintage necklace in her pocket. She usually opted for different weapons, saying a knife served her better than any gold baubles.

At first, she'd refused to accept the antique set of jewelry which their mother, head witch of the coven, gave to each of the triplets on their twenty-first birthdays, seven years ago. In rare attempts to placate Estelle and avoid her rages, Meteor occasionally wore the necklace, but not the bracelets or earrings, making up the talipenlace collection.

Talipenlace, Venus thought again. Where did the term originate? Why had that particular word come to mind tonight? Was she finally going to remember her past four lives? Her mother's best friend, a sister in spirit if not in blood, Diana Yarbro said the memories would come in dreams, fantasies or when Venus finally met her soul-mate. It hadn't happened yet.

Her oldest sister, Astra, claimed not to know much of her history either. Venus eyed the other woman, unsure whether to believe her. She must have driven straight to Everett from the law office in Seattle. Astra still wore navy blue slacks and a jacket that matched her cobalt eyes. She'd coiled her waist-length, strawberry blonde hair into a bun on the back of her head. Her appearance always gave the impression of a woman totally in control.

Other attorneys, judges, politicians and even the media consistently said Astra was on the fast track to success. She planned to be a judge before she turned thirty. She wouldn't stop until she was on the Supreme Court, and it wasn't the one in Washington State. Under the collar of her cream blouse, Venus glimpsed a gold chain. So, Astra expected a *magickal* battle too and arrived prepared.

"All three of you are here? I didn't summon you." Estelle sighed and shook her head. "Why do I think Diana sent you to raise a ruckus? Tell me you don't plan to dance naked in the moonlight in the middle of town."

"Don't ill-speak Diana." Meteor sauntered forward. "She was more of a mother to us than you ever dreamed of being. You didn't have time for us until we came into our powers and joined your coven. She was the one who always listened to our dreams."

"You know we save our sky-clad forms for ceremonies." Astra ranged up beside Meteor. "Stay away from our grove on nights of the full moon and you can pretend we only do the *magick* you order. It's the same thing you do whenever there's a fight at hand."

Anger flickered in Estelle's eyes. "Watch your mouths. The two of you have no respect for your elders and betters most of the time."

"Make that the three of us, Mother." Venus greeted her sisters with quick hugs. Rebellion burned in her heart. She didn't want to be polite or courteous. She longed to return their enemies' evil, a triple *whammy* as Meteor would say. Astra gave a little nod as if she heard the silent wish.

"Enough." It wasn't necessary for Astra to raise her voice. "We're not here to argue with you. We'll do sufficient of that during the next few days of *Samhain*. The doctor says you can see Orion now. Go to him. We'll stay with Venus."

"And that's all I want you to do." Estelle glanced at the doorway as a nurse arrived. "I'm coming." She paused and gazed at her daughters again. "Be good. I need your help, all your help. Don't do anything rash. Just help me and your brother."

"That woman!" Meteor barely waited until Estelle was out of

earshot. "How does she do it? Call for our aid at the same moment she denies who and what we are?"

"Because she's a very smart witch," Astra said. "She always has been and we under-rate her talents. She'll do anything to protect our half-brother, her only son. Do you blame her?"

"Of course not." Meteor's faint smile didn't touch her eyes. "I'd do the same for my children. What happened, Venus? How did the Corbetts get past your protections on Orion and his car?"

"They didn't," Astra said. "If they had, Orion would have died in flames, not gone off the highway in a single car accident. This was brought about by the Corbetts."

The pronouncement in her sister's utterly calm voice eased the guilt in Venus' mind. "I knew they did it and that's not all. We need help on the ranch again. The last hand quit within hours. He hadn't even unpacked when the Corbett loggers frightened him away. Mother needs our help more than she knows or admits."

"What do you offer for payment?" Speculation glittered in Meteor's eyes. "They beat up the last three farmhands. The only one unafraid of them was Kyle Morgan and he's gone for good. The police are just as scared of the Corbetts as everyone else."

"We know they want the Rocking J," Astra said, with obvious impatience. "We've fought this war too many times, in too many lives. The ranch is the last piece of sacred ground with its old-growth cedars and the grove. The county and state politicians are under the Corbett influence. What do you suggest, Meteor?"

"You already know." Meteor crossed to the windows, opened the blinds to reveal the full moon. "Undo what you did when he murdered me the first time."

"What are you talking about?" Venus demanded. "Who killed you? When? We can stop it."

"Not this man," Astra said. "He's killed her in each one of her past four incarnations. She and I blocked his memories to try and keep him from repeating his actions in this life. If he kills her again, she's dead for eternity since she'll refuse to let us bring her back."

Venus took a step forward, leaned into Astra's embrace. "I didn't know any of this. Why haven't you told me before? How do we save our sister?"

"Undo what you did the first time you found me dead," Meteor repeated. "You meted out primitive justice on those who aided my killer, and they escaped the consequences. Undo that. Then, we can start over."

"Three hundred years ago? In 1718?" Astra shook her head. "On this backward planet? These people opted for science over *magick*. They're barely civilized now and most still haven't any respect for the *Craft*. I won't return to those barbaric days or ask Venus to give up her children. There must be another choice."

"My babies gone? Torn from my heart and mind?" Venus shook her head. "No. It keeps Orion and other younglings in the coven from being born too. They're all new witches and wizards who've hardly come into their powers."

"Well, you think of something else. I've got to admit it isn't my favorite option." Meteor shivered, although the room wasn't cold. "Having to forgive him for killing me four times is bad enough. No amount of *Sex Magick* makes up for it, not when I constantly have to watch for traps."

Venus grimaced, pulling free from Astra, and crossing to the window to gaze out at the moon. Tonight, she felt closer to the Goddess than usual. What if she sought protection and aid from a new partner? It was the end of one year, the beginning of the next. She could seek something new, someone different.

If she traded her body to save the family again, so be it. She didn't have to love the man. She had a feeling she'd almost found true love once, then lost it for all time. She was twenty-eight, almost twenty-nine in this particular life-cycle. She hadn't found her soul-mate yet. What were her chances? Slim to none. No man haunted her dreams or fantasies regardless of what Aunt Diana said.

Venus swung around, facing her sisters. "Me. I'll trade me to protect Quaid, Fallyn, and Orion from the Corbetts."

"And Edwin," Meteor said.

"Who?" Venus lifted her chin. "Who is Edwin?"

"Her oldest son." Astra closed her eyes for a moment. She opened them, waved her hand at the door which swung shut. The lights flickered, then dimmed. "Fine, Meteor. It gives us the three younglings and a newly fledged wizard to protect. Let's do it."

"I've never met Edwin," Venus said, reaching for Meteor's hand. "Where is he? Why didn't you bring him to me before?"

"He's coming. You'll know him when he arrives. I want him safe from his father. If he doesn't kill him, he'll ruin Edwin's soul."

"I'll protect him too." Venus grasped her amulet with her free hand. The gold disk warmed until the engraved figure of a primitive warrior on a horse seemed to burn into her palm. She didn't loosen her grip. She felt Astra's arm steal around her waist.

Time to begin, Venus thought. "*On this night and in this hour, I call upon the Ancient Power, that which is mine by birth and blood, that which is known and understood. Lady and Lord, hear my plea. Send a man to fight beside me. A man who battles evil in each day and way, one who looks beyond what is easy to see, one who is right for me—*"

When they finished the spell, Meteor stepped away. "Well, that was heavy-duty and not what I expected, but it should work as well as the *Undoing* one I wanted. We didn't have to travel back to the start." She smiled, kissed Venus' cheek. "I'm going to the party up in Eagleville. It's a good night to hunt Corbetts and return their evil."

"How do you do it without breaking the *Rule of Three*?" Venus asked. "You only have this life left unless you change your mind and return to us for the rest of them."

"I simply send back their evil thrice-fold." Meteor giggled. "Try it sometime. It's better than sex. Blessed be, sisters."

Venus watched her vanish into the shadowy hall. "What else does she know that we don't?"

"Too much." Astra leaned against her. "It's because she linked with her soul-bound mate already, despite the fact she hates him. She knows all our past, but it's forbidden for her to share it. At least, that's what Mother tells me. Does Aunt Diana ward Quaid and Fallyn tonight?"

"Yes, although Mom refers to it as baby-sitting." The heat from the medallion still warmed Venus' palm. "What do you think we did to those who killed her the first time?"

"It couldn't be more than they deserved. I passed judgement. You rendered it. Our spellcasting rebounds on us three-fold as well. The worst punishment we faced was when the Goddess separated us from each another."

"We've been linked since childhood this time around. Did we share any of our past lives with Meteor? Why would we allow anyone to hurt our sister repeatedly? Do you know?"

"An interesting point. I'll scry for an answer for you. I must go. I need to *Forecast* outcomes for my new clients before we celebrate *Samhain*. I've healed Orion as much as I can. I'll *white-light* him too. Remember to set wards around him to keep the Corbetts away."

Venus nodded. "I will. Doesn't anyone wonder why you win so many cases?"

"Not when I only defend the desperate, not the innocent. Those who go free die on the streets or suffer severe consequences for their actions." Astra's confidence didn't waver. "I judge them fairly and they answer for their crimes either in Seattle or in Corbettstown."

"So, you're out for vengeance too. Why haven't you and Meteor shared that before?"

"You're the *Maiden*. We keep you safe and pure to protect us. Tell Mother that our brother will be fine. Blessed be, sister mine."

"Blessed be." Venus drifted to the window after her elder sister left. Astra was right. Orion needed shielding while he recovered in the hospital. Although the oldest of the triplets had apparently departed, she still felt close by and Venus knew her sibling had opted to stay behind on the astral plane, if not the physical.

It was easy for a witch to create psychic barriers in a hospital. So much *Power* swirled in the halls. Venus would only use the positive energies, the love, warmth, concern, devotion, approval, and selflessness. She blocked the negative ones pervading the huge building. So much pain, blood, sorrow, grief, heartbreak, sadness, desolation, misery, and despair clouded the rooms, but she didn't have to surrender to the wretchedness.

Afterwards, she slowly relaxed her grip on the pendant. Why had the real name of the *talipenlace* come to her tonight? Did she and her sisters speak another language, one that only they knew? Where had they traveled from three hundred years ago? Why didn't the idea shock her? How could it simply feel right?

She wasn't sure. Somehow, she knew they'd been sent here from a faraway place. Who traveled with them, other than Meteor's killer? And who was he? Would any of them recognize him?

THANK YOU FOR READING

———

Did you enjoy this book?

We invite you to leave a review at your favorite book site, such as Goodreads, Amazon, Barnes & Noble, etc.

DID YOU KNOW THAT LEAVING A REVIEW…

- Helps other readers find books they may enjoy.
- Gives you a chance to let your voice be heard.
- Gives authors recognition for their hard work.
- Doesn't have to be long. A sentence or two about why you liked the book will do.

ABOUT THE AUTHOR

Josie Malone lives and works at her family's riding stable in Washington State. She's taught children to ride and know about horses for so long that she often discovers she's taught three generations of their families. Her life experiences span adventures from dealing cards in a casino, attending graduate school to get her Masters in Teaching degree, being a substitute teacher, and serving in the Army Reserve - all leading to her second career as a published author. Visit her at her website, www.josiemalone.com to learn about her books.

Subscribe to Josie's Newsletter:
https://sendfox.com/josiemaloneauthor

Contact Josie at:
josiemaloneauthor@outlook.com

www.josiemalone.com

 facebook.com/JosieMaloneAuthor

twitter.com/josmaloneauthor

instagram.com/josiemaloneauthor

amazon.com/Josie-Malone/e/B006HC9VMI

ALSO BY JOSIE MALONE

Baker City Hearts and Haunts

My Sweet Haunt

More Than A Spirit

Family Skeletons

Ghosts of the Past (coming soon!)

———

Liberty Valley Love

A Man's World

Cowboy Spell

The Marshal's Lady

Hero Spell

A Trail Through Time

Time In Between (coming soon!)